Style Queen - Queen's Battle

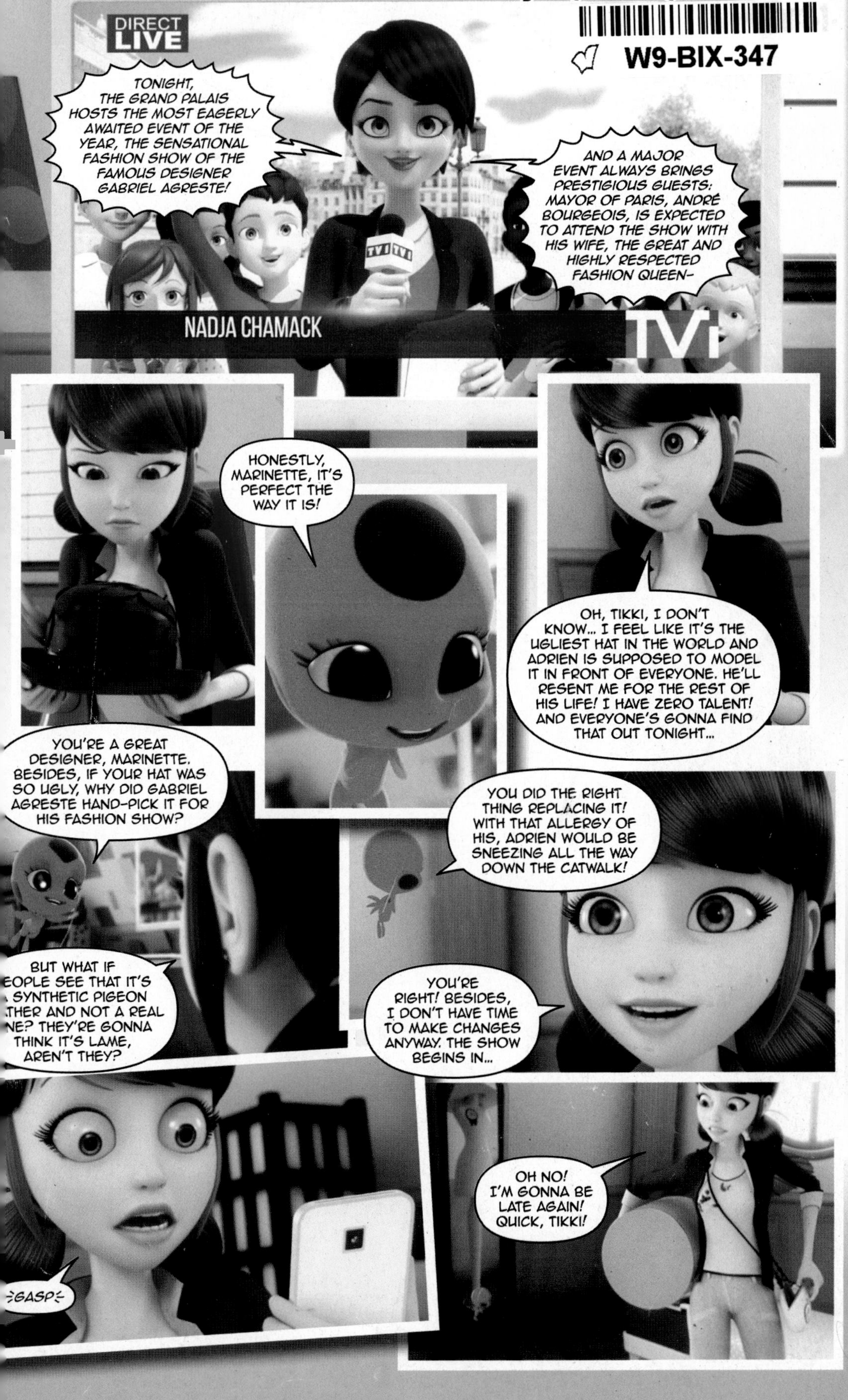
DIRECT
LIVE
TONIGHT, THE GRAND PALAIS HOSTS THE MOST EAGERLY AWAITED EVENT OF THE YEAR, THE SENSATIONAL FASHION SHOW OF THE FAMOUS DESIGNER GABRIEL AGRESTE!
AND A MAJOR EVENT ALWAYS BRINGS PRESTIGIOUS GUESTS: MAYOR OF PARIS, ANDRÉ BOURGEOIS, IS EXPECTED TO ATTEND THE SHOW WITH HIS WIFE, THE GREAT AND HIGHLY RESPECTED FASHION QUEEN–
NADJA CHAMACK
TVi
HONESTLY, MARINETTE, IT'S PERFECT THE WAY IT IS!
OH, TIKKI, I DON'T KNOW... I FEEL LIKE IT'S THE UGLIEST HAT IN THE WORLD AND ADRIEN IS SUPPOSED TO MODEL IT IN FRONT OF EVERYONE. HE'LL RESENT ME FOR THE REST OF HIS LIFE! I HAVE ZERO TALENT! AND EVERYONE'S GONNA FIND THAT OUT TONIGHT...
YOU'RE A GREAT DESIGNER, MARINETTE. BESIDES, IF YOUR HAT WAS SO UGLY, WHY DID GABRIEL AGRESTE HAND-PICK IT FOR HIS FASHION SHOW?
BUT WHAT IF EOPLE SEE THAT IT'S SYNTHETIC PIGEON THER AND NOT A REAL NE? THEY'RE GONNA THINK IT'S LAME, AREN'T THEY?
YOU DID THE RIGHT THING REPLACING IT! WITH THAT ALLERGY OF HIS, ADRIEN WOULD BE SNEEZING ALL THE WAY DOWN THE CATWALK!
YOU'RE RIGHT! BESIDES, I DON'T HAVE TIME TO MAKE CHANGES ANYWAY. THE SHOW BEGINS IN...
GASP
OH NO! I'M GONNA BE LATE AGAIN! QUICK, TIKKI!

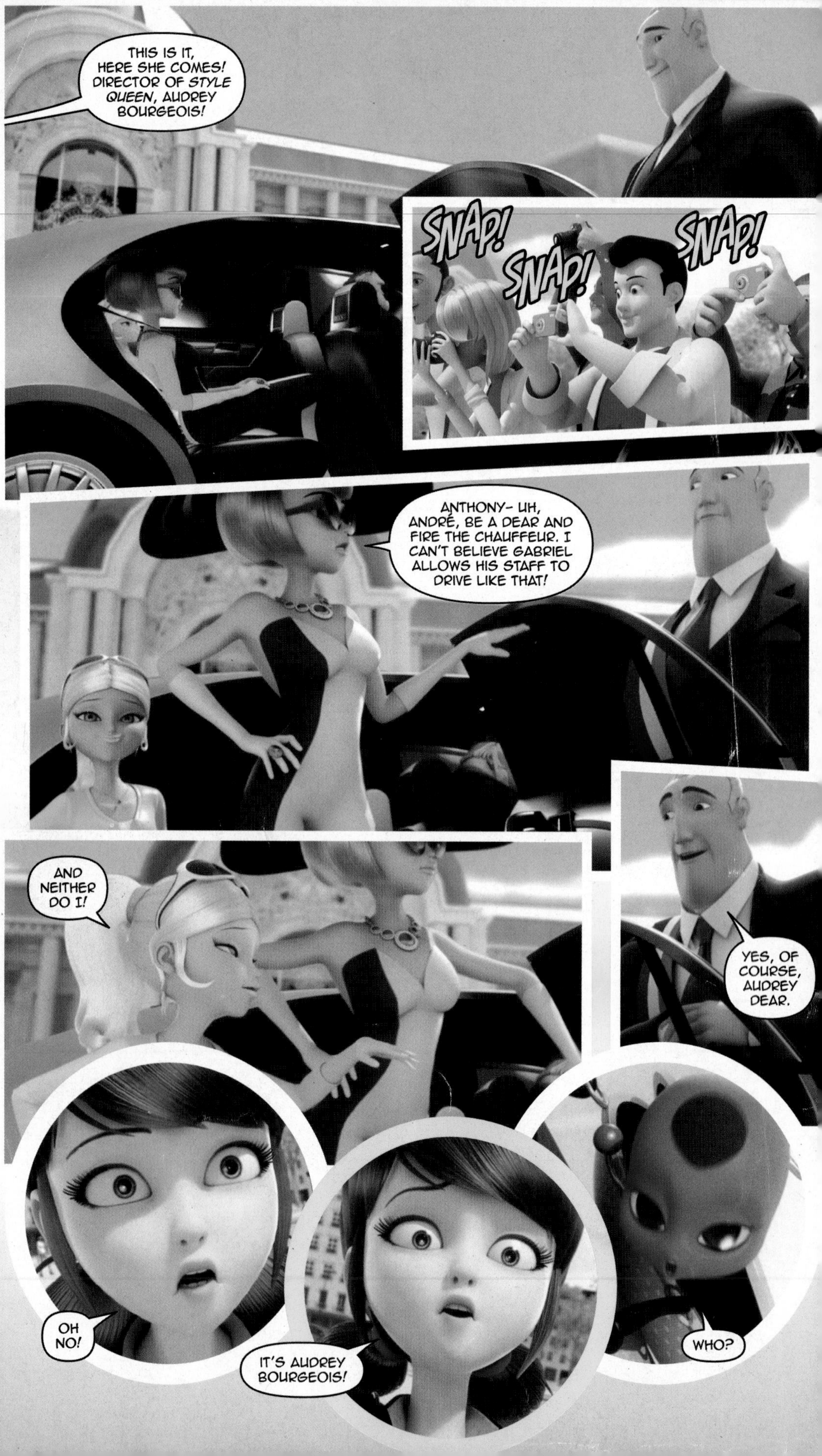
THIS IS IT, HERE SHE COMES! DIRECTOR OF STYLE QUEEN, AUDREY BOURGEOIS!
SNAP!
SNAP!
SNAP!
ANTHONY- UH, ANDRÉ, BE A DEAR AND FIRE THE CHAUFFEUR. I CAN'T BELIEVE GABRIEL ALLOWS HIS STAFF TO DRIVE LIKE THAT!
AND NEITHER DO I!
YES, OF COURSE, AUDREY DEAR.
OH NO!
IT'S AUDREY BOURGEOIS!
WHO?

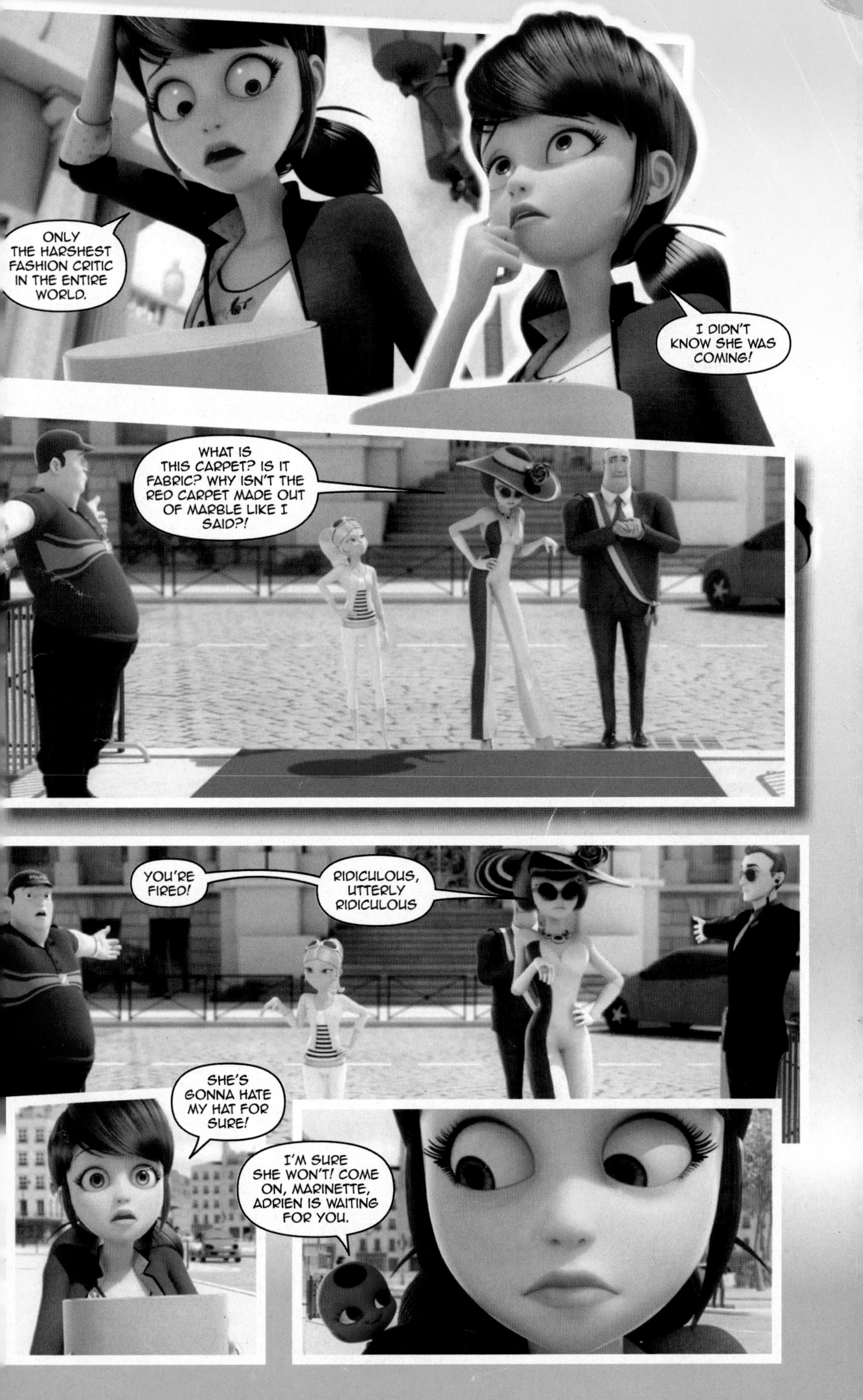
ONLY THE HARSHEST FASHION CRITIC IN THE ENTIRE WORLD.
I DIDN'T KNOW SHE WAS COMING!
WHAT IS THIS CARPET? IS IT FABRIC? WHY ISN'T THE RED CARPET MADE OUT OF MARBLE LIKE I SAID?!
YOU'RE FIRED!
RIDICULOUS, UTTERLY RIDICULOUS
SHE'S GONNA HATE MY HAT FOR SURE!
I'M SURE SHE WON'T! COME ON, MARINETTE, ADRIEN IS WAITING FOR YOU.

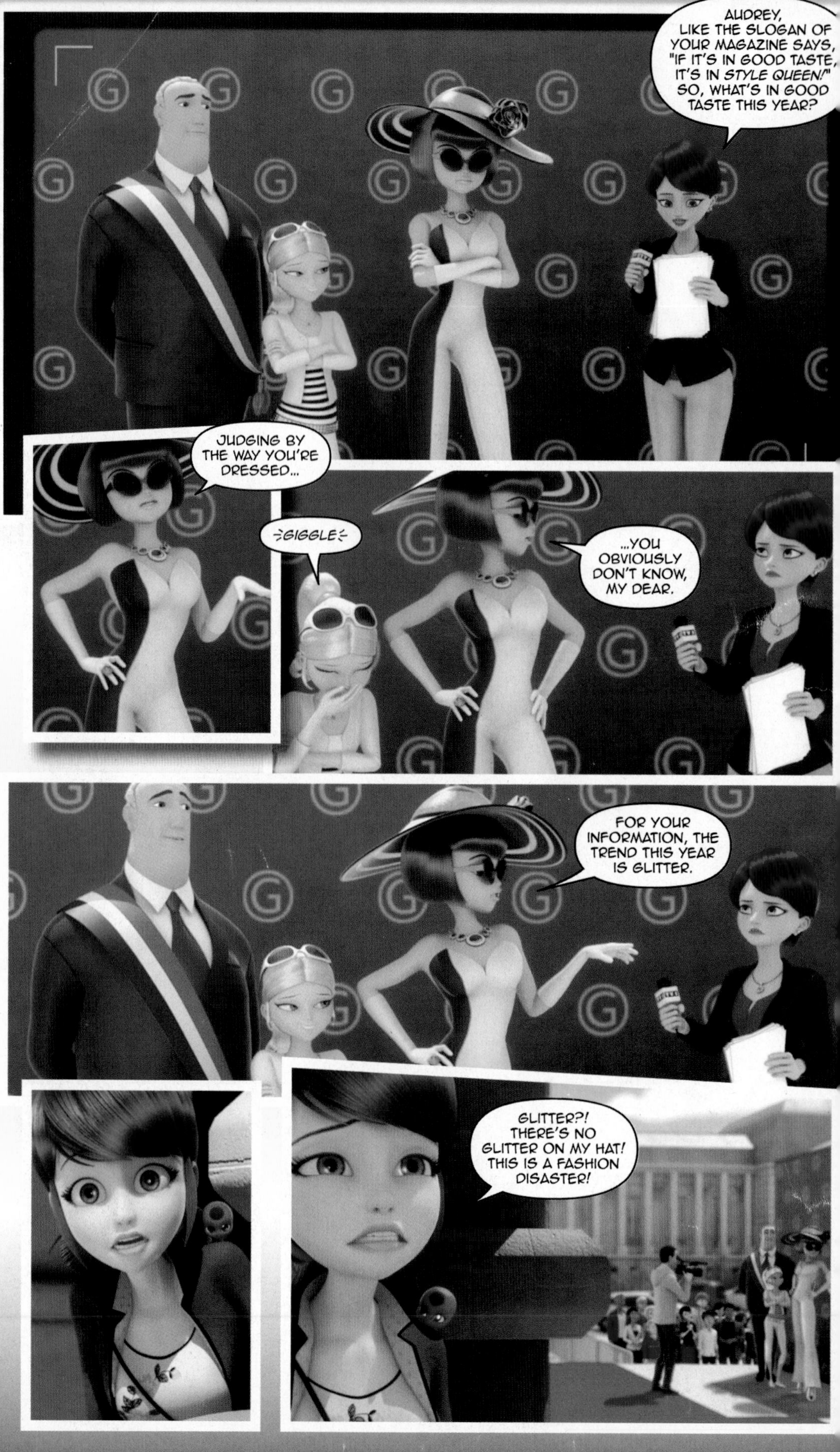
AUDREY, LIKE THE SLOGAN OF YOUR MAGAZINE SAYS, "IF IT'S IN GOOD TASTE, IT'S IN *STYLE QUEEN!*" SO, WHAT'S IN GOOD TASTE THIS YEAR?
JUDGING BY THE WAY YOU'RE DRESSED...
GIGGLE
...YOU OBVIOUSLY DON'T KNOW, MY DEAR.
FOR YOUR INFORMATION, THE TREND THIS YEAR IS GLITTER.
GLITTER?! THERE'S NO GLITTER ON MY HAT! THIS IS A FASHION DISASTER!

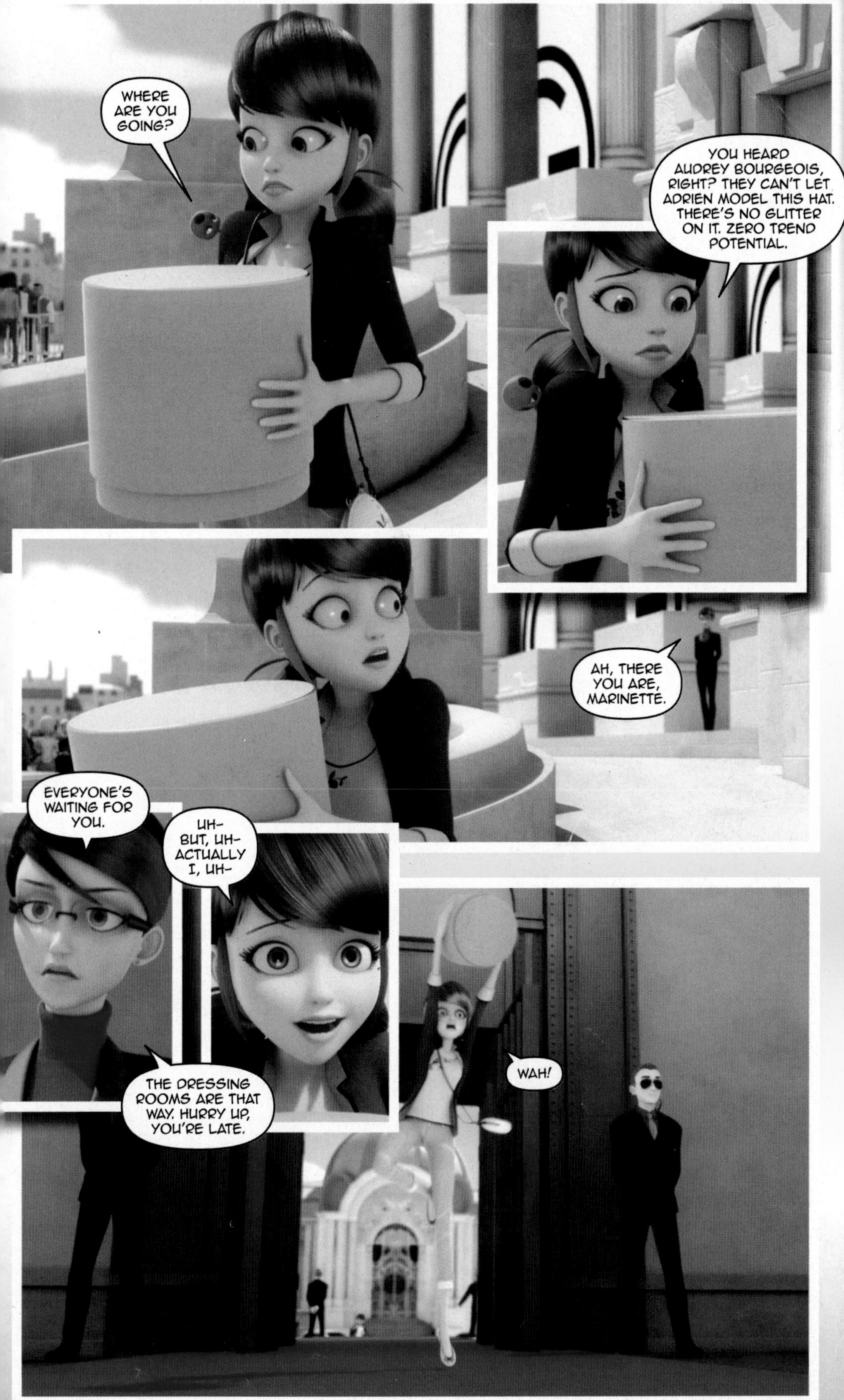
WHERE ARE YOU GOING?
YOU HEARD AUDREY BOURGEOIS, RIGHT? THEY CAN'T LET ADRIEN MODEL THIS HAT. THERE'S NO GLITTER ON IT. ZERO TREND POTENTIAL.
AH, THERE YOU ARE, MARINETTE.
EVERYONE'S WAITING FOR YOU.
UH- BUT, UH- ACTUALLY I, UH-
THE DRESSING ROOMS ARE THAT WAY. HURRY UP, YOU'RE LATE.
WAH!

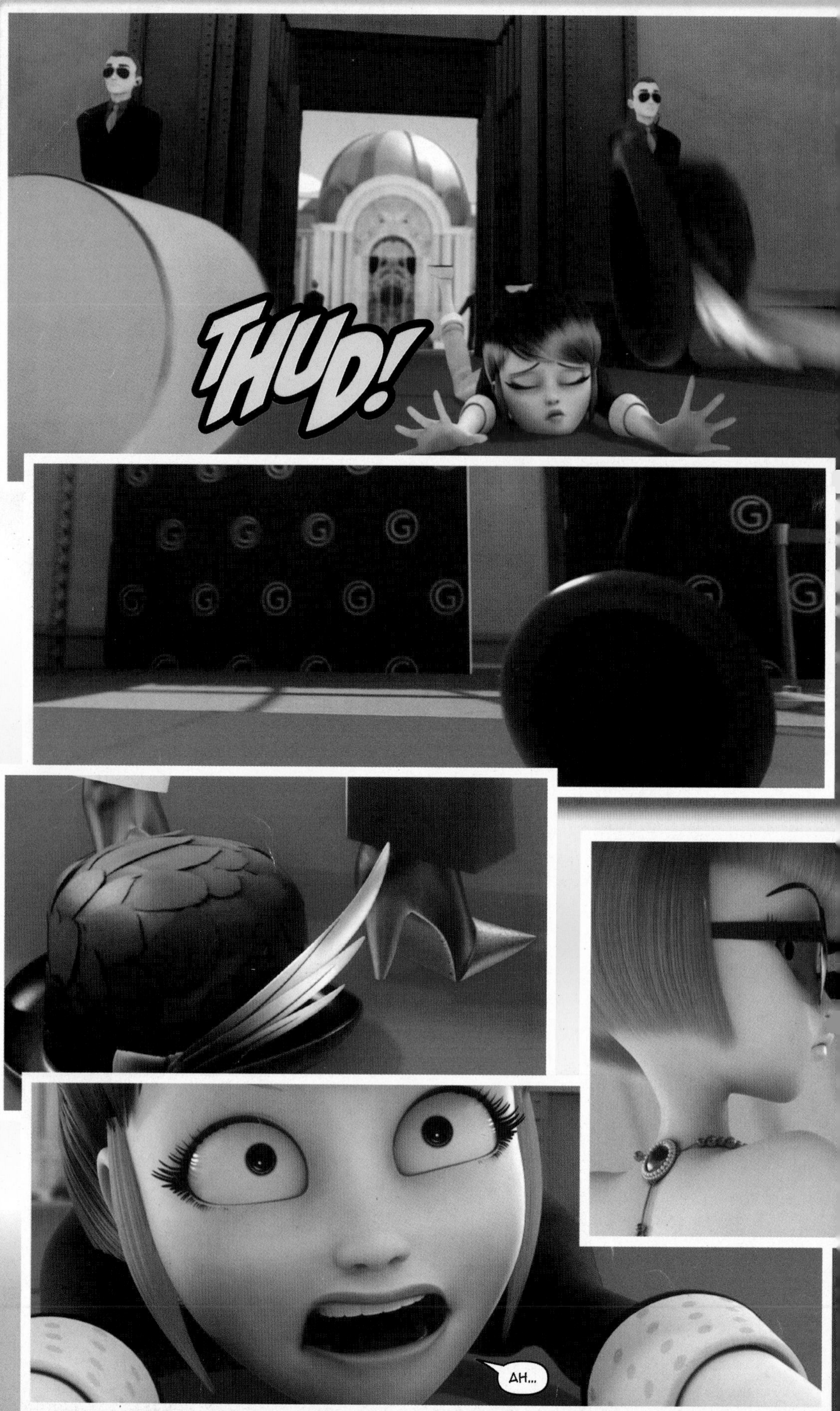
THUD!
AH...

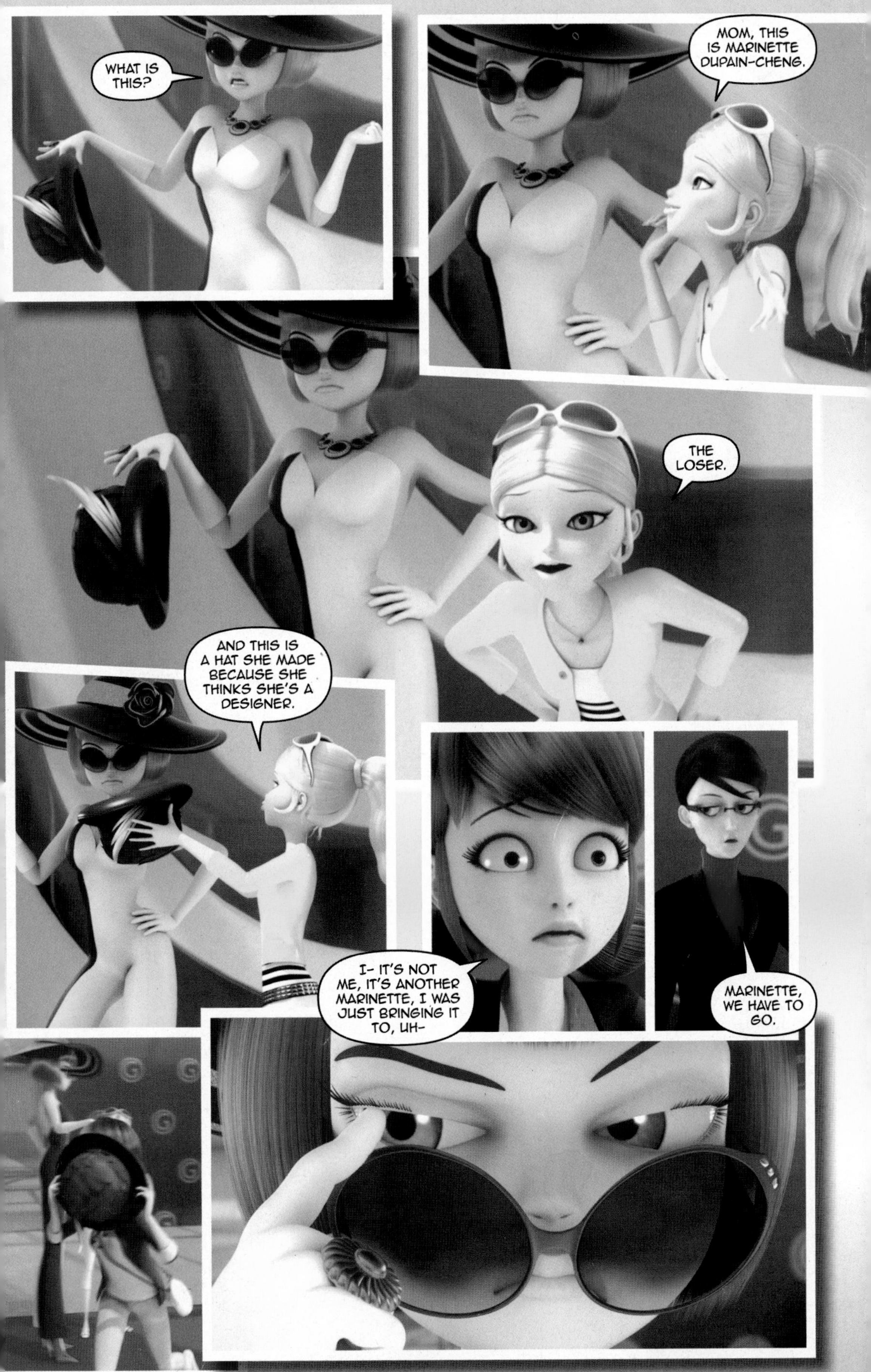
WHAT IS THIS?
MOM, THIS IS MARINETTE DUPAIN-CHENG.
THE LOSER.
AND THIS IS A HAT SHE MADE BECAUSE SHE THINKS SHE'S A DESIGNER.
I- IT'S NOT ME, IT'S ANOTHER MARINETTE, I WAS JUST BRINGING IT TO, UH-
MARINETTE, WE HAVE TO GO.

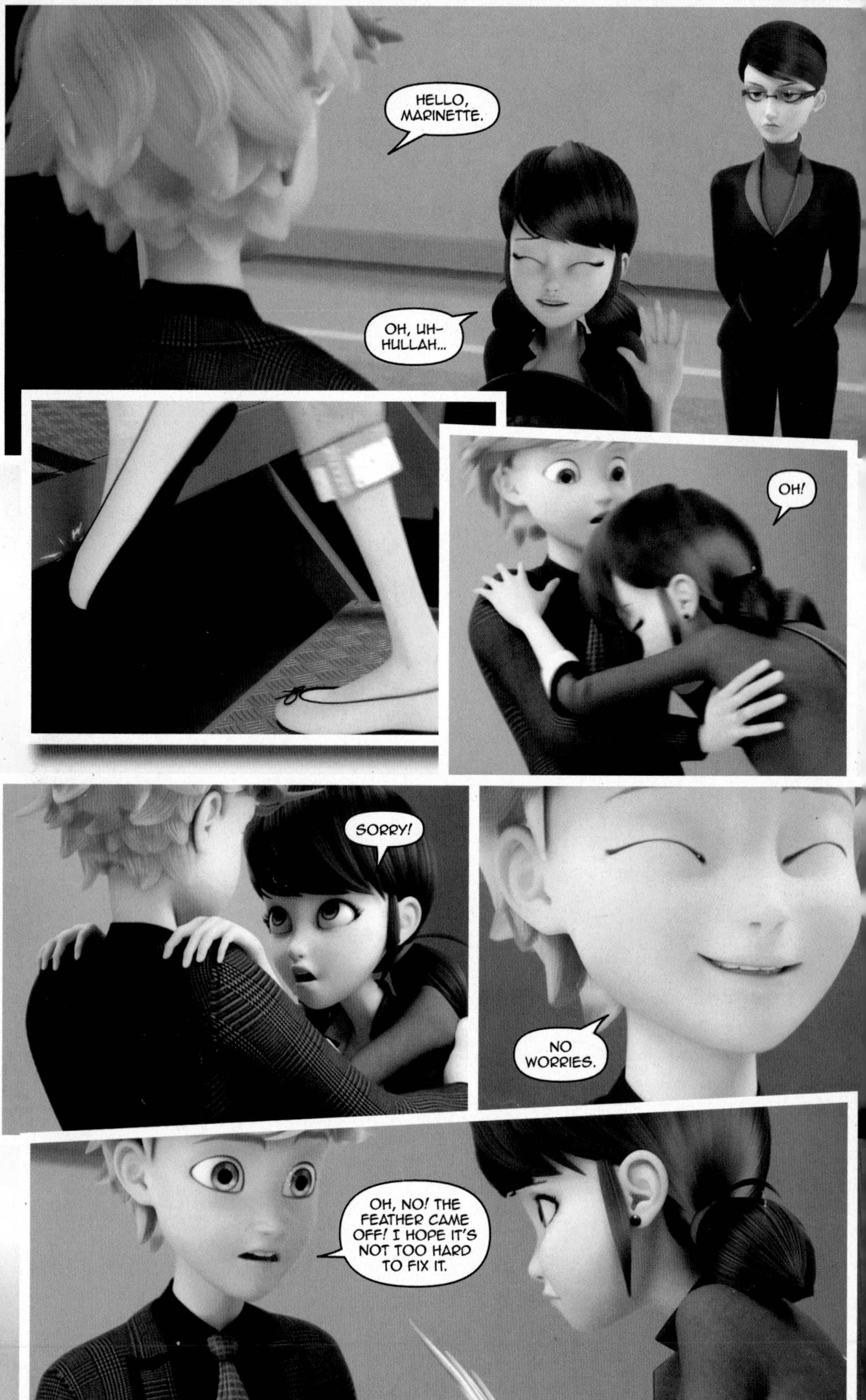
HELLO, MARINETTE.
OH, UH-HULLAH...
OH!
SORRY!
NO WORRIES.
OH, NO! THE FEATHER CAME OFF! I HOPE IT'S NOT TOO HARD TO FIX IT.

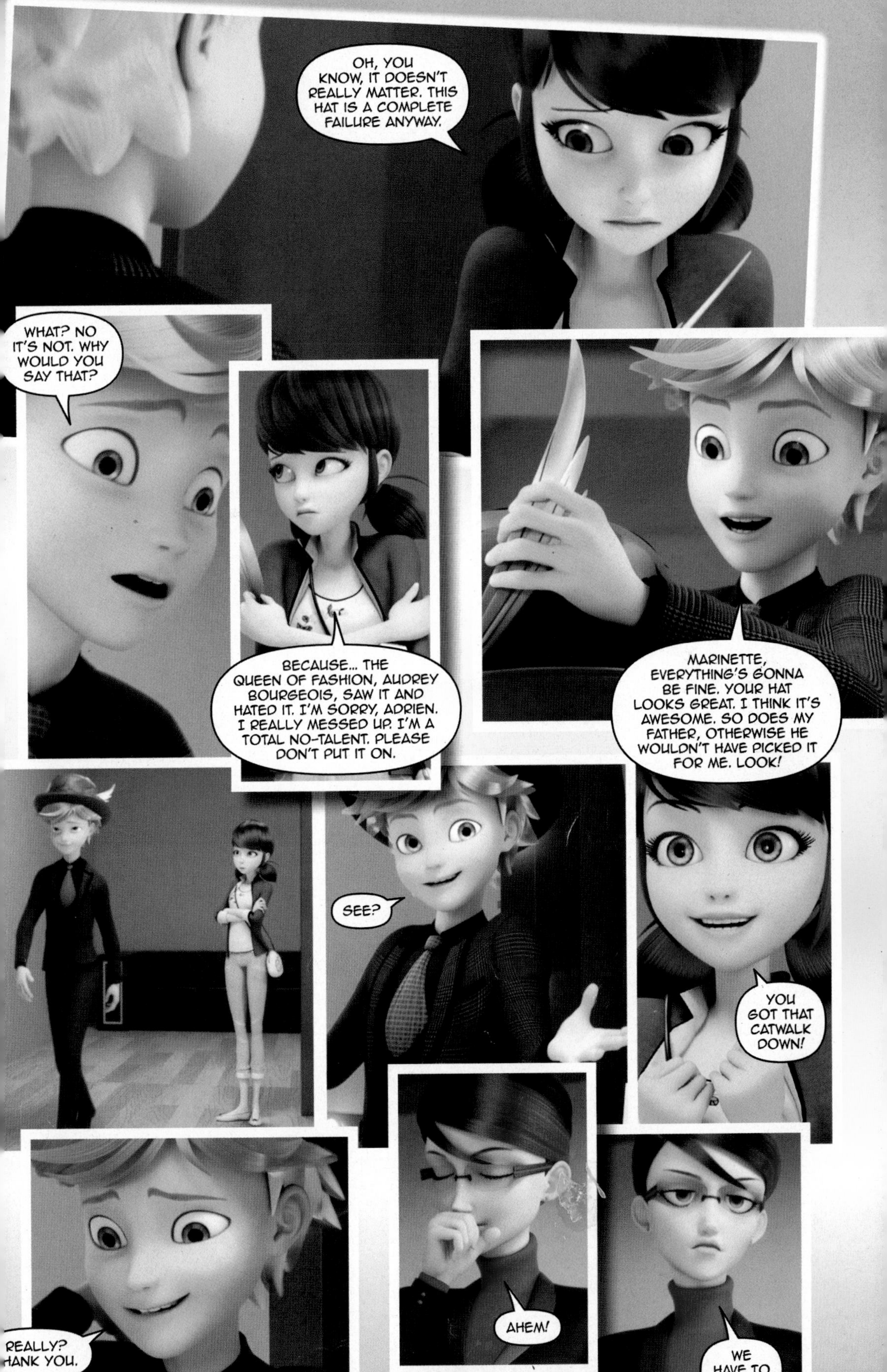
OH, YOU KNOW, IT DOESN'T REALLY MATTER. THIS HAT IS A COMPLETE FAILURE ANYWAY.
WHAT? NO IT'S NOT. WHY WOULD YOU SAY THAT?
BECAUSE... THE QUEEN OF FASHION, AUDREY BOURGEOIS, SAW IT AND HATED IT. I'M SORRY, ADRIEN. I REALLY MESSED UP. I'M A TOTAL NO-TALENT. PLEASE DON'T PUT IT ON.
MARINETTE, EVERYTHING'S GONNA BE FINE. YOUR HAT LOOKS GREAT. I THINK IT'S AWESOME. SO DOES MY FATHER, OTHERWISE HE WOULDN'T HAVE PICKED IT FOR ME. LOOK!
SEE?
YOU GOT THAT CATWALK DOWN!
REALLY? HANK YOU.
AHEM!
WE HAVE TO GO.

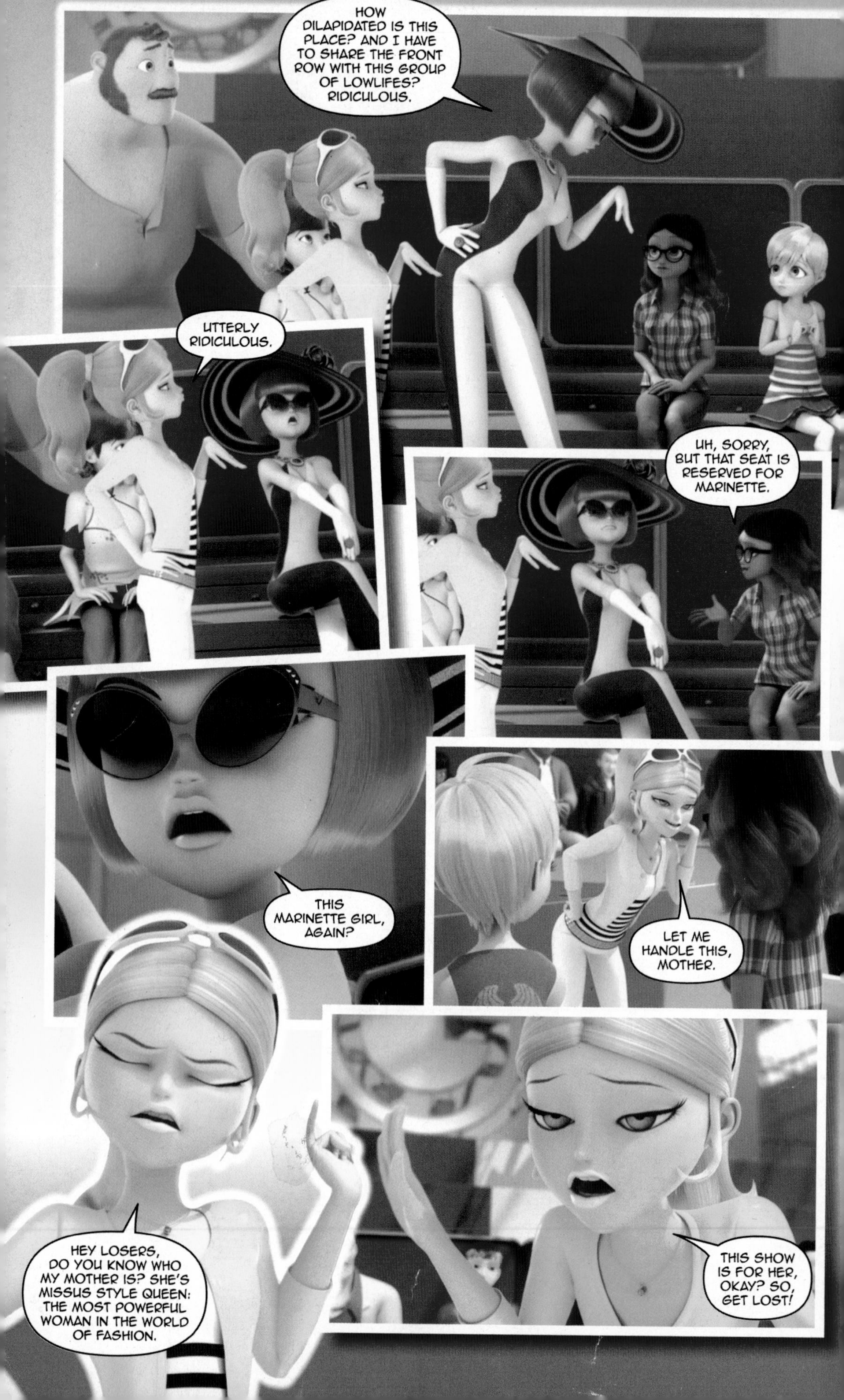
HOW DILAPIDATED IS THIS PLACE? AND I HAVE TO SHARE THE FRONT ROW WITH THIS GROUP OF LOWLIFES? RIDICULOUS.
UTTERLY RIDICULOUS.
UH, SORRY, BUT THAT SEAT IS RESERVED FOR MARINETTE.
THIS MARINETTE GIRL, AGAIN?
LET ME HANDLE THIS, MOTHER.
HEY LOSERS, DO YOU KNOW WHO MY MOTHER IS? SHE'S MISSUS STYLE QUEEN: THE MOST POWERFUL WOMAN IN THE WORLD OF FASHION.
THIS SHOW IS FOR HER, OKAY? SO, GET LOST!

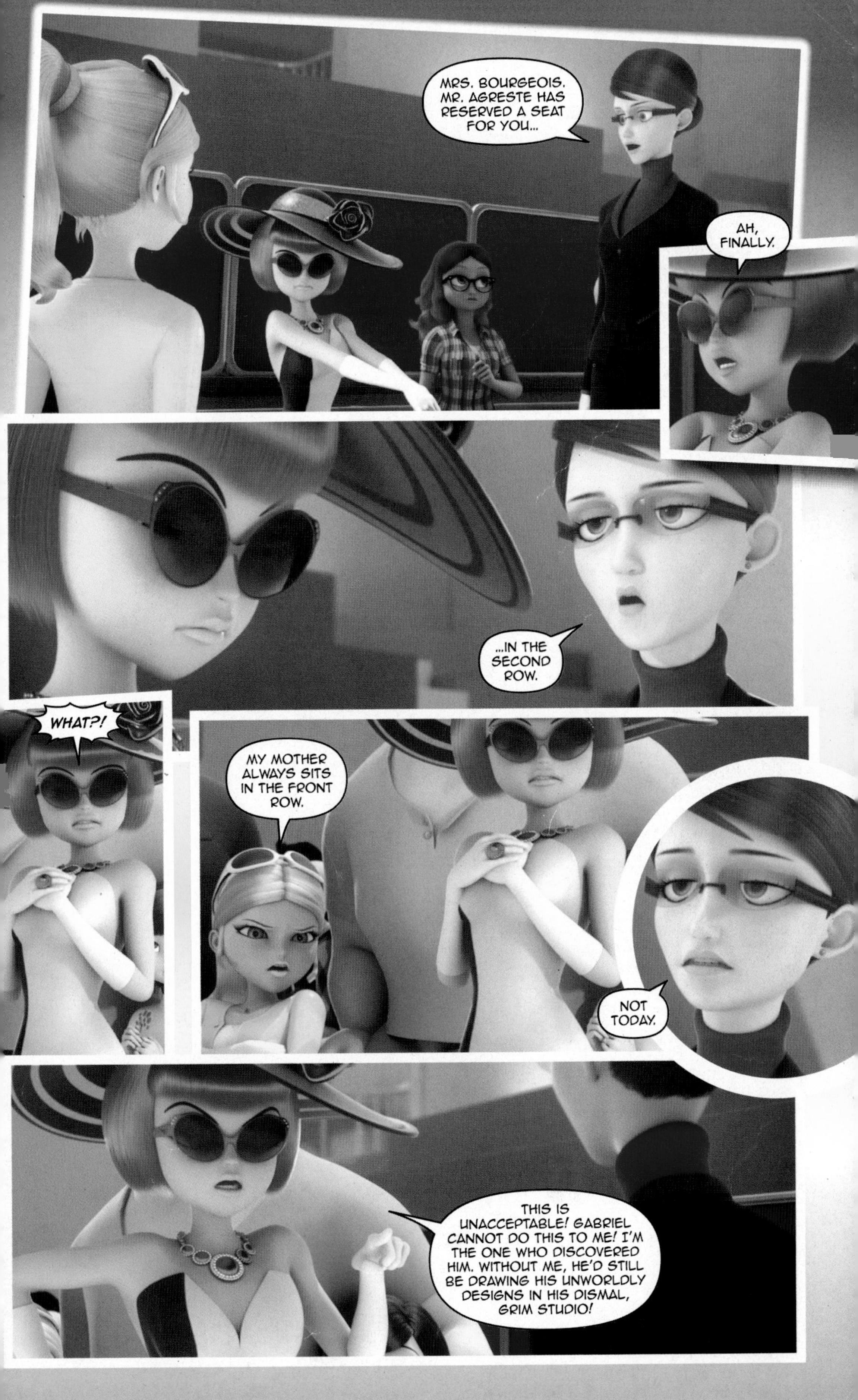
MRS. BOURGEOIS. MR. AGRESTE HAS RESERVED A SEAT FOR YOU...
AH, FINALLY.
...IN THE SECOND ROW.
WHAT?!
MY MOTHER ALWAYS SITS IN THE FRONT ROW.
NOT TODAY.
THIS IS UNACCEPTABLE! GABRIEL CANNOT DO THIS TO ME! I'M THE ONE WHO DISCOVERED HIM. WITHOUT ME, HE'D STILL BE DRAWING HIS UNWORLDLY DESIGNS IN HIS DISMAL, GRIM STUDIO!

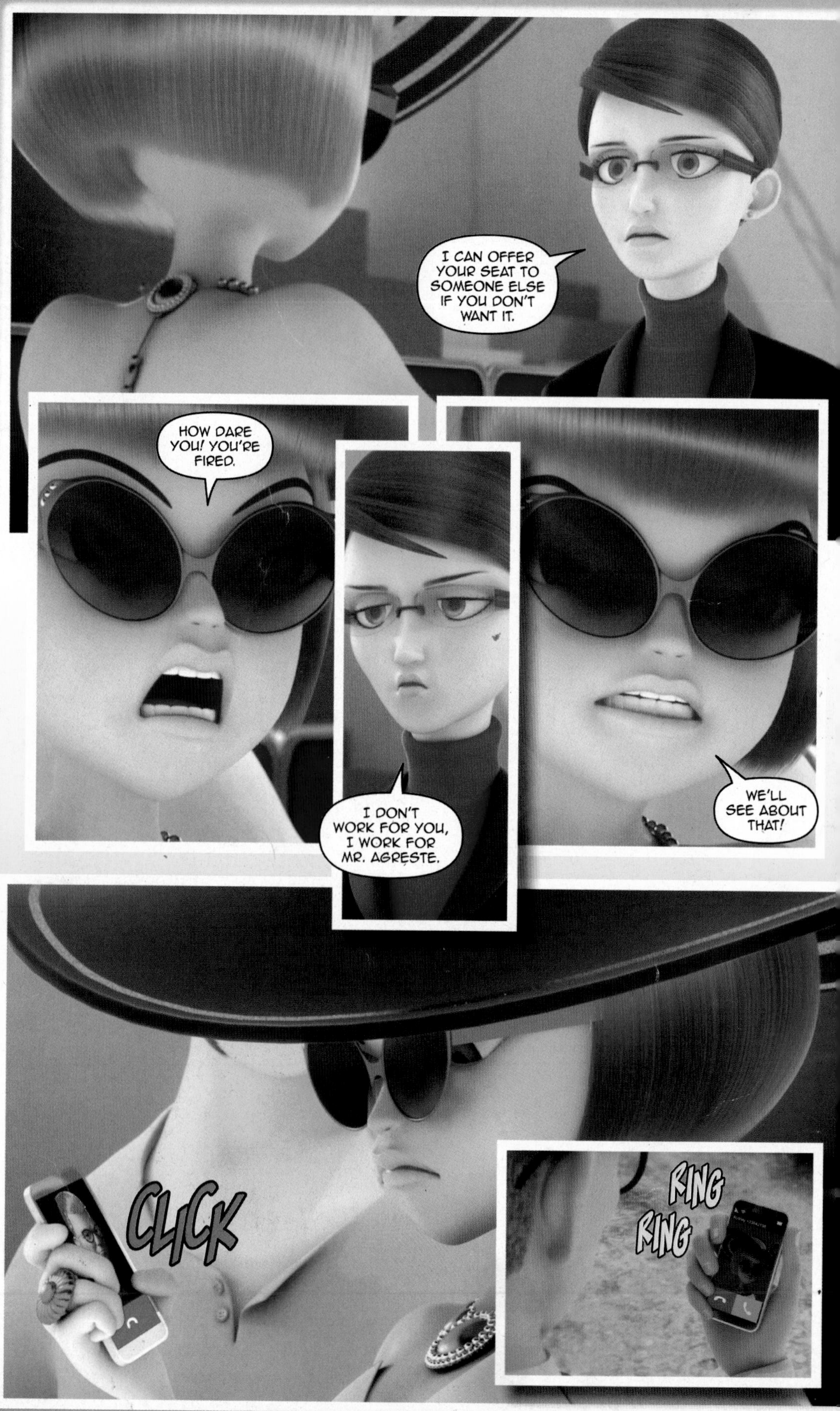
I CAN OFFER YOUR SEAT TO SOMEONE ELSE IF YOU DON'T WANT IT.
HOW DARE YOU! YOU'RE FIRED.
I DON'T WORK FOR YOU, I WORK FOR MR. AGRESTE.
WE'LL SEE ABOUT THAT!
CLICK
RING RING

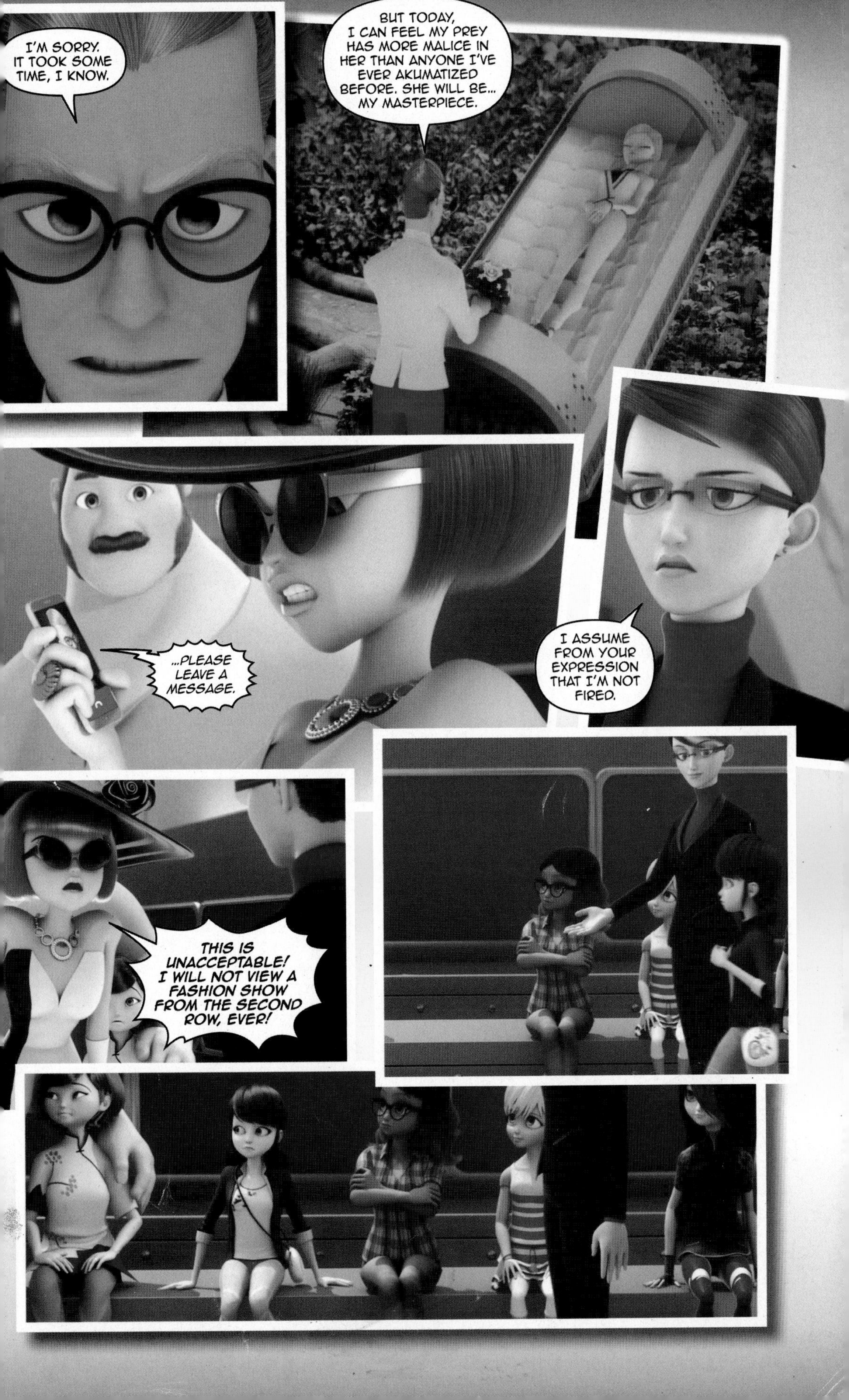

I'M SORRY. IT TOOK SOME TIME, I KNOW.
BUT TODAY, I CAN FEEL MY PREY HAS MORE MALICE IN HER THAN ANYONE I'VE EVER AKUMATIZED BEFORE. SHE WILL BE... MY MASTERPIECE.
...PLEASE LEAVE A MESSAGE.
I ASSUME FROM YOUR EXPRESSION THAT I'M NOT FIRED.
THIS IS UNACCEPTABLE! I WILL NOT VIEW A FASHION SHOW FROM THE SECOND ROW, EVER!

TELL ME, MY DEAR AKUMAS...
...WHAT WILL BE THE TREND TONIGHT?
WWZZING
FLY AWAY, MY LITTLE AKUMA, AND EVILIZE THIS WONDERFULLY VILE QUEEN.

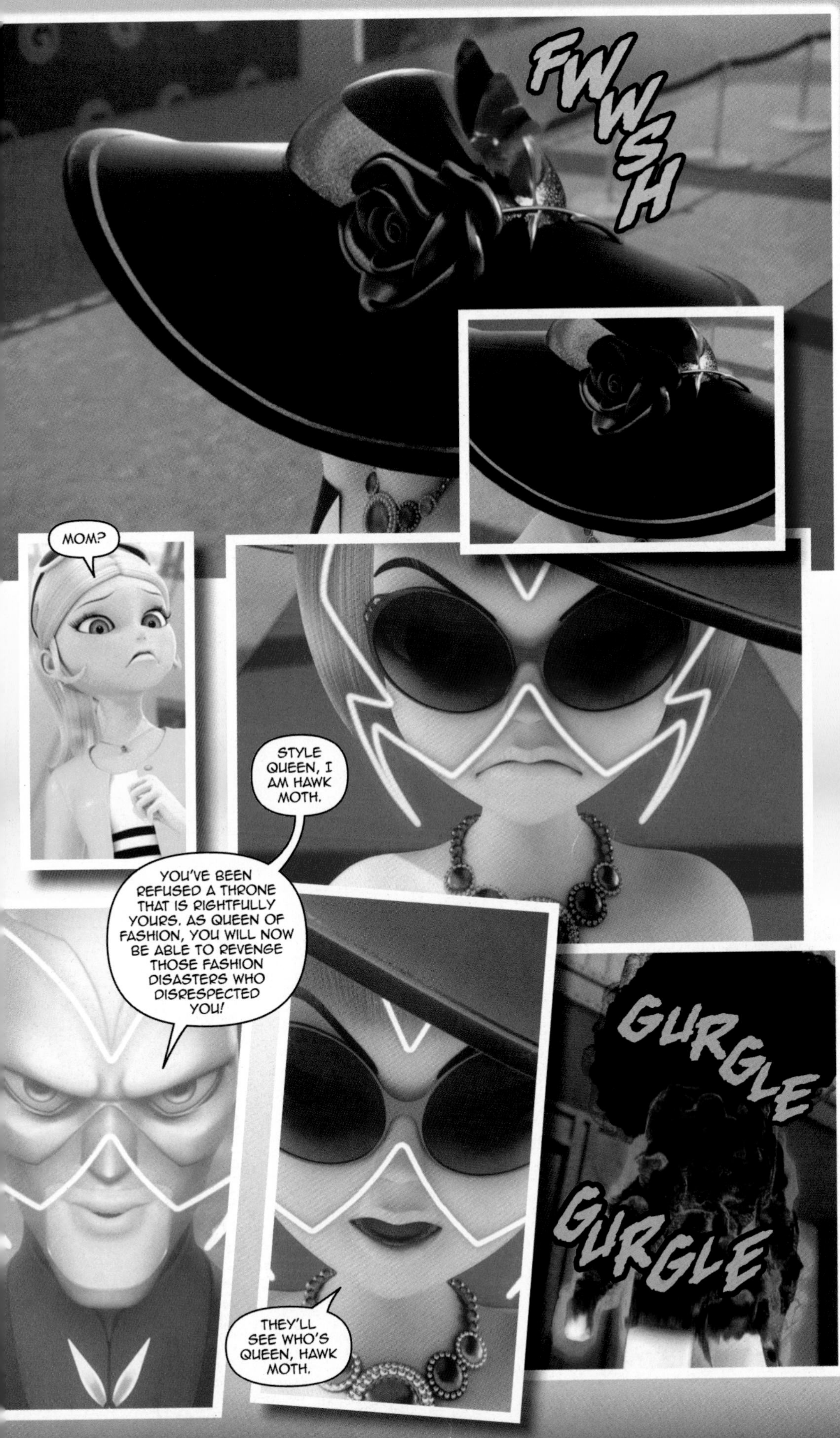
FWWSH
MOM?
STYLE QUEEN, I AM HAWK MOTH.
YOU'VE BEEN REFUSED A THRONE THAT IS RIGHTFULLY YOURS. AS QUEEN OF FASHION, YOU WILL NOW BE ABLE TO REVENGE THOSE FASHION DISASTERS WHO DISRESPECTED YOU!
THEY'LL SEE WHO'S QUEEN, HAWK MOTH.
GURGLE
GURGLE

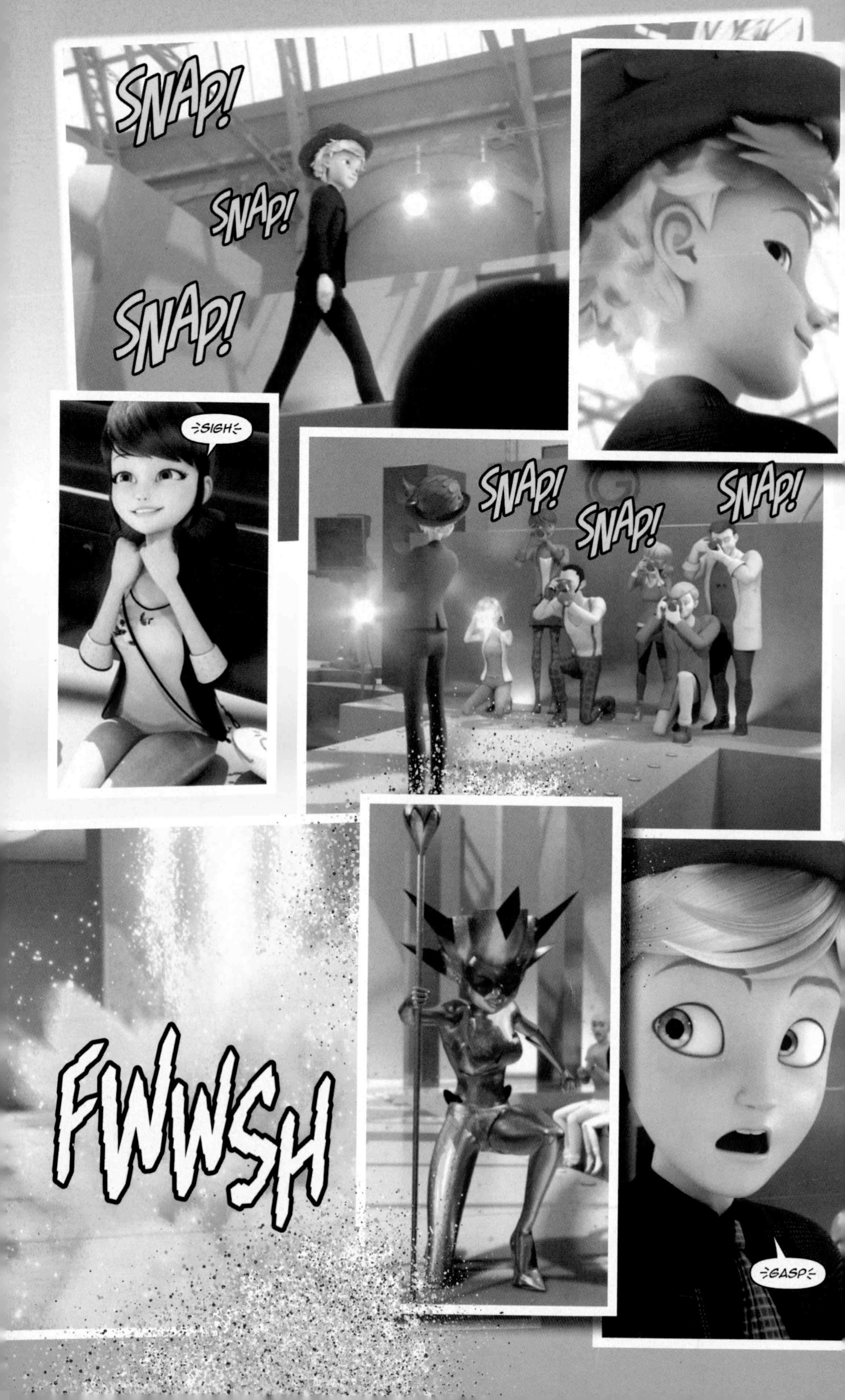
SNAP!
SNAP!
SNAP!
⫘SIGH⫘
SNAP!
SNAP!
SNAP!
FWWSH
⫘GASP⫘

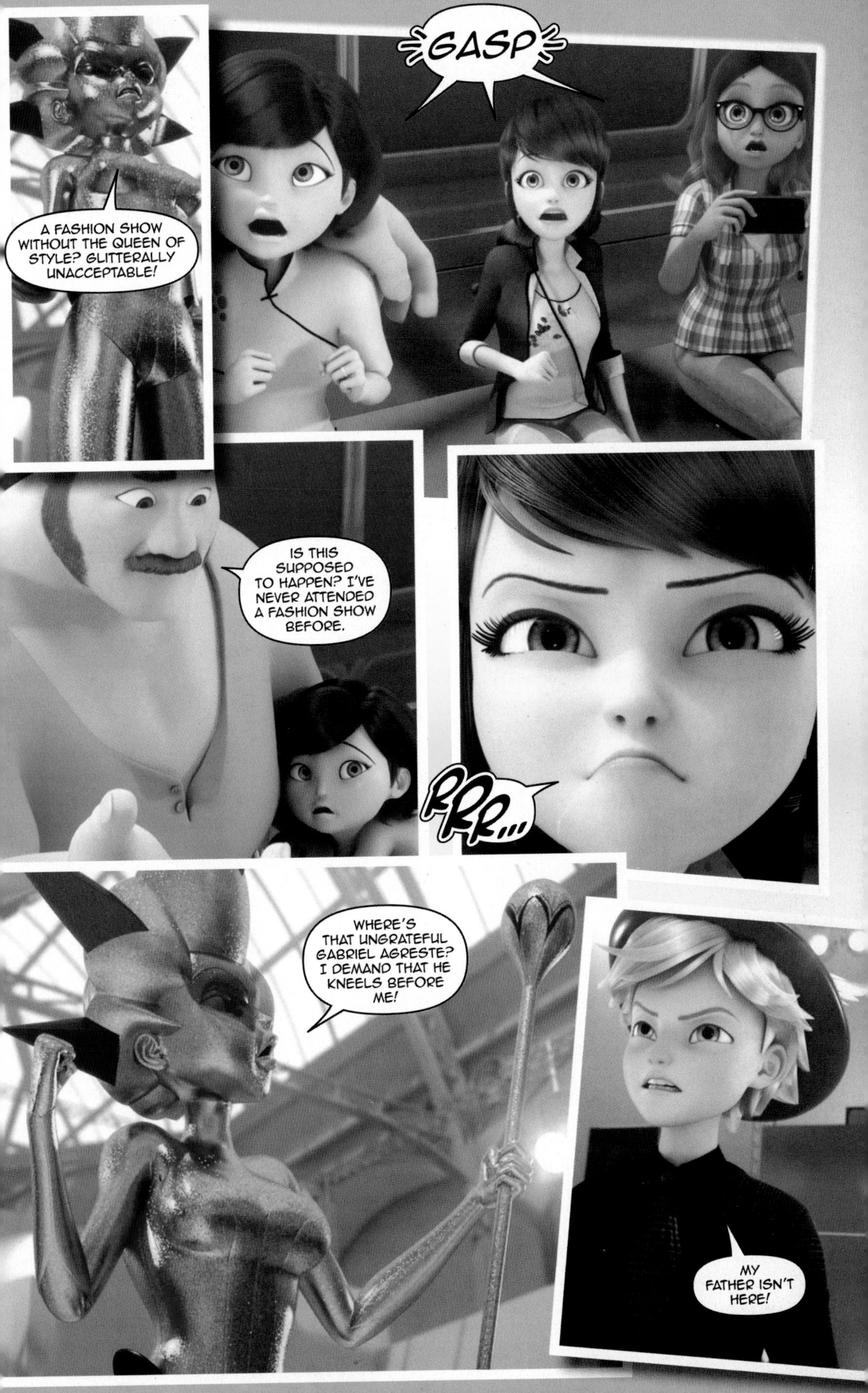
A FASHION SHOW WITHOUT THE QUEEN OF STYLE? GLITTERALLY UNACCEPTABLE!
GASP
IS THIS SUPPOSED TO HAPPEN? I'VE NEVER ATTENDED A FASHION SHOW BEFORE.
RRR...
WHERE'S THAT UNGRATEFUL GABRIEL AGRESTE? I DEMAND THAT HE KNEELS BEFORE ME!
MY FATHER ISN'T HERE!

WELL THEN, IF FASHION-DISASTER DADDY ISN'T HERE, I'LL JUST HAVE TO SETTLE FOR AGRESTE JUNIOR!
YOU'RE FIRED!
FWOOM!
ADRIEN!
UH-OH, WE'VE GOT A PROBLEM!
ADRIEN!
WE NO LONGER HAVE A CHOICE. STYLE QUEEN, YOU MUST DEFEAT LADYBUG AND CAT NOIR AS SOON AS POSSIBLE.

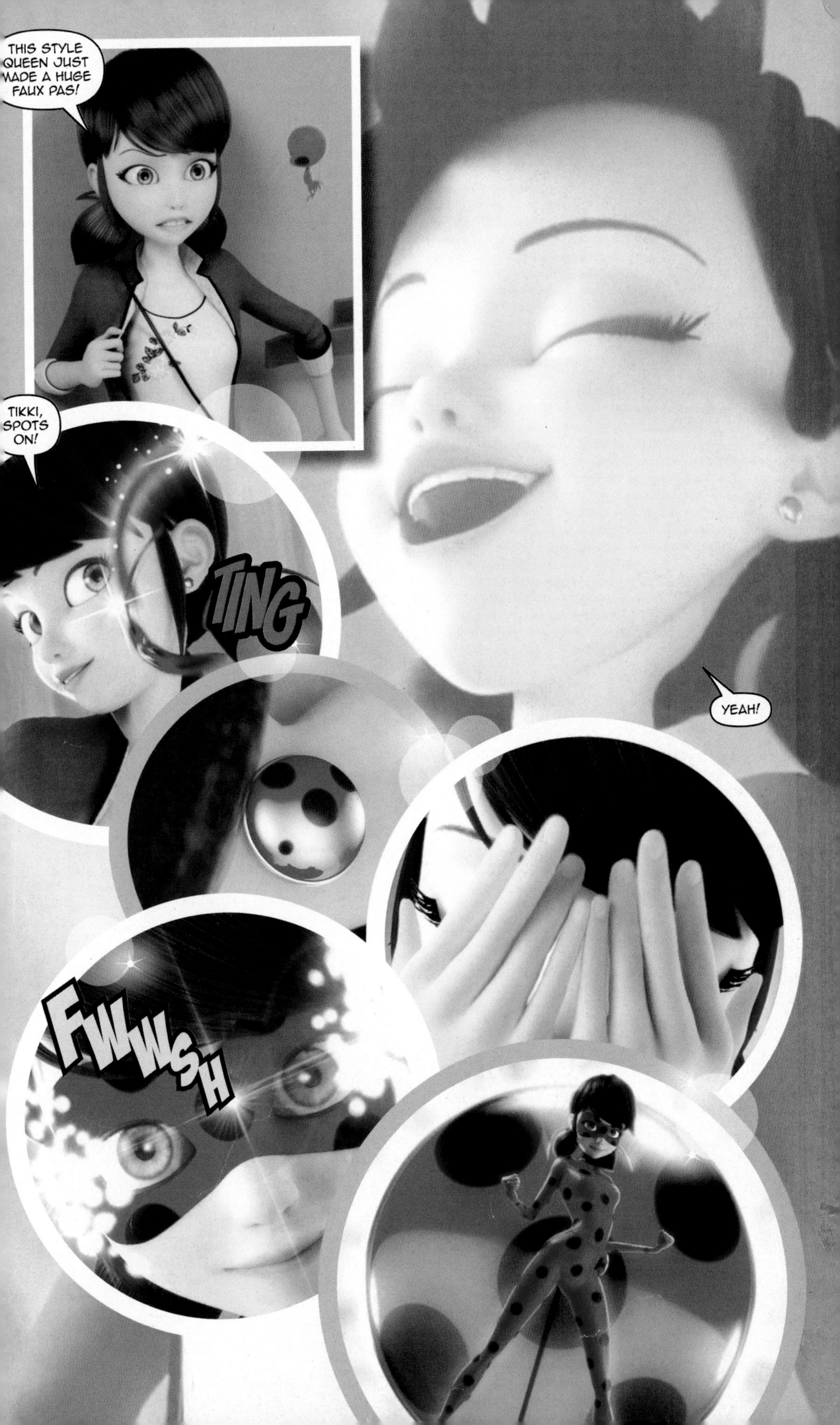
THIS STYLE QUEEN JUST MADE A HUGE FAUX PAS!
TIKKI, SPOTS ON!
TING
YEAH!
FWWSH

AUDREY, DEAR! DARLING, SWEETHEART, PLEASE STOP THIS MADNESS!

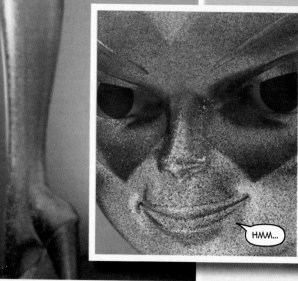

HMM...

FWOOSH

FIRED!

MOM.

CLAUDINE— UH, CHLOÉ, I'M NOT MOM. I AM STYLE QUEEN. DO YOU WANT TO BE FIRED, TOO?

NO, NO, I REALLY DON'T, STYLE QUEEN.

UH, BESIDES, DON'T YOU NEED AN ASSISTANT?

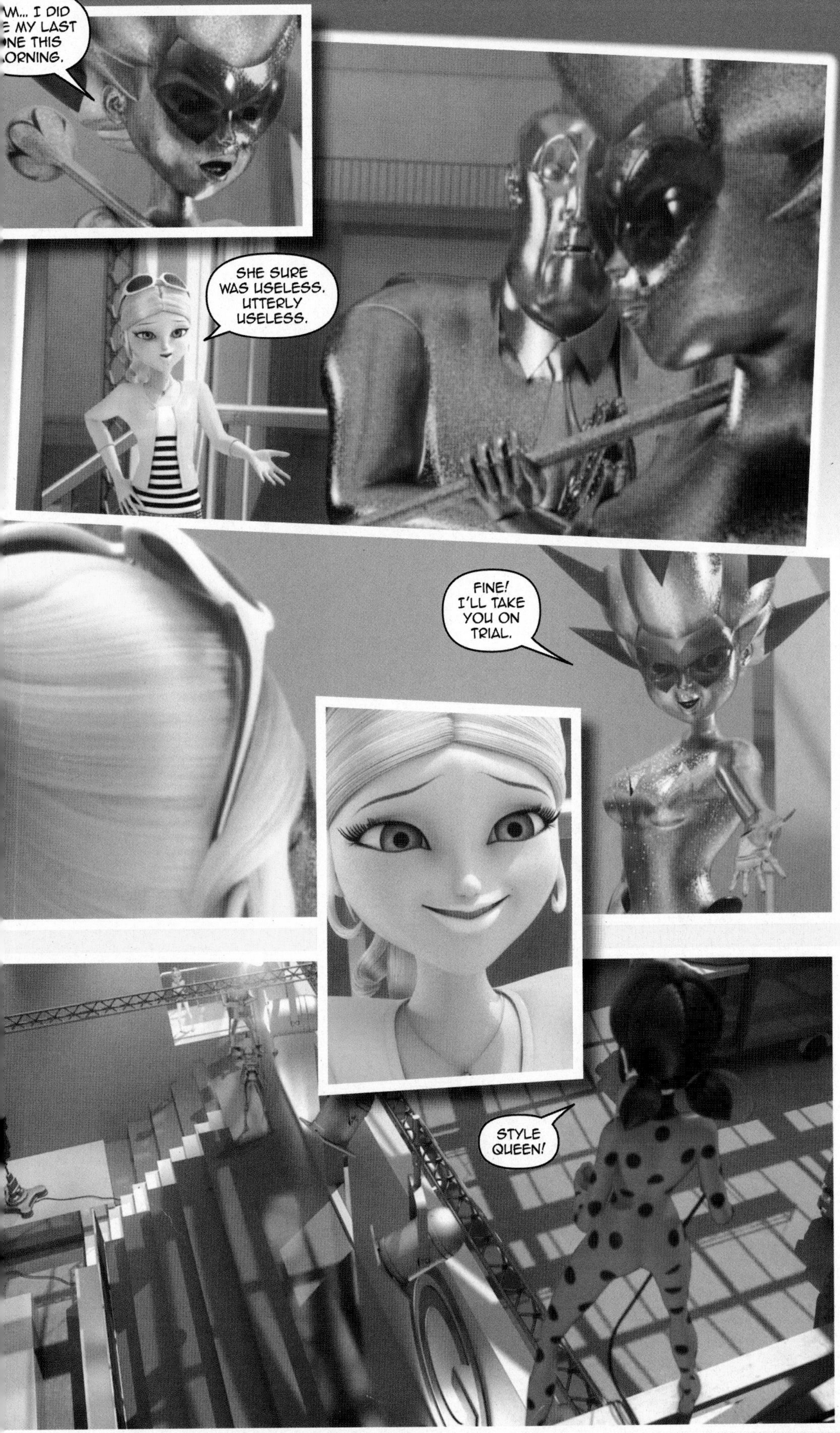
M... I DID E MY LAST NE THIS ORNING.
SHE SURE WAS USELESS. UTTERLY USELESS.
FINE! I'LL TAKE YOU ON TRIAL.
STYLE QUEEN!

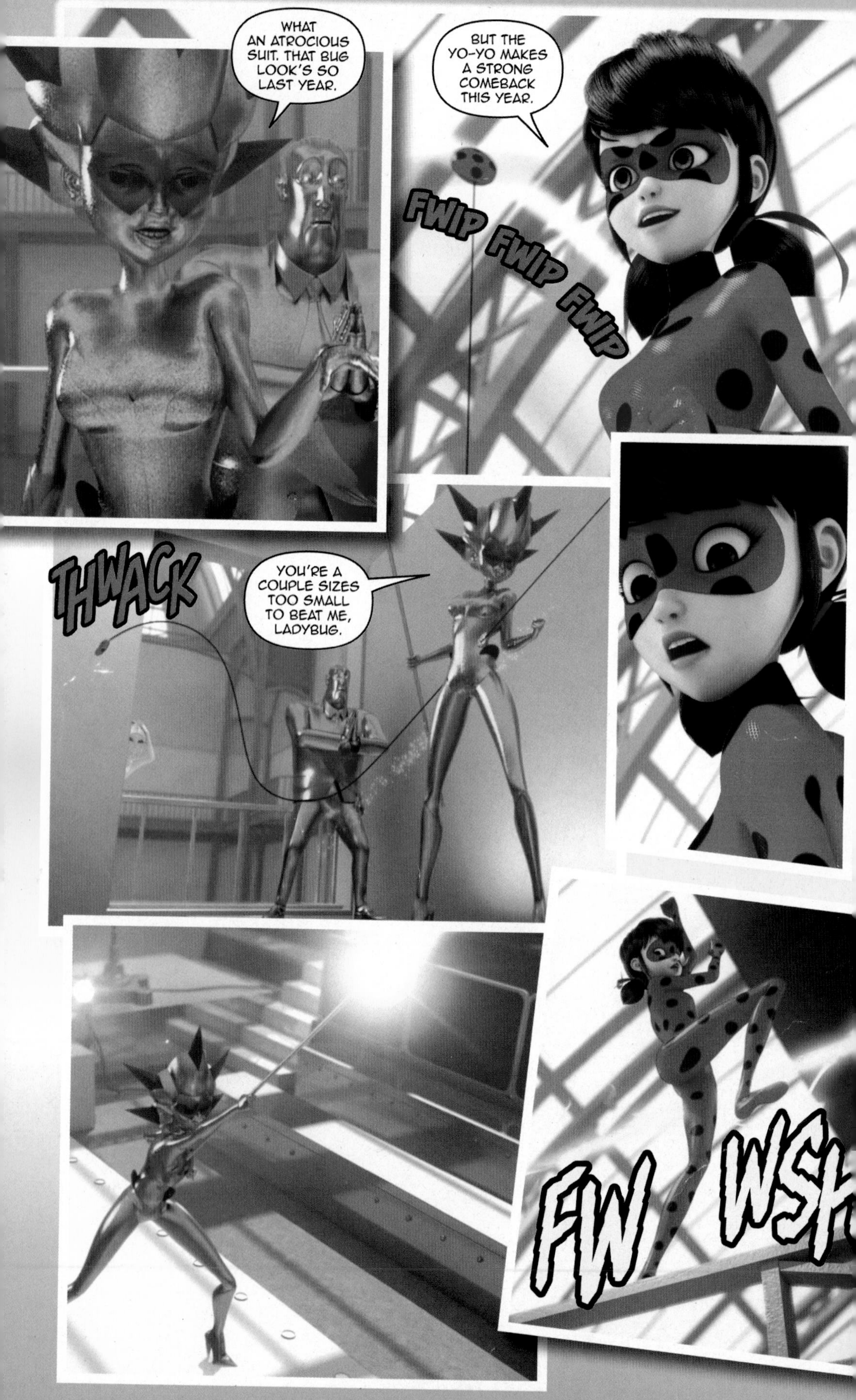
WHAT AN ATROCIOUS SUIT. THAT BUG LOOK'S SO LAST YEAR.
BUT THE YO-YO MAKES A STRONG COMEBACK THIS YEAR.
FWIP FWIP FWIP
THWACK
YOU'RE A COUPLE SIZES TOO SMALL TO BEAT ME, LADYBUG.
FW WSH

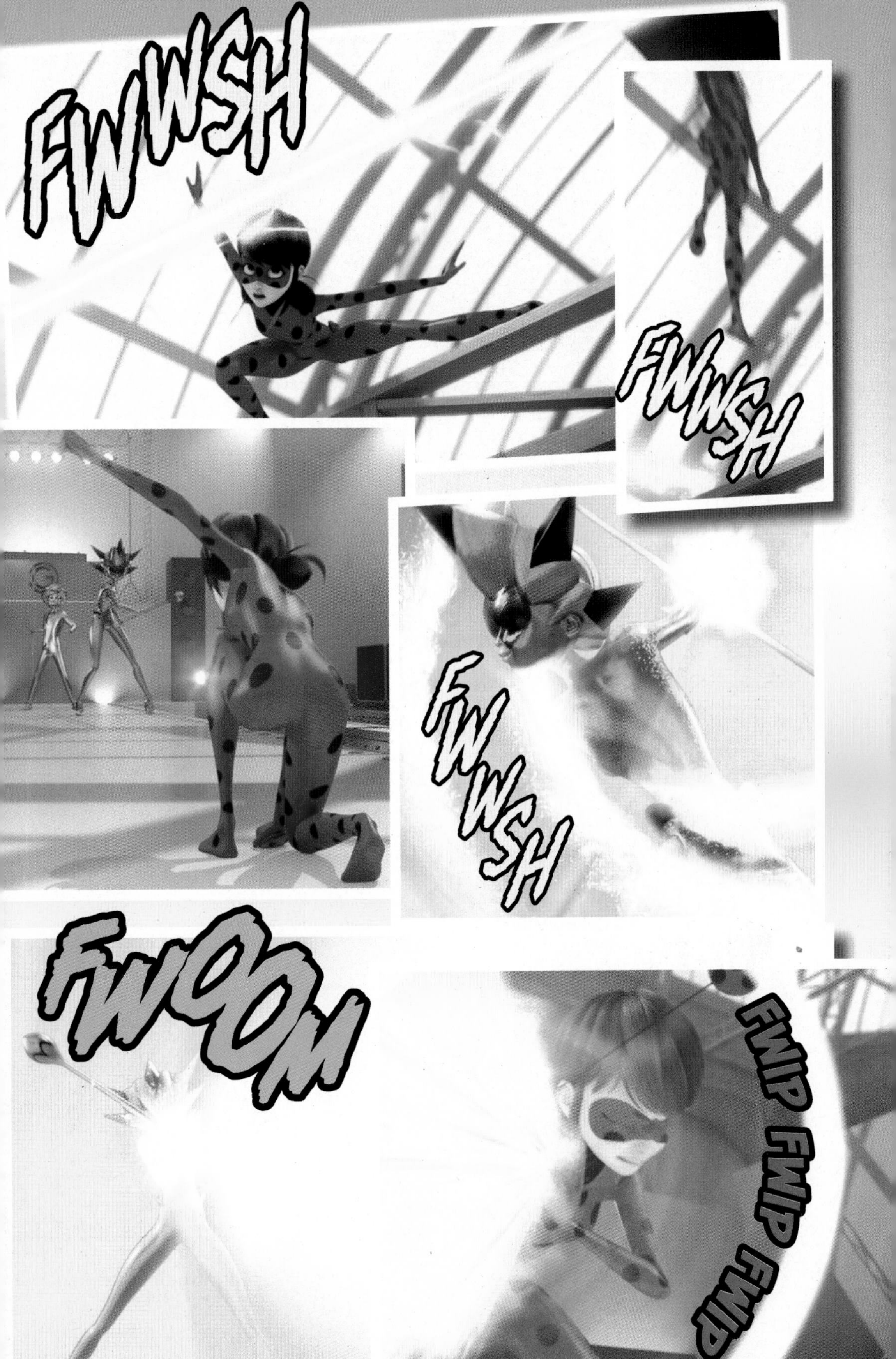

FWWSH
FWWSH
FWWSH
FWOOM
FWIP FWIP FWIP

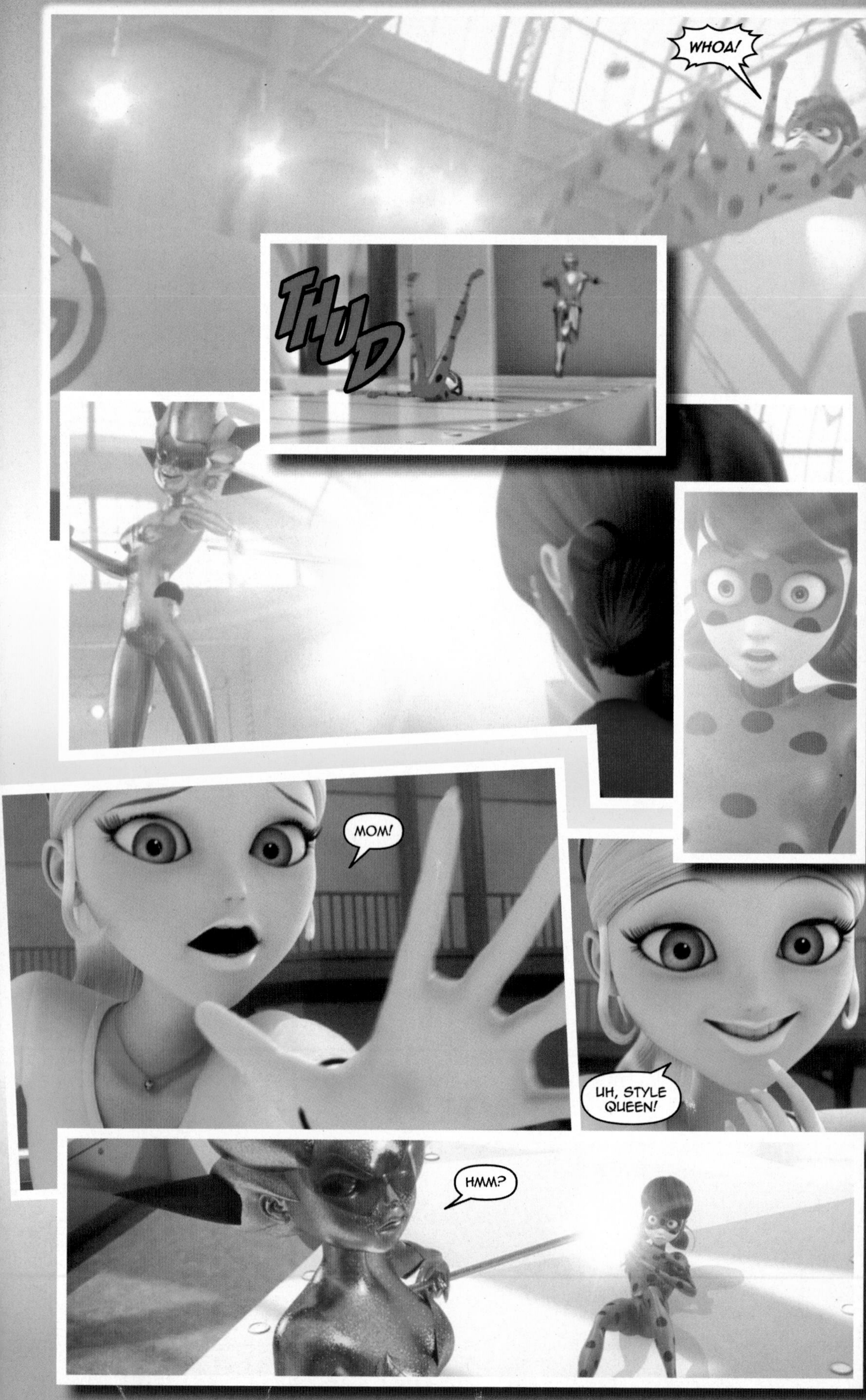
WHOA!
THUD
MOM!
UH, STYLE QUEEN!
HMM?

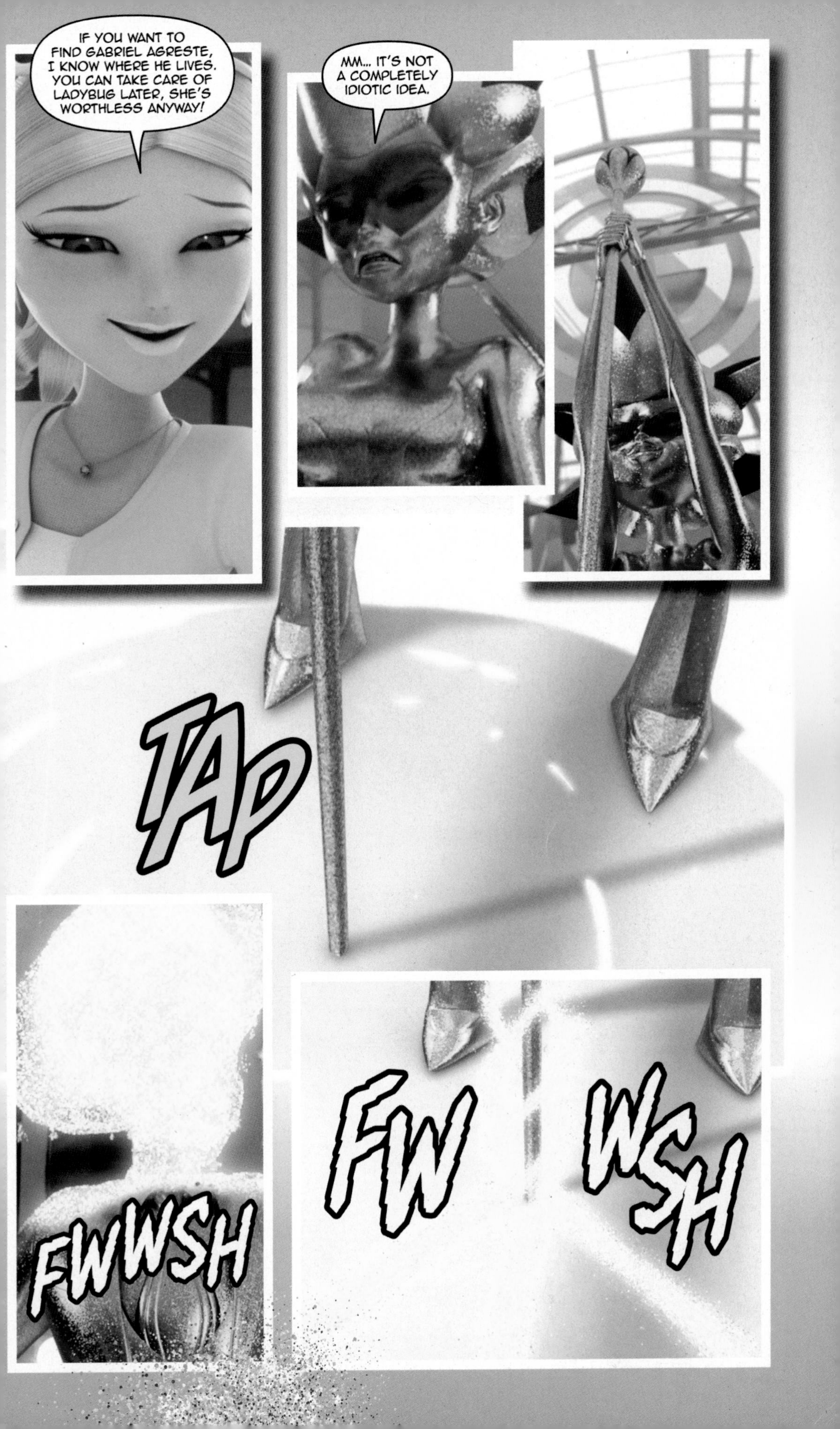
IF YOU WANT TO FIND GABRIEL AGRESTE, I KNOW WHERE HE LIVES. YOU CAN TAKE CARE OF LADYBUG LATER, SHE'S WORTHLESS ANYWAY!
MM... IT'S NOT A COMPLETELY IDIOTIC IDEA.
TAP
FWWSH
FW
WSH

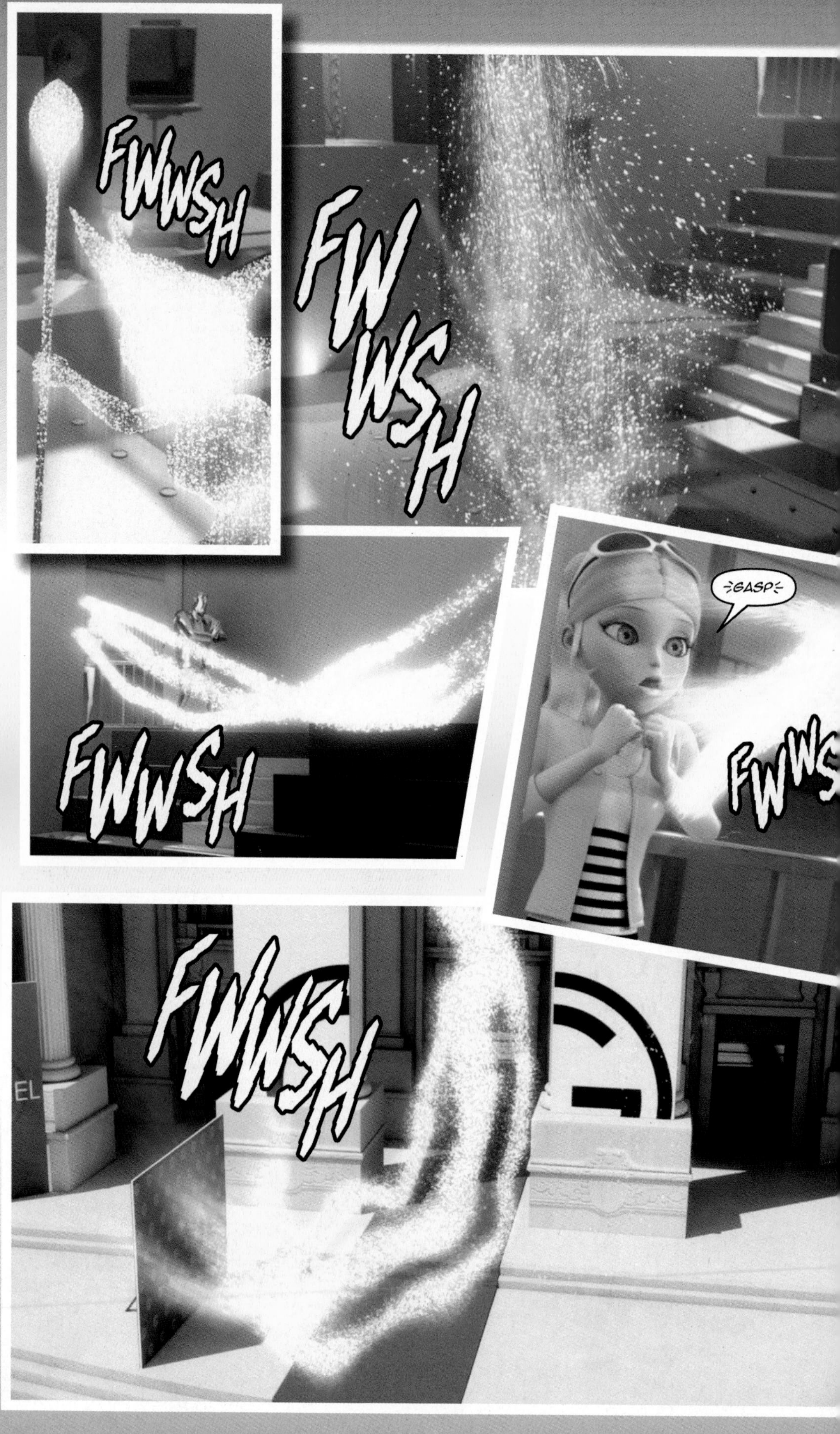
FWWSH
FWWSH
FWWSH
GASP
FWWS
FWWSH
EL

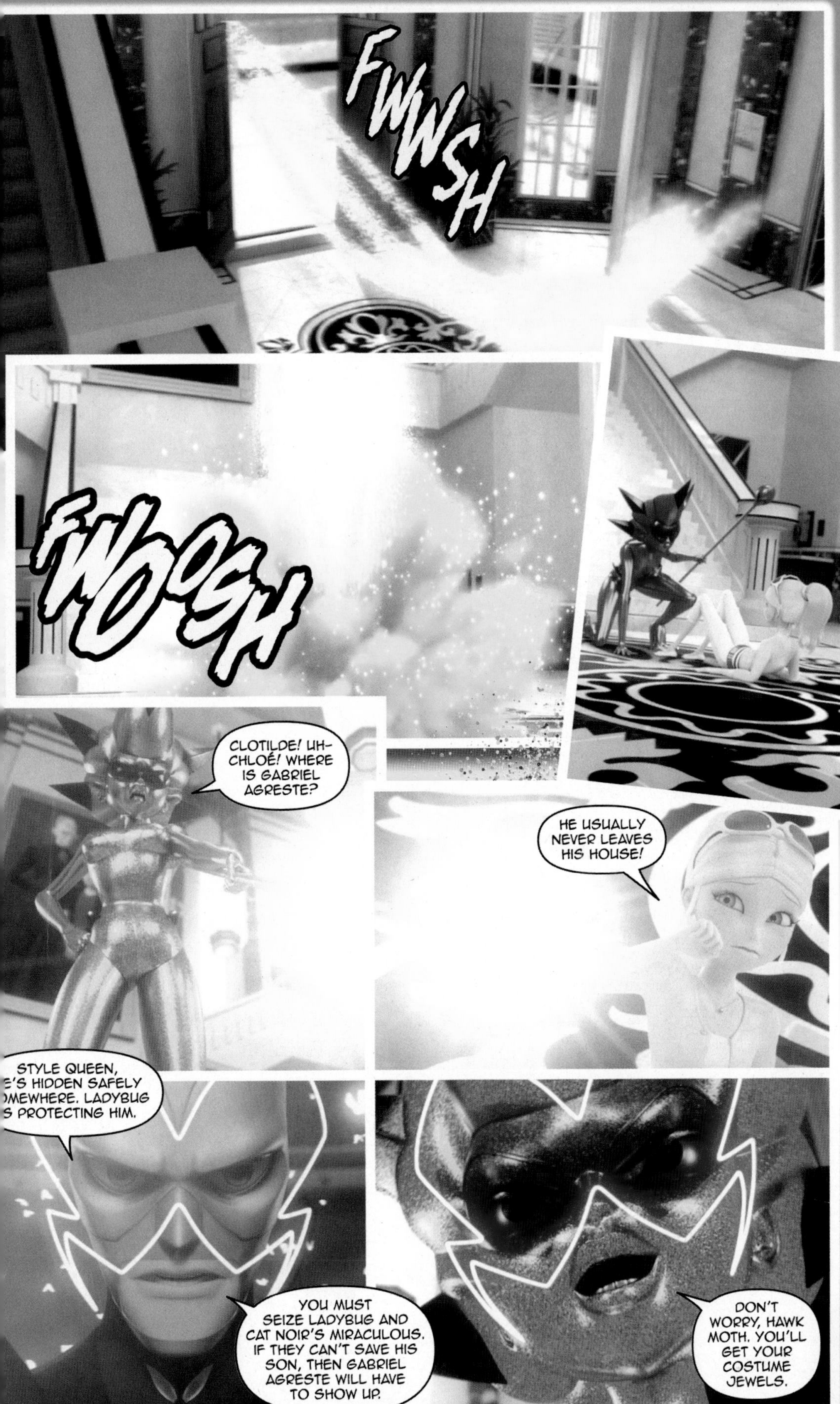
FWWSH
FWOOSH
CLOTILDE! UH- CHLOÉ! WHERE IS GABRIEL AGRESTE?
HE USUALLY NEVER LEAVES HIS HOUSE!
STYLE QUEEN, E'S HIDDEN SAFELY OMEWHERE. LADYBUG S PROTECTING HIM.
YOU MUST SEIZE LADYBUG AND CAT NOIR'S MIRACULOUS. IF THEY CAN'T SAVE HIS SON, THEN GABRIEL AGRESTE WILL HAVE TO SHOW UP.
DON'T WORRY, HAWK MOTH. YOU'LL GET YOUR COSTUME JEWELS.

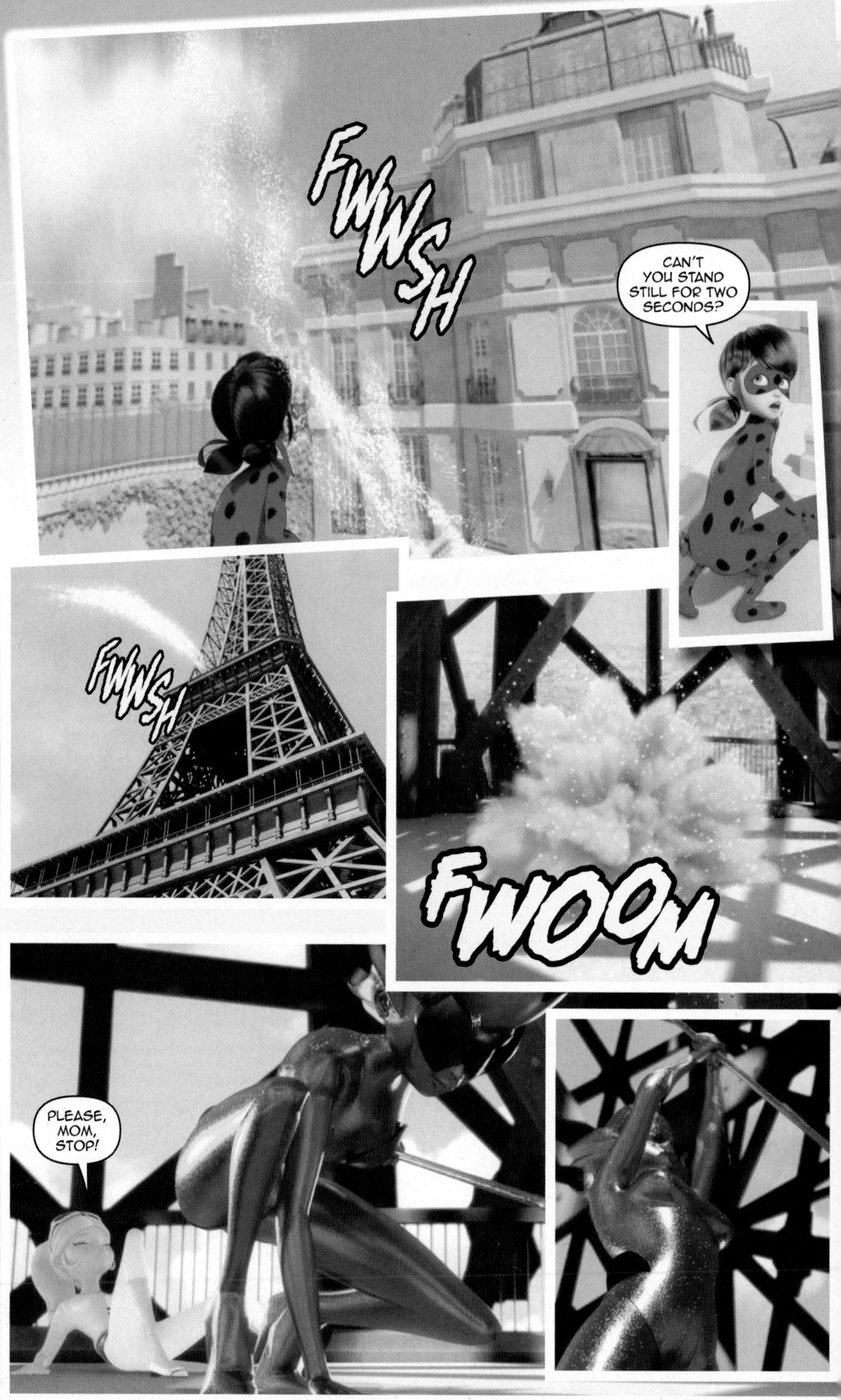
FWWSH
CAN'T YOU STAND STILL FOR TWO SECONDS?
FWWSH
FWOOM
PLEASE, MOM, STOP!

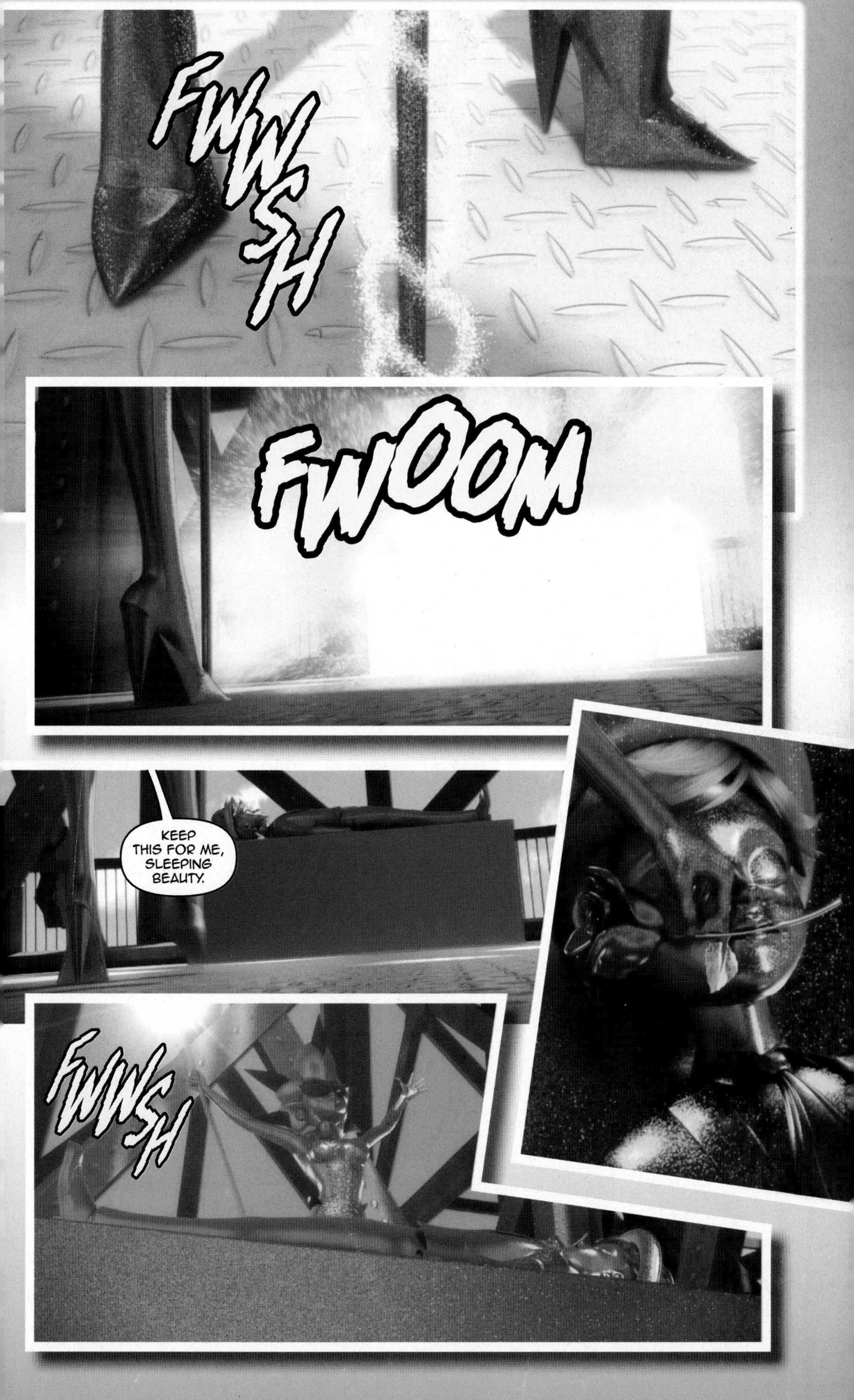
FWWSH
FWOOM
KEEP THIS FOR ME, SLEEPING BEAUTY.
FWWSH

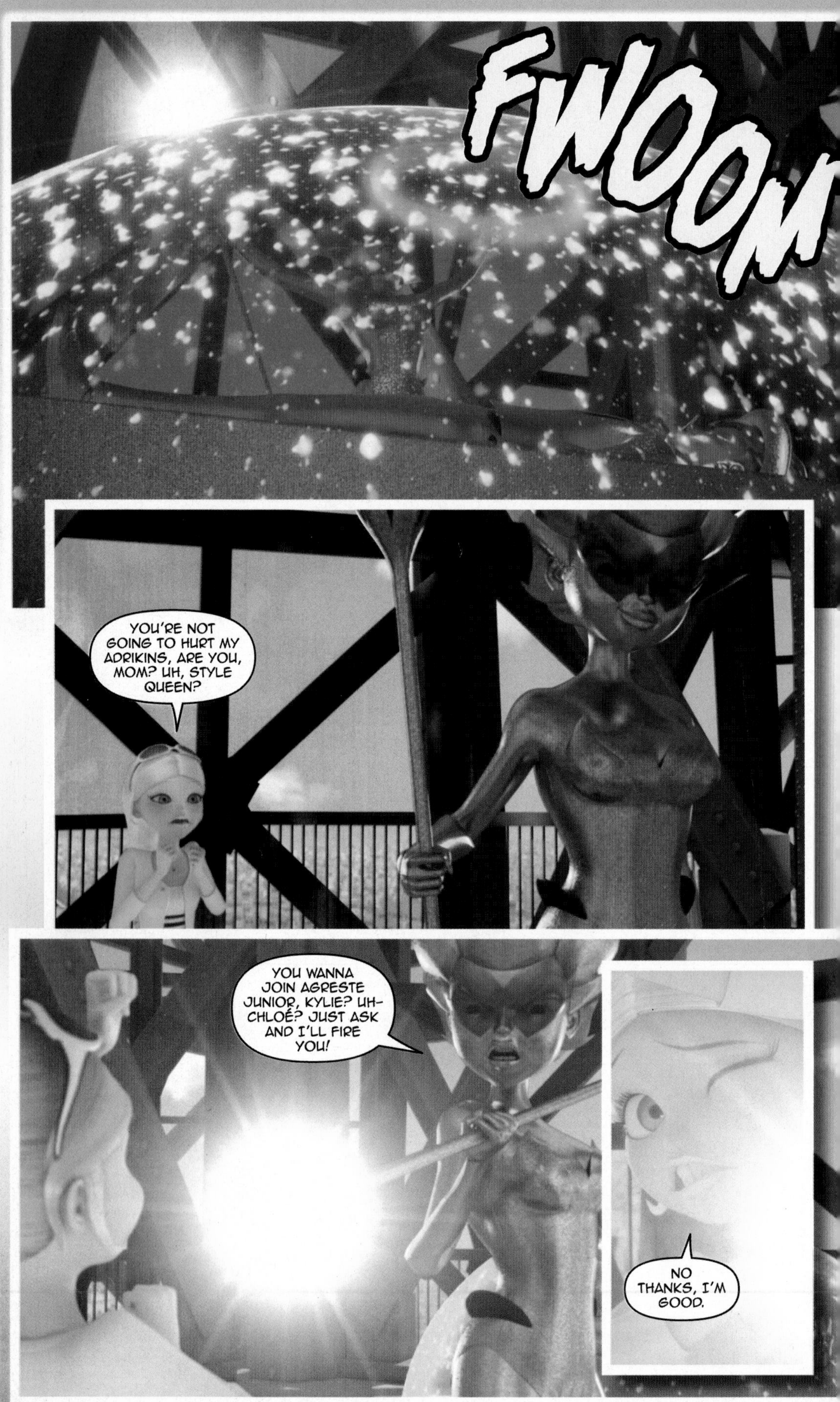
FWOOM
YOU'RE NOT GOING TO HURT MY ADRIKINS, ARE YOU, MOM? UH, STYLE QUEEN?
YOU WANNA JOIN AGRESTE JUNIOR, KYLIE? UH-CHLOÉ? JUST ASK AND I'LL FIRE YOU!
NO THANKS, I'M GOOD.

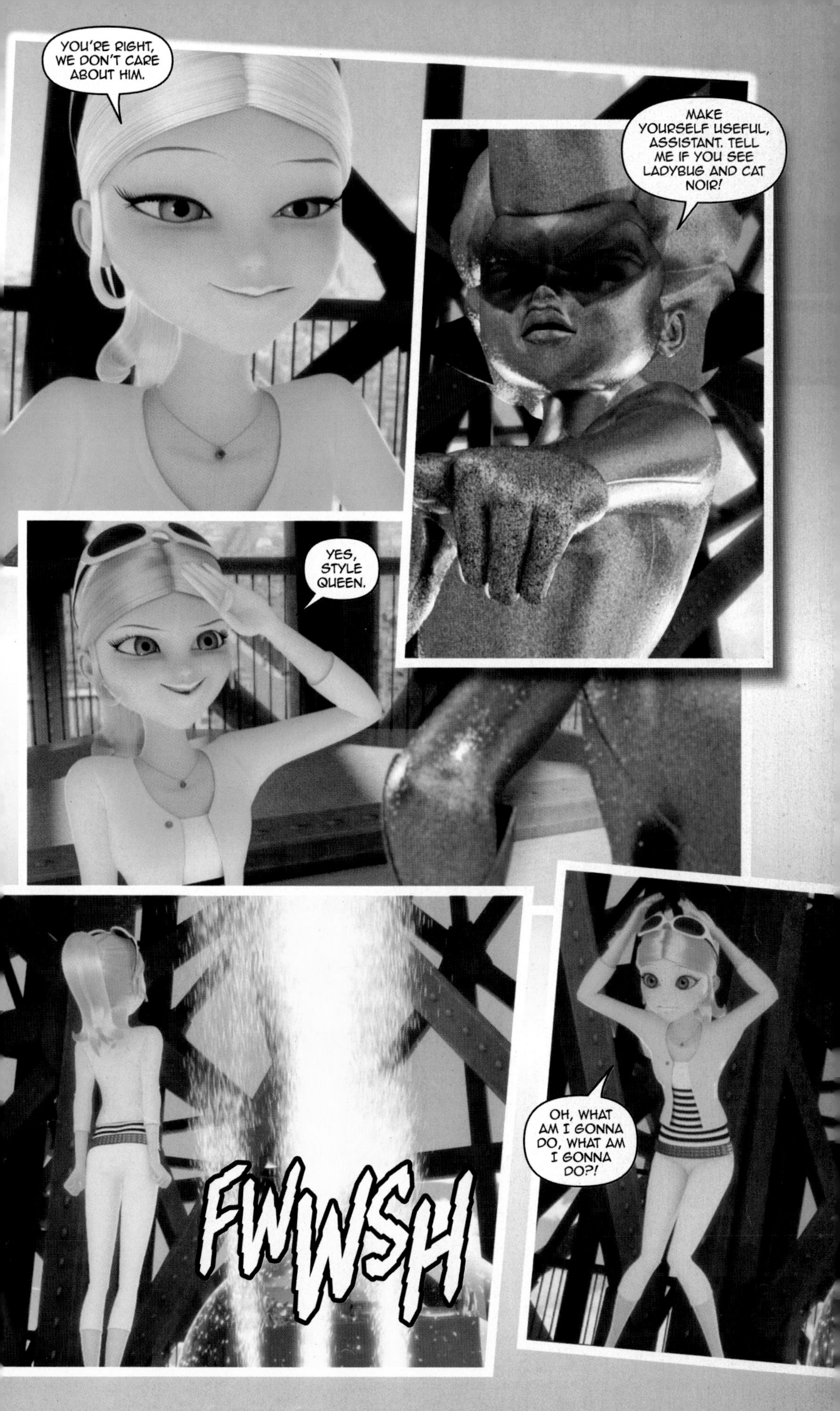
YOU'RE RIGHT, WE DON'T CARE ABOUT HIM.
MAKE YOURSELF USEFUL, ASSISTANT. TELL ME IF YOU SEE LADYBUG AND CAT NOIR!
YES, STYLE QUEEN.
FWWSH
OH, WHAT AM I GONNA DO, WHAT AM I GONNA DO?!

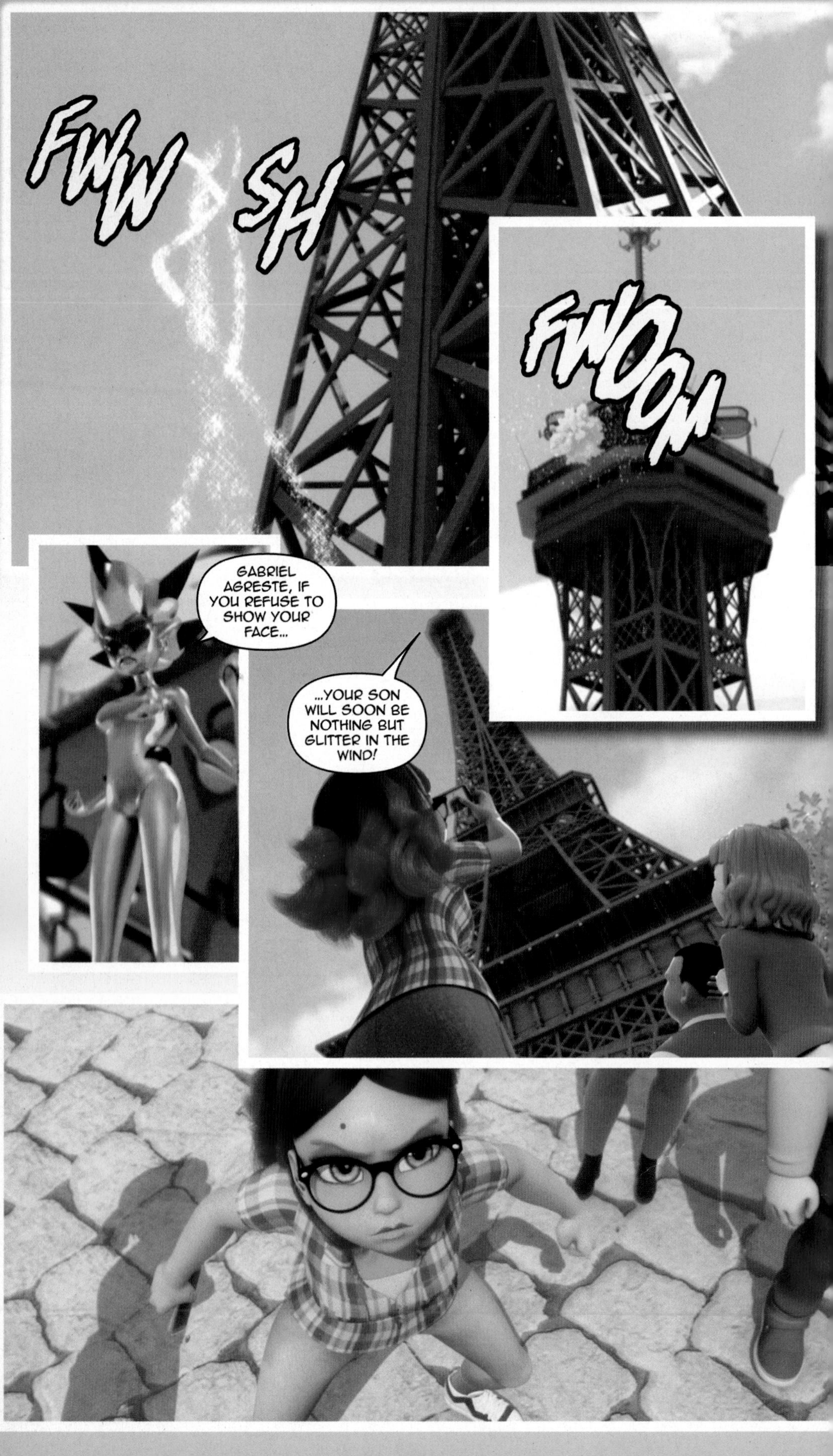
FWWSH
FWOOM
GABRIEL AGRESTE, IF YOU REFUSE TO SHOW YOUR FACE...
...YOUR SON WILL SOON BE NOTHING BUT GLITTER IN THE WIND!

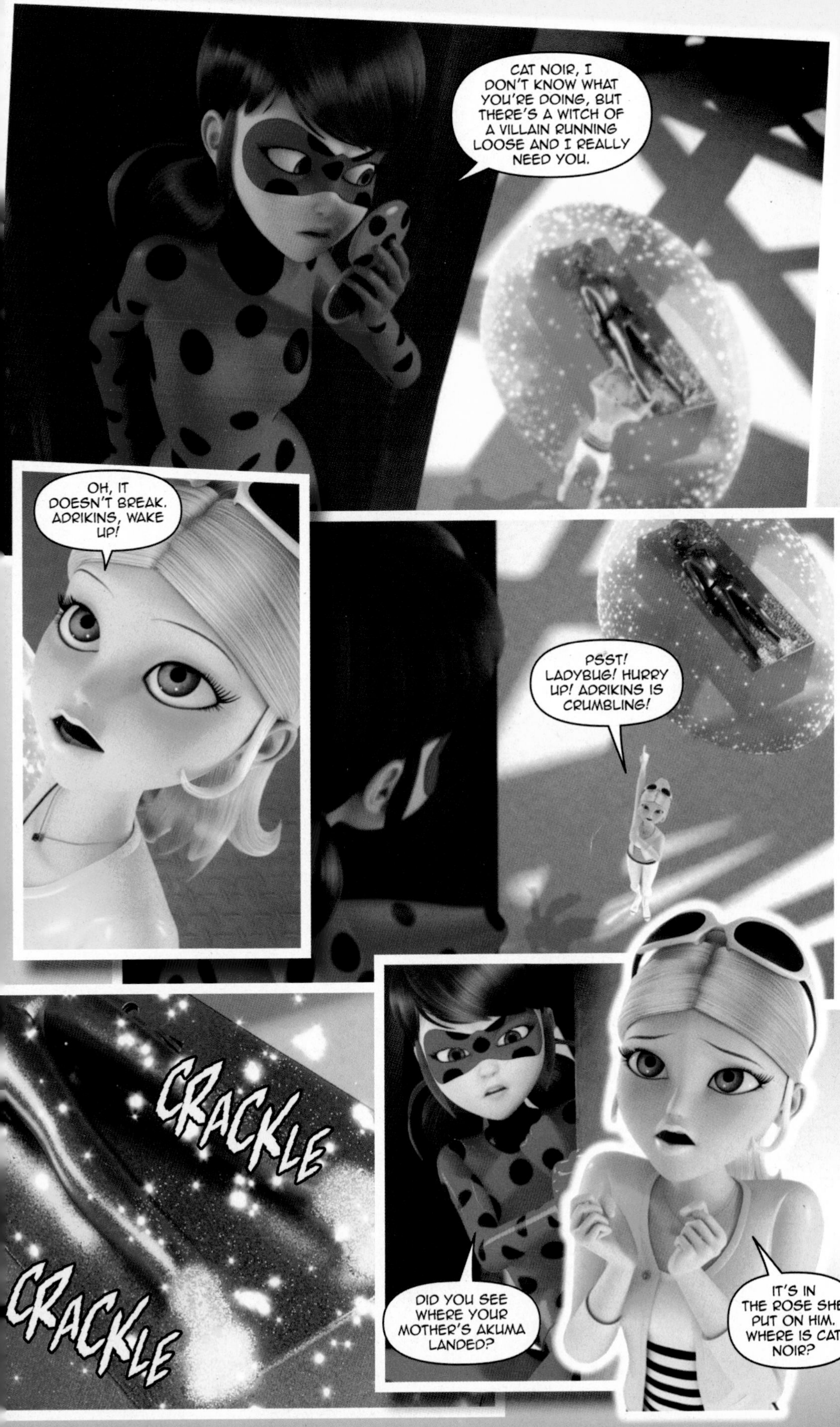
CAT NOIR, I DON'T KNOW WHAT YOU'RE DOING, BUT THERE'S A WITCH OF A VILLAIN RUNNING LOOSE AND I REALLY NEED YOU.
OH, IT DOESN'T BREAK. ADRIKINS, WAKE UP!
PSST! LADYBUG! HURRY UP! ADRIKINS IS CRUMBLING!
CRACKLE
CRACKLE
DID YOU SEE WHERE YOUR MOTHER'S AKUMA LANDED?
IT'S IN THE ROSE SHE PUT ON HIM. WHERE IS CAT NOIR?

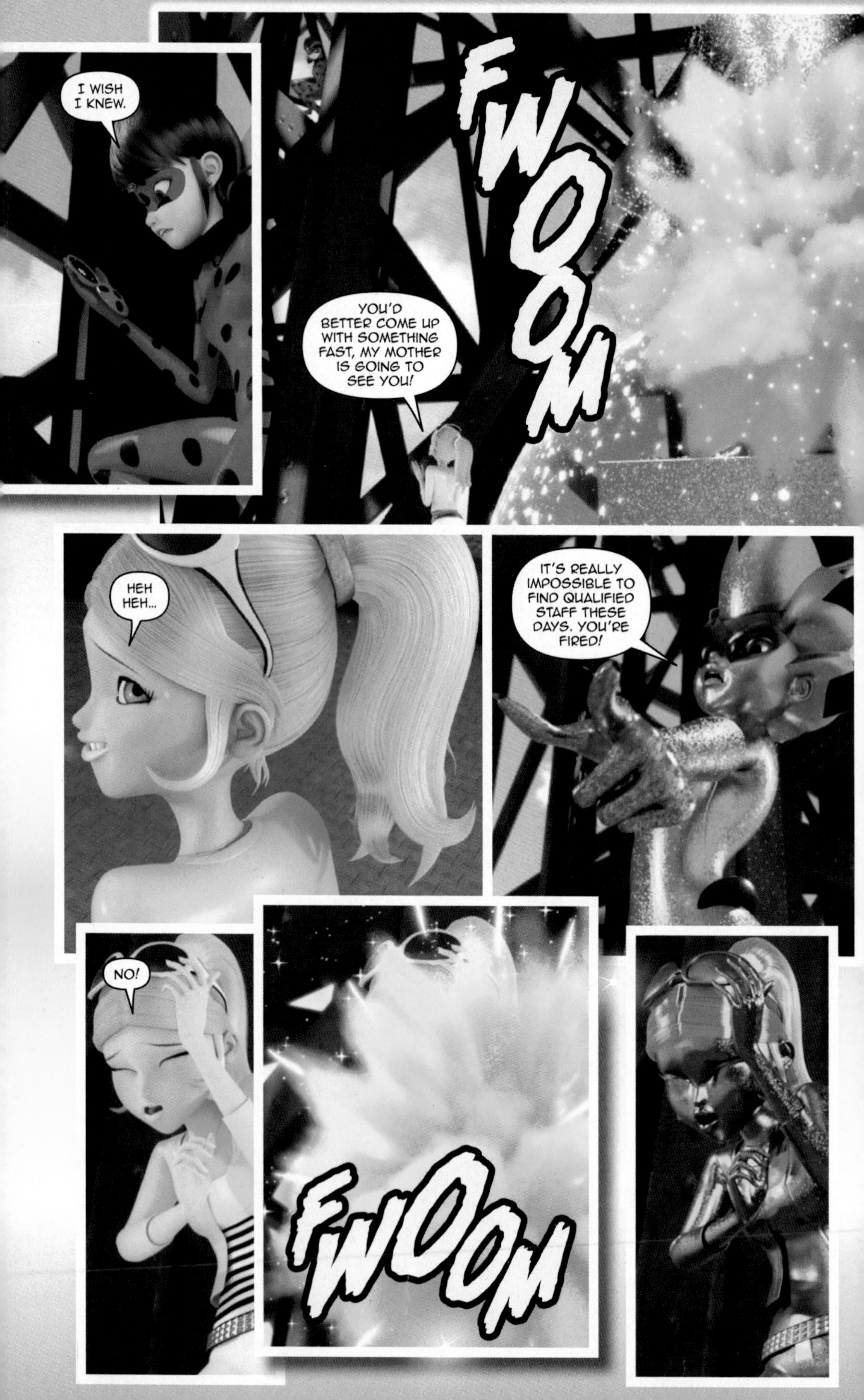
I WISH I KNEW.
YOU'D BETTER COME UP WITH SOMETHING FAST, MY MOTHER IS GOING TO SEE YOU!
FWOOOM
HEH HEH...
IT'S REALLY IMPOSSIBLE TO FIND QUALIFIED STAFF THESE DAYS. YOU'RE FIRED!
NO!
FWOOOM

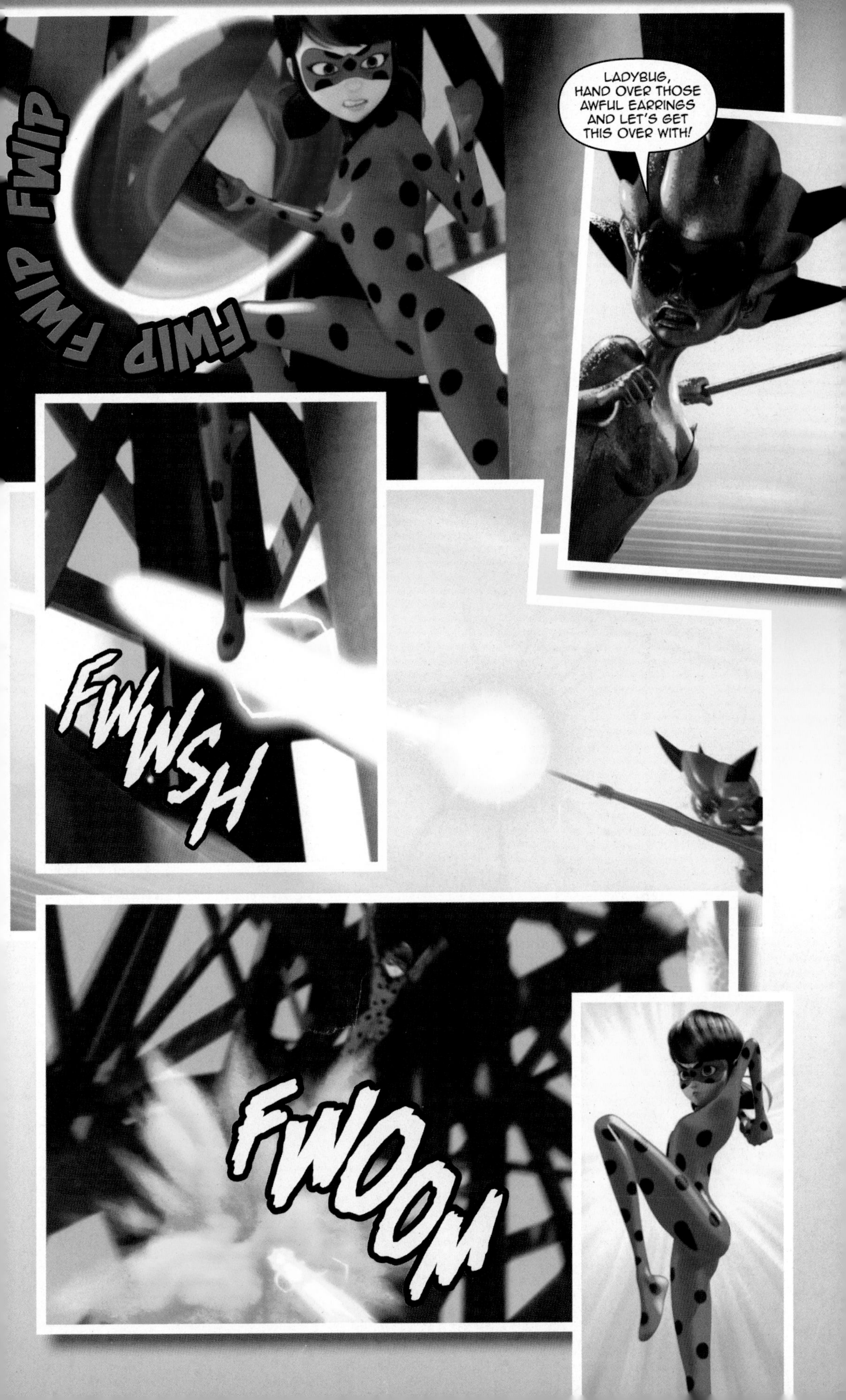

FWIP FWIP FWIP
LADYBUG, HAND OVER THOSE AWFUL EARRINGS AND LET'S GET THIS OVER WITH!
FWWSH
FWOOM

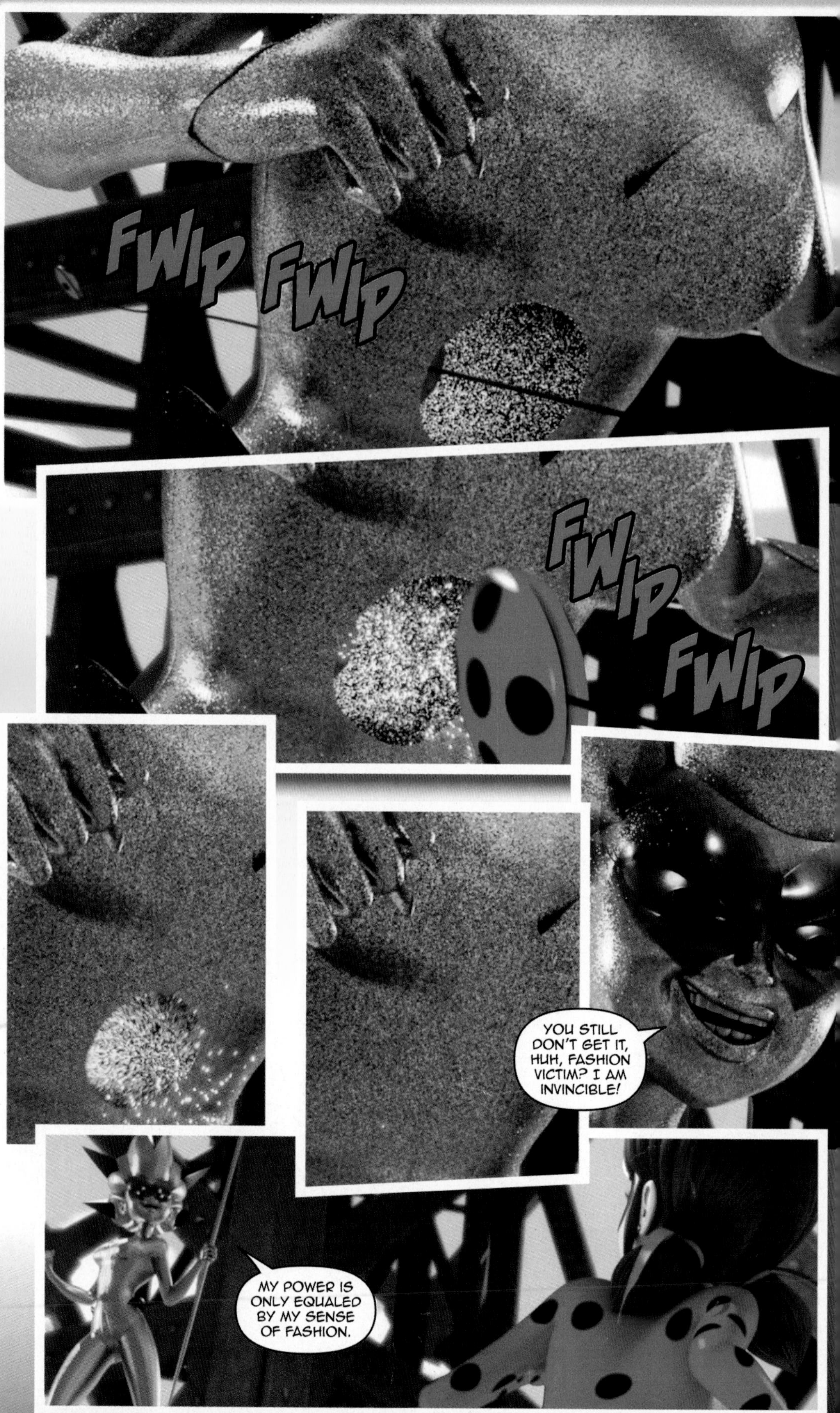
FWIP FWIP
FWIP FWIP
YOU STILL DON'T GET IT, HUH, FASHION VICTIM? I AM INVINCIBLE!
MY POWER IS ONLY EQUALED BY MY SENSE OF FASHION.

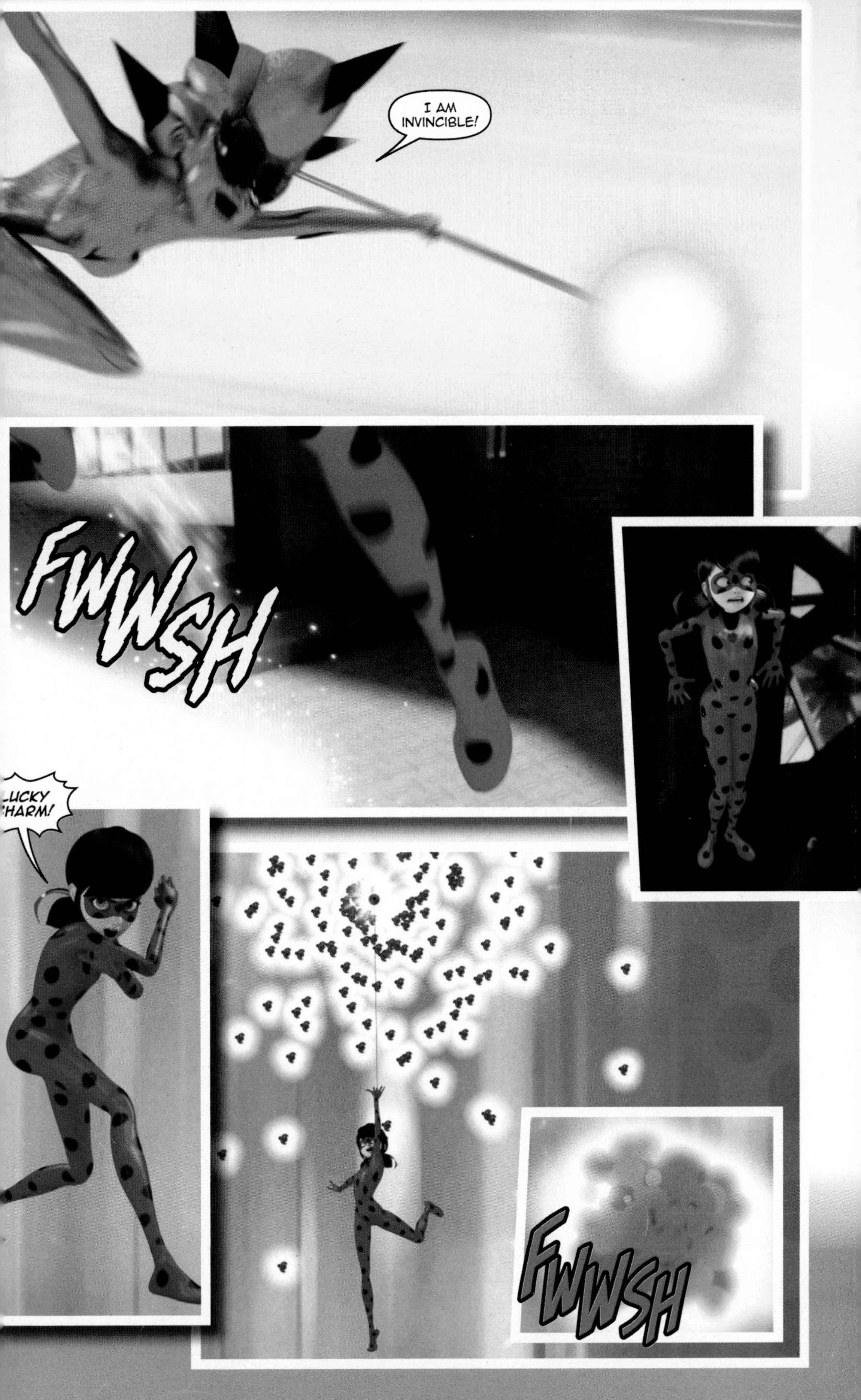
I AM INVINCIBLE!
FWWSH
LUCKY CHARM!
FWWSH

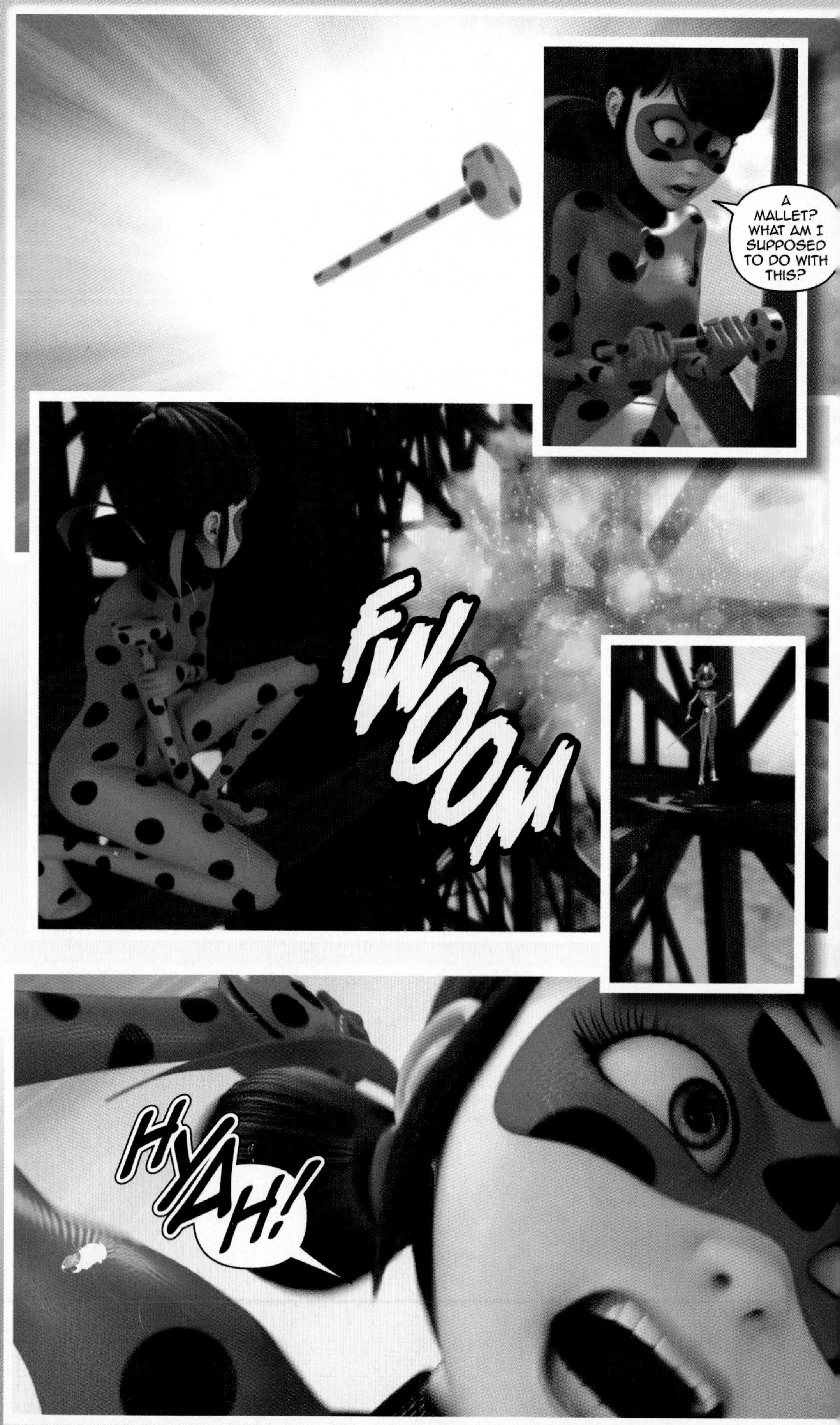
A MALLET? WHAT AM I SUPPOSED TO DO WITH THIS?
FWOOM
HYAH!

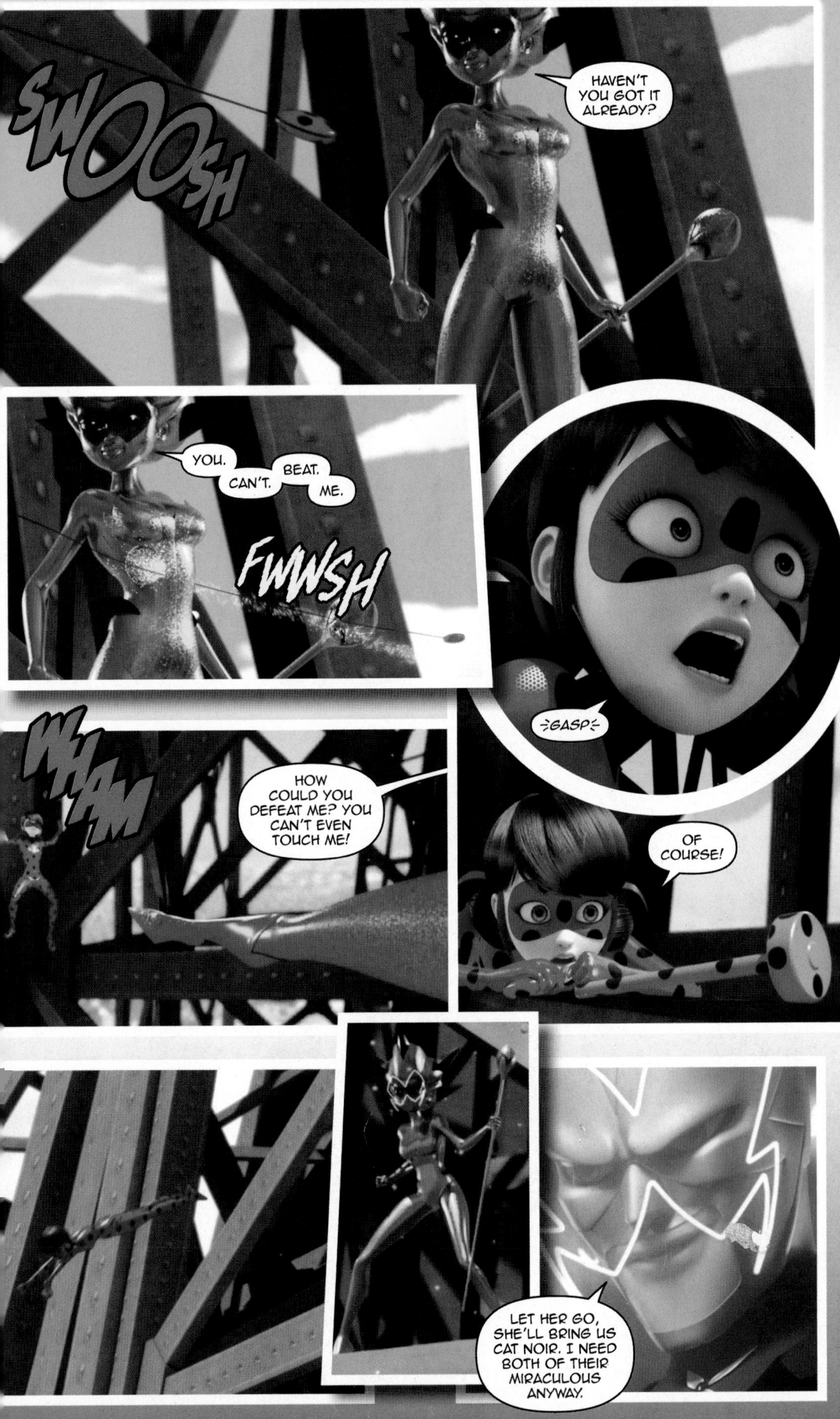
SWOOSH
HAVEN'T YOU GOT IT ALREADY?
YOU. CAN'T. BEAT. ME.
FWWSH
GASP
WHAM
HOW COULD YOU DEFEAT ME? YOU CAN'T EVEN TOUCH ME!
OF COURSE!
LET HER GO, SHE'LL BRING US CAT NOIR. I NEED BOTH OF THEIR MIRACULOUS ANYWAY.

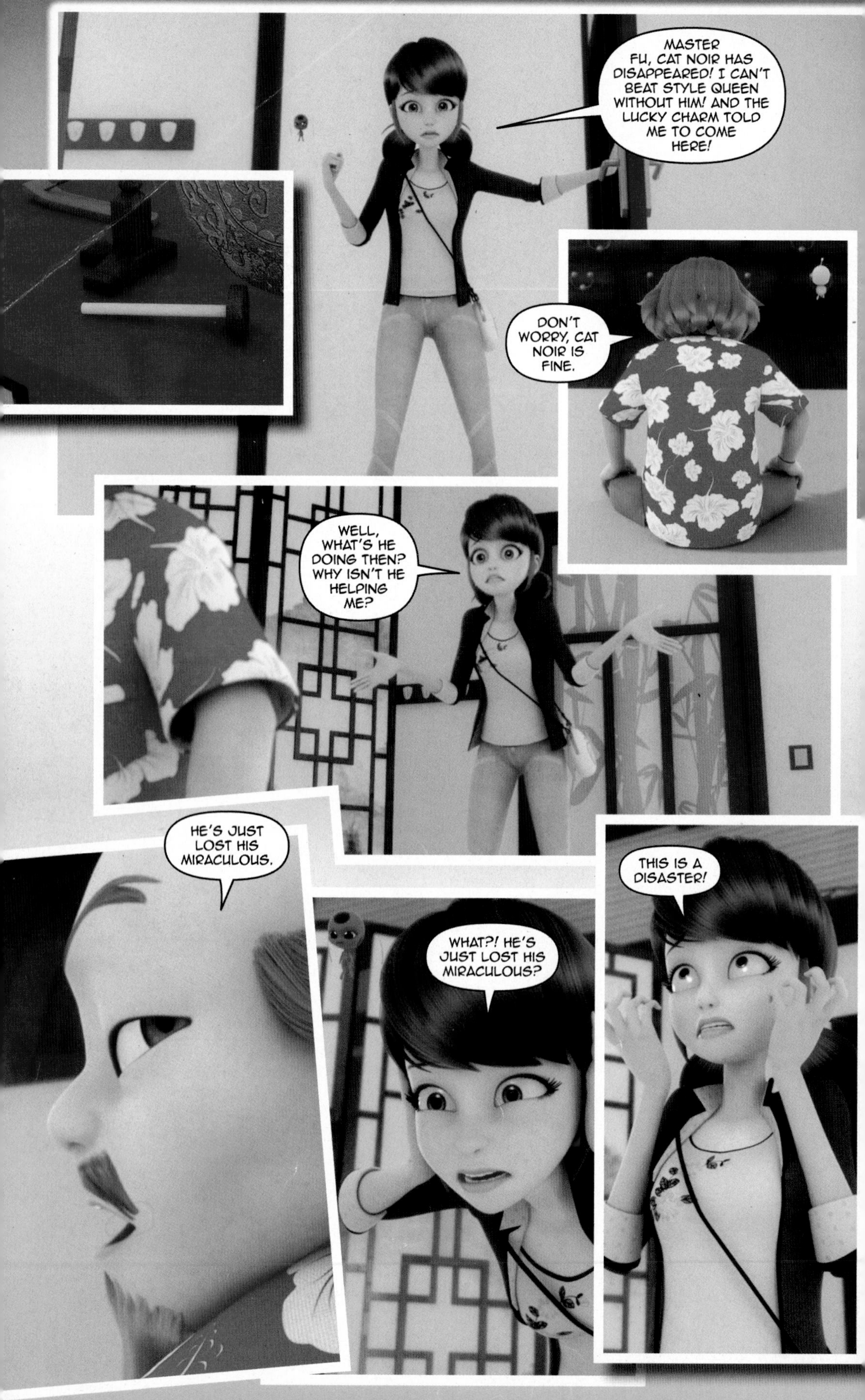
MASTER FU, CAT NOIR HAS DISAPPEARED! I CAN'T BEAT STYLE QUEEN WITHOUT HIM! AND THE LUCKY CHARM TOLD ME TO COME HERE!
DON'T WORRY, CAT NOIR IS FINE.
WELL, WHAT'S HE DOING THEN? WHY ISN'T HE HELPING ME?
HE'S JUST LOST HIS MIRACULOUS.
WHAT?! HE'S JUST LOST HIS MIRACULOUS?
THIS IS A DISASTER!

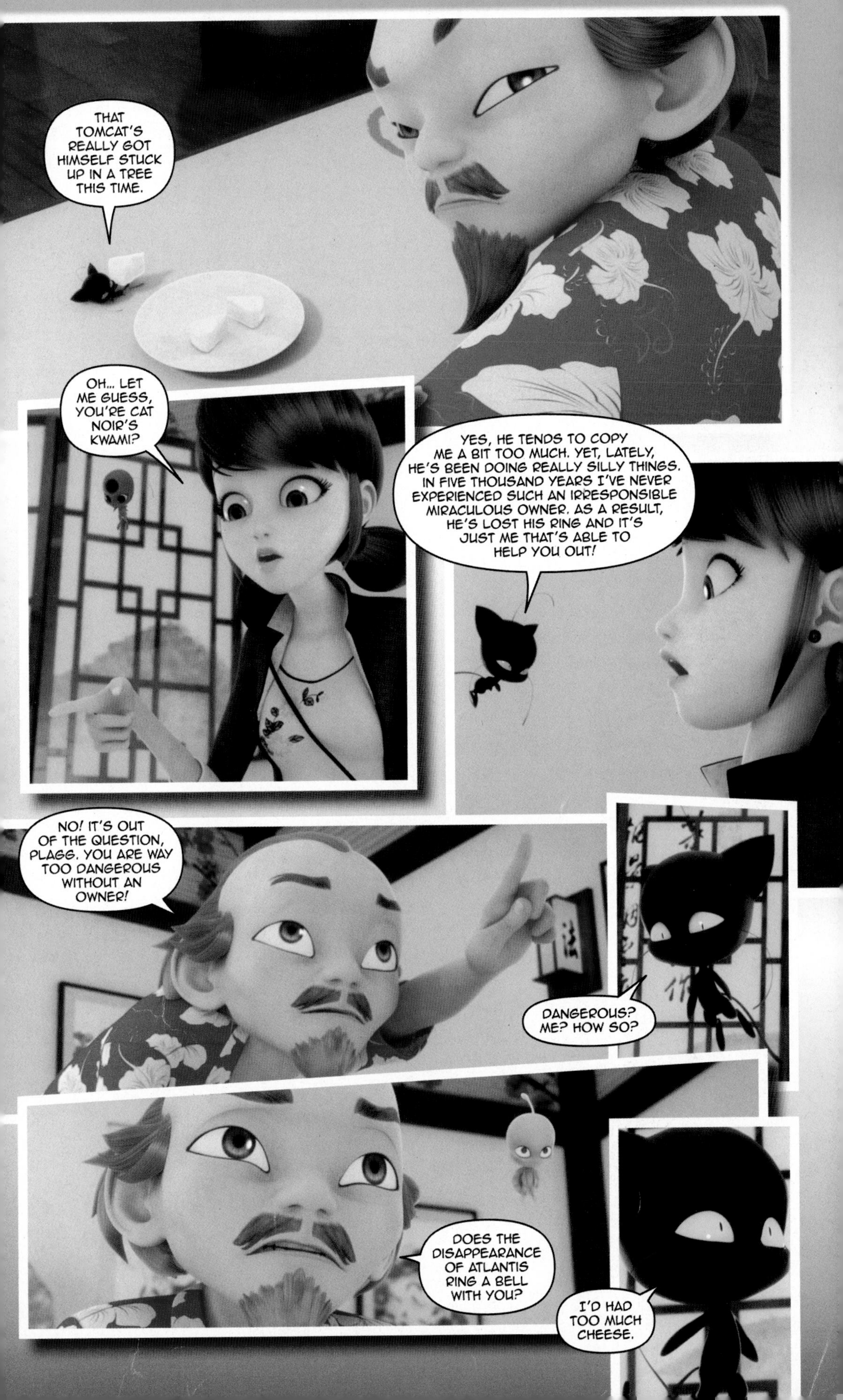
THAT TOMCAT'S REALLY GOT HIMSELF STUCK UP IN A TREE THIS TIME.
OH... LET ME GUESS, YOU'RE CAT NOIR'S KWAMI?
YES, HE TENDS TO COPY ME A BIT TOO MUCH. YET, LATELY, HE'S BEEN DOING REALLY SILLY THINGS. IN FIVE THOUSAND YEARS I'VE NEVER EXPERIENCED SUCH AN IRRESPONSIBLE MIRACULOUS OWNER. AS A RESULT, HE'S LOST HIS RING AND IT'S JUST ME THAT'S ABLE TO HELP YOU OUT!
NO! IT'S OUT OF THE QUESTION, PLAGG. YOU ARE WAY TOO DANGEROUS WITHOUT AN OWNER!
DANGEROUS? ME? HOW SO?
DOES THE DISAPPEARANCE OF ATLANTIS RING A BELL WITH YOU?
I'D HAD TOO MUCH CHEESE.

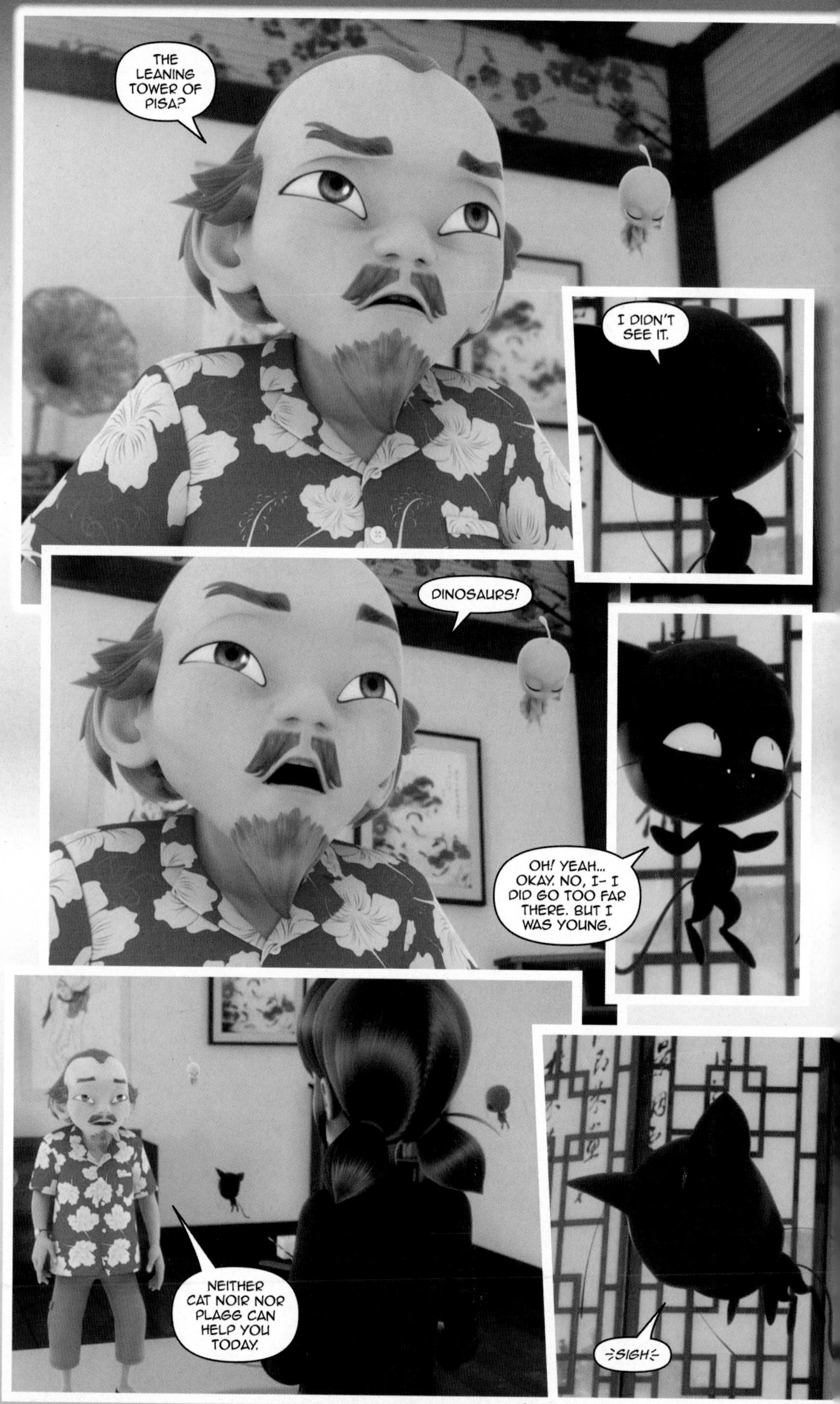
THE LEANING TOWER OF PISA?
I DIDN'T SEE IT.
DINOSAURS!
OH! YEAH... OKAY. NO, I- I DID GO TOO FAR THERE. BUT I WAS YOUNG.
NEITHER CAT NOIR NOR PLAGG CAN HELP YOU TODAY.
-SIGH-

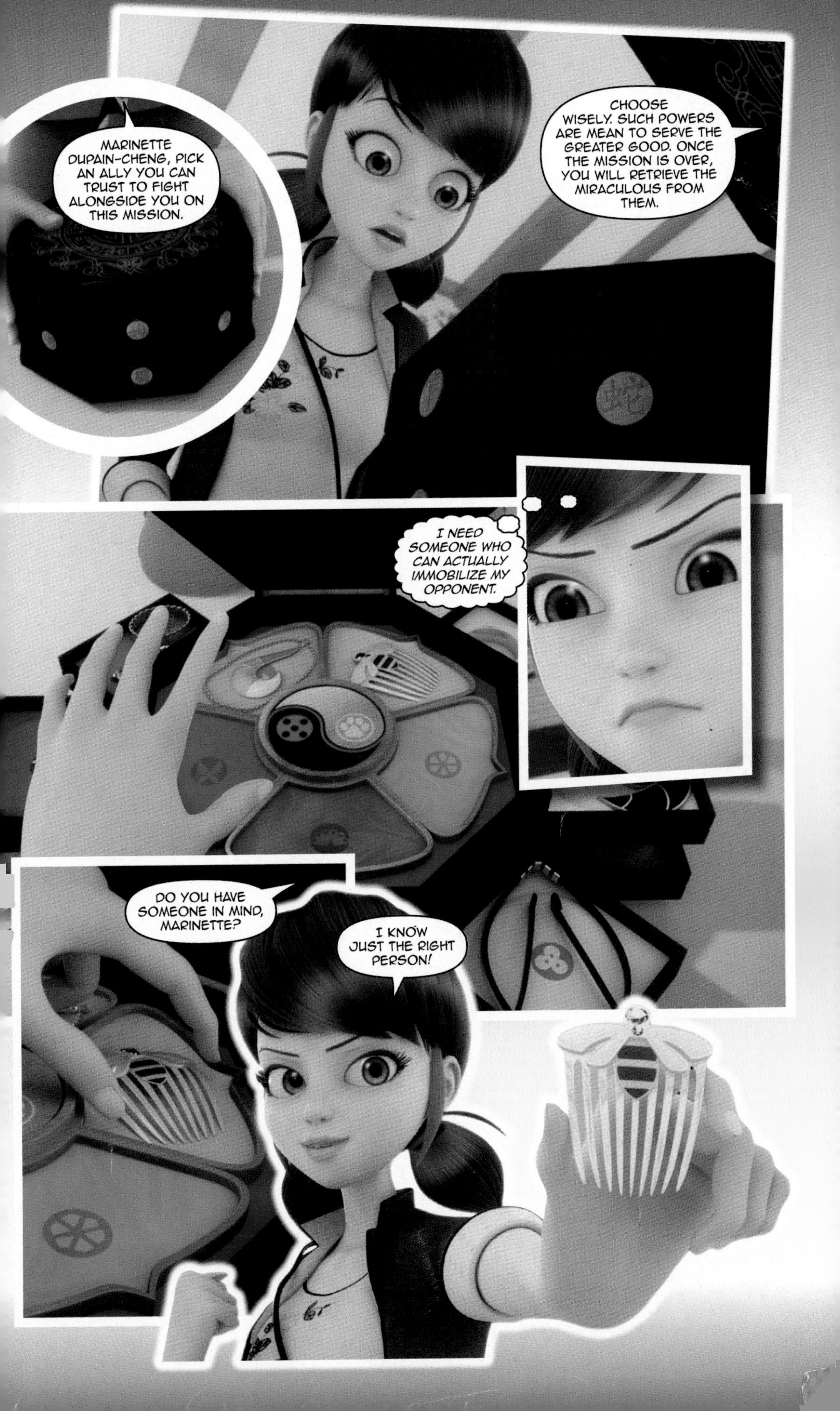
MARINETTE DUPAIN-CHENG, PICK AN ALLY YOU CAN TRUST TO FIGHT ALONGSIDE YOU ON THIS MISSION.
CHOOSE WISELY. SUCH POWERS ARE MEAN TO SERVE THE GREATER GOOD. ONCE THE MISSION IS OVER, YOU WILL RETRIEVE THE MIRACULOUS FROM THEM.
I NEED SOMEONE WHO CAN ACTUALLY IMMOBILIZE MY OPPONENT.
DO YOU HAVE SOMEONE IN MIND, MARINETTE?
I KNOW JUST THE RIGHT PERSON!

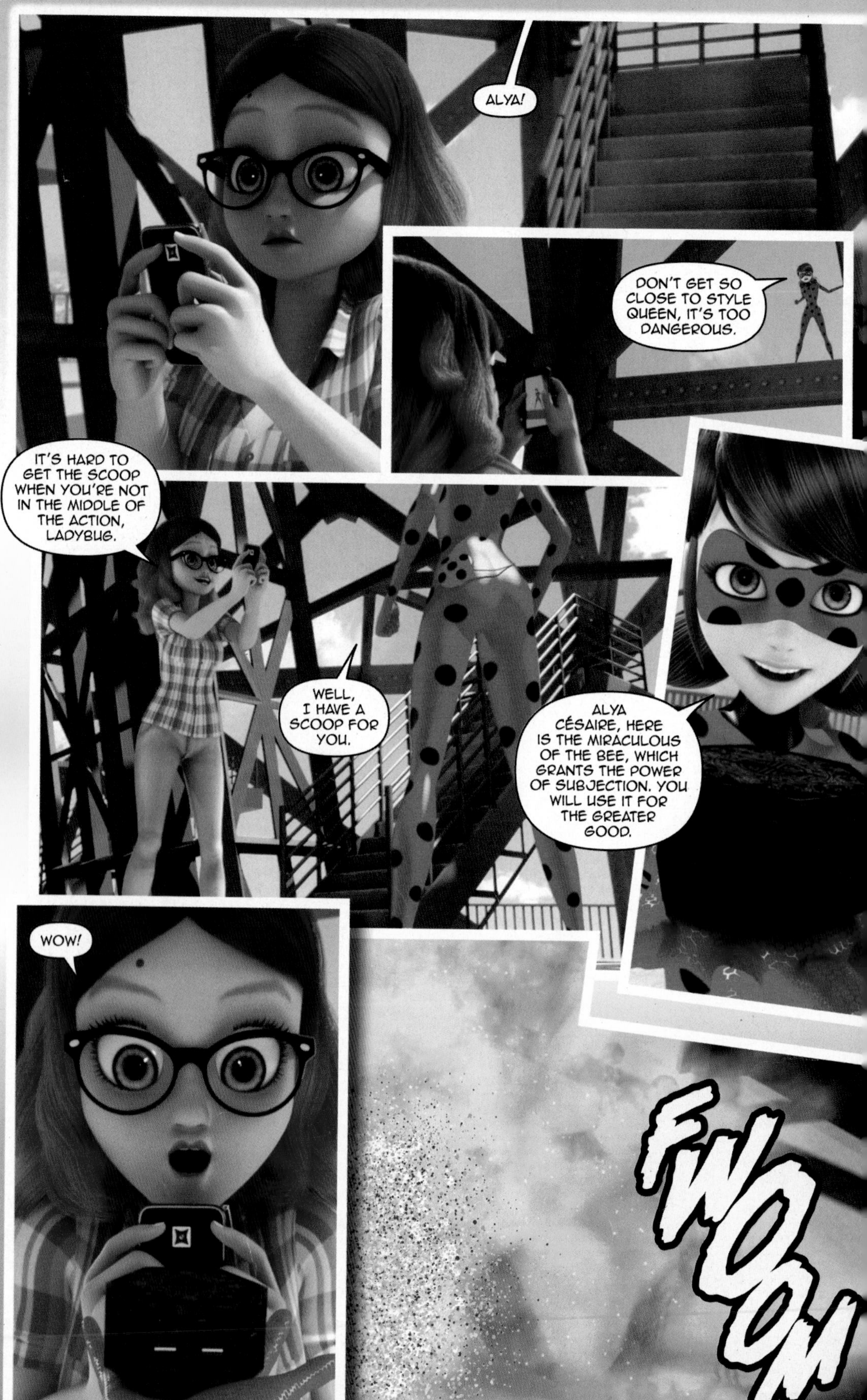
ALYA!
DON'T GET SO CLOSE TO STYLE QUEEN, IT'S TOO DANGEROUS.
IT'S HARD TO GET THE SCOOP WHEN YOU'RE NOT IN THE MIDDLE OF THE ACTION, LADYBUG.
WELL, I HAVE A SCOOP FOR YOU.
ALYA CÉSAIRE, HERE IS THE MIRACULOUS OF THE BEE, WHICH GRANTS THE POWER OF SUBJECTION. YOU WILL USE IT FOR THE GREATER GOOD.
WOW!
FWOOM

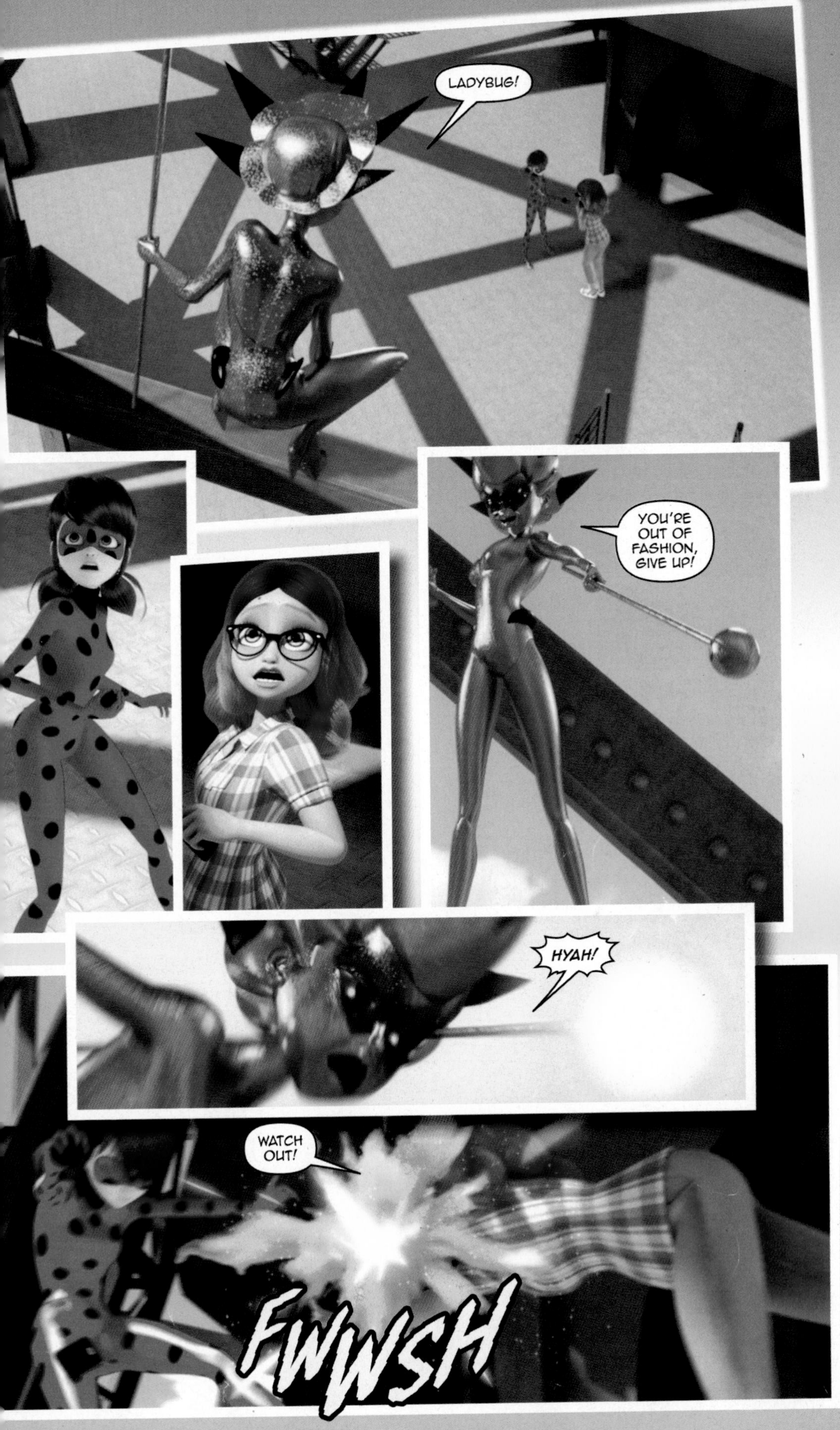
LADYBUG!
YOU'RE OUT OF FASHION, GIVE UP!
HYAH!
WATCH OUT!
FWWSH

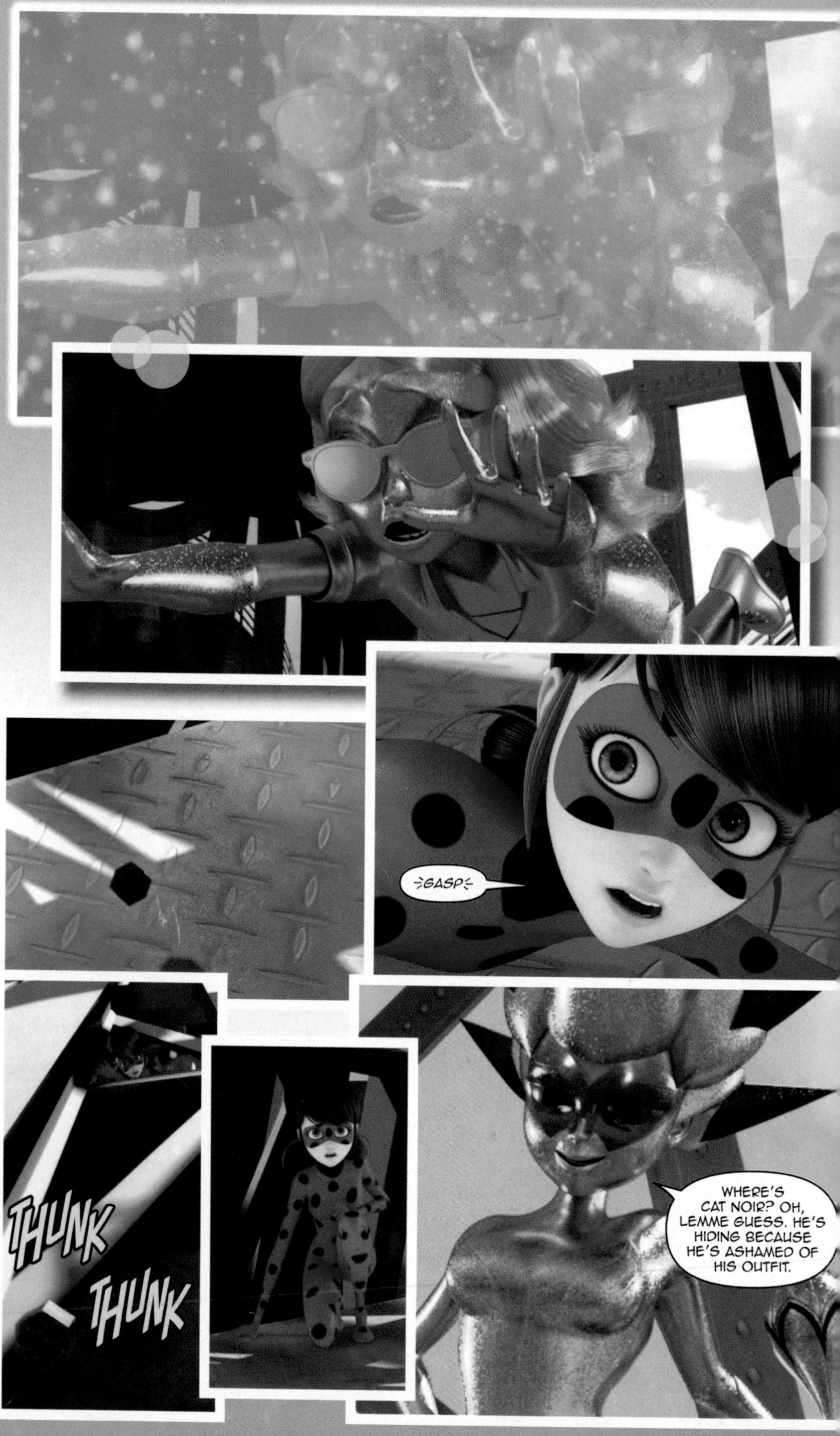
GASP
THUNK
THUNK
WHERE'S CAT NOIR? OH, LEMME GUESS. HE'S HIDING BECAUSE HE'S ASHAMED OF HIS OUTFIT.

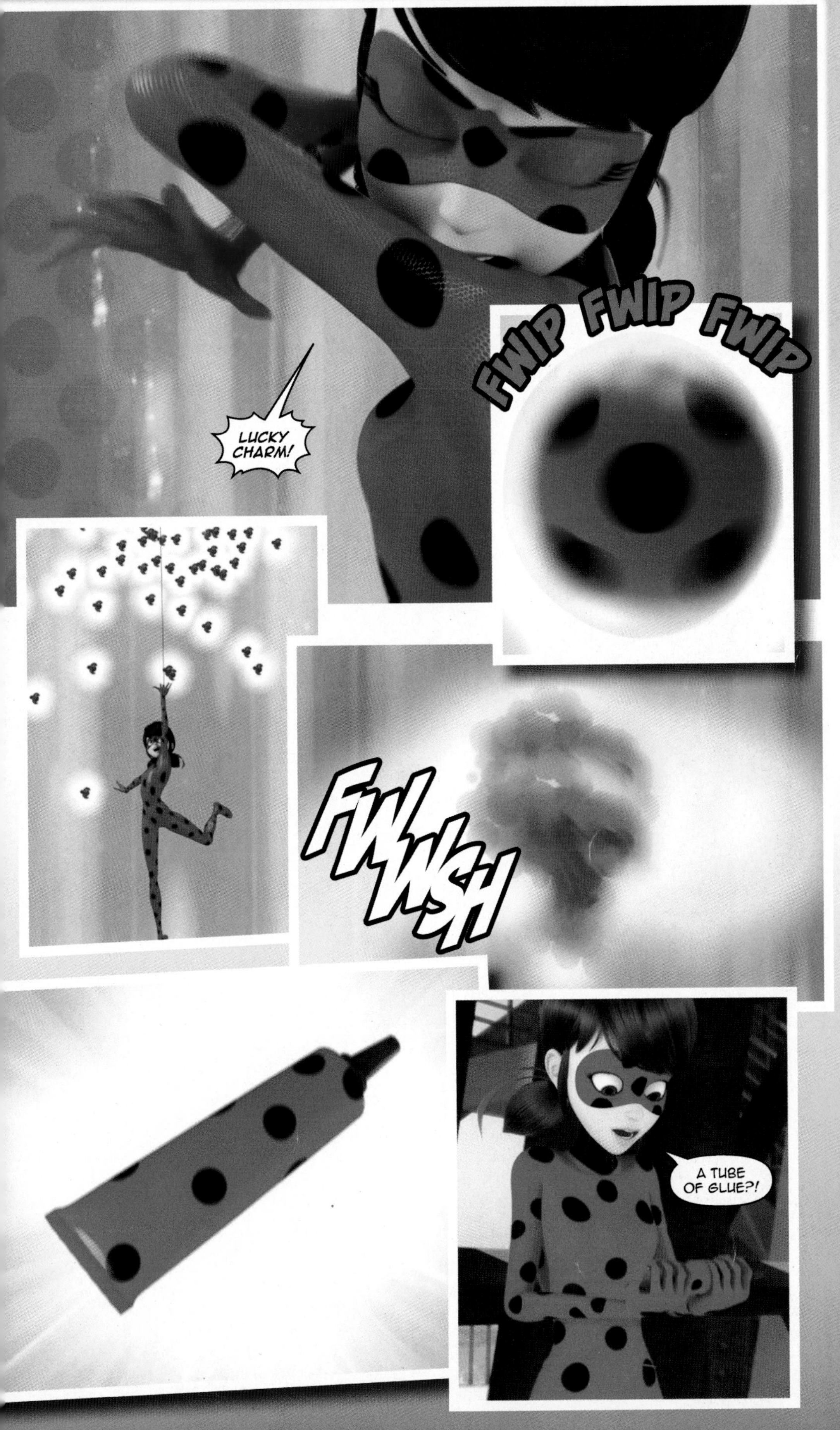
LUCKY CHARM!
FWIP FWIP FWIP
FWUSH
A TUBE OF GLUE?!

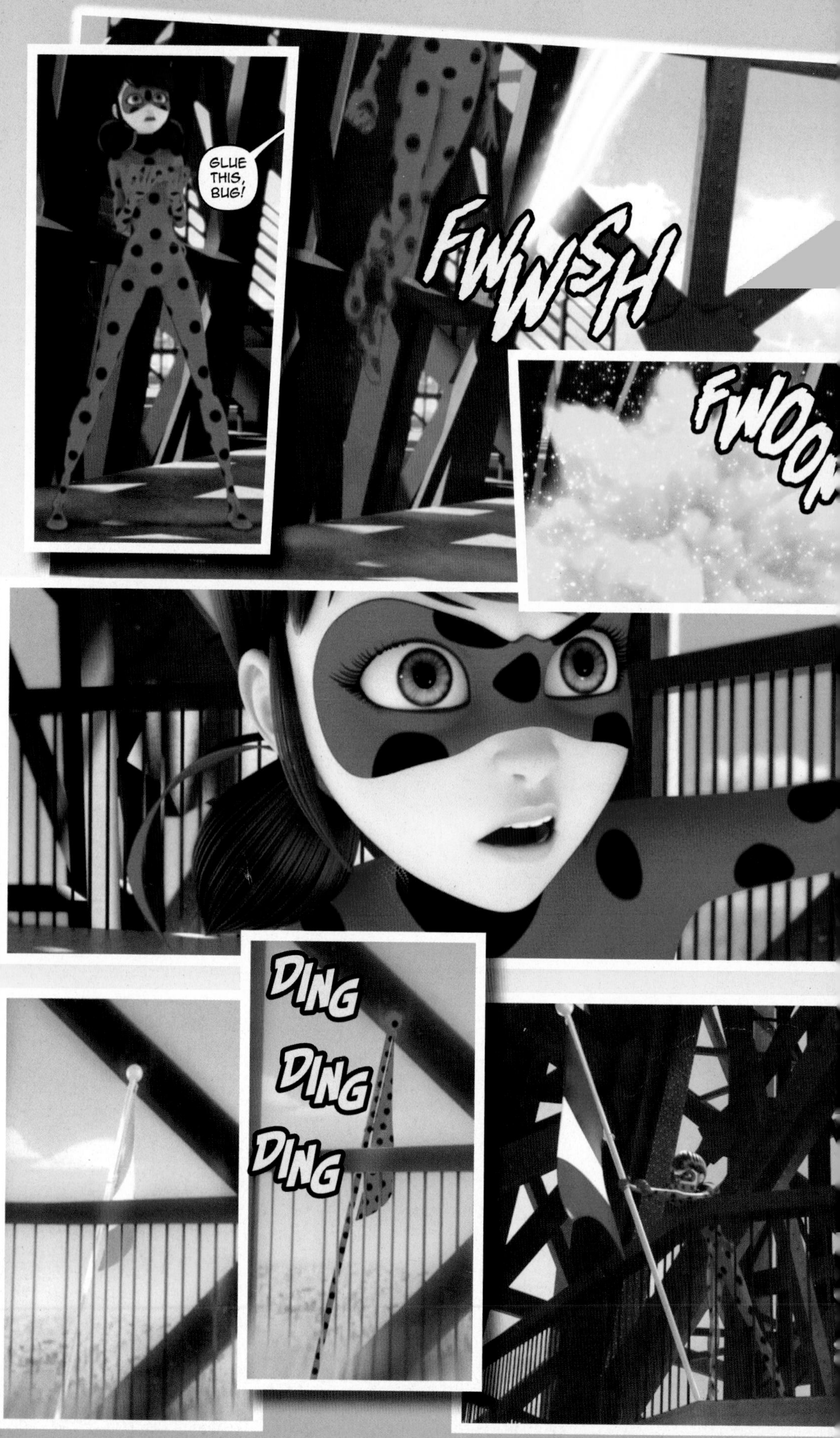
GLUE THIS, BUG!
FWWSH
FWOOM
DING
DING
DING

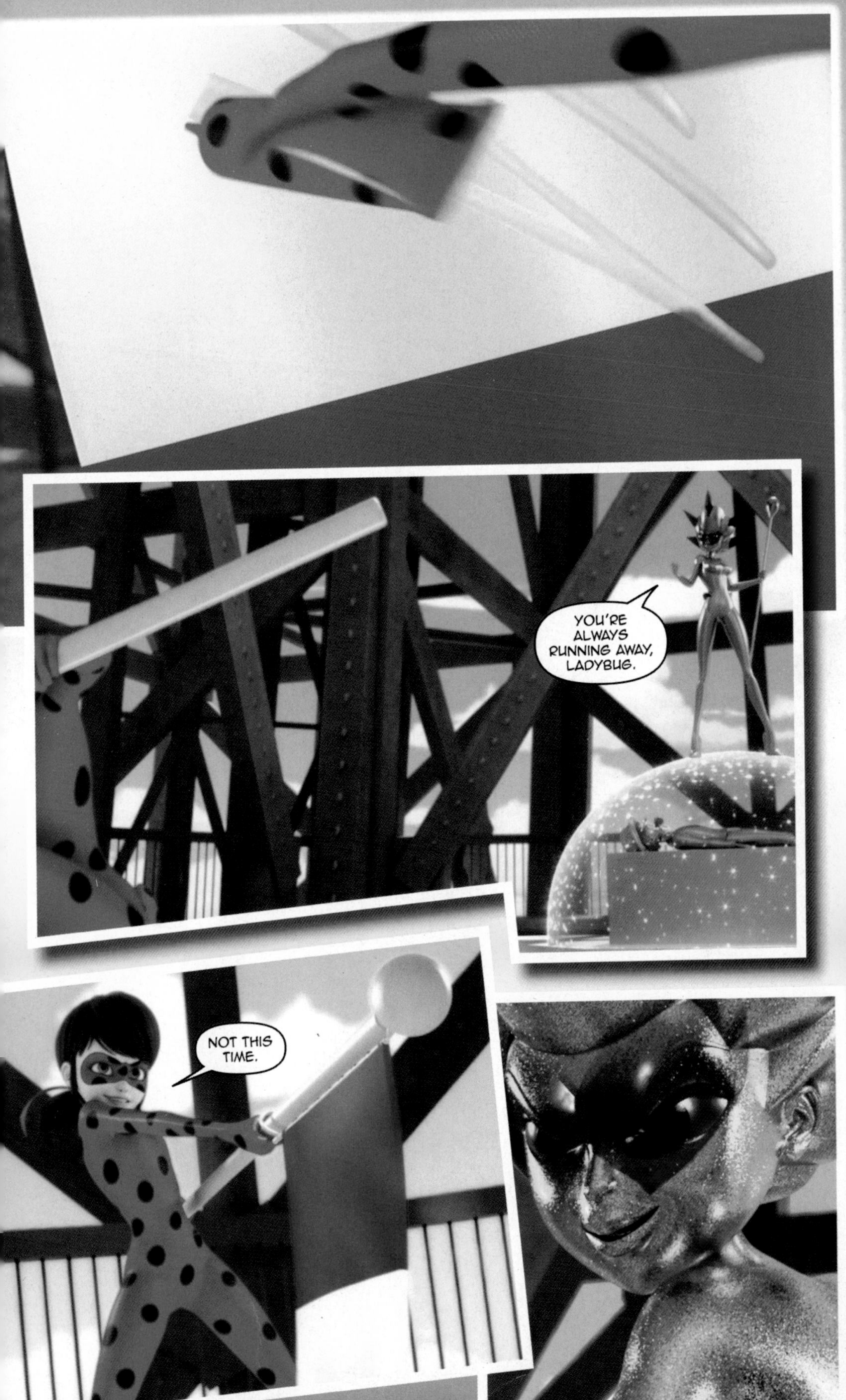
YOU'RE ALWAYS RUNNING AWAY, LADYBUG.
NOT THIS TIME.

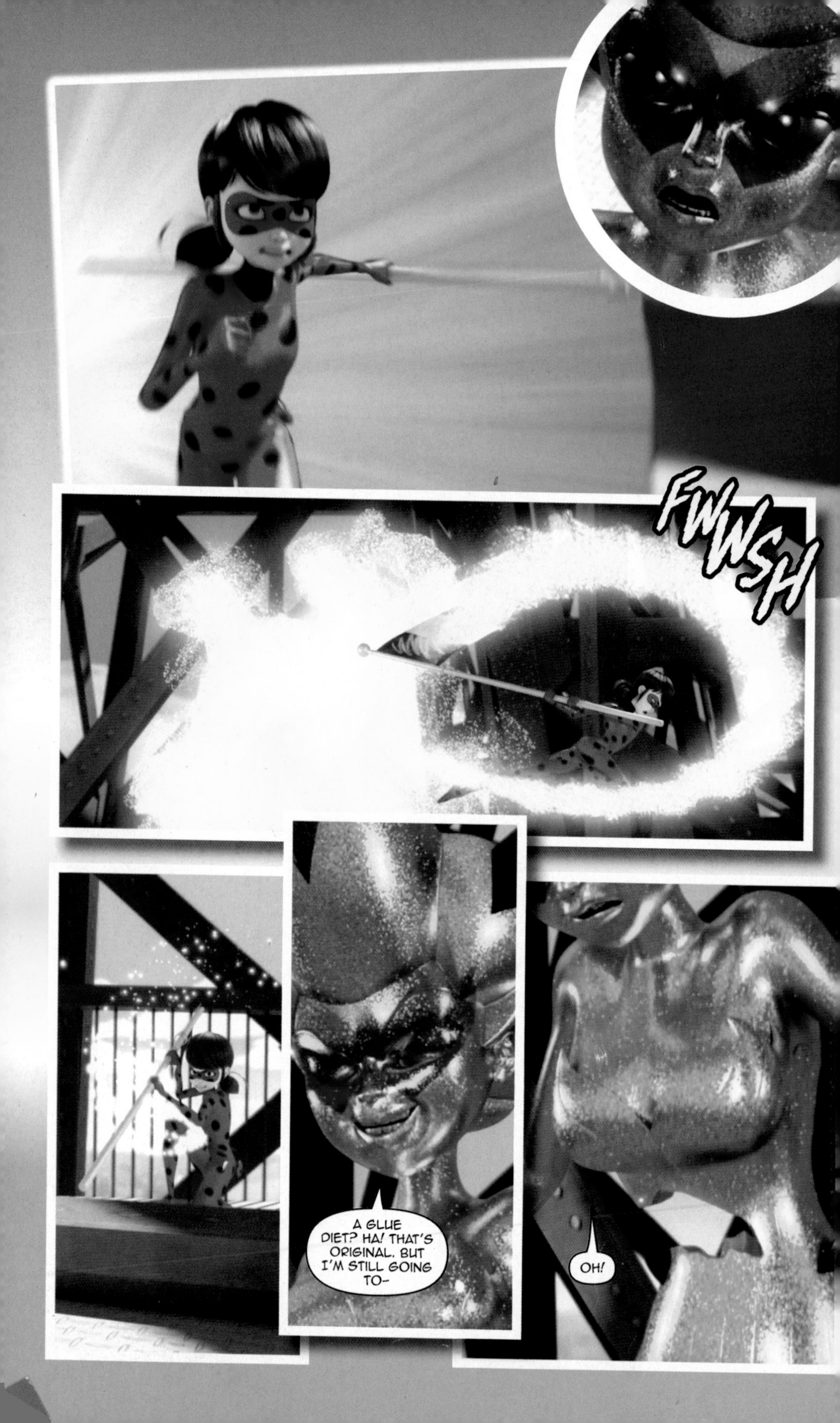
FWWSH
A GLUE DIET? HA! THAT'S ORIGINAL. BUT I'M STILL GOING TO-
OH!

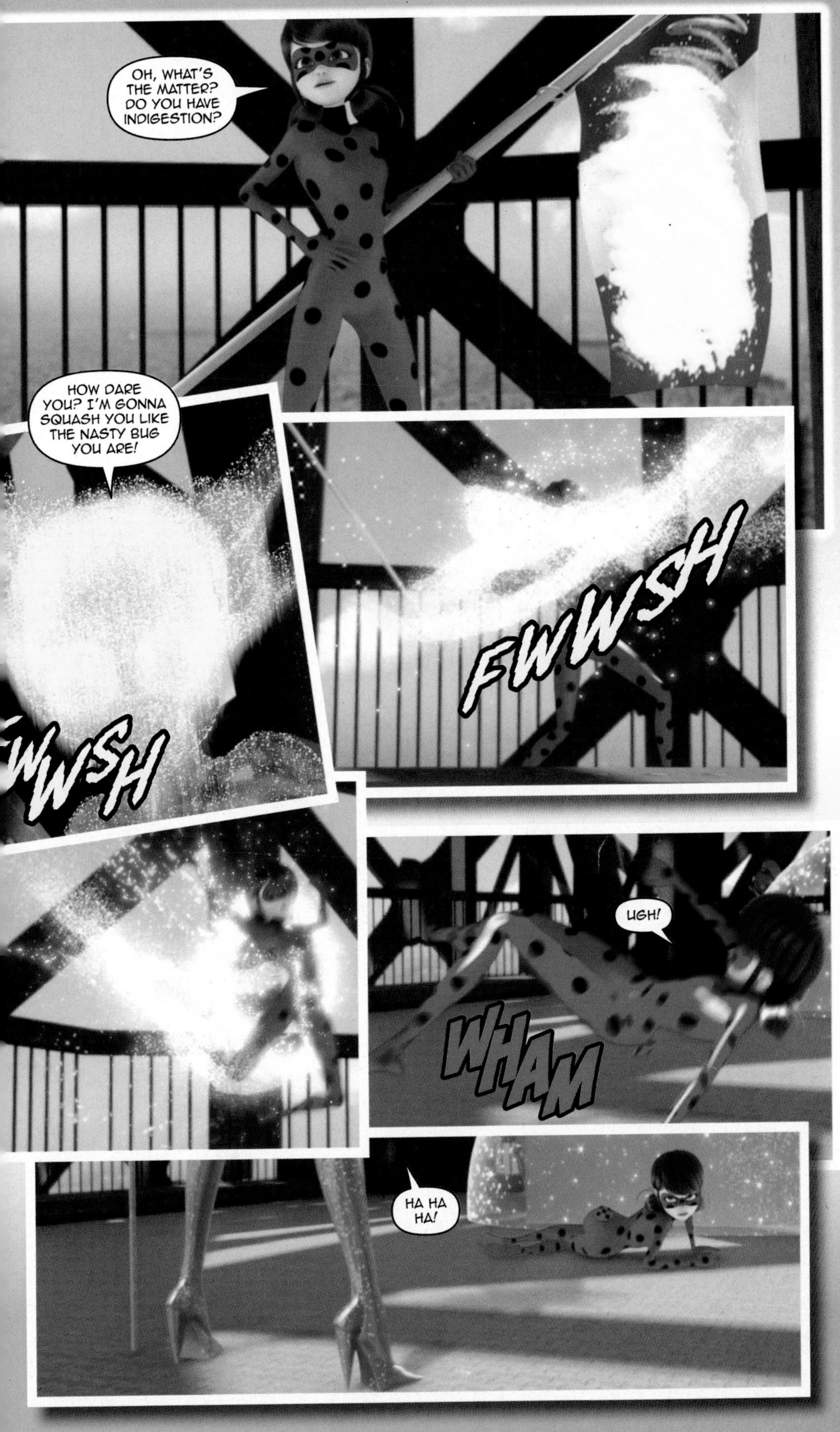
OH, WHAT'S THE MATTER? DO YOU HAVE INDIGESTION?
HOW DARE YOU? I'M GONNA SQUASH YOU LIKE THE NASTY BUG YOU ARE!
FWWSH
FWWSH
UGH!
WHAM
HA HA HA!

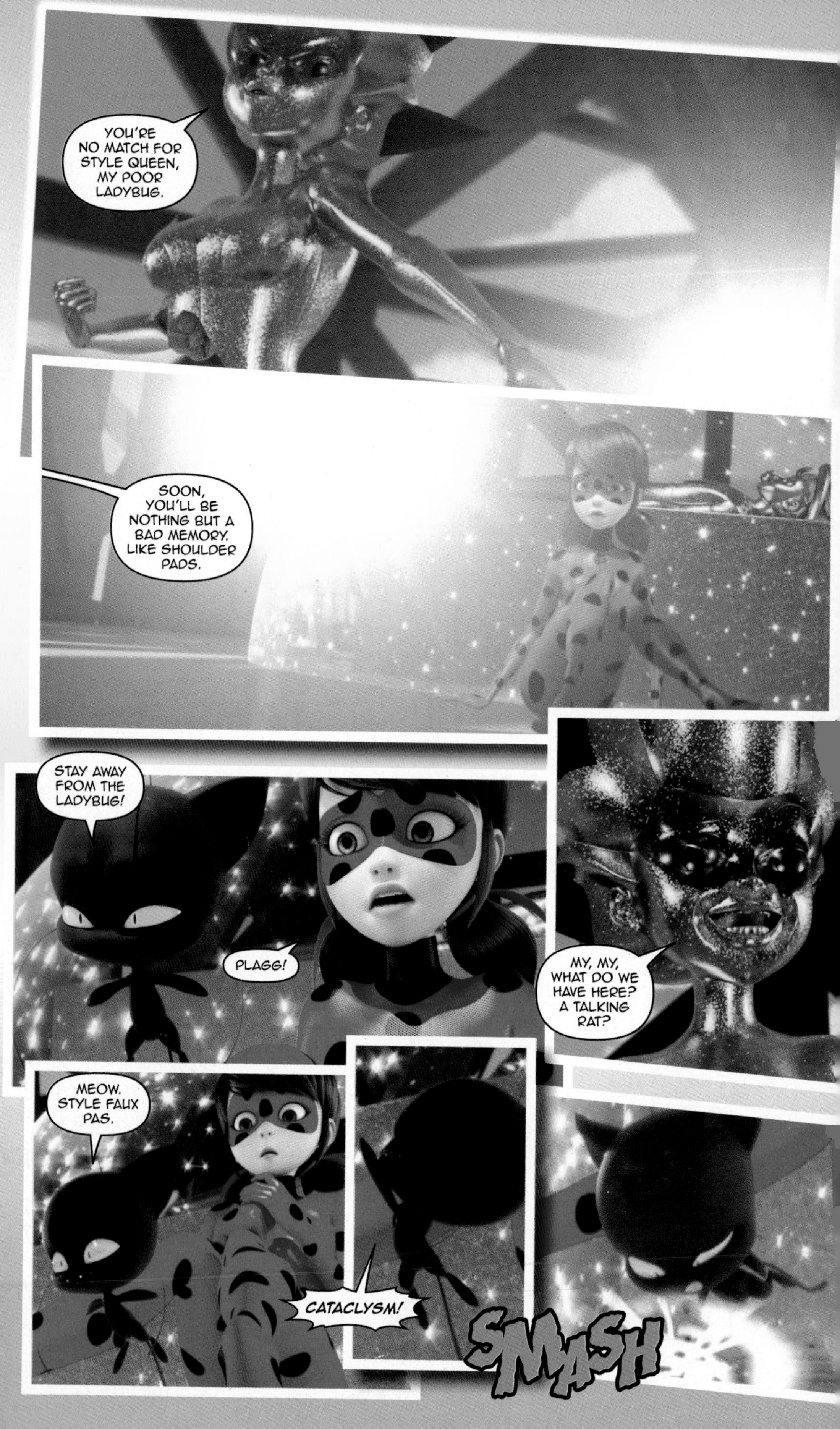
YOU'RE NO MATCH FOR STYLE QUEEN, MY POOR LADYBUG.
SOON, YOU'LL BE NOTHING BUT A BAD MEMORY. LIKE SHOULDER PADS.
STAY AWAY FROM THE LADYBUG!
PLAGG!
MY, MY, WHAT DO WE HAVE HERE? A TALKING RAT?
MEOW. STYLE FAUX PAS.
CATACLYSM!
SMASH

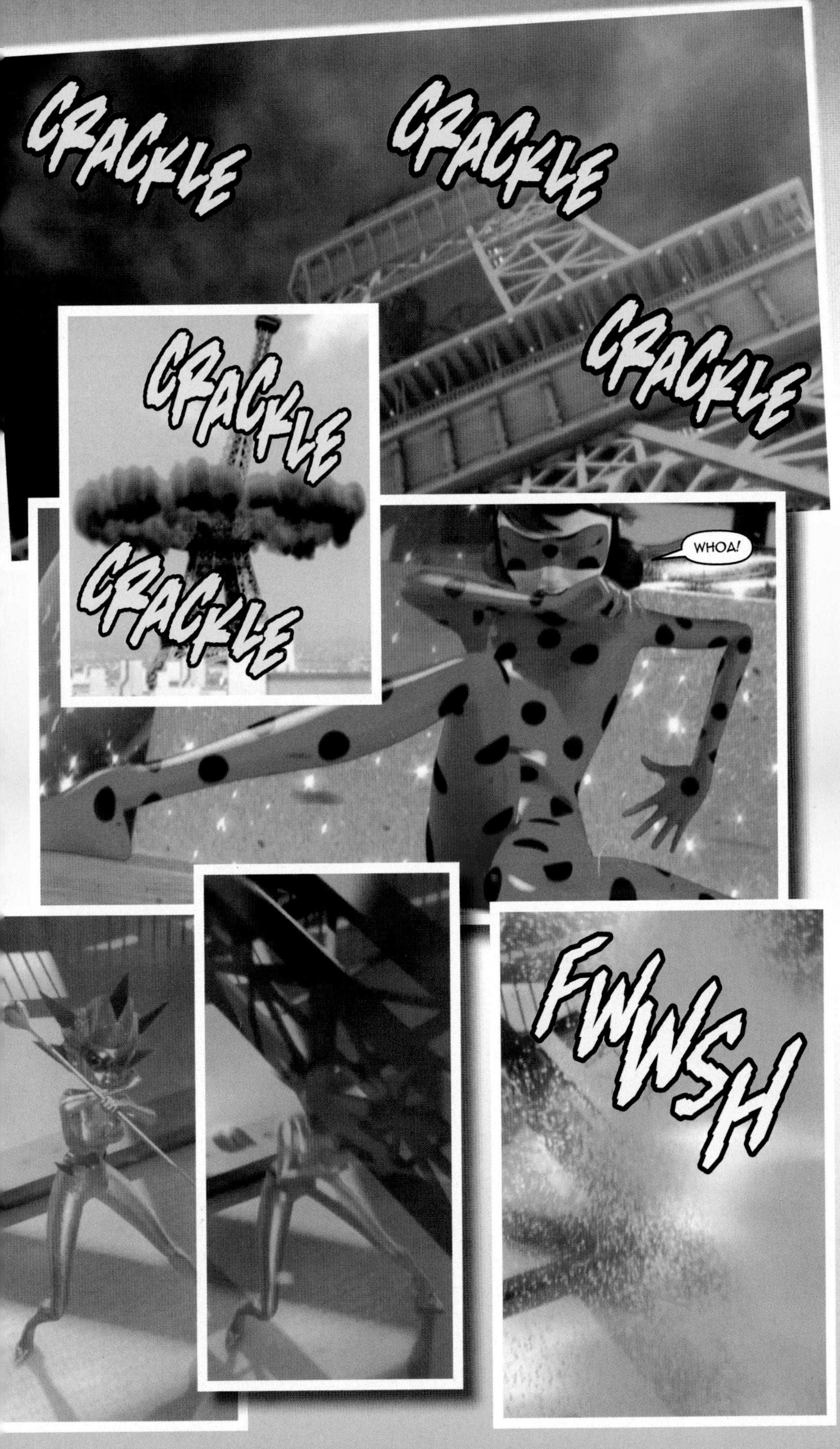
CRACKLE
CRACKLE
CRACKLE
CRACKLE
CRACKLE
WHOA!
FWWSH

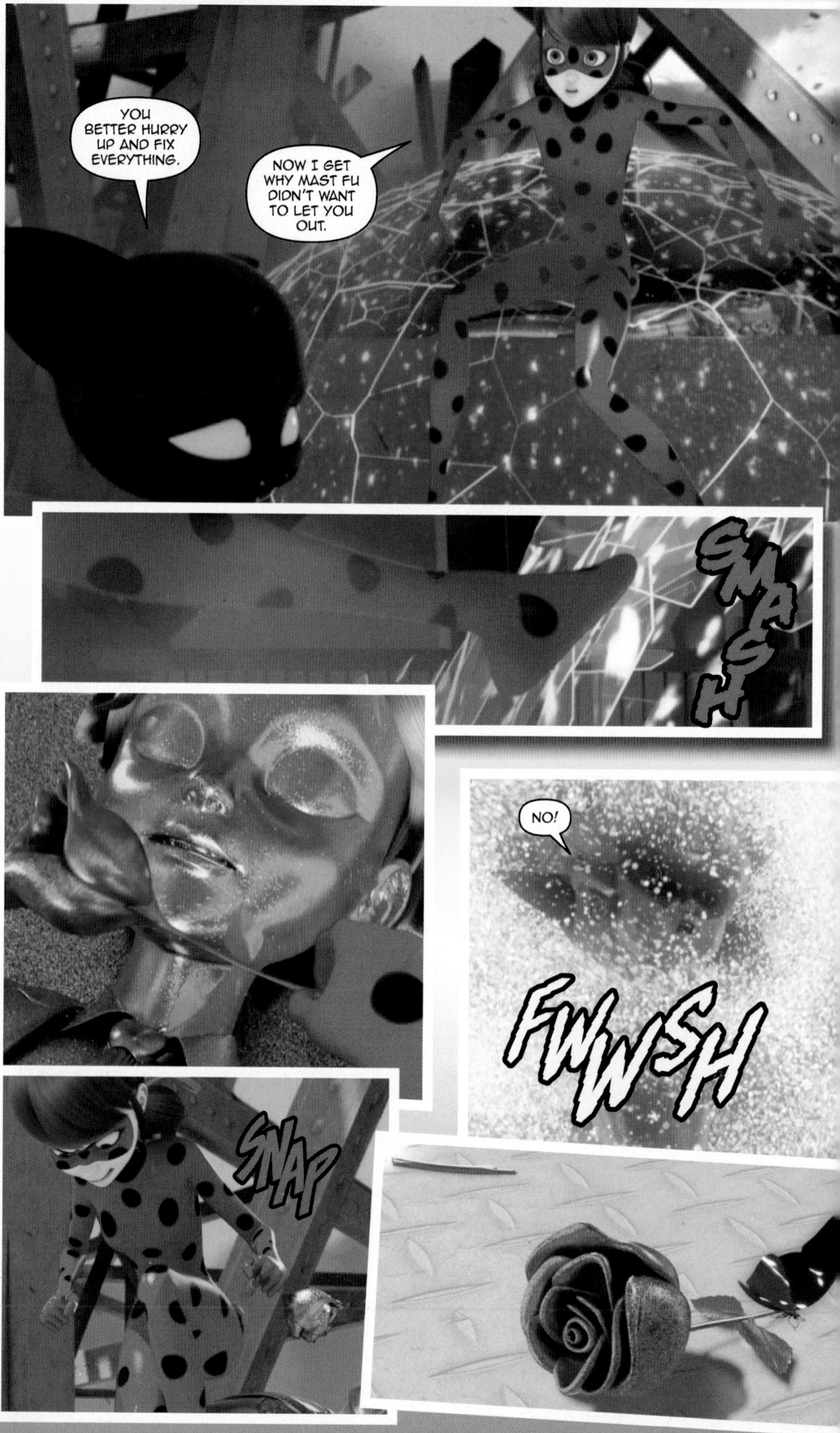
YOU BETTER HURRY UP AND FIX EVERYTHING.
NOW I GET WHY MAST FU DIDN'T WANT TO LET YOU OUT.
SMASH
NO!
FWWSH
SNAP

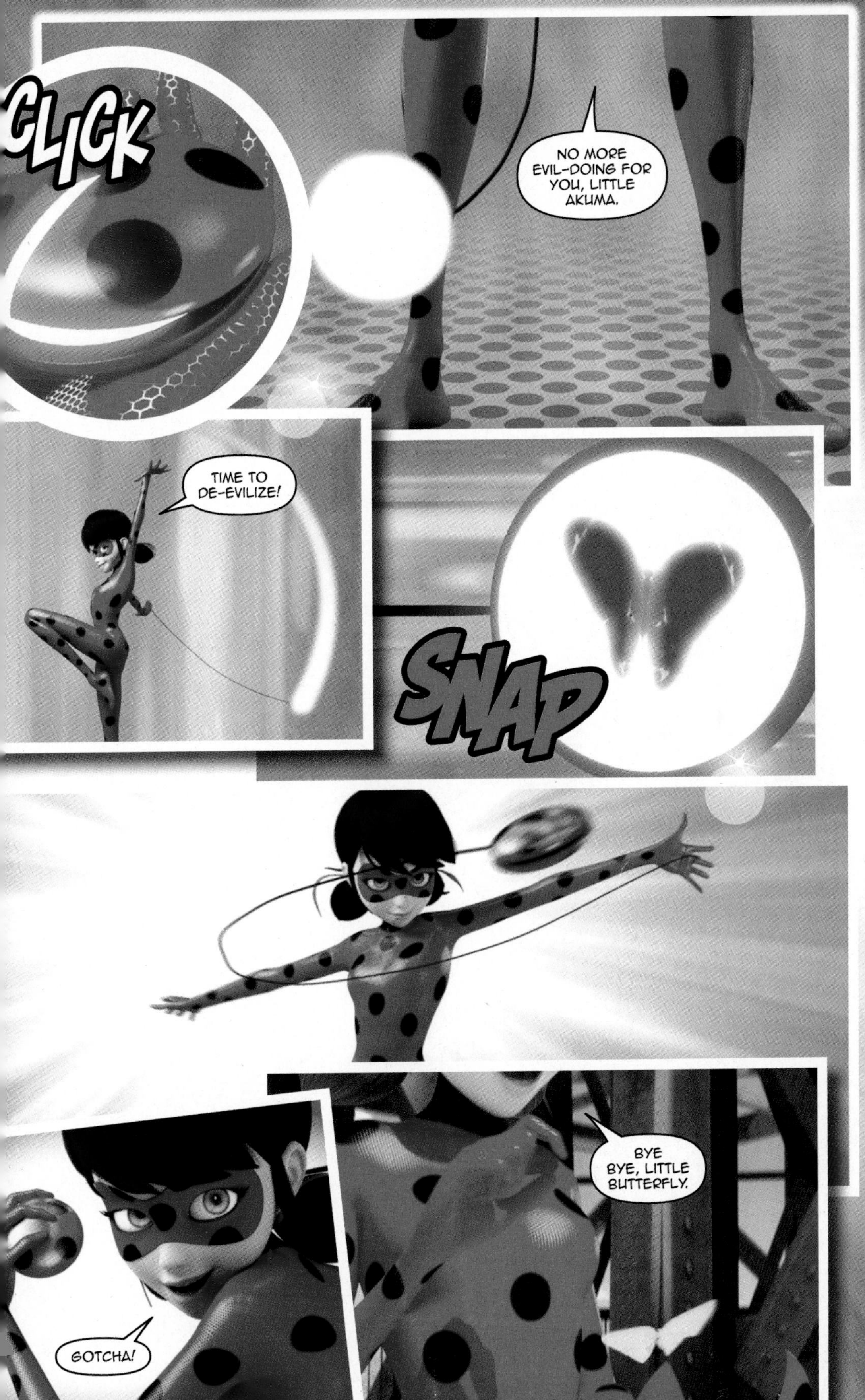
CLICK
NO MORE EVIL-DOING FOR YOU, LITTLE AKUMA.
TIME TO DE-EVILIZE!
SNAP
BYE BYE, LITTLE BUTTERFLY.
GOTCHA!

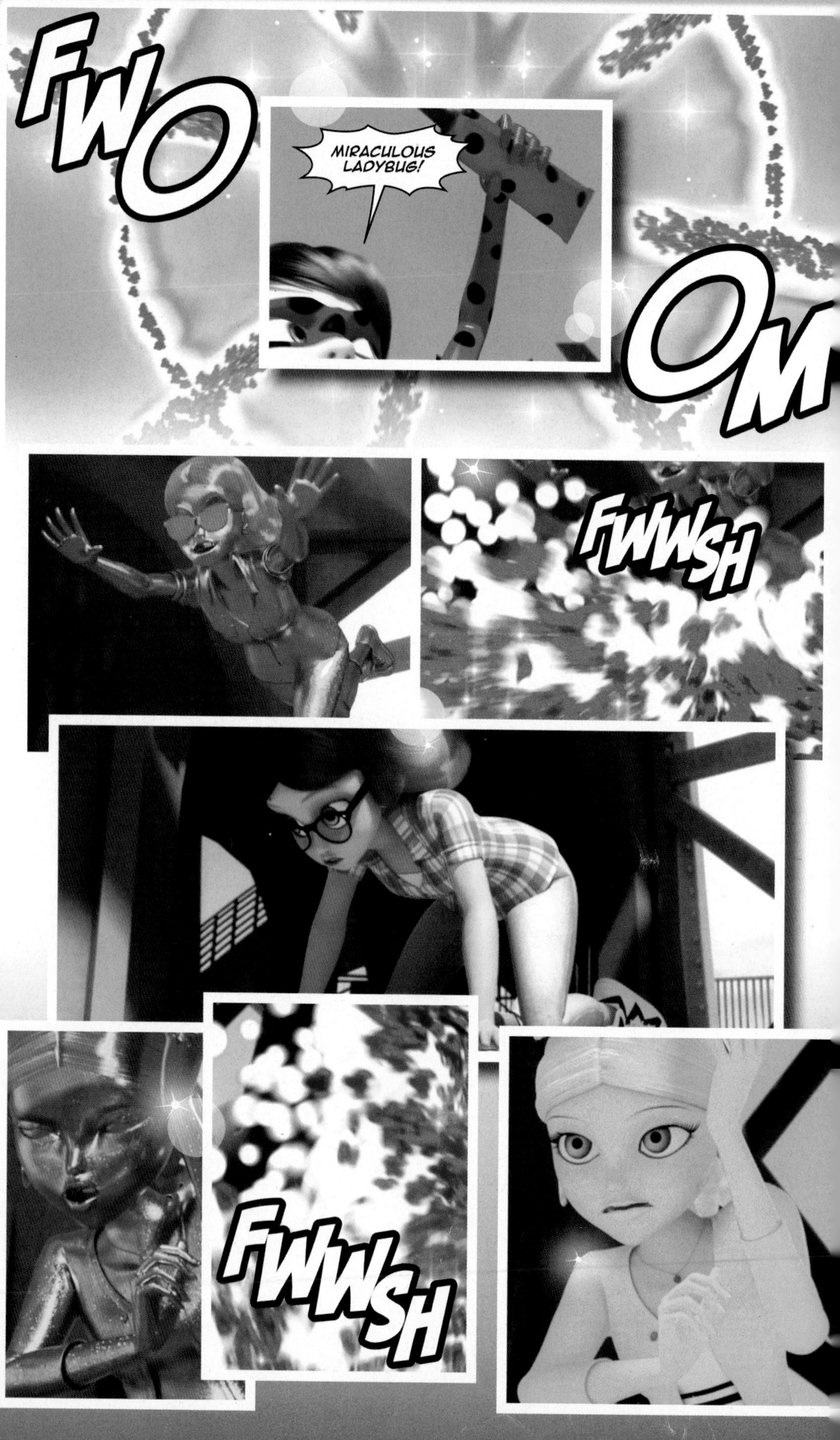
FWOOM
MIRACULOUS LADYBUG!
FWWSH
FWWSH

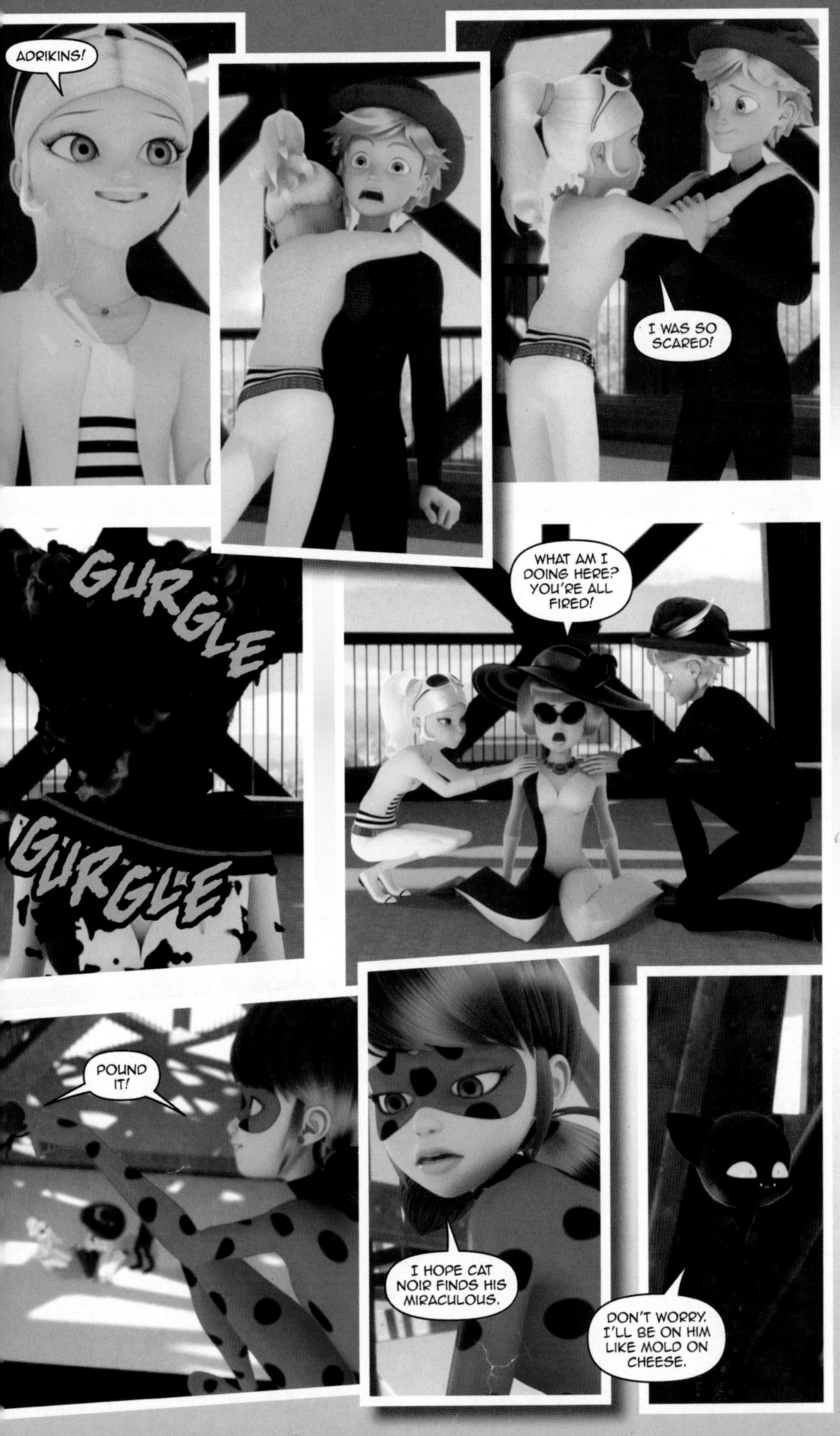
ADRIKINS!
I WAS SO SCARED!
GURGLE
GURGLE
WHAT AM I DOING HERE? YOU'RE ALL FIRED!
POUND IT!
I HOPE CAT NOIR FINDS HIS MIRACULOUS.
DON'T WORRY. I'LL BE ON HIM LIKE MOLD ON CHEESE.

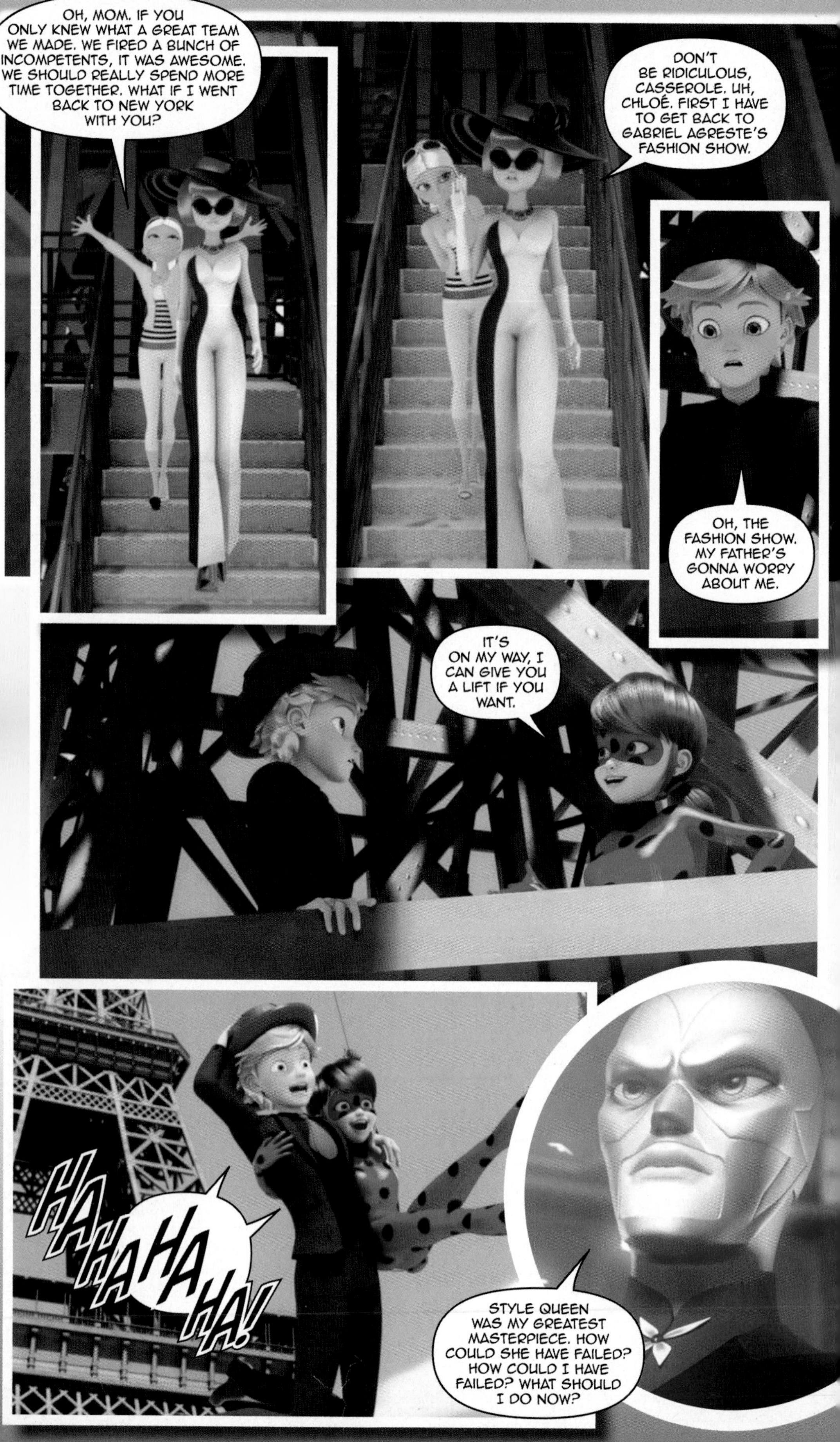
OH, MOM. IF YOU ONLY KNEW WHAT A GREAT TEAM WE MADE. WE FIRED A BUNCH OF INCOMPETENTS, IT WAS AWESOME. WE SHOULD REALLY SPEND MORE TIME TOGETHER. WHAT IF I WENT BACK TO NEW YORK WITH YOU?
DON'T BE RIDICULOUS, CASSEROLE. UH, CHLOÉ. FIRST I HAVE TO GET BACK TO GABRIEL AGRESTE'S FASHION SHOW.
OH, THE FASHION SHOW. MY FATHER'S GONNA WORRY ABOUT ME.
IT'S ON MY WAY, I CAN GIVE YOU A LIFT IF YOU WANT.
HAHAHAHAHA!
STYLE QUEEN WAS MY GREATEST MASTERPIECE. HOW COULD SHE HAVE FAILED? HOW COULD I HAVE FAILED? WHAT SHOULD I DO NOW?

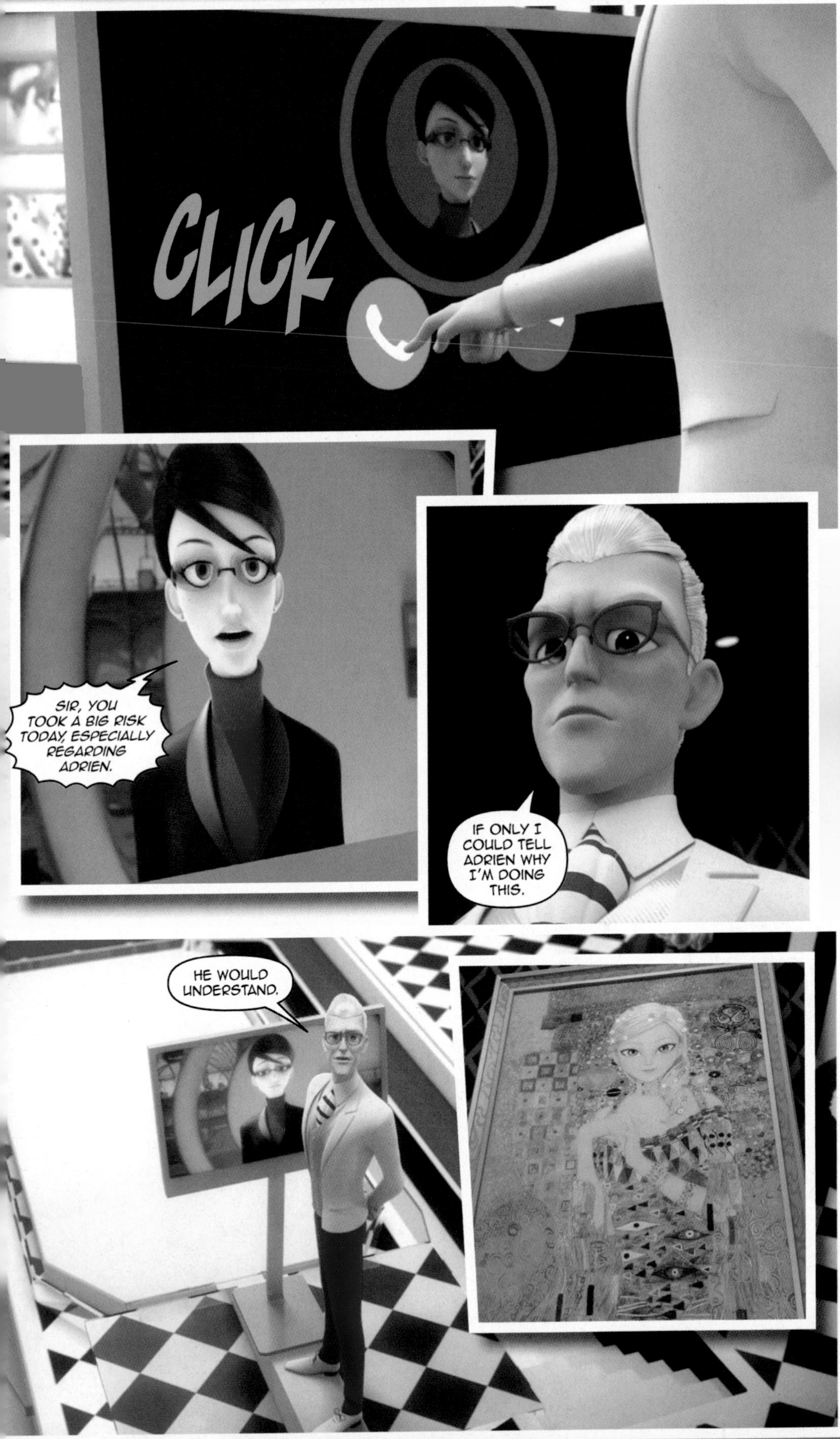
CLICK
SIR, YOU TOOK A BIG RISK TODAY, ESPECIALLY REGARDING ADRIEN.
IF ONLY I COULD TELL ADRIEN WHY I'M DOING THIS.
HE WOULD UNDERSTAND.

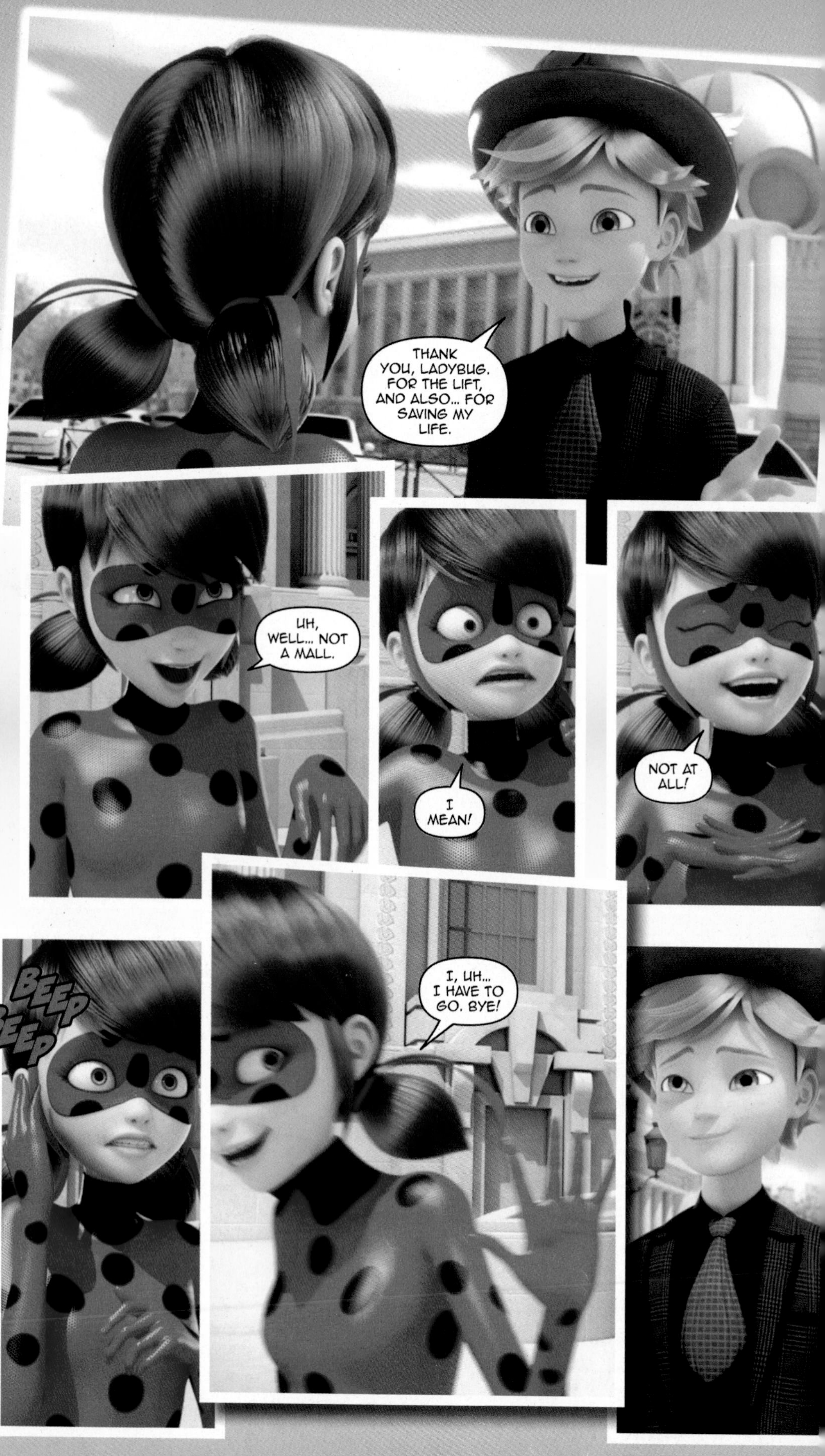
THANK YOU, LADYBUG. FOR THE LIFT, AND ALSO... FOR SAVING MY LIFE.
UH, WELL... NOT A MALL.
I MEAN!
NOT AT ALL!
BEEP BEEP
I, UH... I HAVE TO GO. BYE!

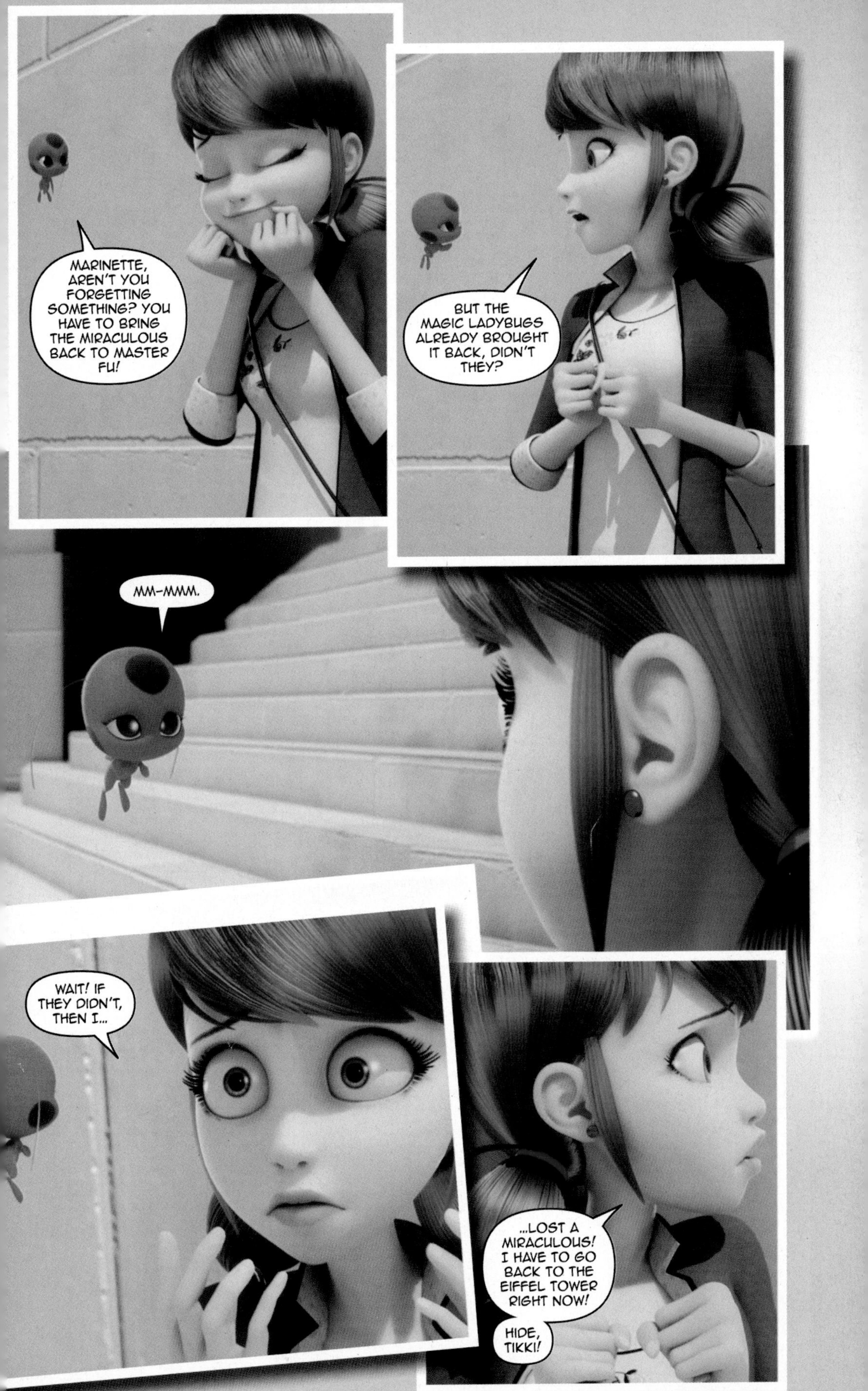
MARINETTE, AREN'T YOU FORGETTING SOMETHING? YOU HAVE TO BRING THE MIRACULOUS BACK TO MASTER FU!
BUT THE MAGIC LADYBUGS ALREADY BROUGHT IT BACK, DIDN'T THEY?
MM-MMM.
WAIT! IF THEY DIDN'T, THEN I...
...LOST A MIRACULOUS! I HAVE TO GO BACK TO THE EIFFEL TOWER RIGHT NOW!
HIDE, TIKKI!

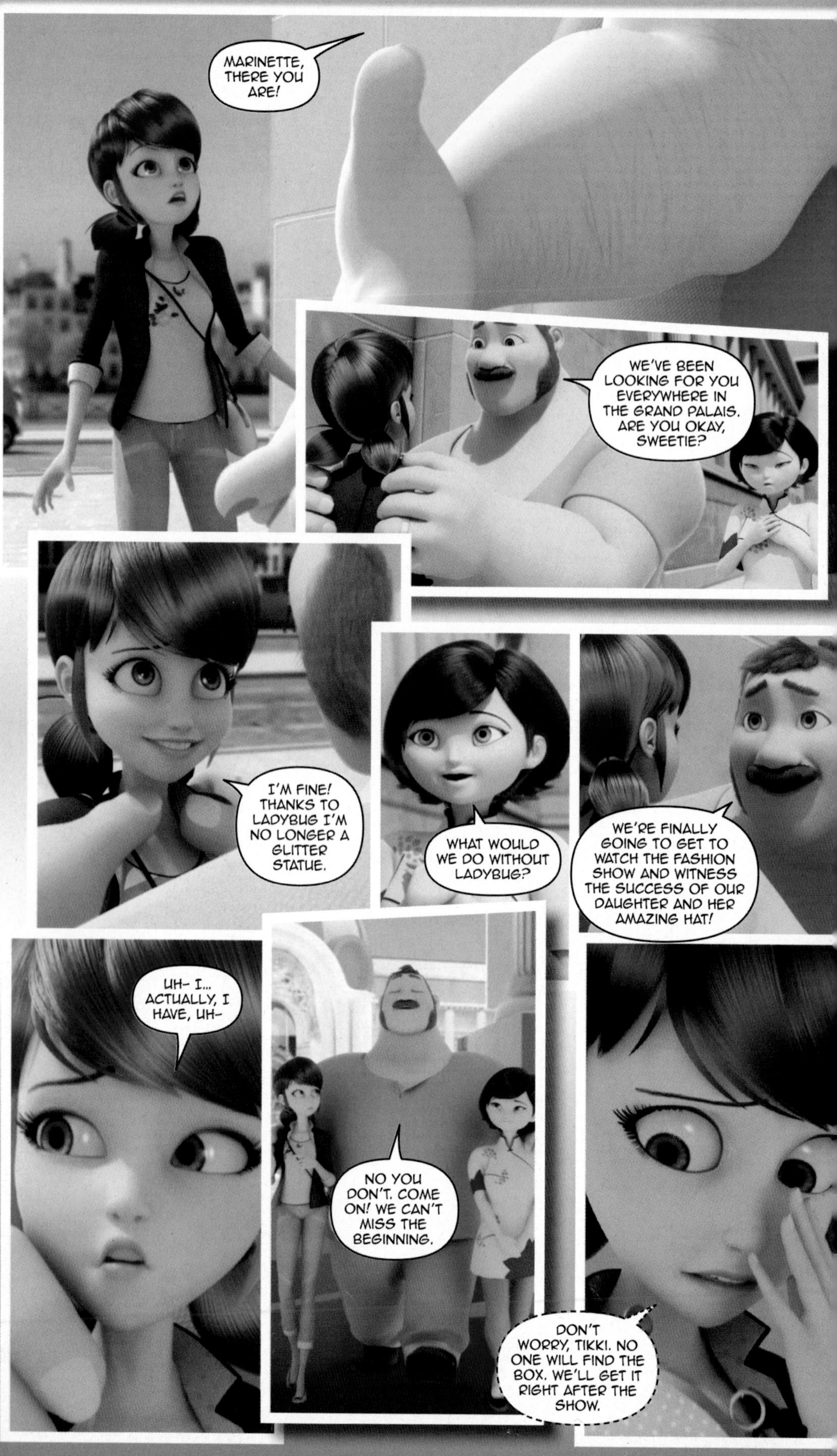
MARINETTE, THERE YOU ARE!
WE'VE BEEN LOOKING FOR YOU EVERYWHERE IN THE GRAND PALAIS. ARE YOU OKAY, SWEETIE?
I'M FINE! THANKS TO LADYBUG I'M NO LONGER A GLITTER STATUE.
WHAT WOULD WE DO WITHOUT LADYBUG?
WE'RE FINALLY GOING TO GET TO WATCH THE FASHION SHOW AND WITNESS THE SUCCESS OF OUR DAUGHTER AND HER AMAZING HAT!
UH- I... ACTUALLY, I HAVE, UH-
NO YOU DON'T. COME ON! WE CAN'T MISS THE BEGINNING.
DON'T WORRY, TIKKI. NO ONE WILL FIND THE BOX. WE'LL GET IT RIGHT AFTER THE SHOW.

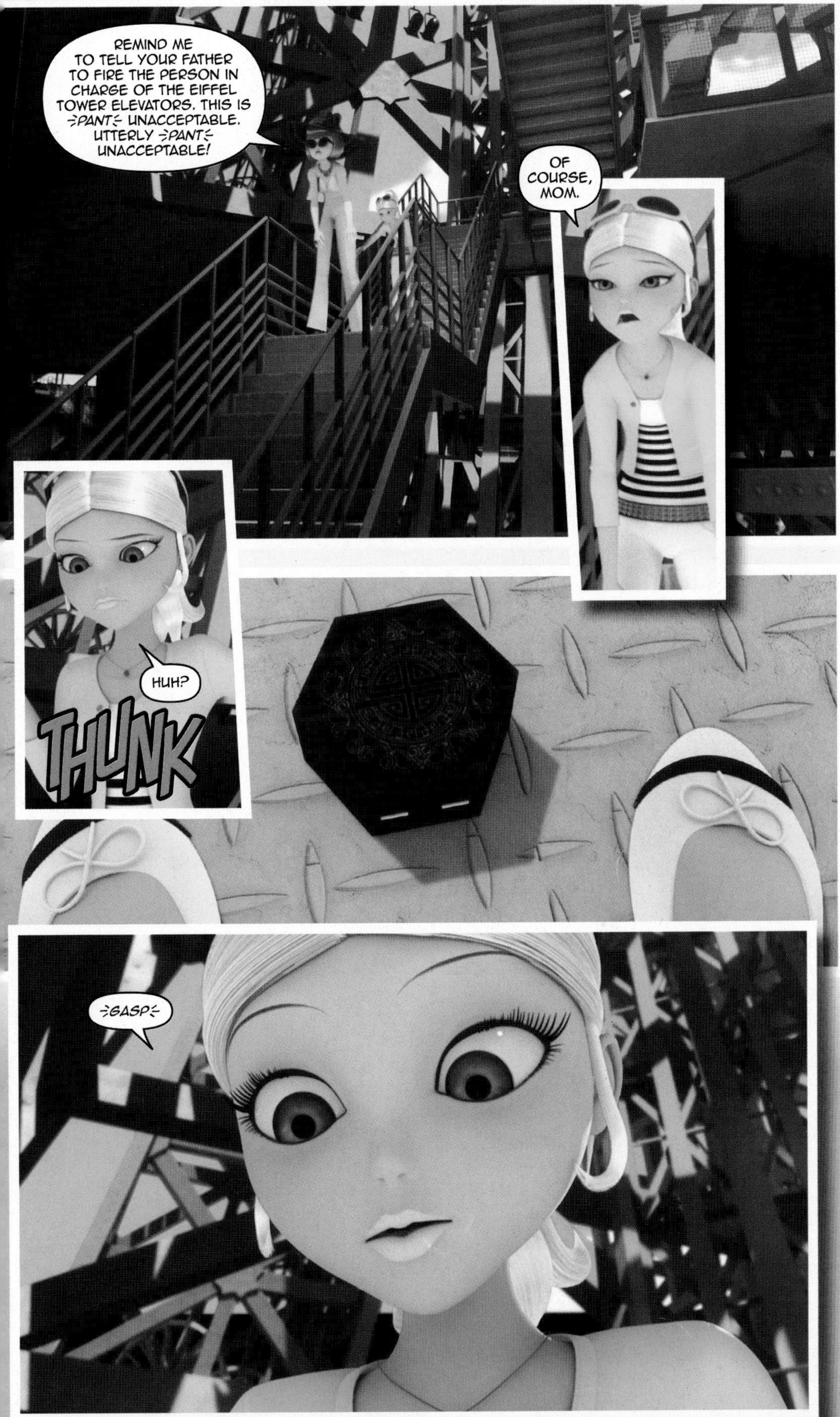
REMIND ME TO TELL YOUR FATHER TO FIRE THE PERSON IN CHARGE OF THE EIFFEL TOWER ELEVATORS. THIS IS ⩦PANT⩧ UNACCEPTABLE. UTTERLY ⩦PANT⩧ UNACCEPTABLE!
OF COURSE, MOM.
HUH?
THUNK
⩦GASP⩧

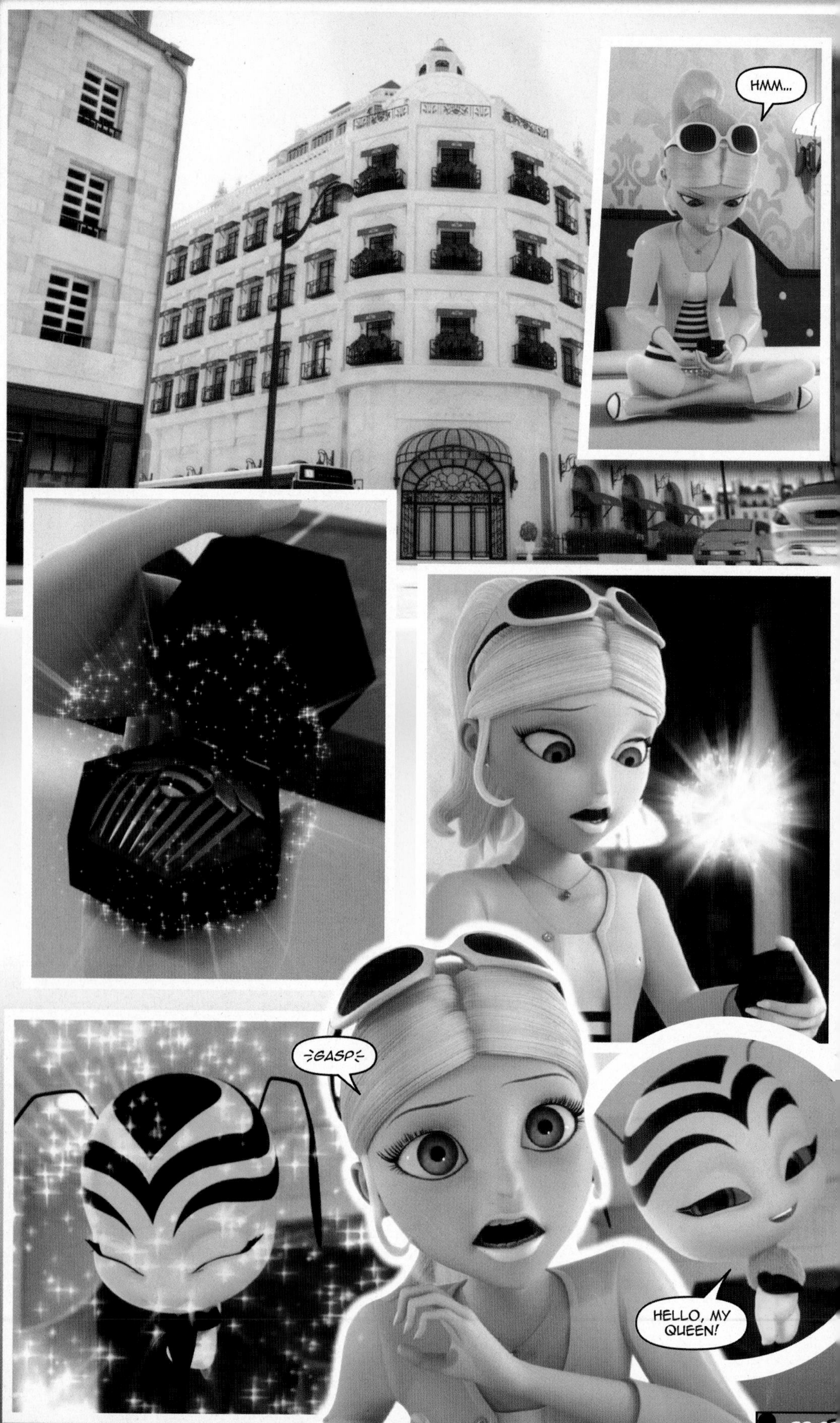
HMM...
GASP
HELLO, MY QUEEN!
TO BE CONTINU

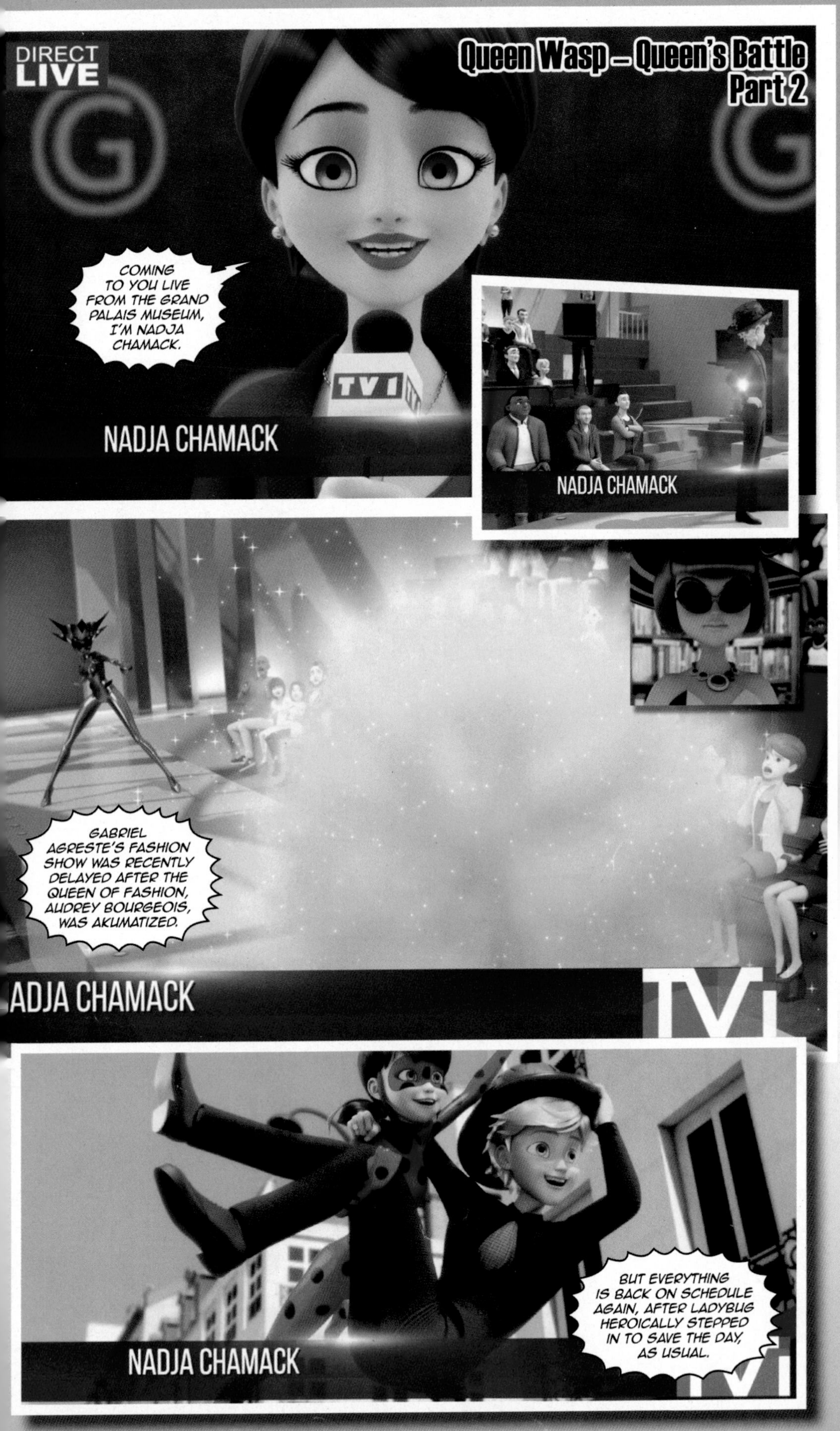
DIRECT LIVE
Queen Wasp – Queen's Battle
Part 2
COMING TO YOU LIVE FROM THE GRAND PALAIS MUSEUM, I'M NADJA CHAMACK.
TV1
NADJA CHAMACK
NADJA CHAMACK
GABRIEL AGRESTE'S FASHION SHOW WAS RECENTLY DELAYED AFTER THE QUEEN OF FASHION, AUDREY BOURGEOIS, WAS AKUMATIZED.
ADJA CHAMACK
BUT EVERYTHING IS BACK ON SCHEDULE AGAIN, AFTER LADYBUG HEROICALLY STEPPED IN TO SAVE THE DAY, AS USUAL.
NADJA CHAMACK

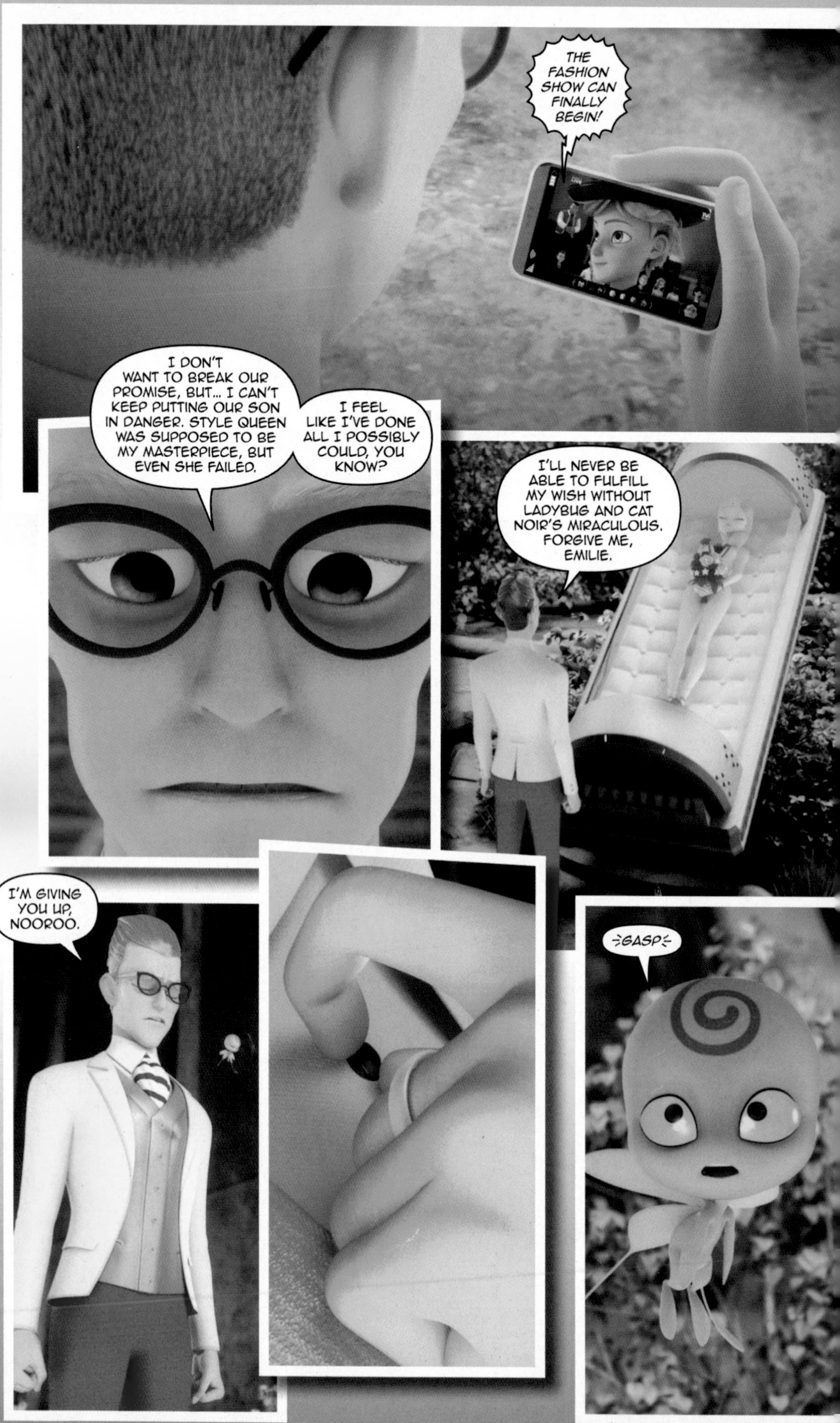
THE FASHION SHOW CAN FINALLY BEGIN!
I DON'T WANT TO BREAK OUR PROMISE, BUT... I CAN'T KEEP PUTTING OUR SON IN DANGER. STYLE QUEEN WAS SUPPOSED TO BE MY MASTERPIECE, BUT EVEN SHE FAILED.
I FEEL LIKE I'VE DONE ALL I POSSIBLY COULD, YOU KNOW?
I'LL NEVER BE ABLE TO FULFILL MY WISH WITHOUT LADYBUG AND CAT NOIR'S MIRACULOUS. FORGIVE ME, EMILIE.
I'M GIVING YOU UP, NOOROO.
GASP

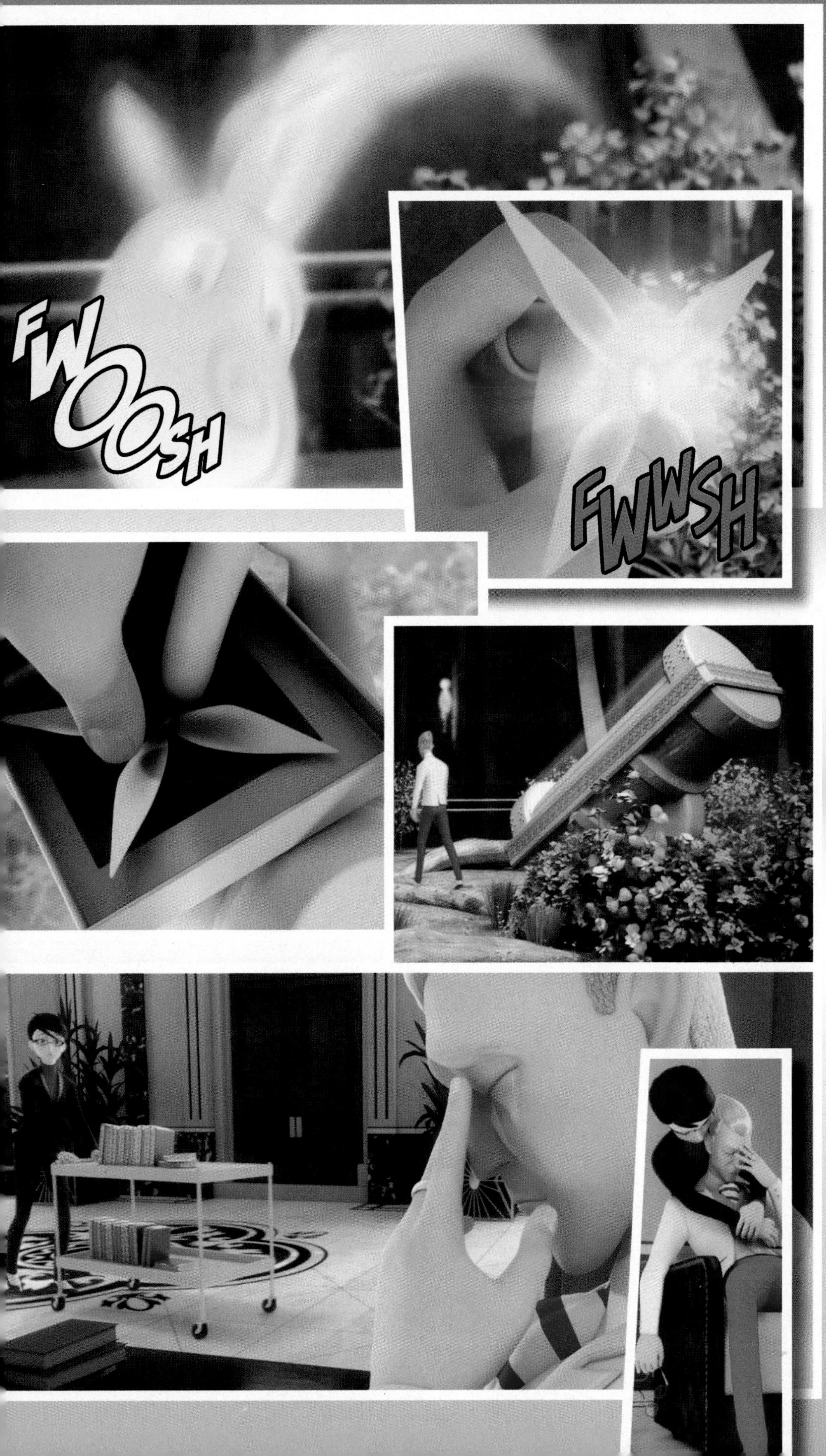
FWOOSH
FWWSH

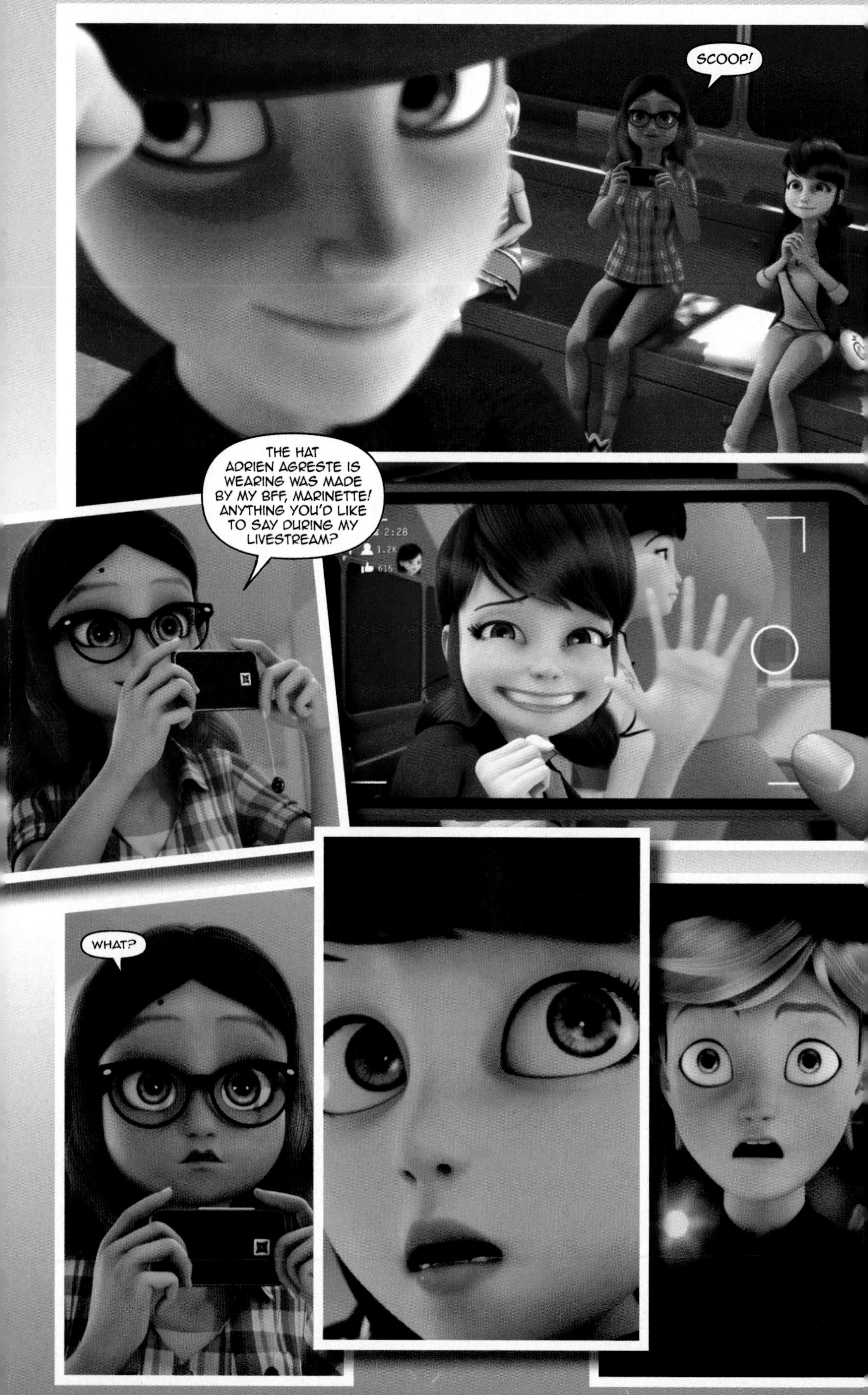
SCOOP!
THE HAT ADRIEN AGRESTE IS WEARING WAS MADE BY MY BFF, MARINETTE! ANYTHING YOU'D LIKE TO SAY DURING MY LIVESTREAM?
2:28
1.2K
615
WHAT?

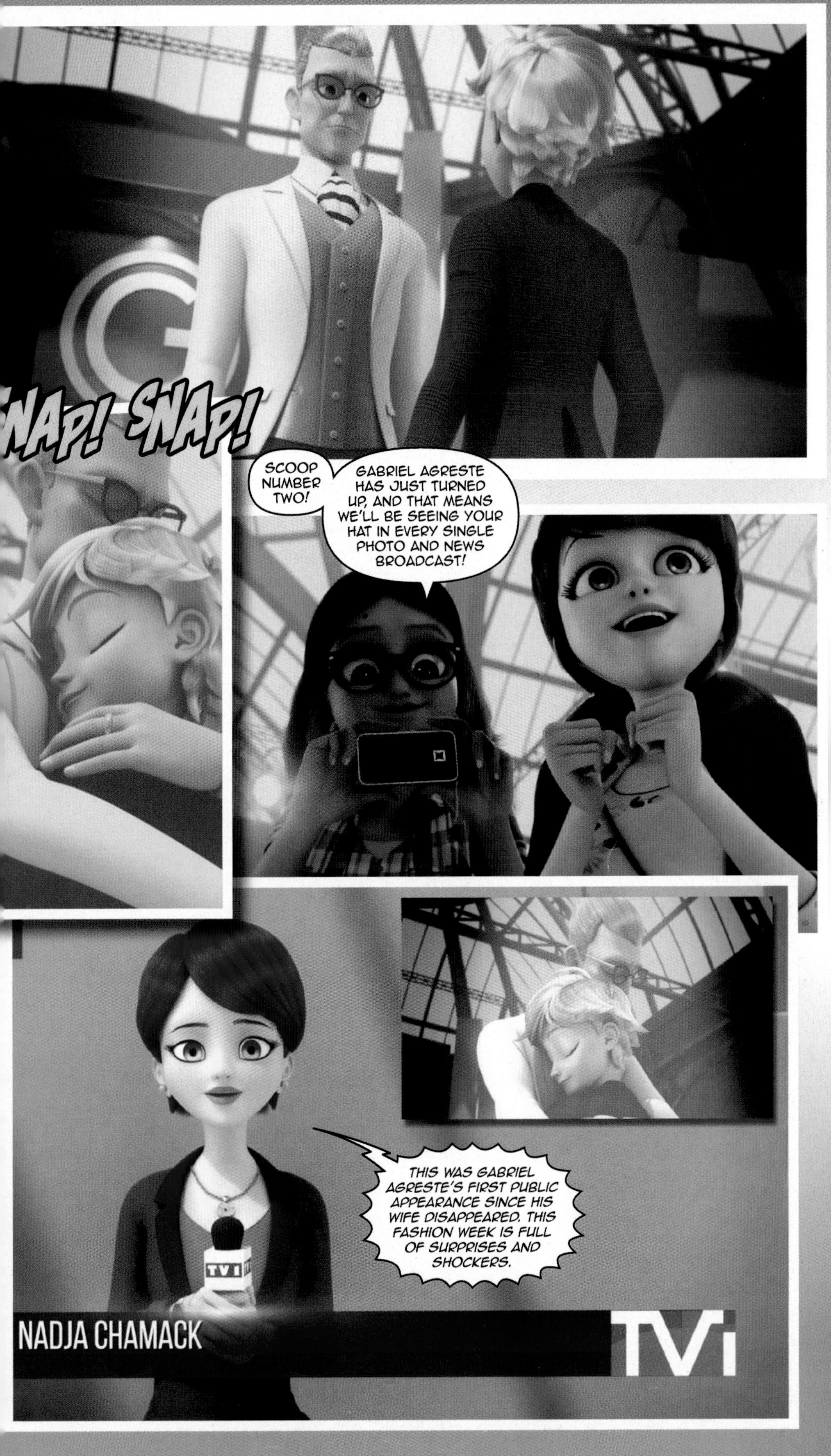
SNAP! SNAP!
SCOOP NUMBER TWO!
GABRIEL AGRESTE HAS JUST TURNED UP, AND THAT MEANS WE'LL BE SEEING YOUR HAT IN EVERY SINGLE PHOTO AND NEWS BROADCAST!
THIS WAS GABRIEL AGRESTE'S FIRST PUBLIC APPEARANCE SINCE HIS WIFE DISAPPEARED. THIS FASHION WEEK IS FULL OF SURPRISES AND SHOCKERS.
TVi
NADJA CHAMACK
TVi

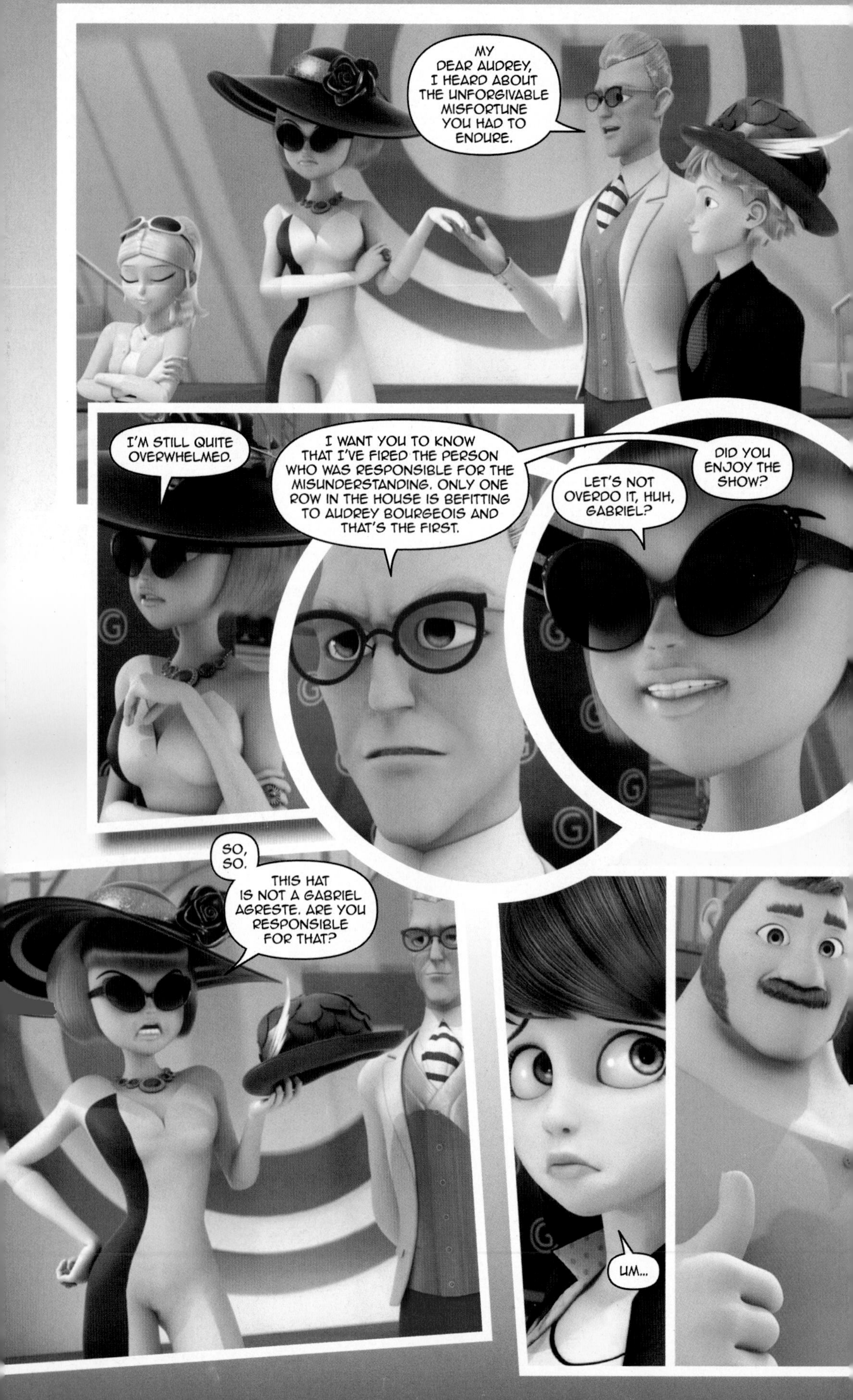
MY DEAR AUDREY, I HEARD ABOUT THE UNFORGIVABLE MISFORTUNE YOU HAD TO ENDURE.
I'M STILL QUITE OVERWHELMED.
I WANT YOU TO KNOW THAT I'VE FIRED THE PERSON WHO WAS RESPONSIBLE FOR THE MISUNDERSTANDING. ONLY ONE ROW IN THE HOUSE IS BEFITTING TO AUDREY BOURGEOIS AND THAT'S THE FIRST.
LET'S NOT OVERDO IT, HUH, GABRIEL?
DID YOU ENJOY THE SHOW?
SO, SO.
THIS HAT IS NOT A GABRIEL AGRESTE. ARE YOU RESPONSIBLE FOR THAT?
UM...

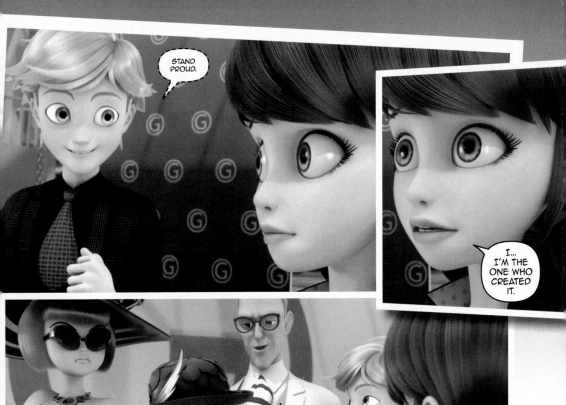

STAND PROUD.

I... I'M THE ONE WHO CREATED IT.

MARINETTE WON A FASHION DESIGN COMPETITION.

IT'S THE MOST...

...EXCEPTIONAL THING I'VE EVER SEEN!

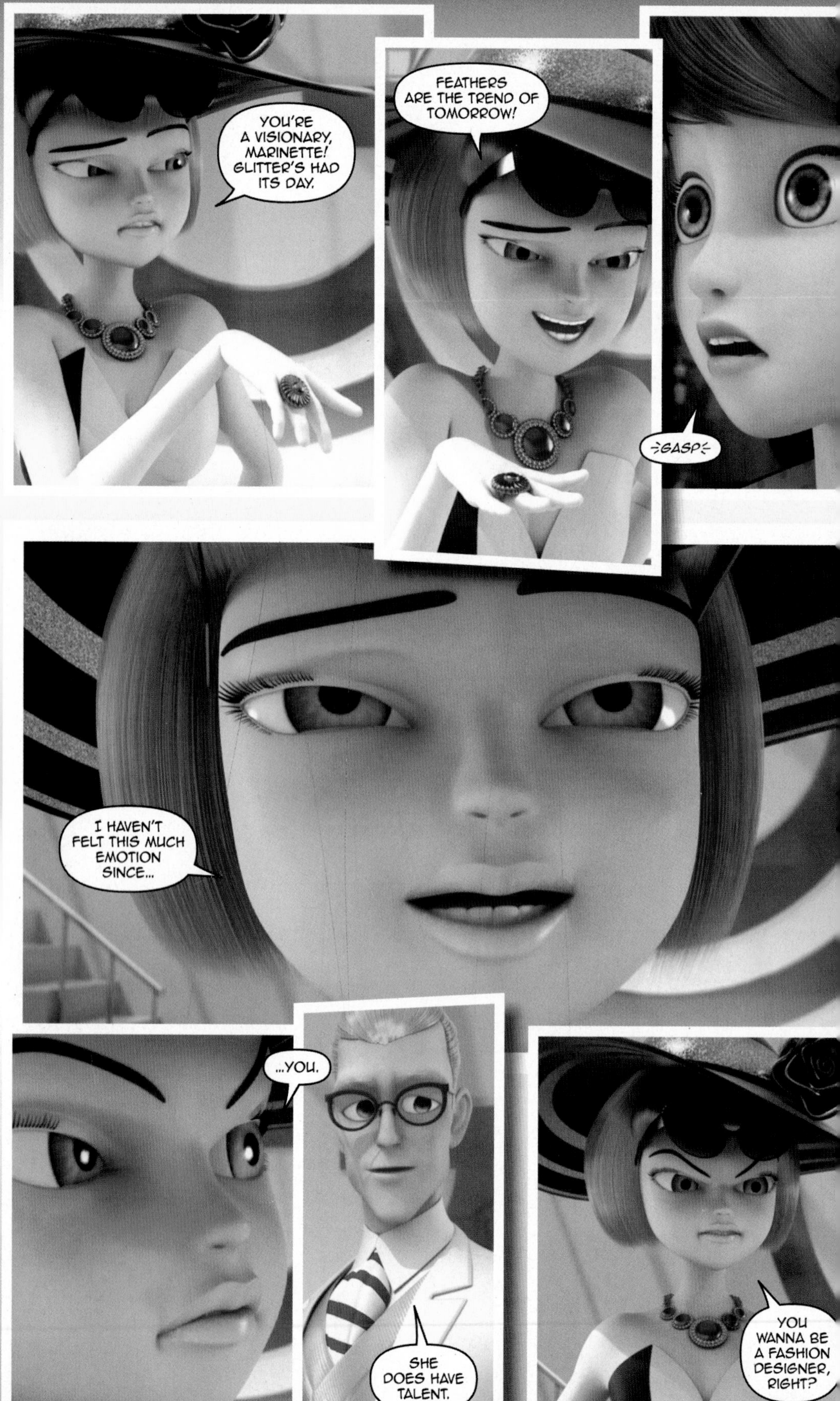
YOU'RE A VISIONARY, MARINETTE! GLITTER'S HAD ITS DAY.
FEATHERS ARE THE TREND OF TOMORROW!
GASP
I HAVEN'T FELT THIS MUCH EMOTION SINCE...
...YOU.
SHE DOES HAVE TALENT.
YOU WANNA BE A FASHION DESIGNER, RIGHT?

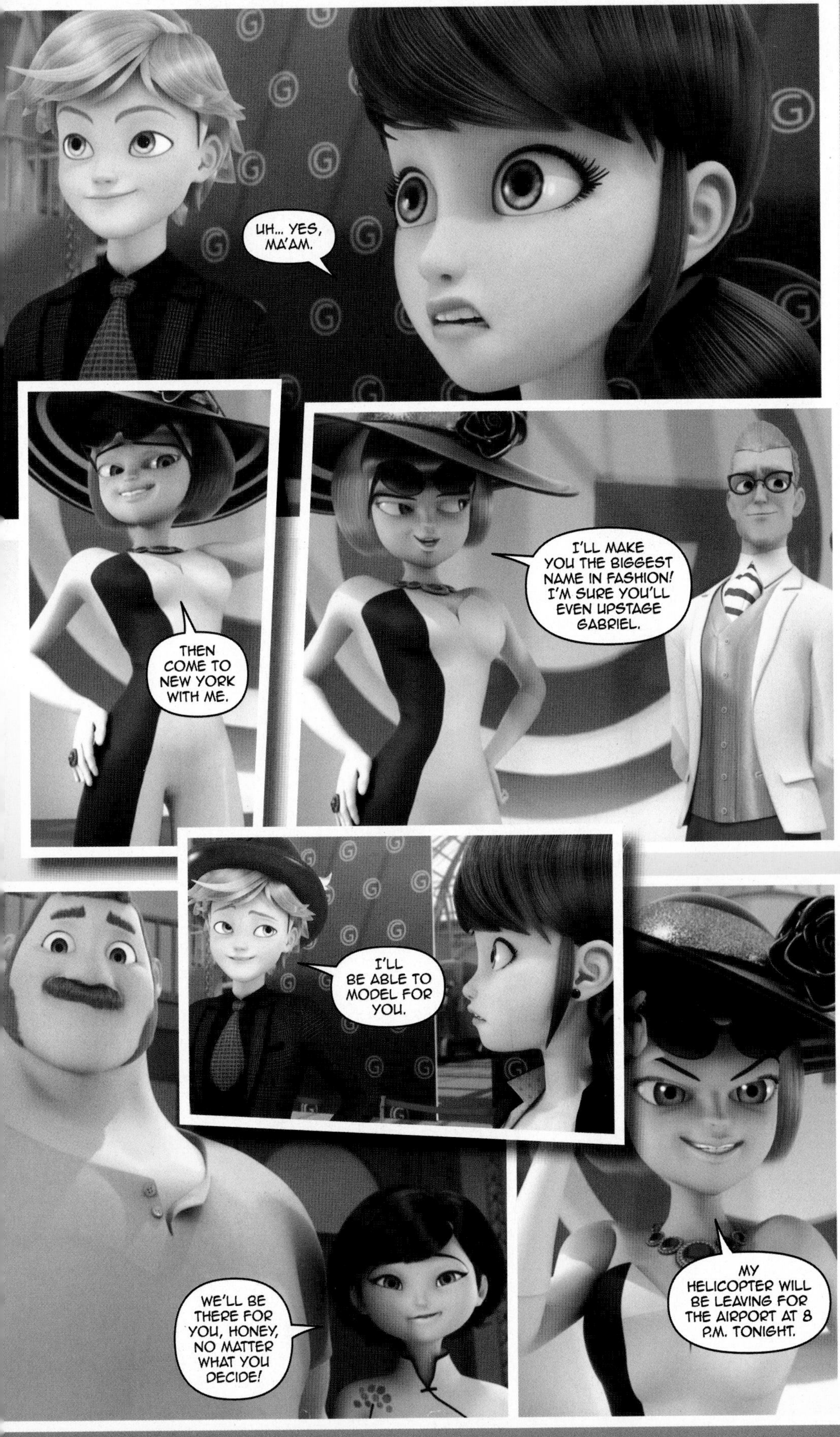
UH... YES, MA'AM.
THEN COME TO NEW YORK WITH ME.
I'LL MAKE YOU THE BIGGEST NAME IN FASHION! I'M SURE YOU'LL EVEN UPSTAGE GABRIEL.
I'LL BE ABLE TO MODEL FOR YOU.
WE'LL BE THERE FOR YOU, HONEY, NO MATTER WHAT YOU DECIDE!
MY HELICOPTER WILL BE LEAVING FOR THE AIRPORT AT 8 P.M. TONIGHT.

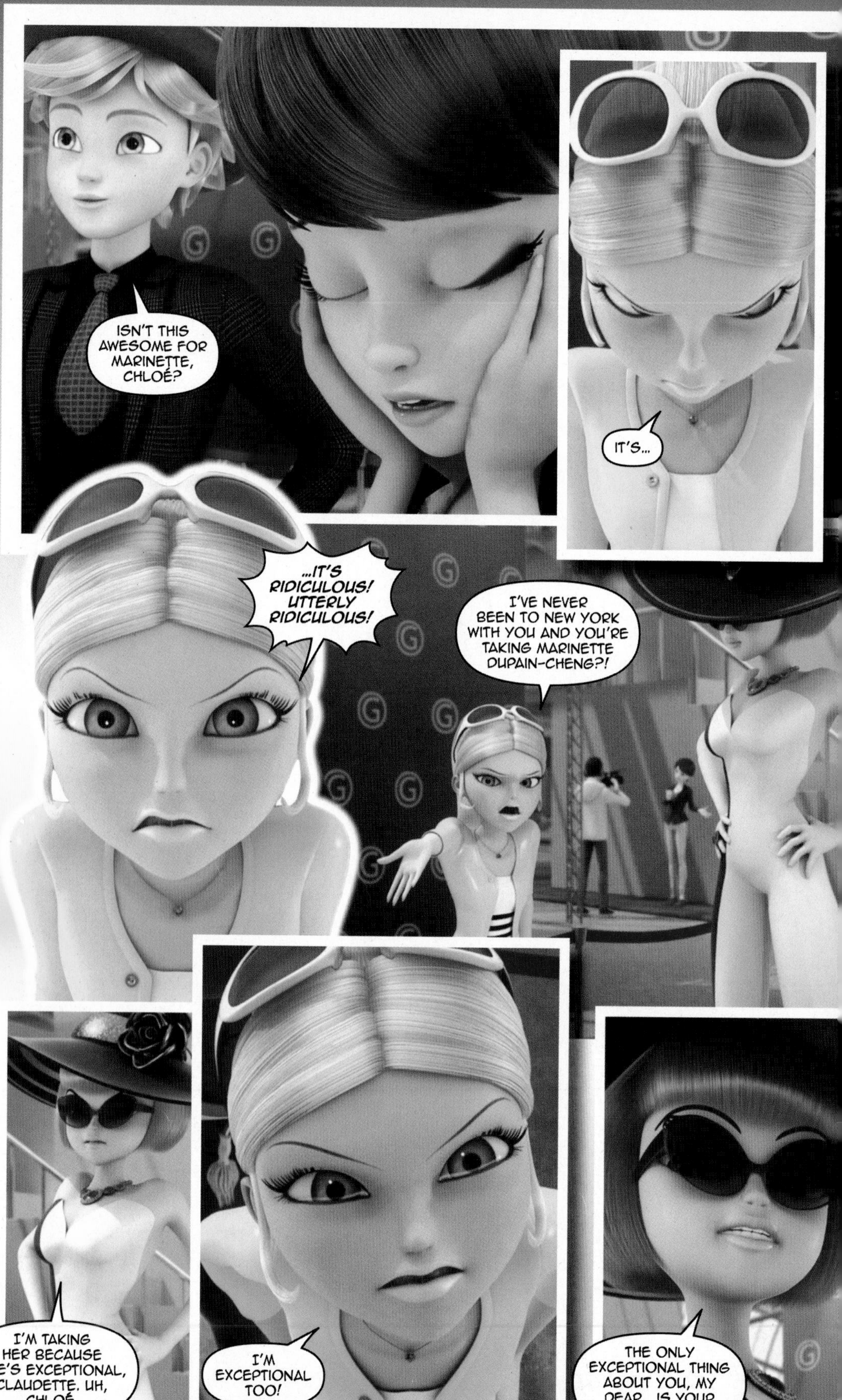
ISN'T THIS AWESOME FOR MARINETTE, CHLOÉ?
IT'S...
...IT'S RIDICULOUS! UTTERLY RIDICULOUS!
I'VE NEVER BEEN TO NEW YORK WITH YOU AND YOU'RE TAKING MARINETTE DUPAIN-CHENG?!
I'M TAKING HER BECAUSE SHE'S EXCEPTIONAL, CLAUDETTE. UH, CHLOÉ.
I'M EXCEPTIONAL TOO!
THE ONLY EXCEPTIONAL THING ABOUT YOU, MY DEAR... IS YOUR MOTHER.

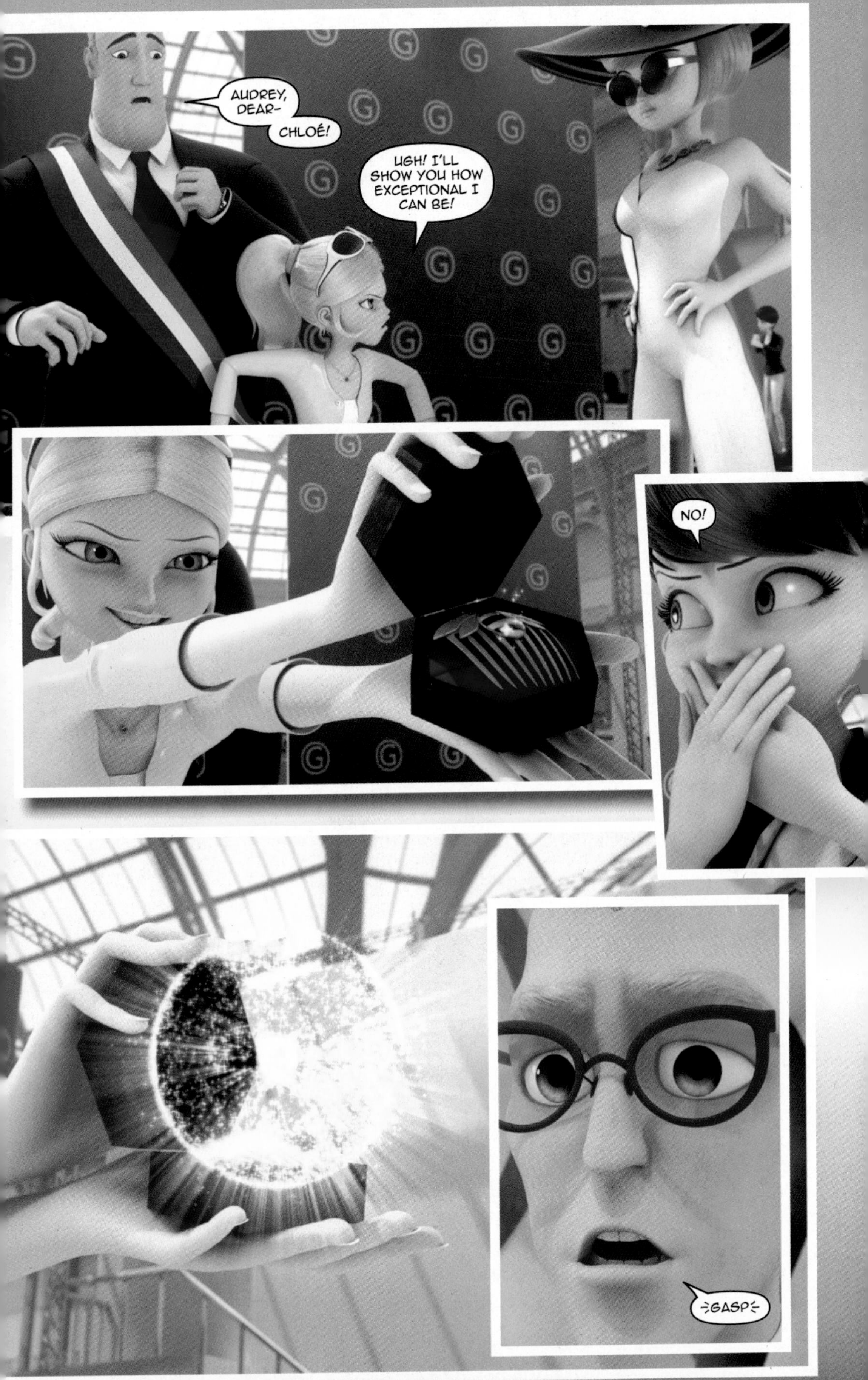
AUDREY, DEAR-
CHLOÉ!
UGH! I'LL SHOW YOU HOW EXCEPTIONAL I CAN BE!
NO!
GASP

HOW MAY I PLEASE YOU, MY QUEEN?

WHAT IS THAT THING?

CHLOÉ... WHAT ARE YOU DOING?!

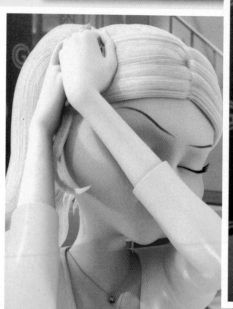

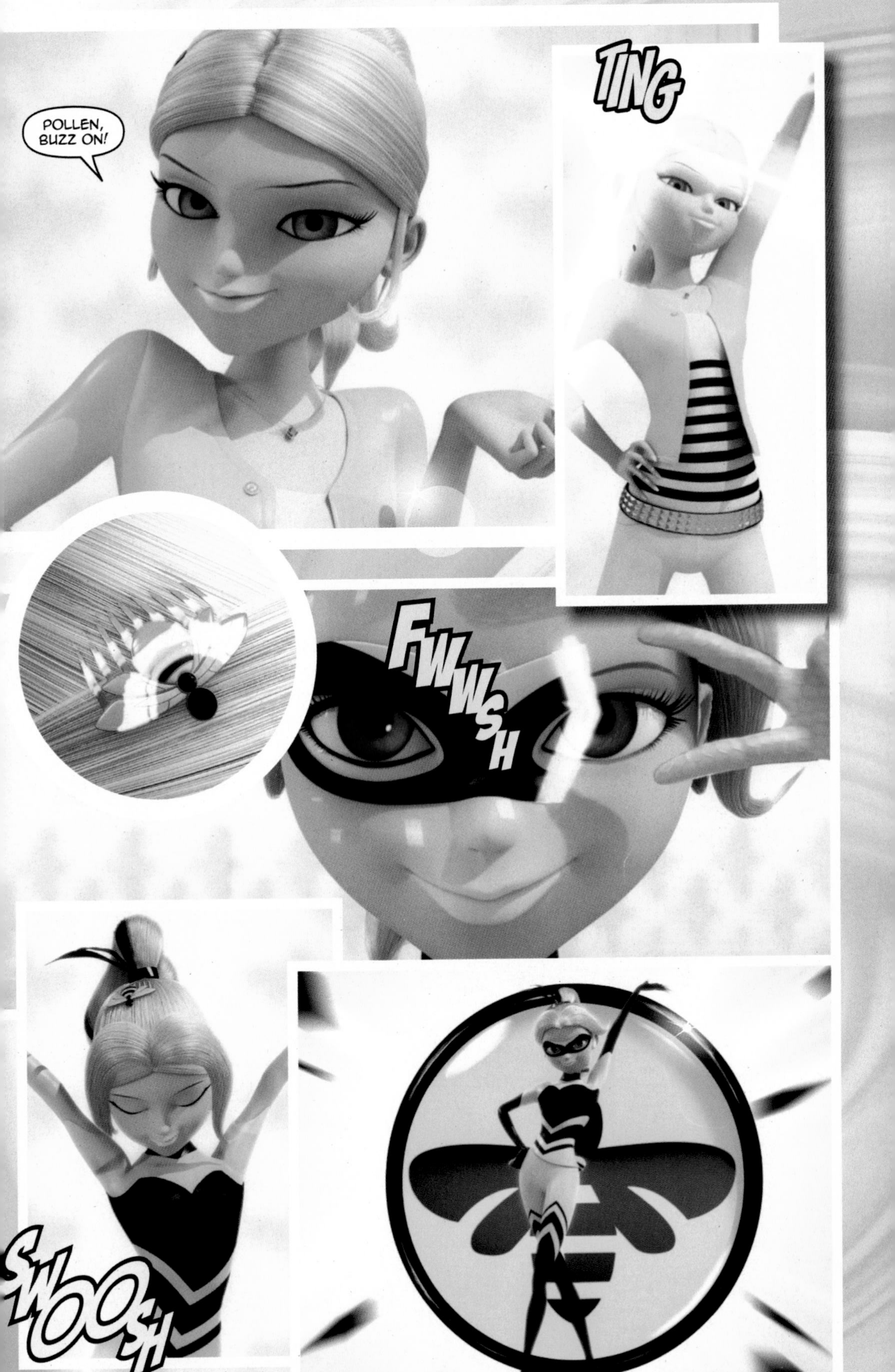
POLLEN, BUZZ ON!
TING
FWWSH
SWOOSH

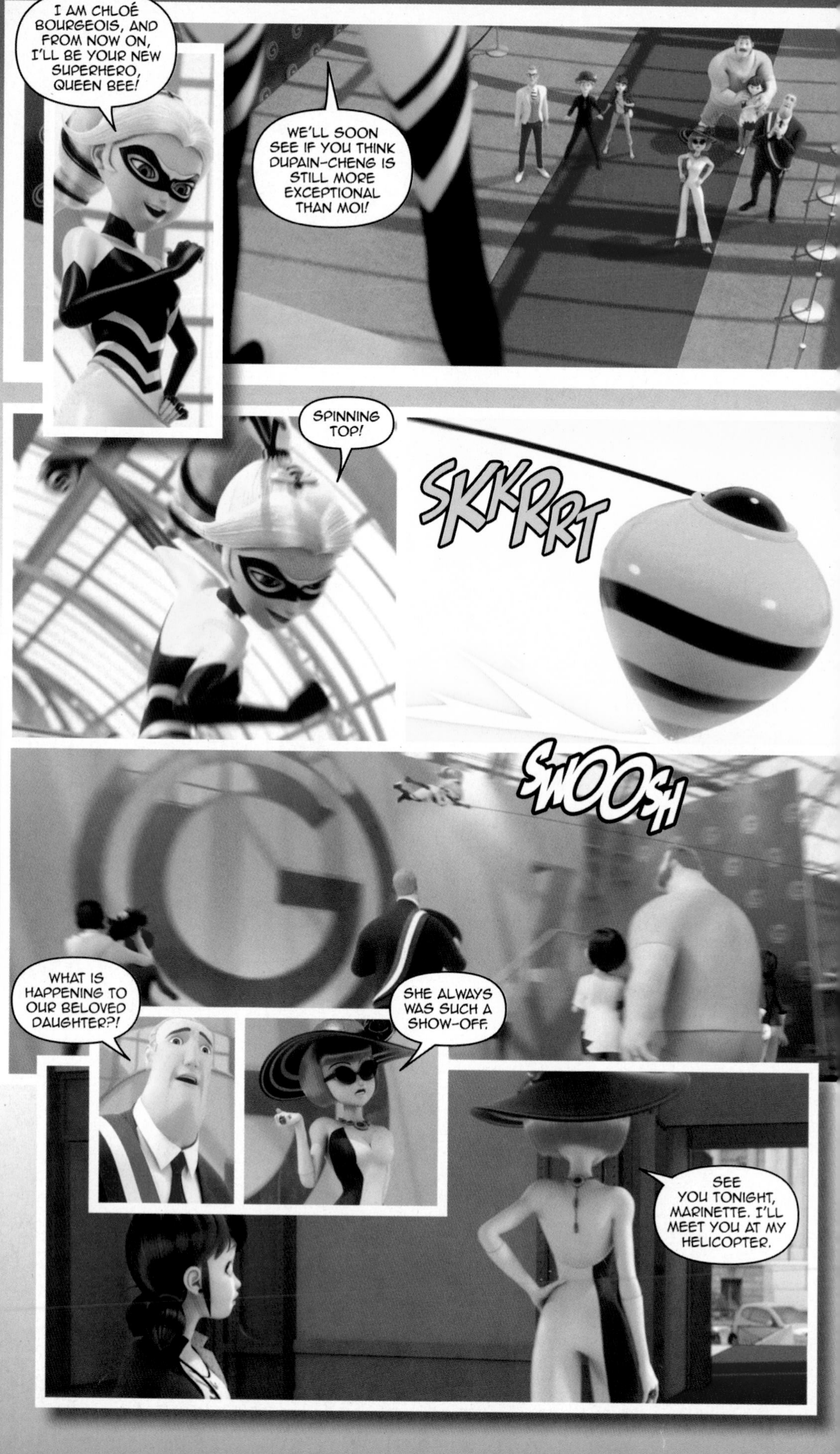
I AM CHLOÉ BOURGEOIS, AND FROM NOW ON, I'LL BE YOUR NEW SUPERHERO, QUEEN BEE!
WE'LL SOON SEE IF YOU THINK DUPAIN-CHENG IS STILL MORE EXCEPTIONAL THAN MOI!
SPINNING TOP!
SKKRRT
SWOOSH
WHAT IS HAPPENING TO OUR BELOVED DAUGHTER?!
SHE ALWAYS WAS SUCH A SHOW-OFF.
SEE YOU TONIGHT, MARINETTE. I'LL MEET YOU AT MY HELICOPTER.

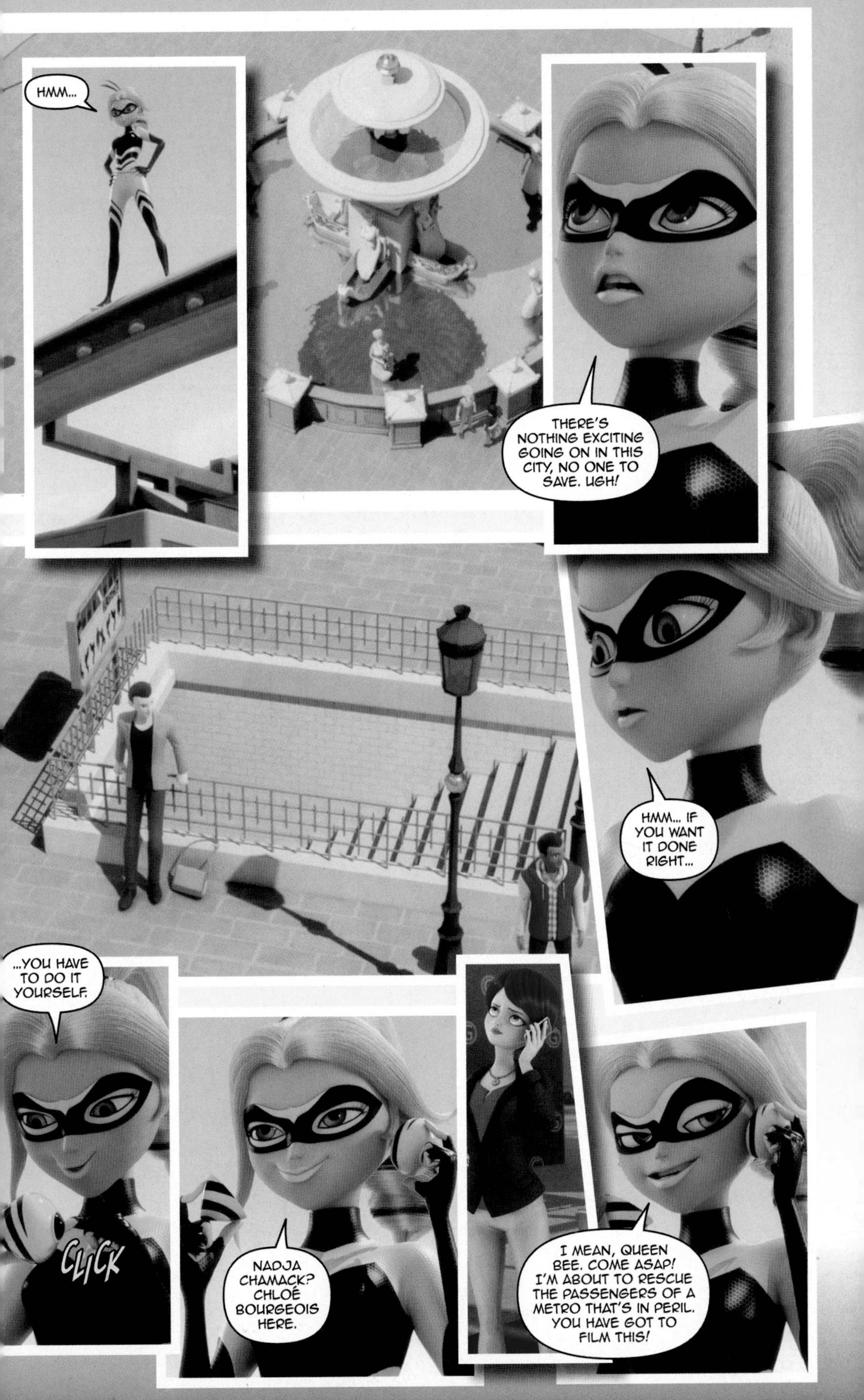
HMM...
THERE'S NOTHING EXCITING GOING ON IN THIS CITY, NO ONE TO SAVE. UGH!
HMM... IF YOU WANT IT DONE RIGHT...
...YOU HAVE TO DO IT YOURSELF.
CLICK
NADJA CHAMACK? CHLOÉ BOURGEOIS HERE.
I MEAN, QUEEN BEE. COME ASAP! I'M ABOUT TO RESCUE THE PASSENGERS OF A METRO THAT'S IN PERIL. YOU HAVE GOT TO FILM THIS!

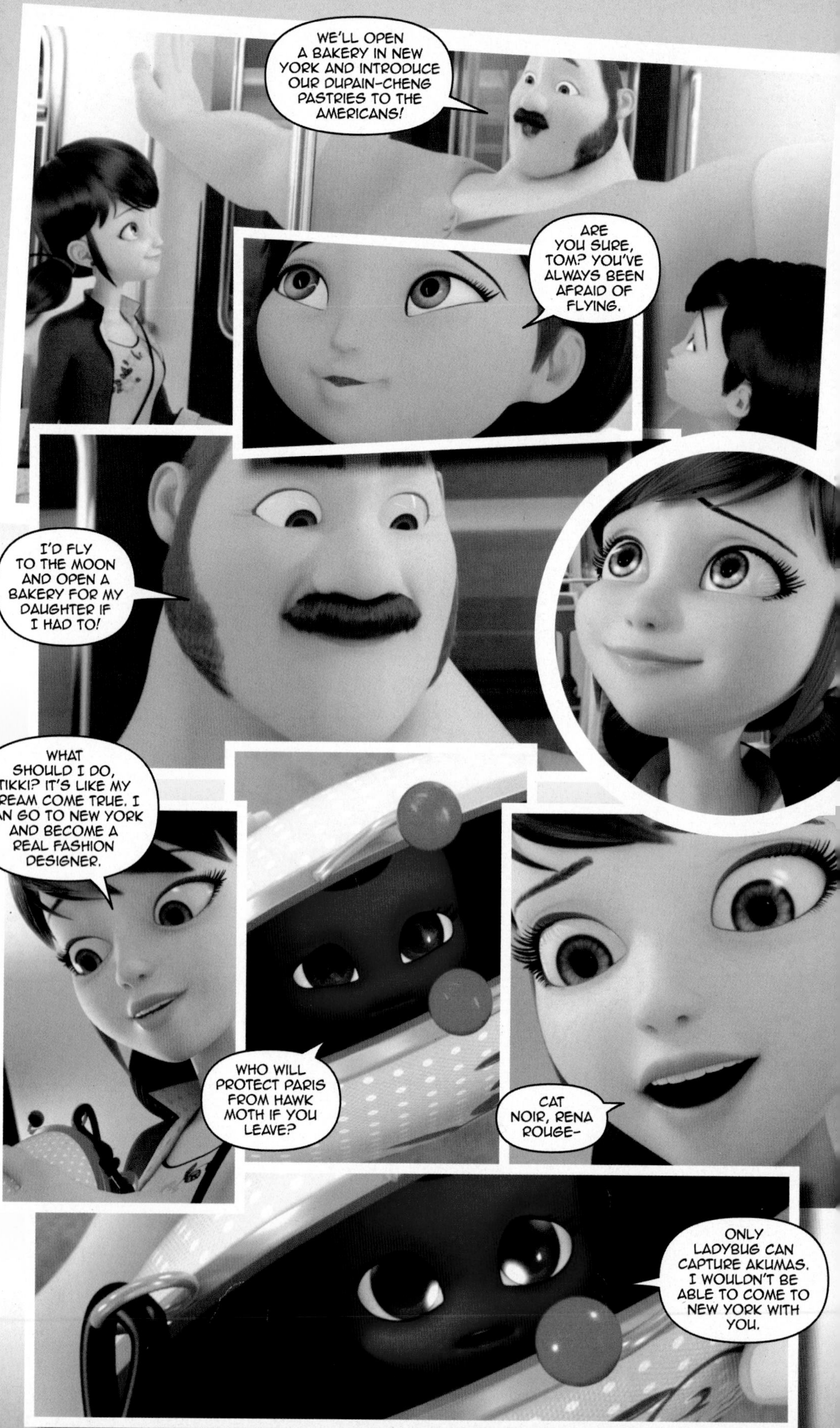
WE'LL OPEN A BAKERY IN NEW YORK AND INTRODUCE OUR DUPAIN-CHENG PASTRIES TO THE AMERICANS!
ARE YOU SURE, TOM? YOU'VE ALWAYS BEEN AFRAID OF FLYING.
I'D FLY TO THE MOON AND OPEN A BAKERY FOR MY DAUGHTER IF I HAD TO!
WHAT SHOULD I DO, TIKKI? IT'S LIKE MY DREAM COME TRUE. I CAN GO TO NEW YORK AND BECOME A REAL FASHION DESIGNER.
WHO WILL PROTECT PARIS FROM HAWK MOTH IF YOU LEAVE?
CAT NOIR, RENA ROUGE-
ONLY LADYBUG CAN CAPTURE AKUMAS. I WOULDN'T BE ABLE TO COME TO NEW YORK WITH YOU.

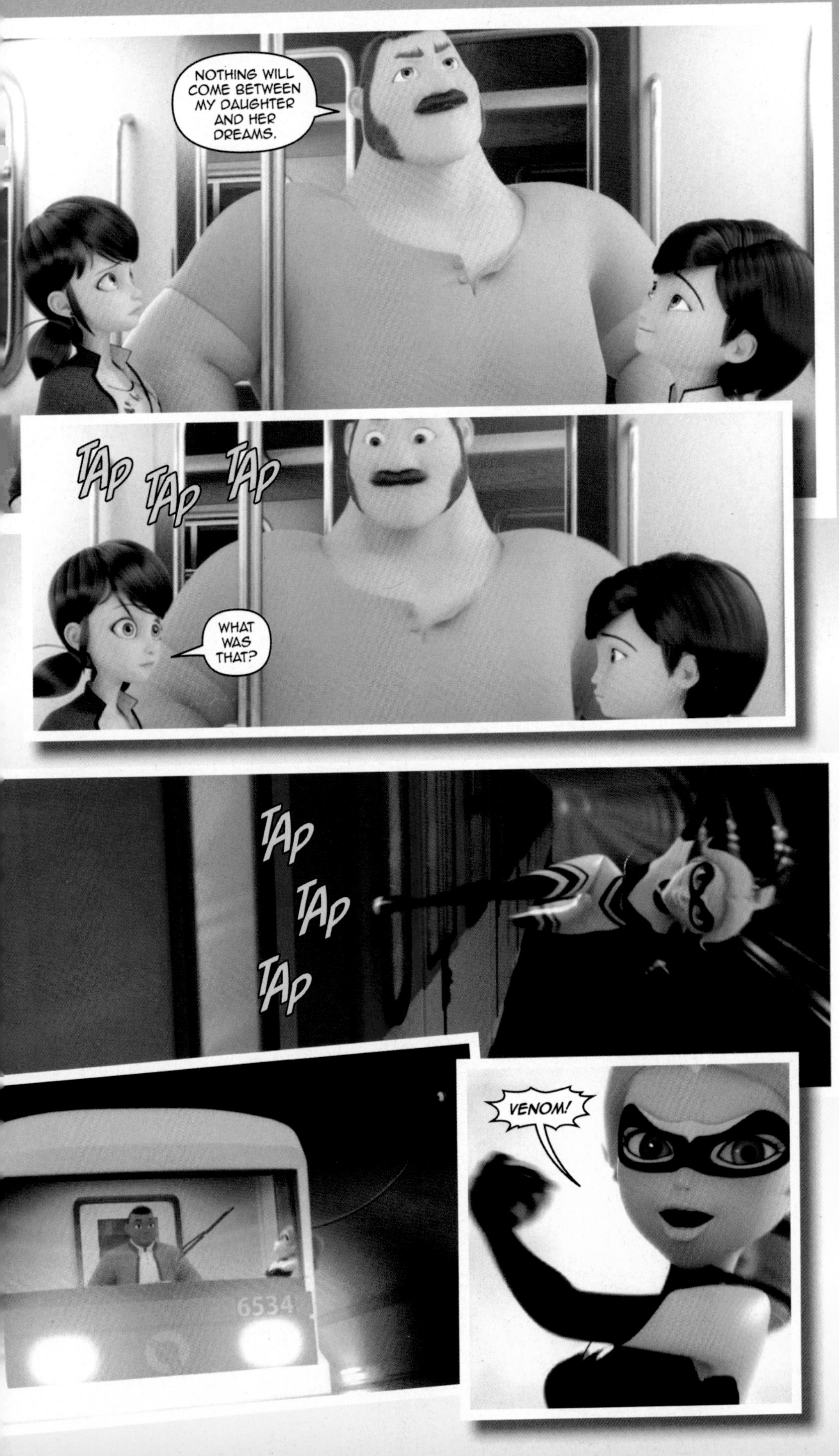
NOTHING WILL COME BETWEEN MY DAUGHTER AND HER DREAMS.
TAP TAP TAP
WHAT WAS THAT?
TAP TAP TAP
6534
VENOM!

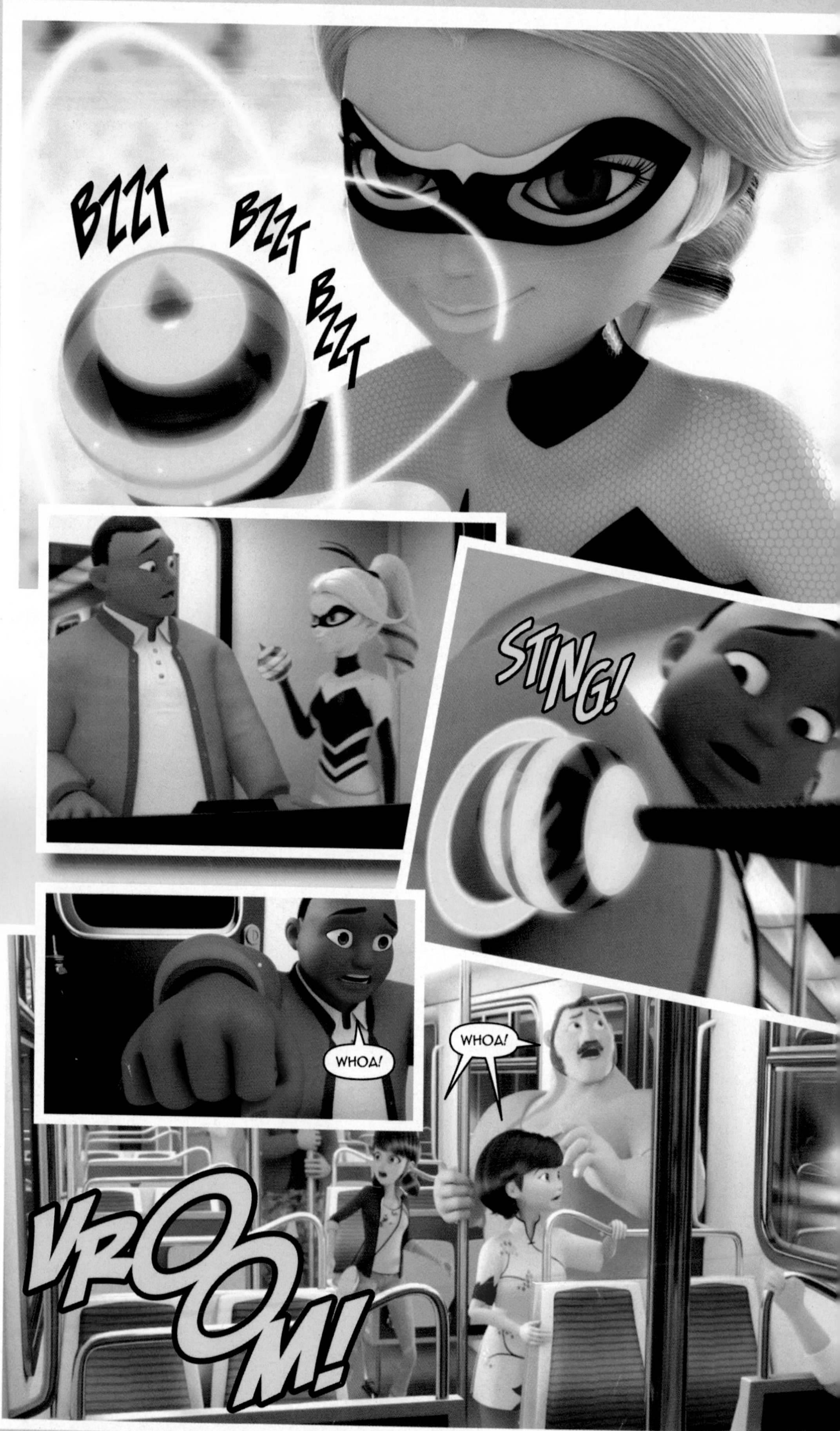
BZZT
BZZT
BZZT
STING!
WHOA!
WHOA!
VROOOM!

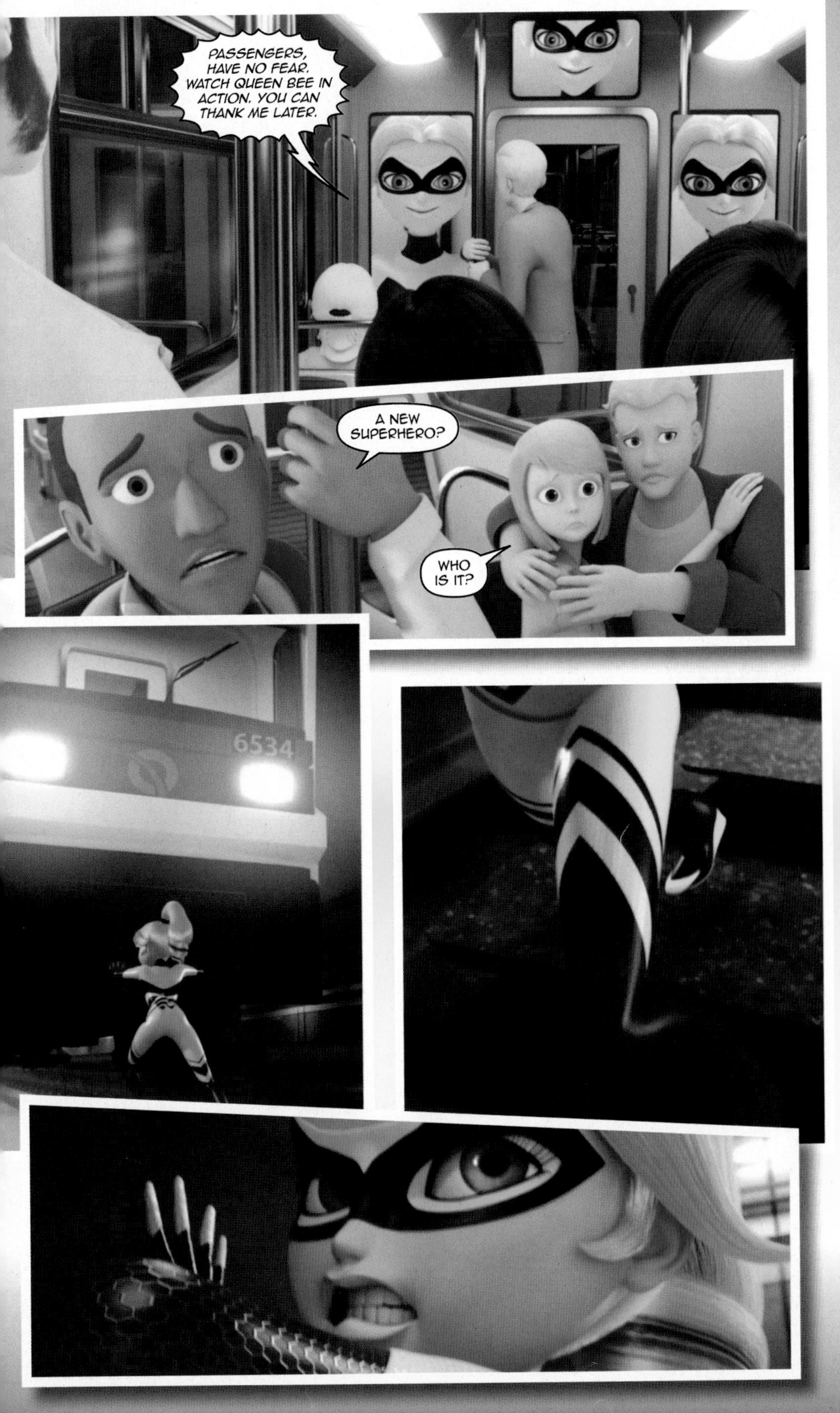
PASSENGERS, HAVE NO FEAR. WATCH QUEEN BEE IN ACTION. YOU CAN THANK ME LATER.
A NEW SUPERHERO?
WHO IS IT?
6534

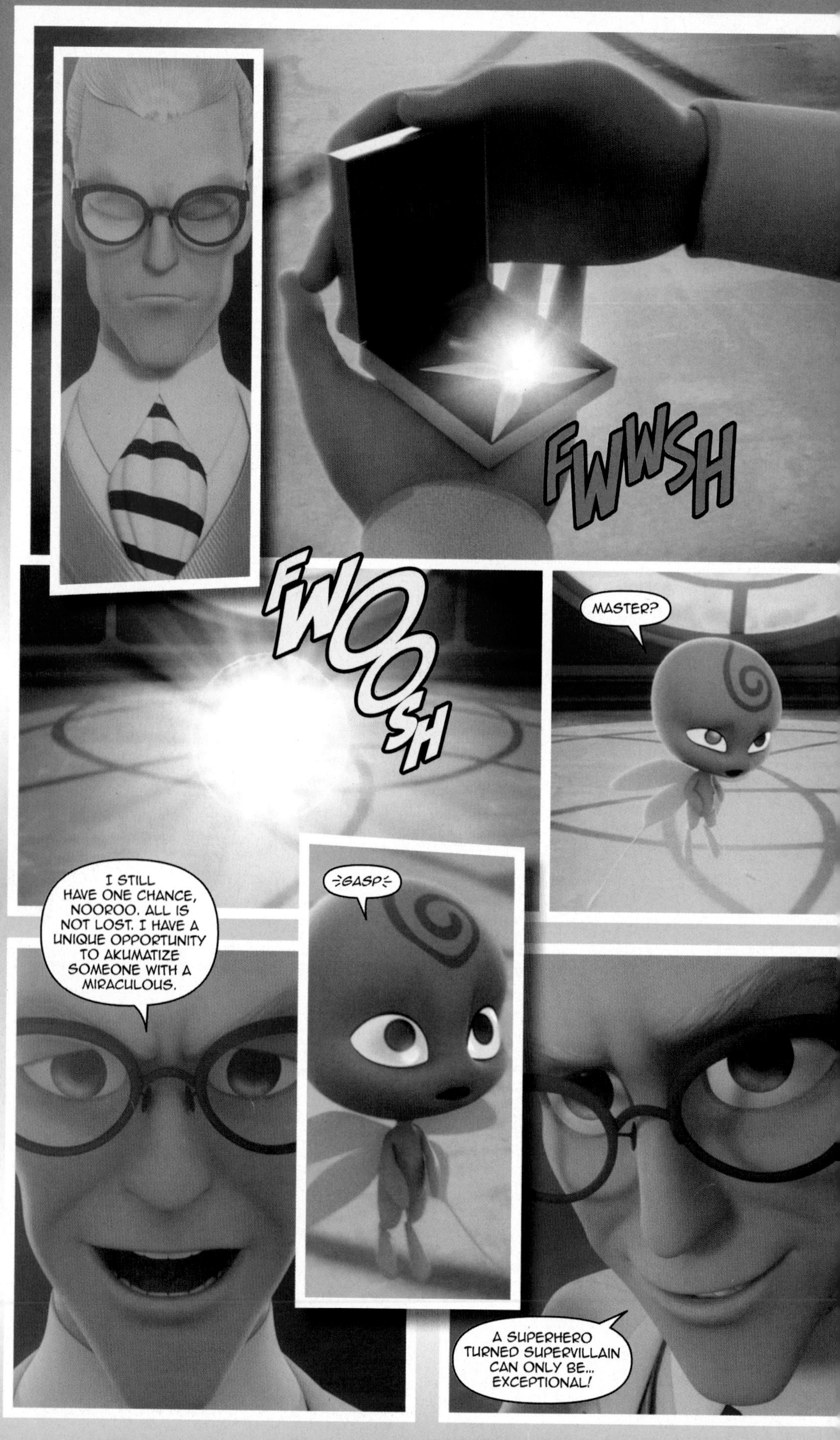
FWWSH
FWOOSH
MASTER?
I STILL HAVE ONE CHANCE, NOOROO. ALL IS NOT LOST. I HAVE A UNIQUE OPPORTUNITY TO AKUMATIZE SOMEONE WITH A MIRACULOUS.
GASP
A SUPERHERO TURNED SUPERVILLAIN CAN ONLY BE... EXCEPTIONAL!

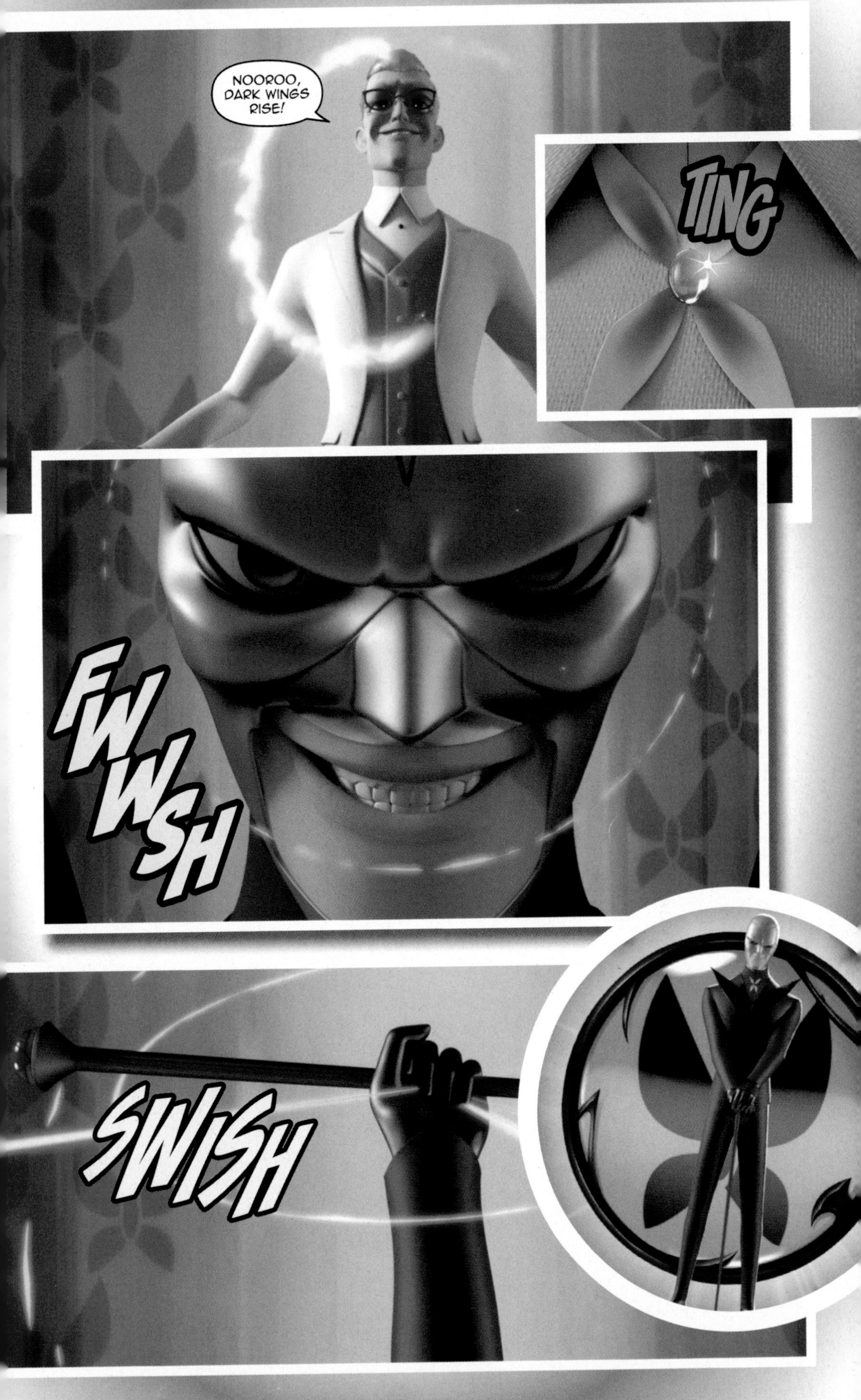
NOOROO, DARK WINGS RISE!
TING
FWWSH
SWISH

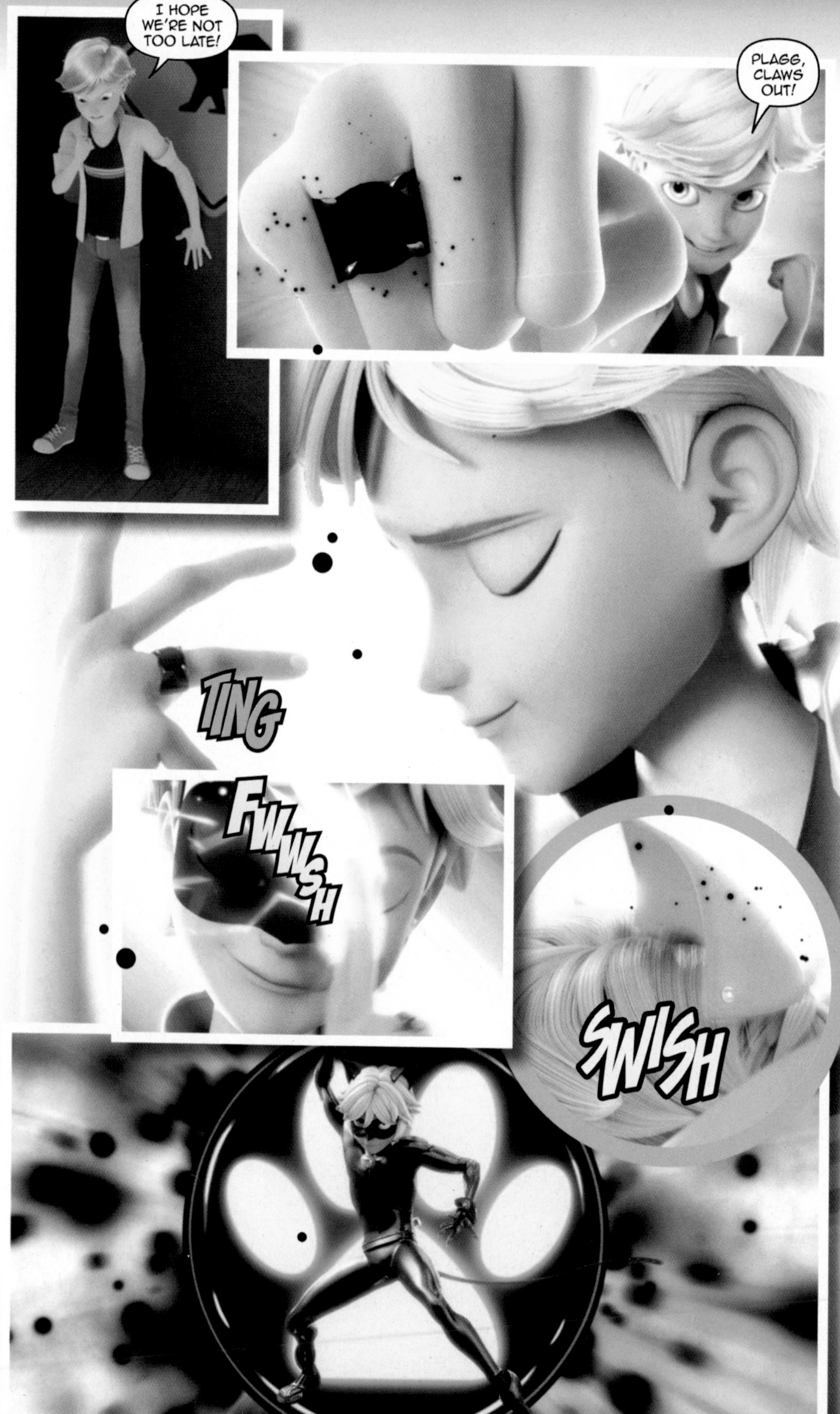
I HOPE WE'RE NOT TOO LATE!
PLAGG, CLAWS OUT!
TING
FWWSH
SWISH

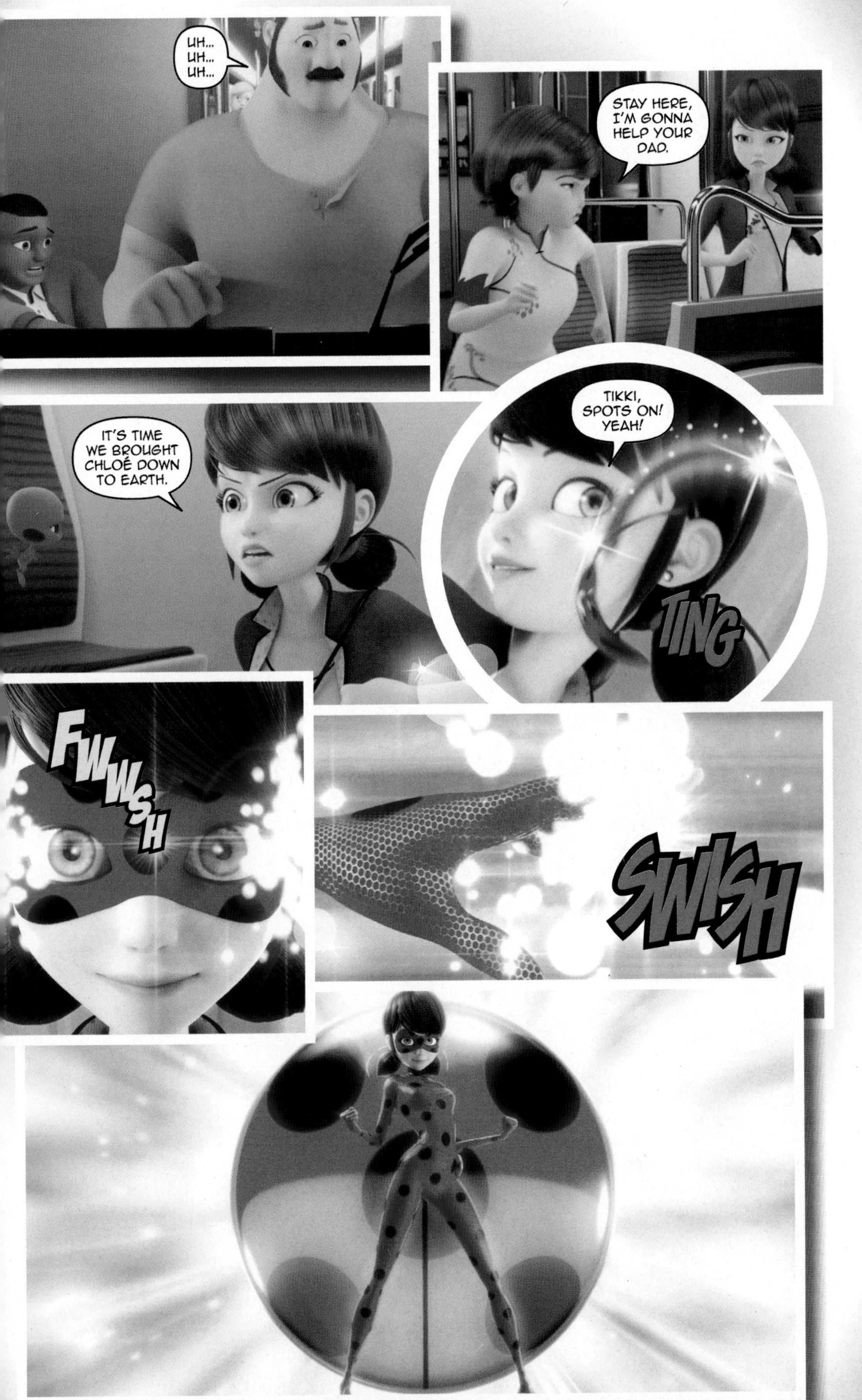
UH...
UH...
UH...
STAY HERE, I'M GONNA HELP YOUR DAD.
IT'S TIME WE BROUGHT CHLOÉ DOWN TO EARTH.
TIKKI, SPOTS ON! YEAH!
TING
FWWSH
SWISH

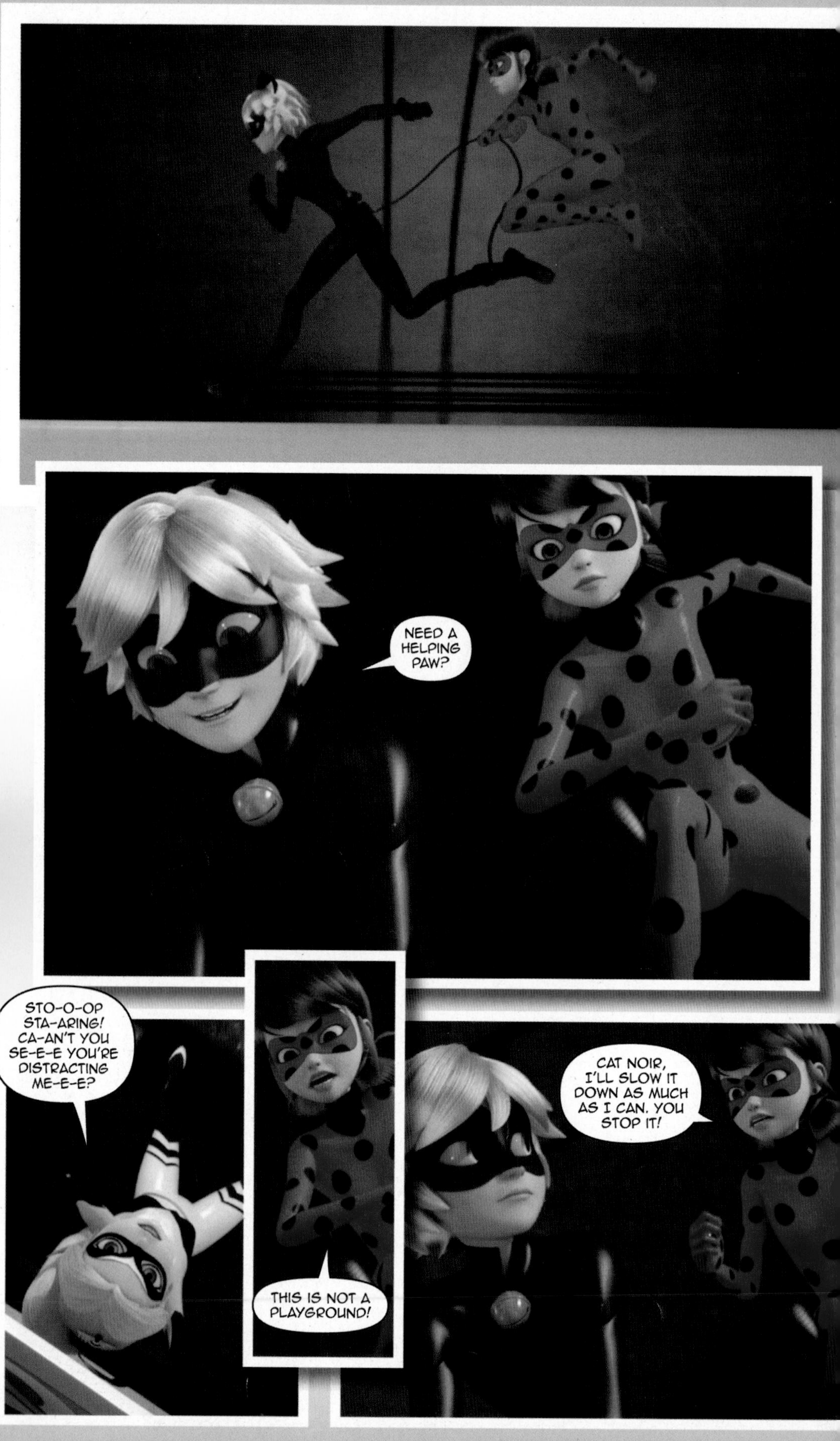
NEED A HELPING PAW?
STO-O-OP STA-ARING! CA-AN'T YOU SE-E-E YOU'RE DISTRACTING ME-E-E?
THIS IS NOT A PLAYGROUND!
CAT NOIR, I'LL SLOW IT DOWN AS MUCH AS I CAN. YOU STOP IT!

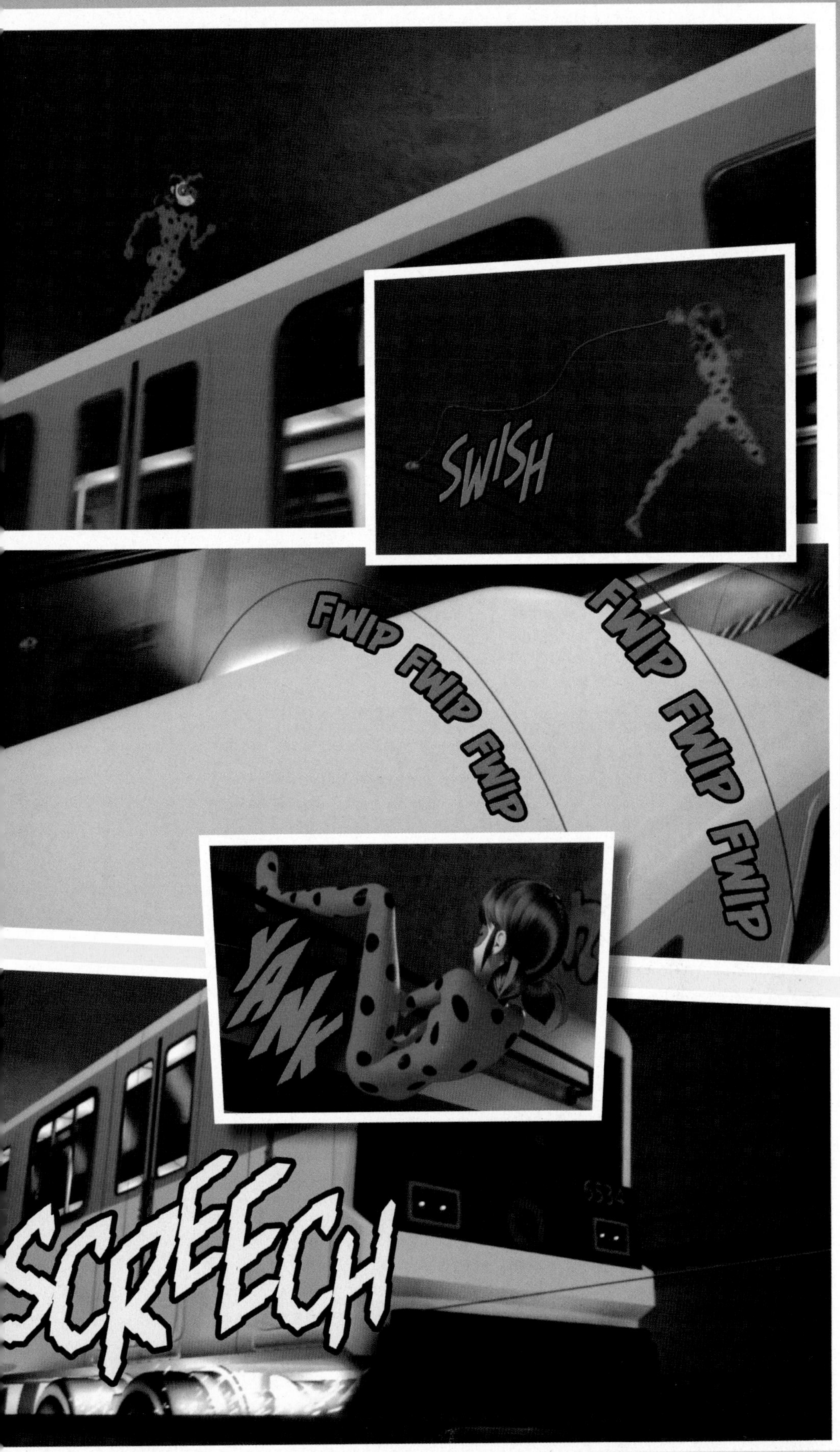
SWISH
FWIP FWIP FWIP
FWIP FWIP FWIP
YANK
SCREECH

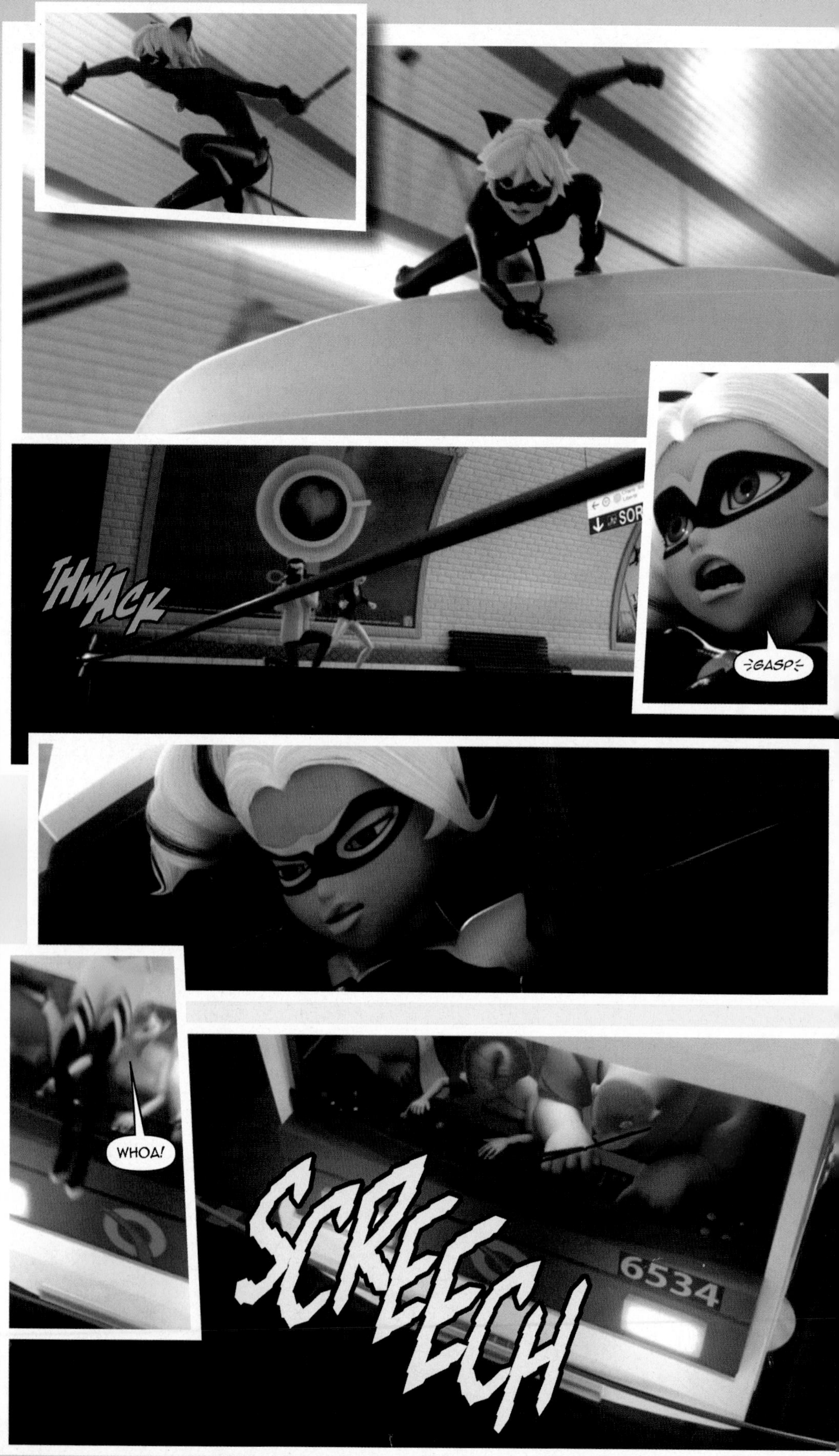
THWACK
GASP
WHOA!
SCREECH
6534

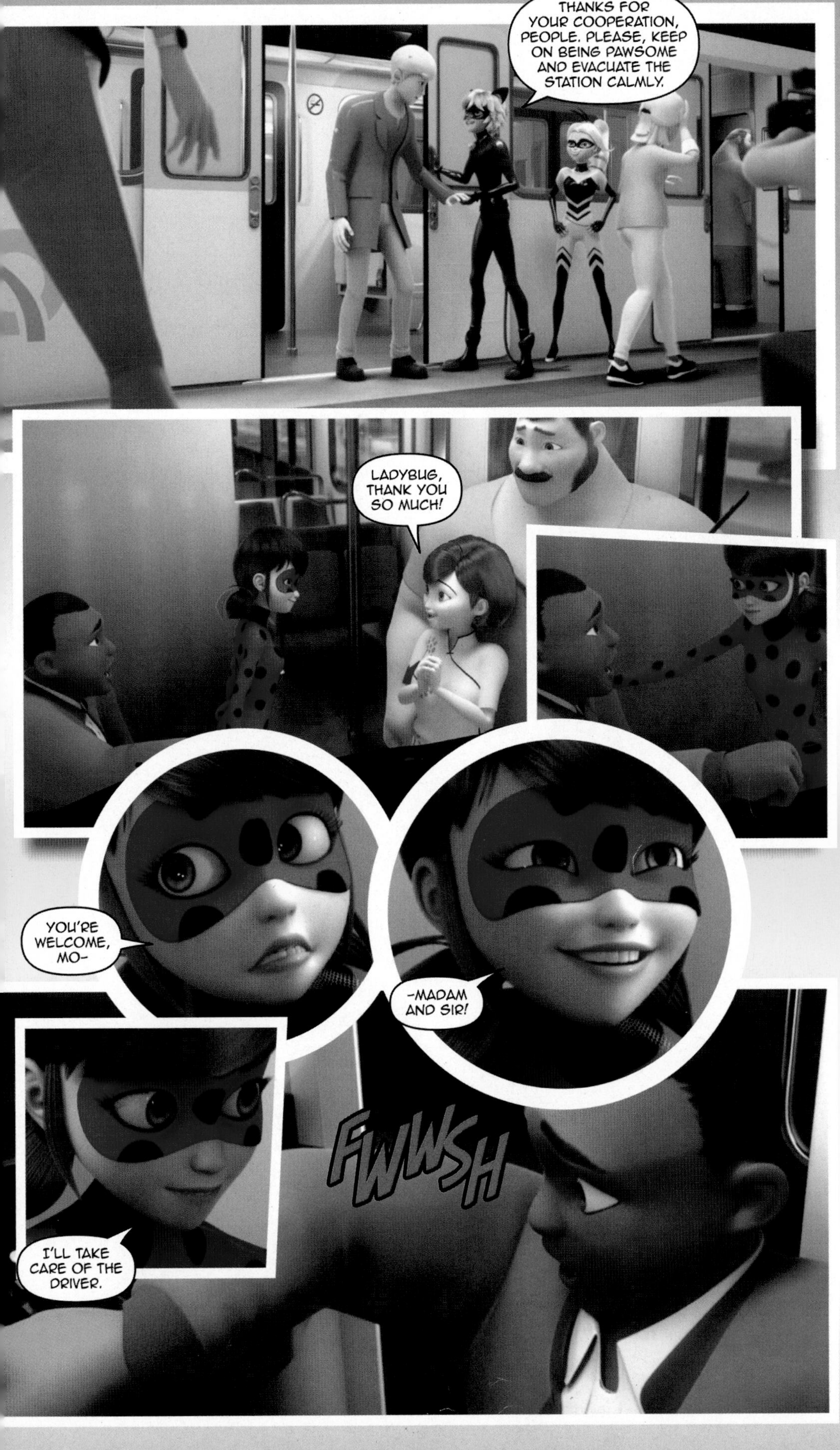
THANKS FOR YOUR COOPERATION, PEOPLE. PLEASE, KEEP ON BEING PAWSOME AND EVACUATE THE STATION CALMLY.
LADYBUG, THANK YOU SO MUCH!
YOU'RE WELCOME, MO-
-MADAM AND SIR!
FWWSH
I'LL TAKE CARE OF THE DRIVER.

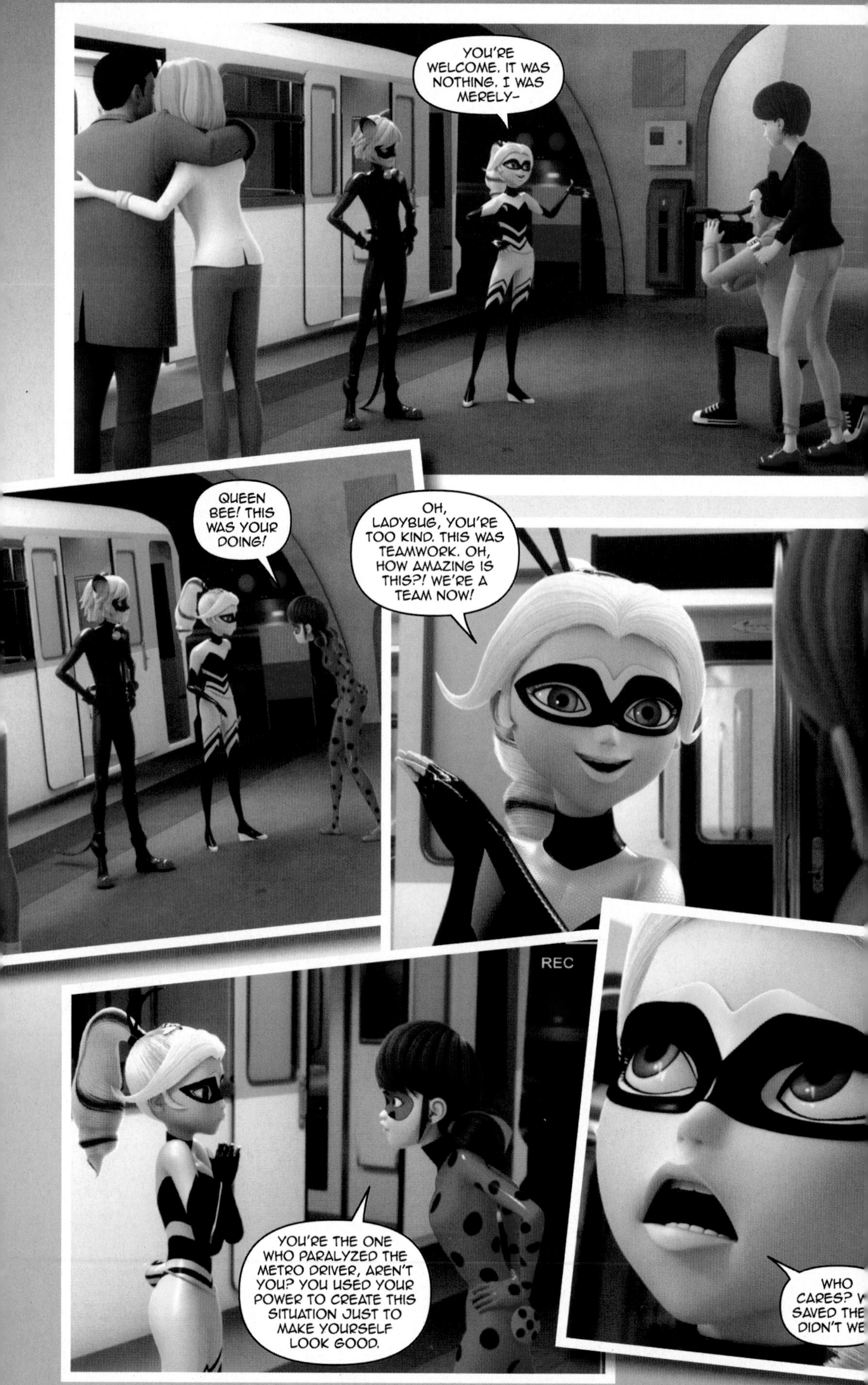
YOU'RE WELCOME. IT WAS NOTHING. I WAS MERELY-
QUEEN BEE! THIS WAS YOUR DOING!
OH, LADYBUG, YOU'RE TOO KIND. THIS WAS TEAMWORK. OH, HOW AMAZING IS THIS?! WE'RE A TEAM NOW!
REC
YOU'RE THE ONE WHO PARALYZED THE METRO DRIVER, AREN'T YOU? YOU USED YOUR POWER TO CREATE THIS SITUATION JUST TO MAKE YOURSELF LOOK GOOD.
WHO CARES? SAVED THE DIDN'T WE

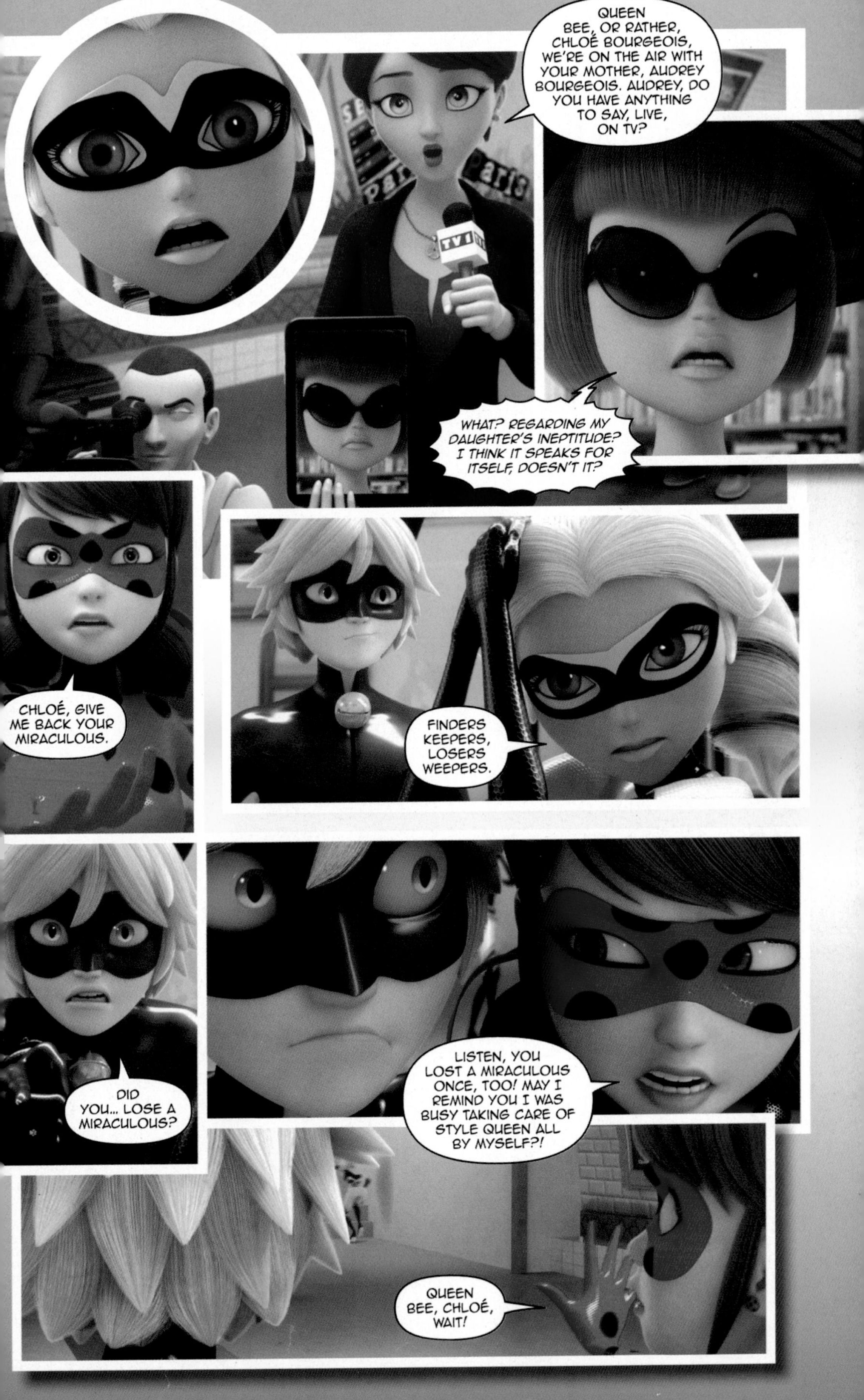
QUEEN BEE, OR RATHER, CHLOÉ BOURGEOIS, WE'RE ON THE AIR WITH YOUR MOTHER, AUDREY BOURGEOIS. AUDREY, DO YOU HAVE ANYTHING TO SAY, LIVE, ON TV?
WHAT? REGARDING MY DAUGHTER'S INEPTITUDE? I THINK IT SPEAKS FOR ITSELF, DOESN'T IT?
CHLOÉ, GIVE ME BACK YOUR MIRACULOUS.
FINDERS KEEPERS, LOSERS WEEPERS.
DID YOU... LOSE A MIRACULOUS?
LISTEN, YOU LOST A MIRACULOUS ONCE, TOO! MAY I REMIND YOU I WAS BUSY TAKING CARE OF STYLE QUEEN ALL BY MYSELF?!
QUEEN BEE, CHLOÉ, WAIT!

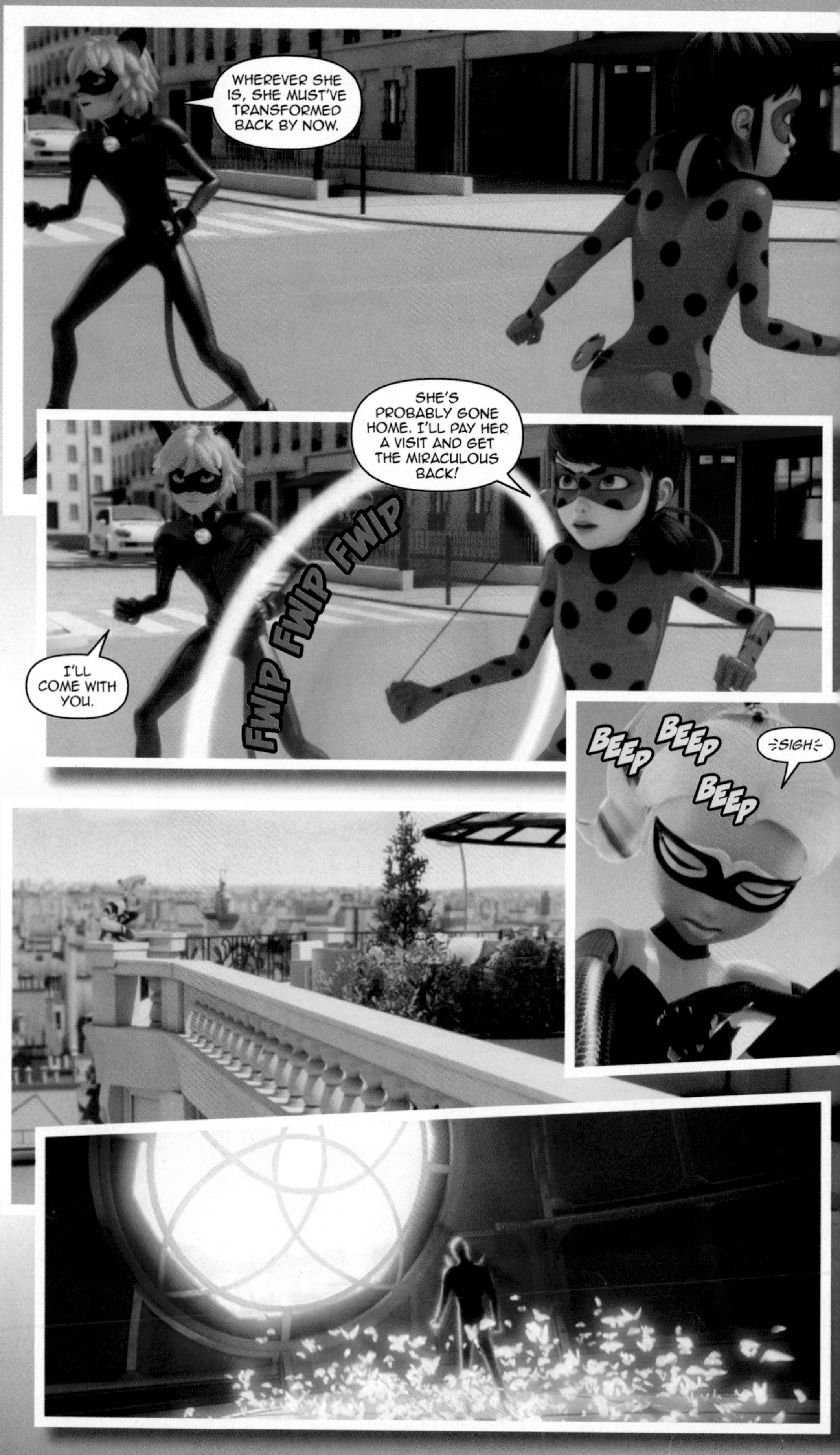
WHEREVER SHE IS, SHE MUST'VE TRANSFORMED BACK BY NOW.
SHE'S PROBABLY GONE HOME. I'LL PAY HER A VISIT AND GET THE MIRACULOUS BACK!
I'LL COME WITH YOU.
FWIP FWIP FWIP
BEEP BEEP BEEP
SIGH

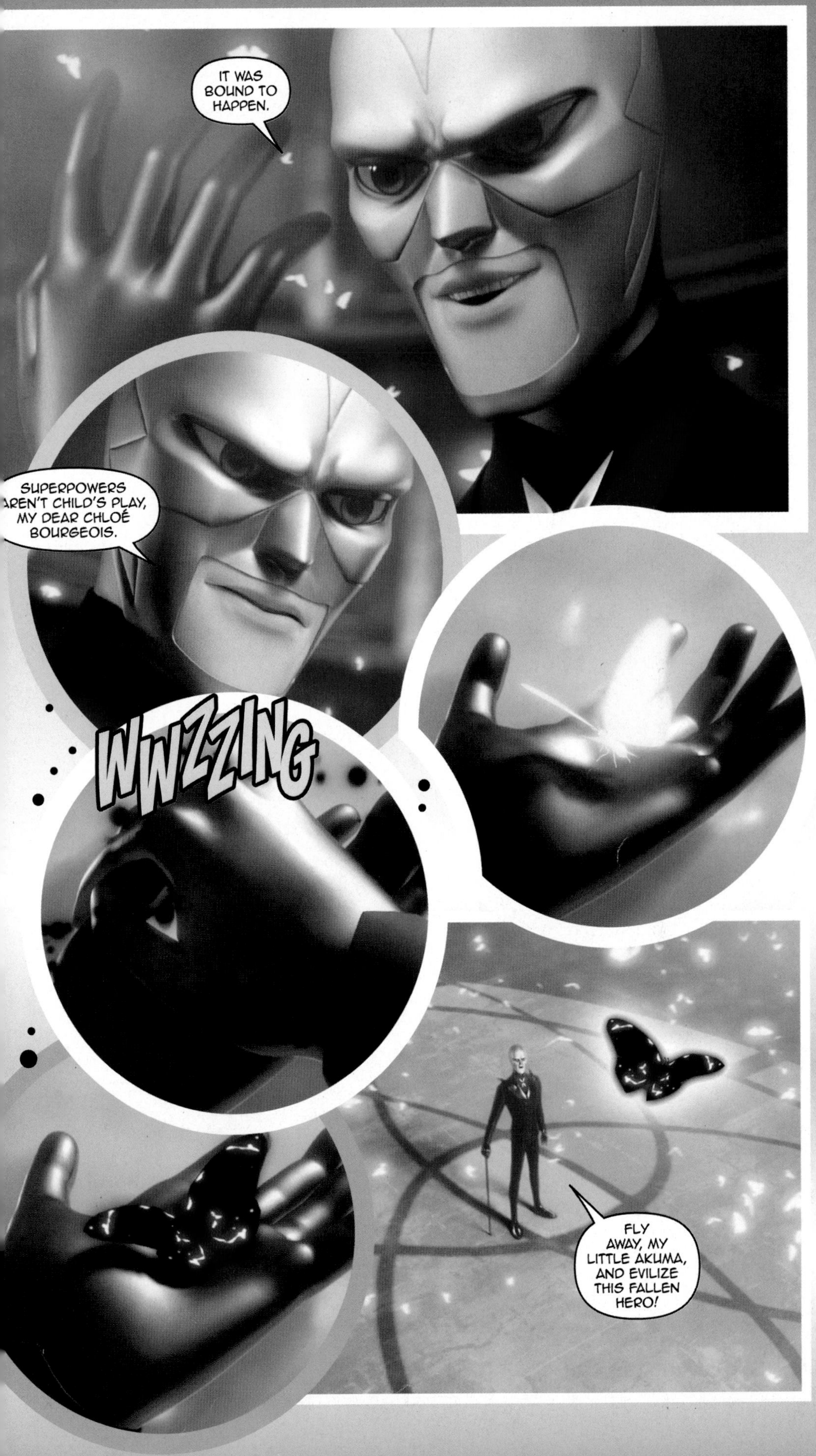
IT WAS BOUND TO HAPPEN.
SUPERPOWERS AREN'T CHILD'S PLAY, MY DEAR CHLOÉ BOURGEOIS.
WWZZING
FLY AWAY, MY LITTLE AKUMA, AND EVILIZE THIS FALLEN HERO!

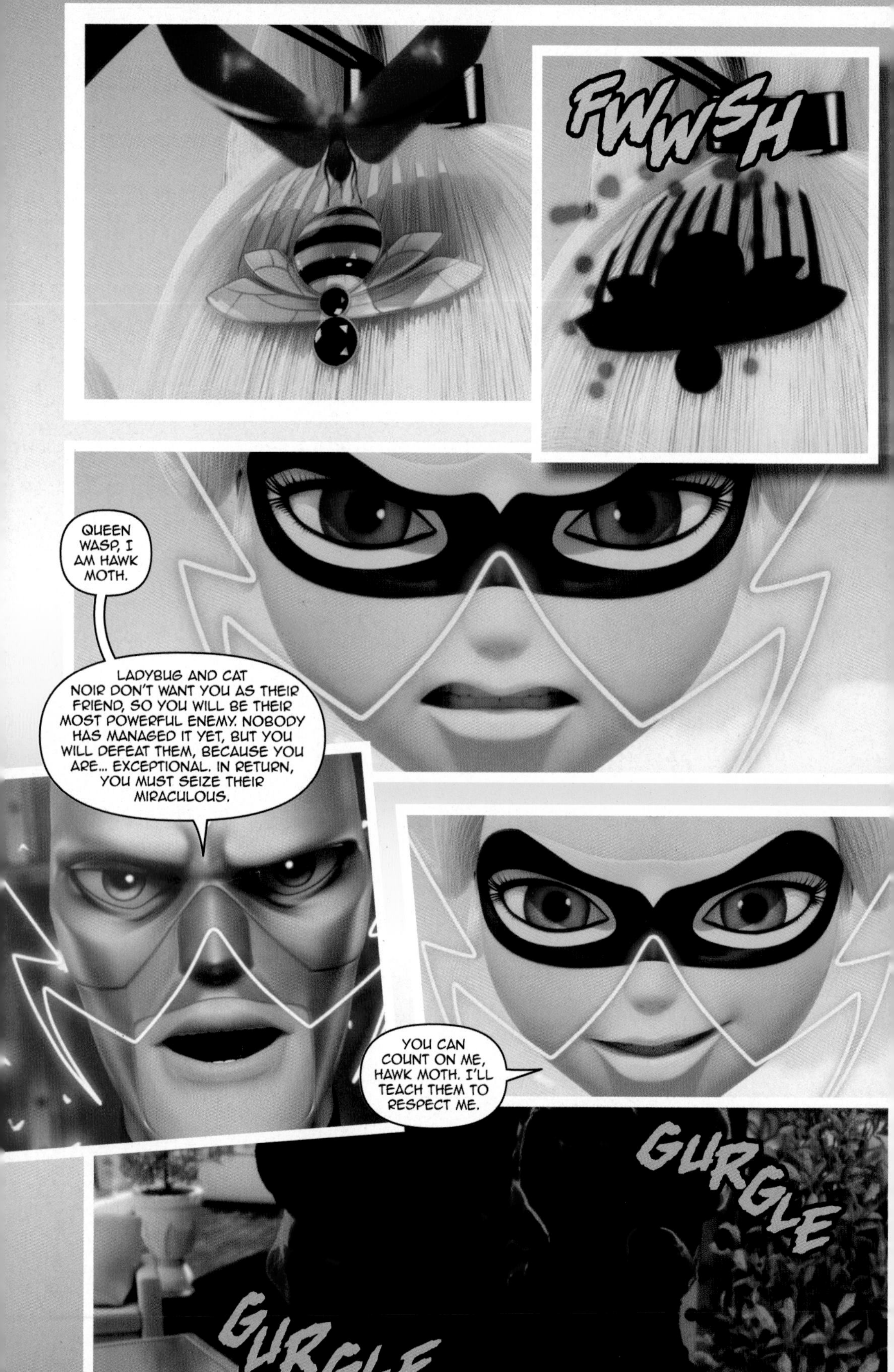
FWWSH
QUEEN WASP, I AM HAWK MOTH.
LADYBUG AND CAT NOIR DON'T WANT YOU AS THEIR FRIEND, SO YOU WILL BE THEIR MOST POWERFUL ENEMY. NOBODY HAS MANAGED IT YET, BUT YOU WILL DEFEAT THEM, BECAUSE YOU ARE... EXCEPTIONAL. IN RETURN, YOU MUST SEIZE THEIR MIRACULOUS.
YOU CAN COUNT ON ME, HAWK MOTH. I'LL TEACH THEM TO RESPECT ME.
GURGLE
GURGLE

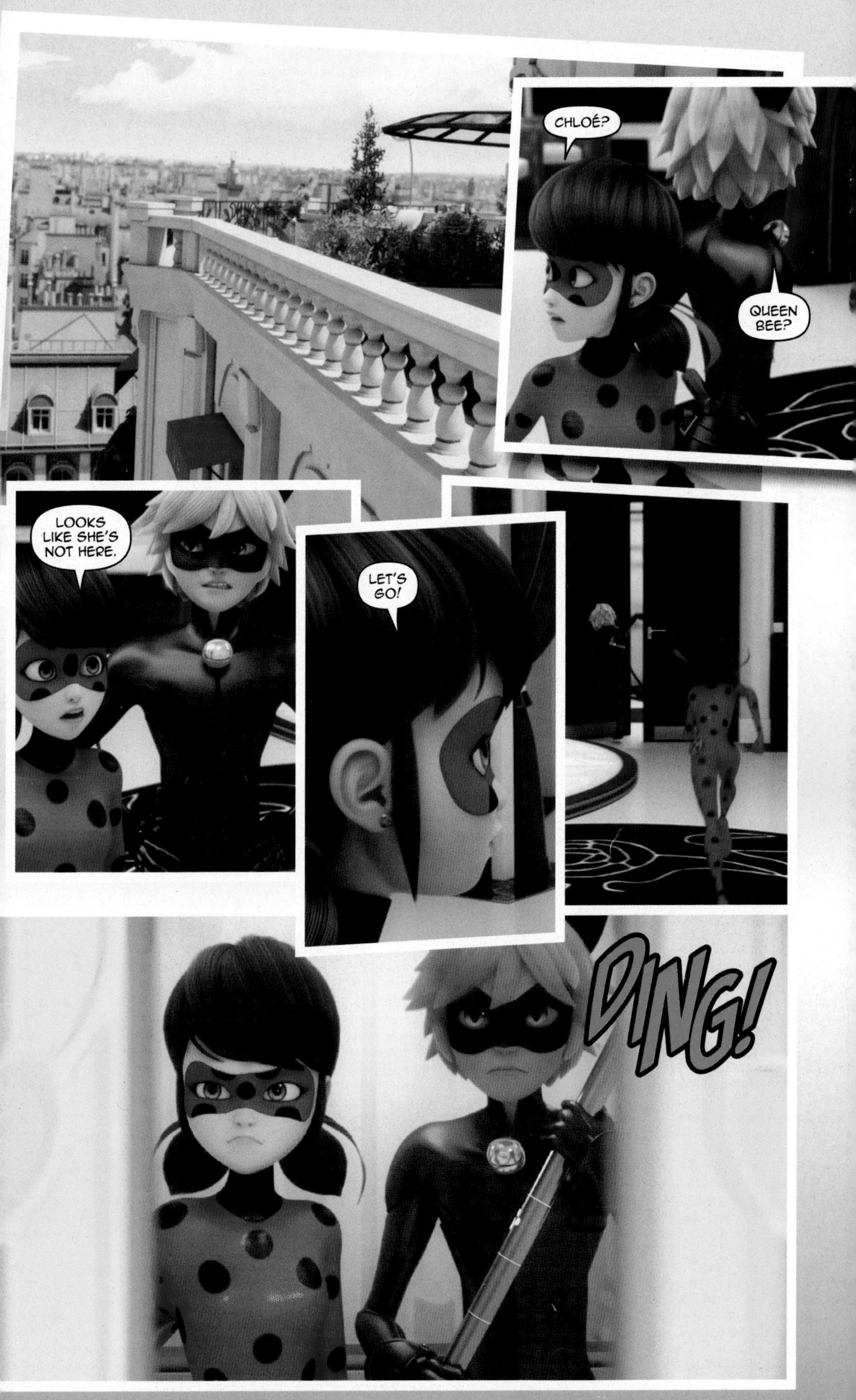

CHLOÉ?
QUEEN BEE?
LOOKS LIKE SHE'S NOT HERE.
LET'S GO!
DING!

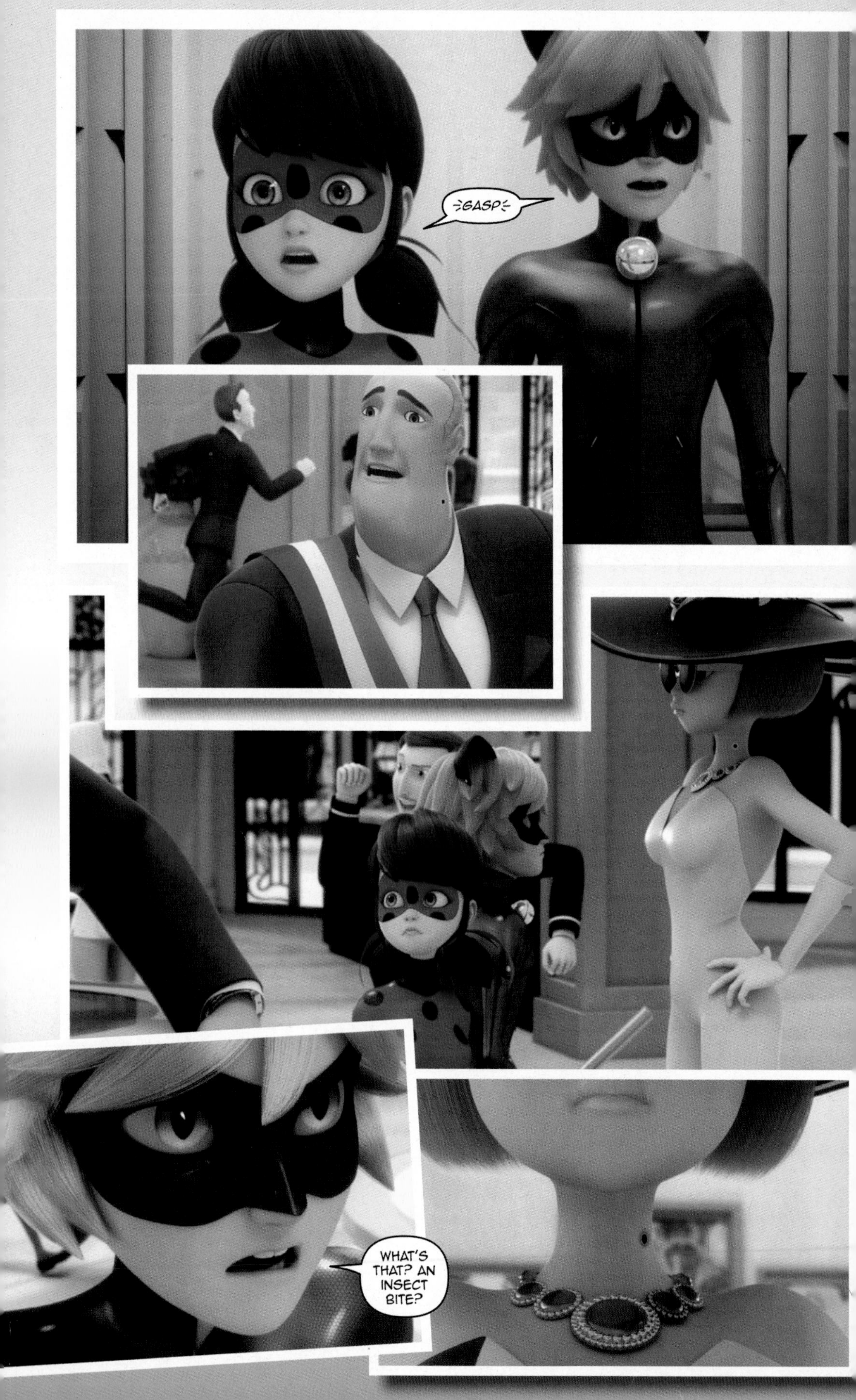
GASP
WHAT'S THAT? AN INSECT BITE?

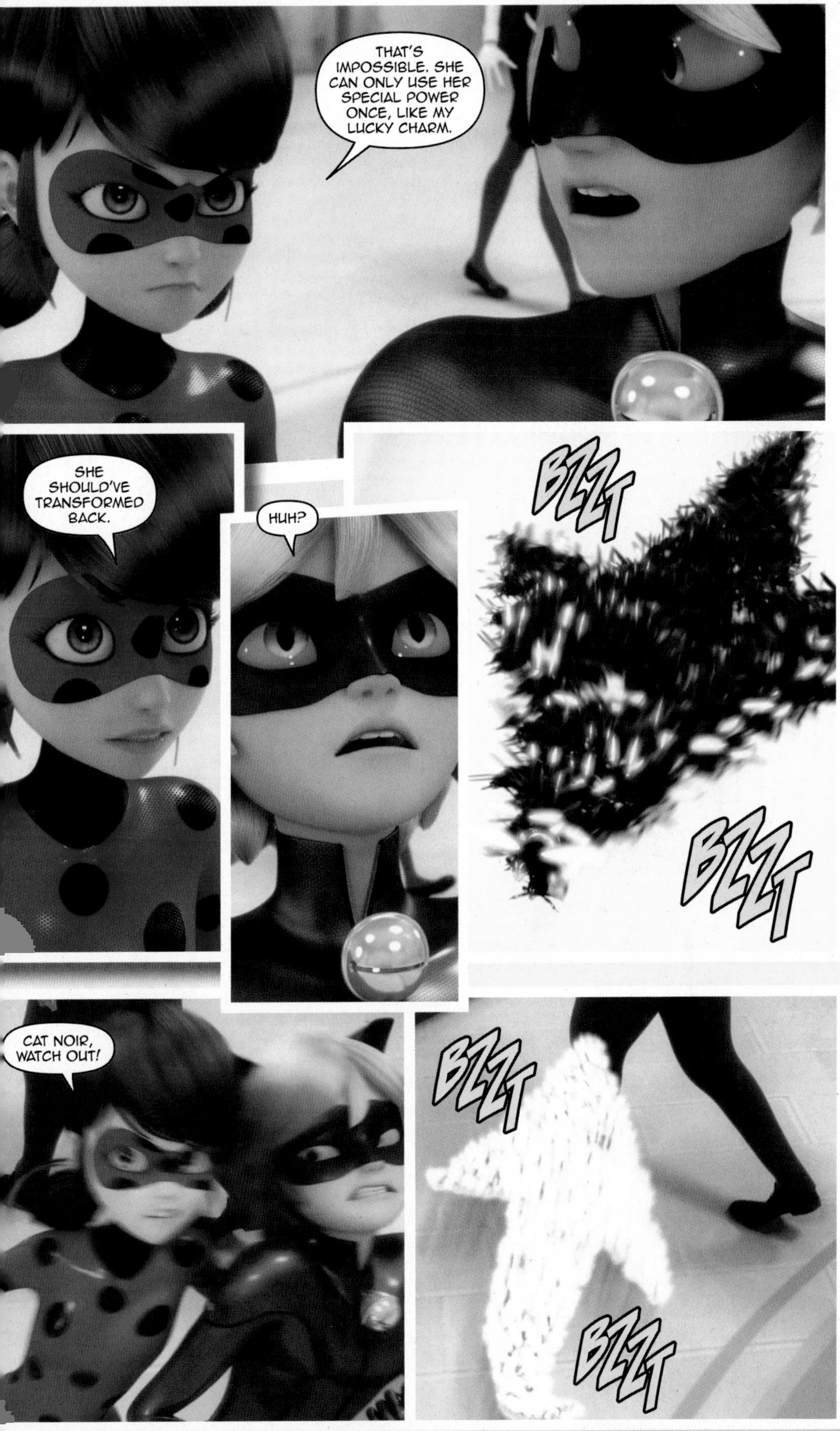
THAT'S IMPOSSIBLE. SHE CAN ONLY USE HER SPECIAL POWER ONCE, LIKE MY LUCKY CHARM.
SHE SHOULD'VE TRANSFORMED BACK.
HUH?
BZZT
BZZT
CAT NOIR, WATCH OUT!
BZZT
BZZT

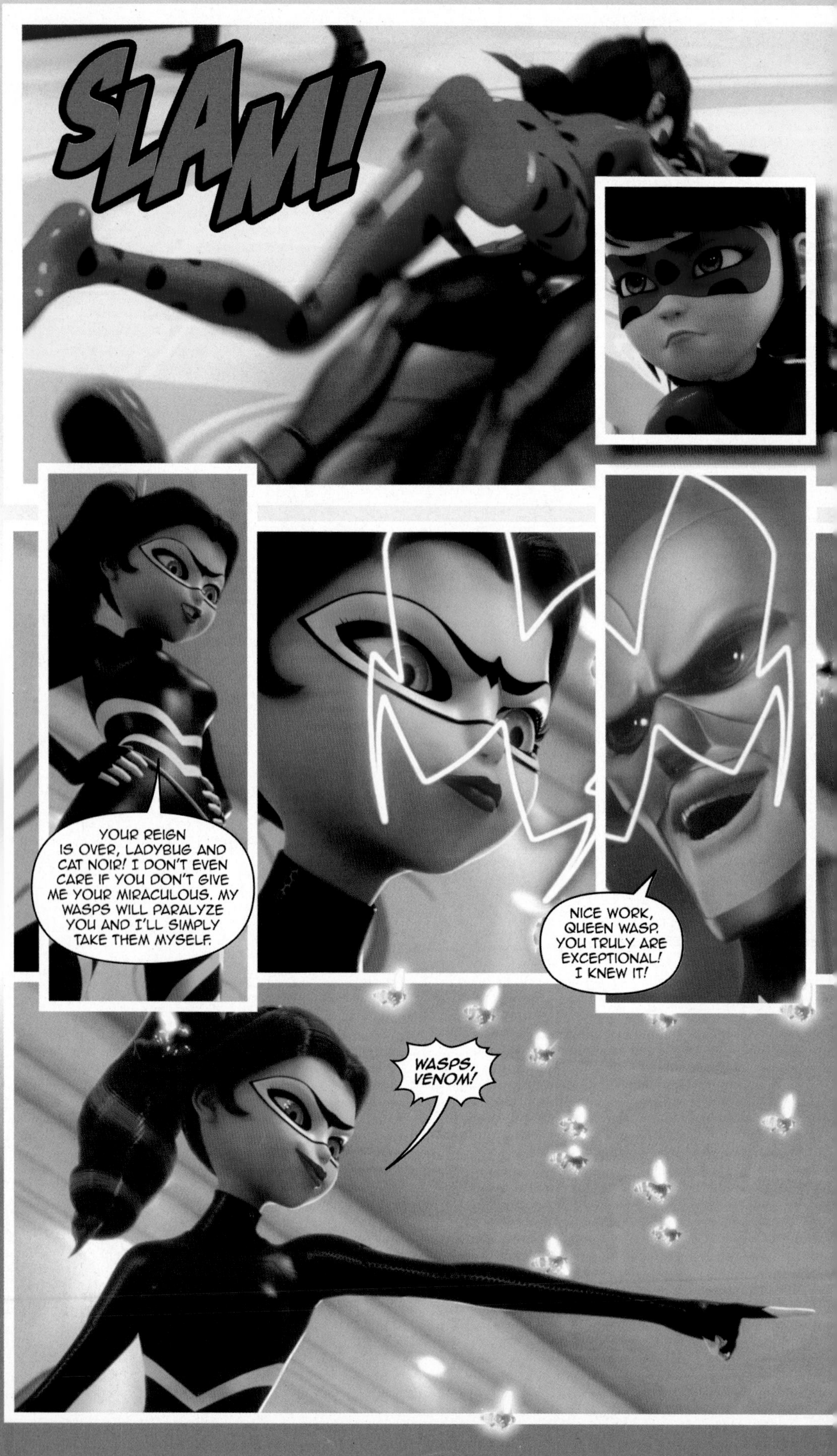
SLAM!
YOUR REIGN IS OVER, LADYBUG AND CAT NOIR! I DON'T EVEN CARE IF YOU DON'T GIVE ME YOUR MIRACULOUS. MY WASPS WILL PARALYZE YOU AND I'LL SIMPLY TAKE THEM MYSELF.
NICE WORK, QUEEN WASP. YOU TRULY ARE EXCEPTIONAL! I KNEW IT!
WASPS, VENOM!

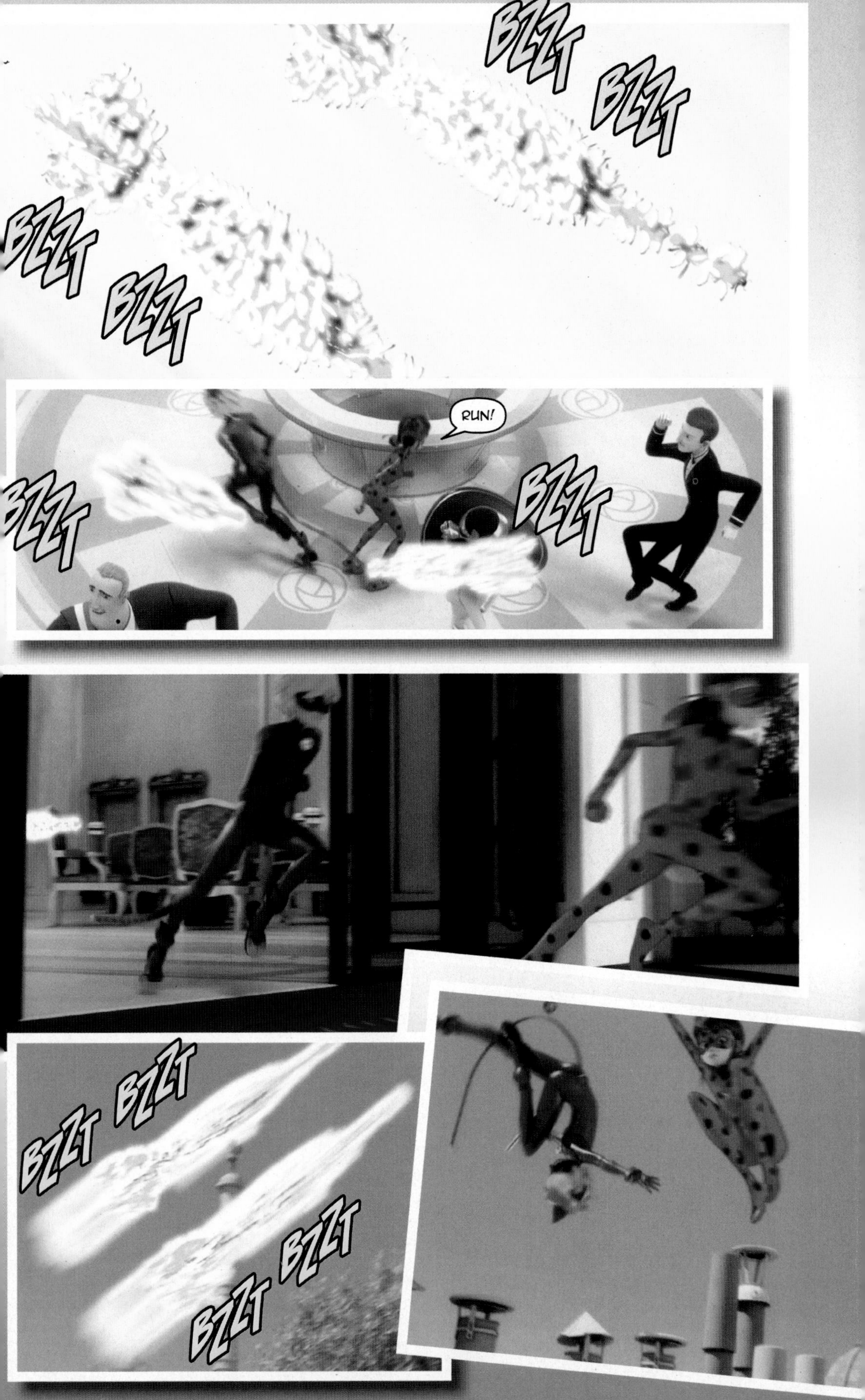
BZZT
BZZT
BZZT
BZZT
BZZT
RUN!
BZZT
BZZT BZZT
BZZT BZZT

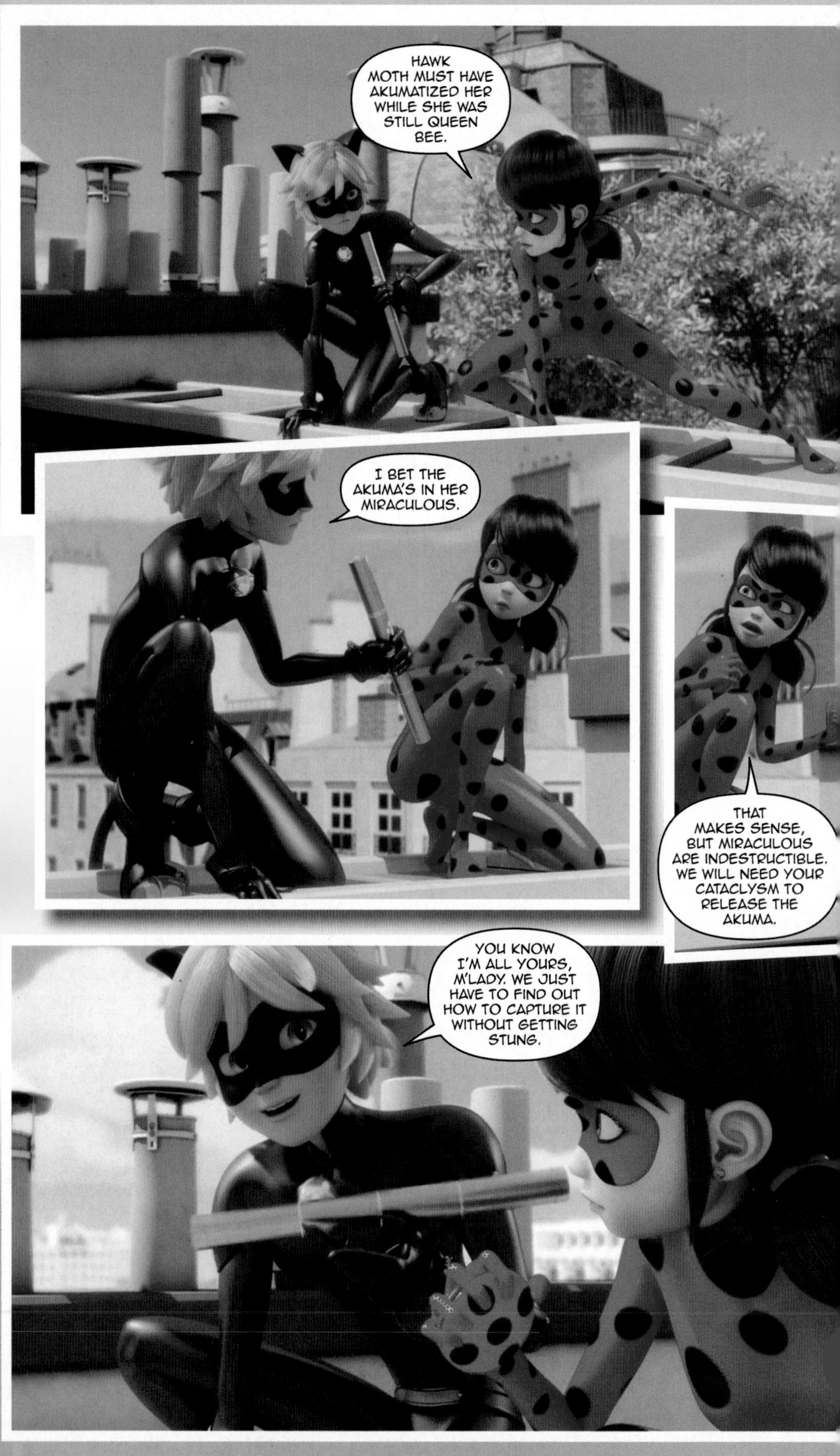
HAWK MOTH MUST HAVE AKUMATIZED HER WHILE SHE WAS STILL QUEEN BEE.
I BET THE AKUMA'S IN HER MIRACULOUS.
THAT MAKES SENSE, BUT MIRACULOUS ARE INDESTRUCTIBLE. WE WILL NEED YOUR CATACLYSM TO RELEASE THE AKUMA.
YOU KNOW I'M ALL YOURS, M'LADY. WE JUST HAVE TO FIND OUT HOW TO CAPTURE IT WITHOUT GETTING STUNG.

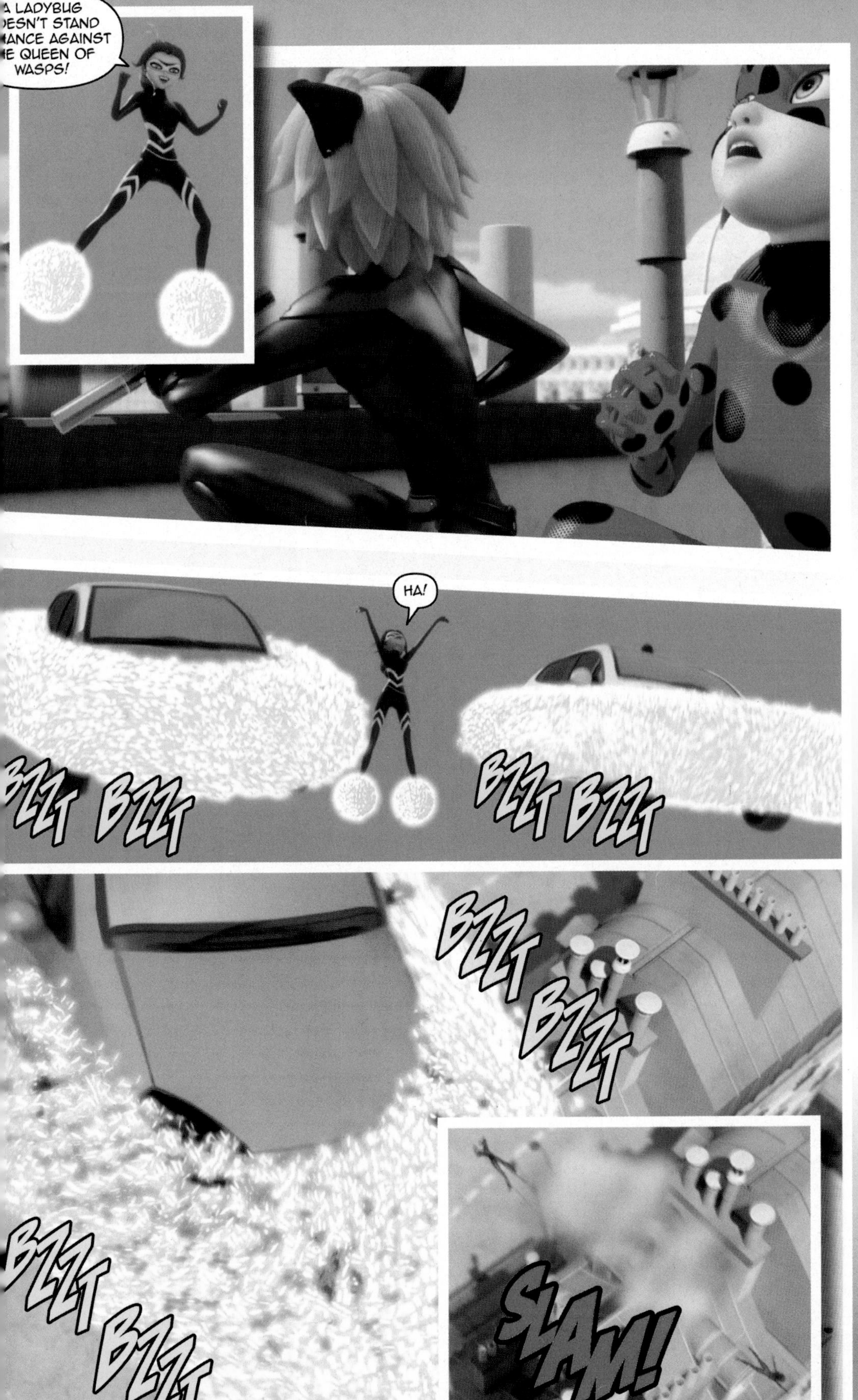
A LADYBUG
ESN'T STAND
ANCE AGAINST
E QUEEN OF
WASPS!
HA!
BZZT BZZT
BZZT BZZT
BZZT
BZZT
BZZT
BZZT
SLAM!

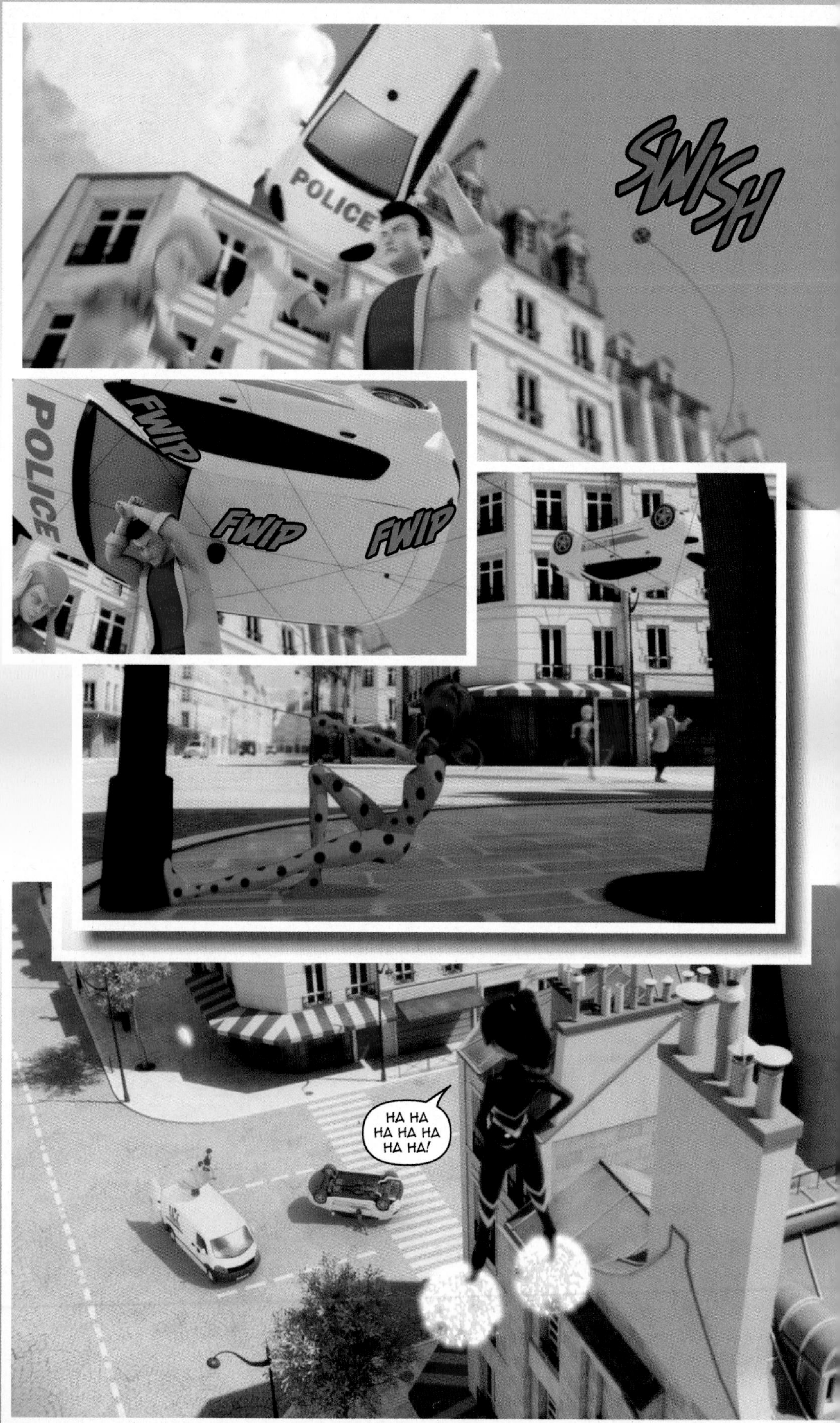
SWISH
FWIP
FWIP
FWIP
HA HA
HA HA HA
HA HA!

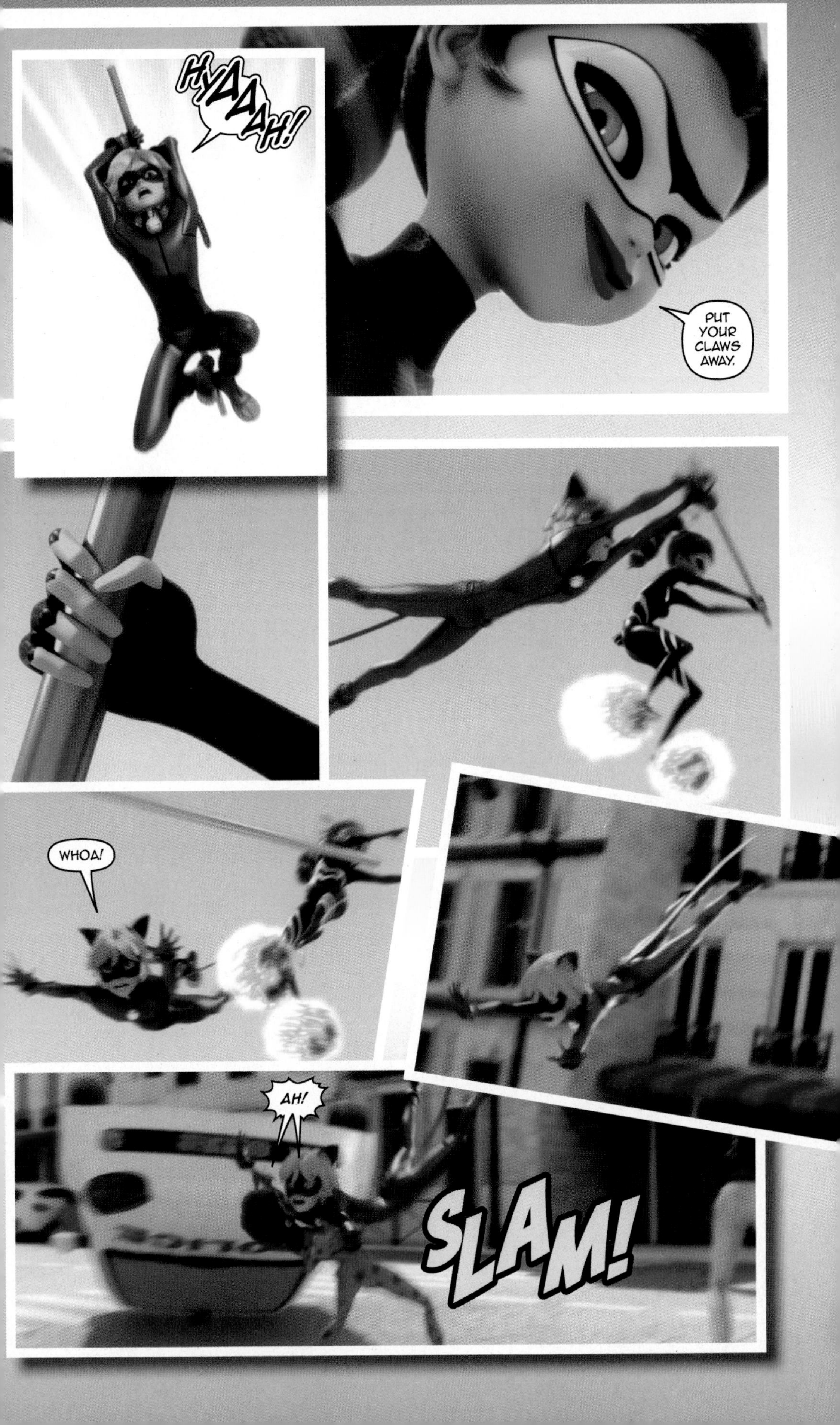
HYAAAH!
PUT YOUR CLAWS AWAY.
WHOA!
AH!
SLAM!

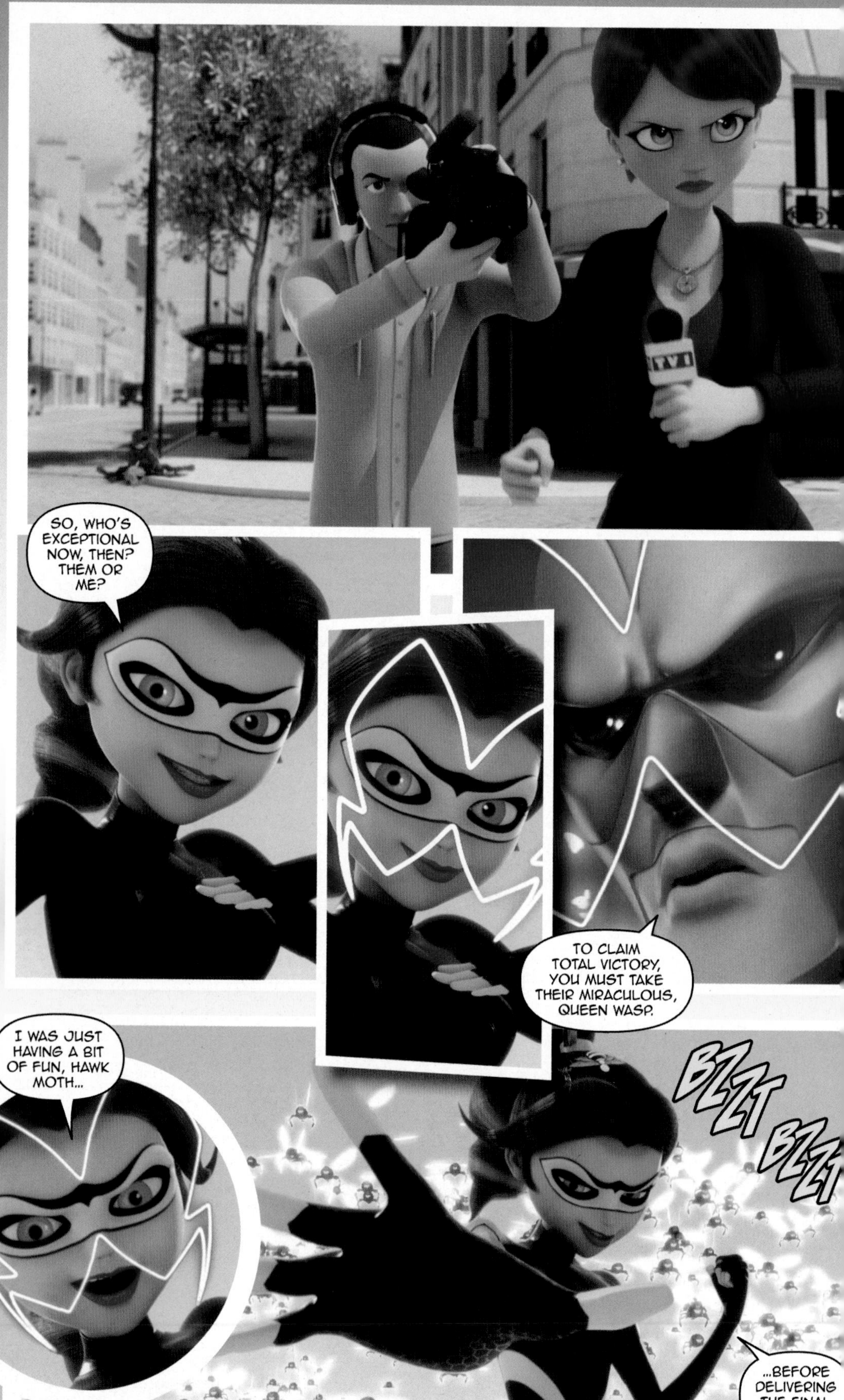
SO, WHO'S EXCEPTIONAL NOW, THEN? THEM OR ME?
TO CLAIM TOTAL VICTORY, YOU MUST TAKE THEIR MIRACULOUS, QUEEN WASP.
I WAS JUST HAVING A BIT OF FUN, HAWK MOTH...
BZZT BZZT
...BEFORE DELIVERING THE FINAL STING!

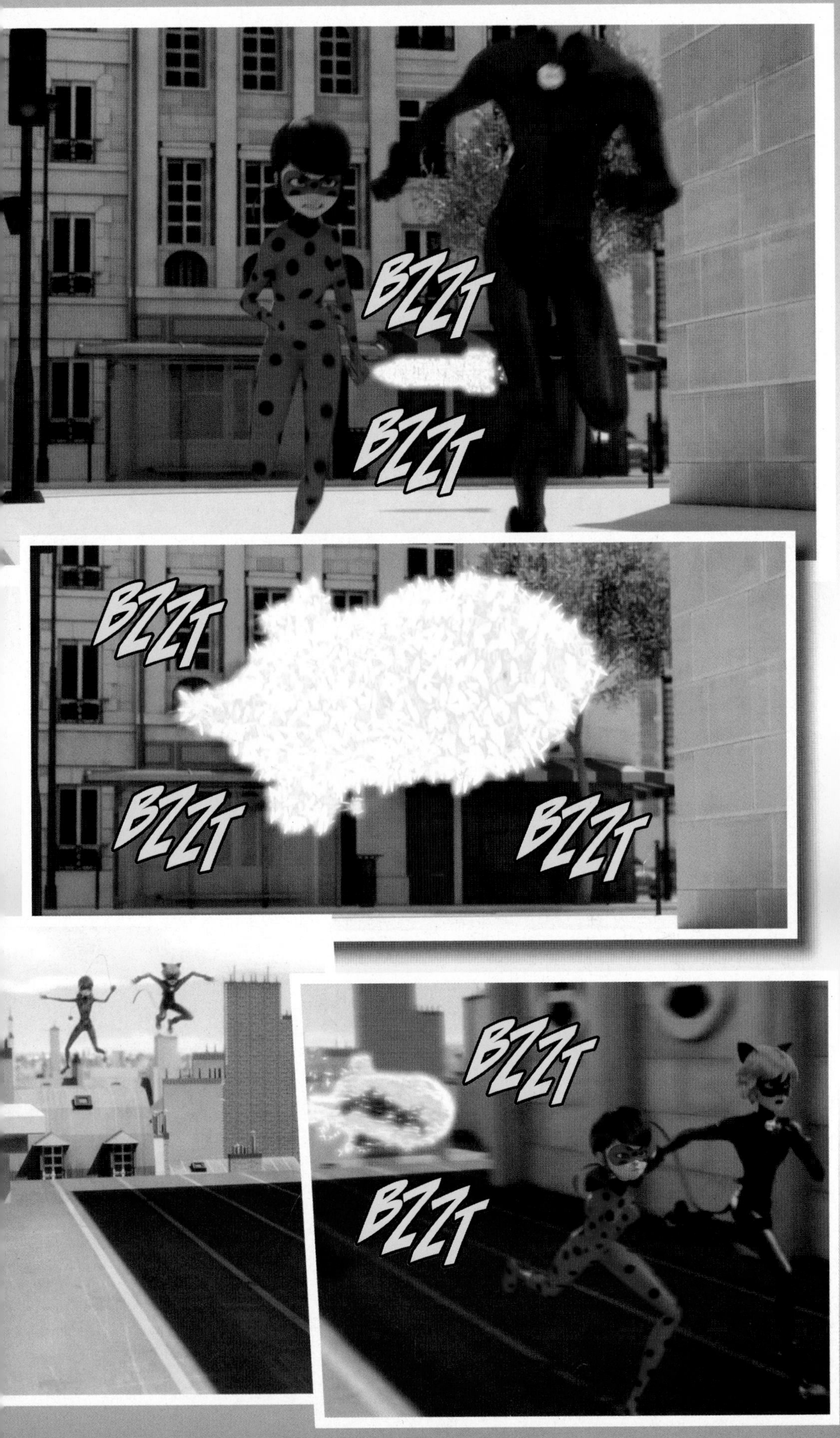
BZZT
BZZT
BZZT
BZZT
BZZT
BZZT
BZZT

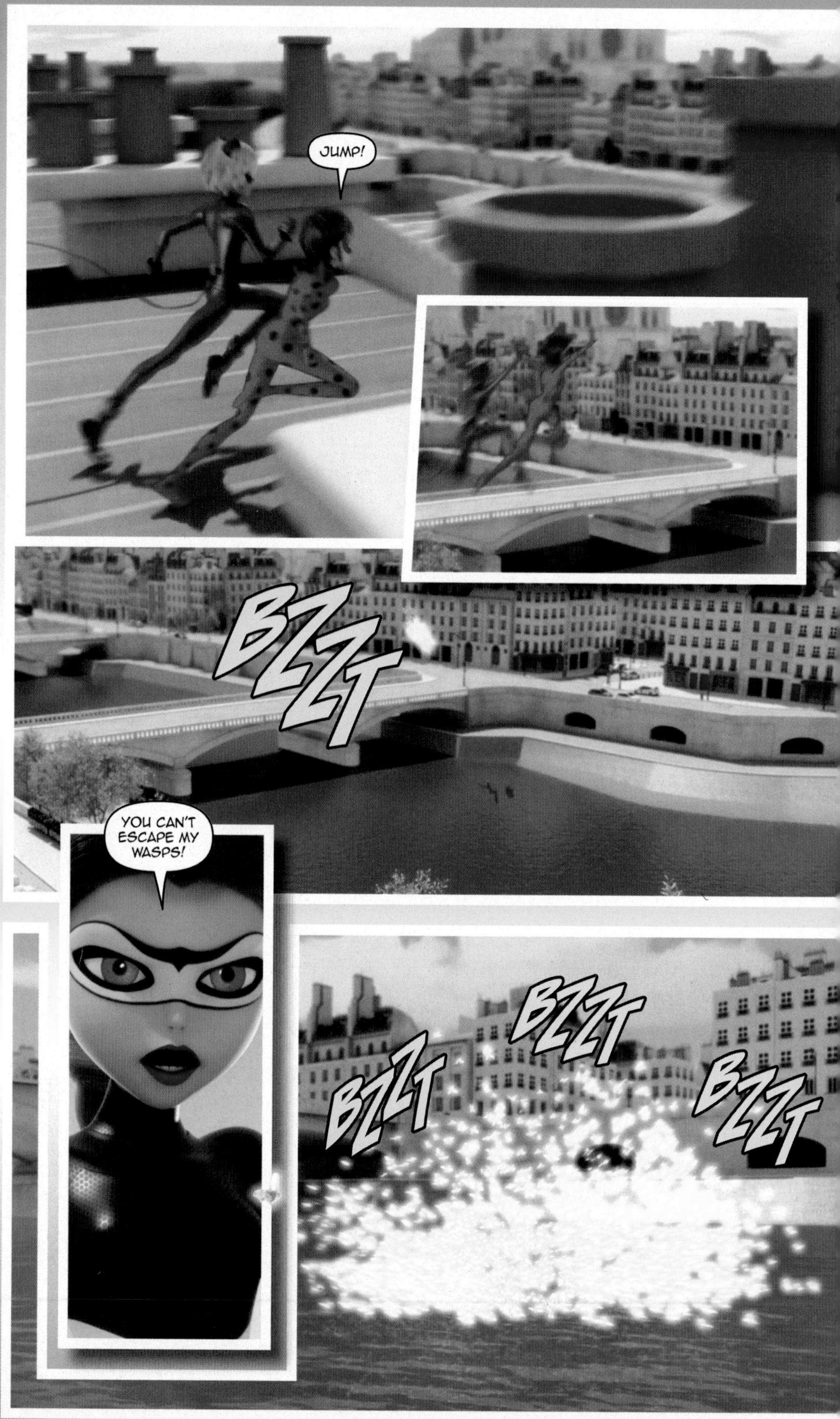
JUMP!
BZZT
YOU CAN'T ESCAPE MY WASPS!
BZZT
BZZT
BZZT

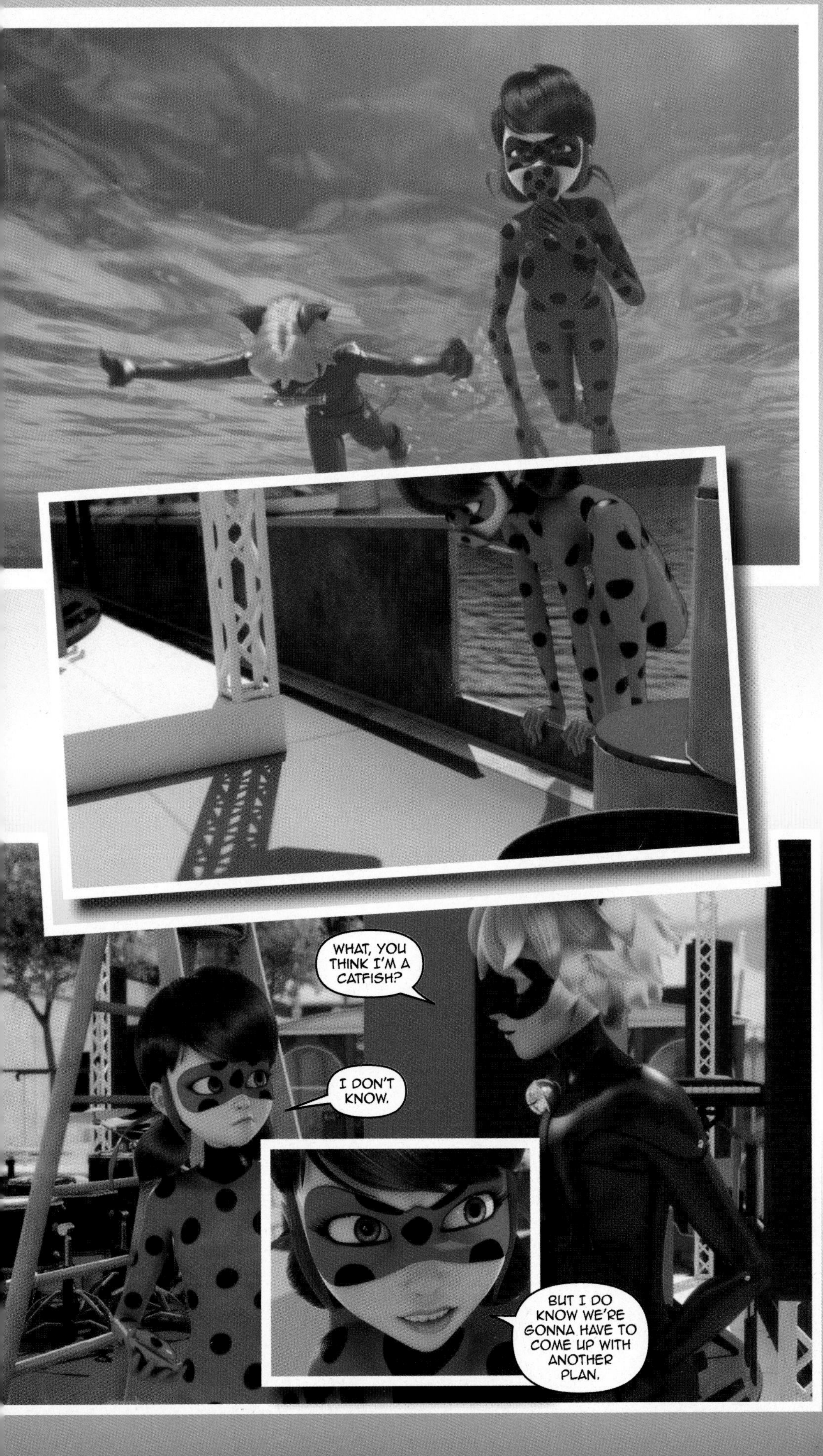
WHAT, YOU THINK I'M A CATFISH?
I DON'T KNOW.
BUT I DO KNOW WE'RE GONNA HAVE TO COME UP WITH ANOTHER PLAN.

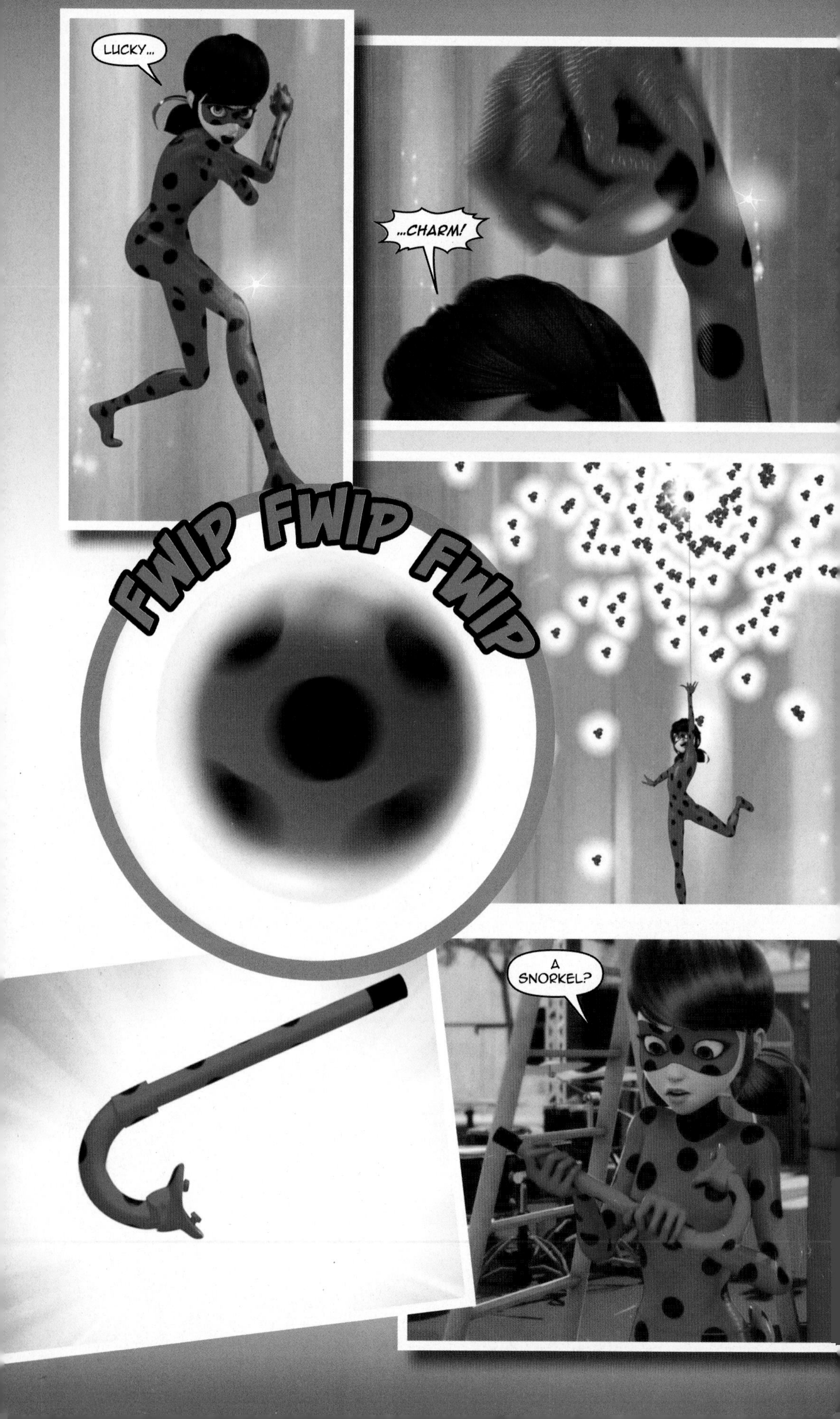
LUCKY...
...CHARM!
FWIP FWIP FWIP
A SNORKEL?

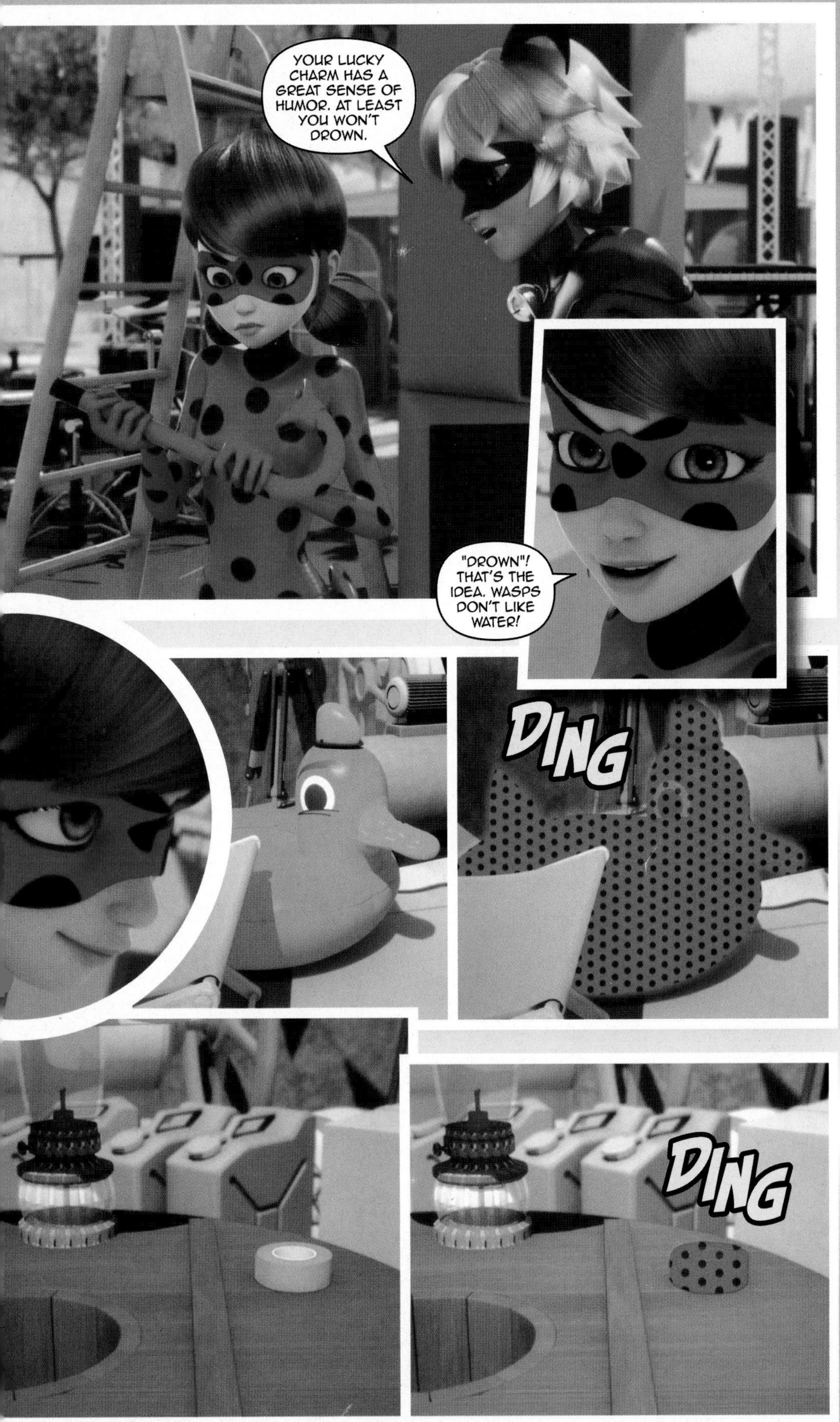
YOUR LUCKY CHARM HAS A GREAT SENSE OF HUMOR. AT LEAST YOU WON'T DROWN.
"DROWN"! THAT'S THE IDEA. WASPS DON'T LIKE WATER!
DING
DING

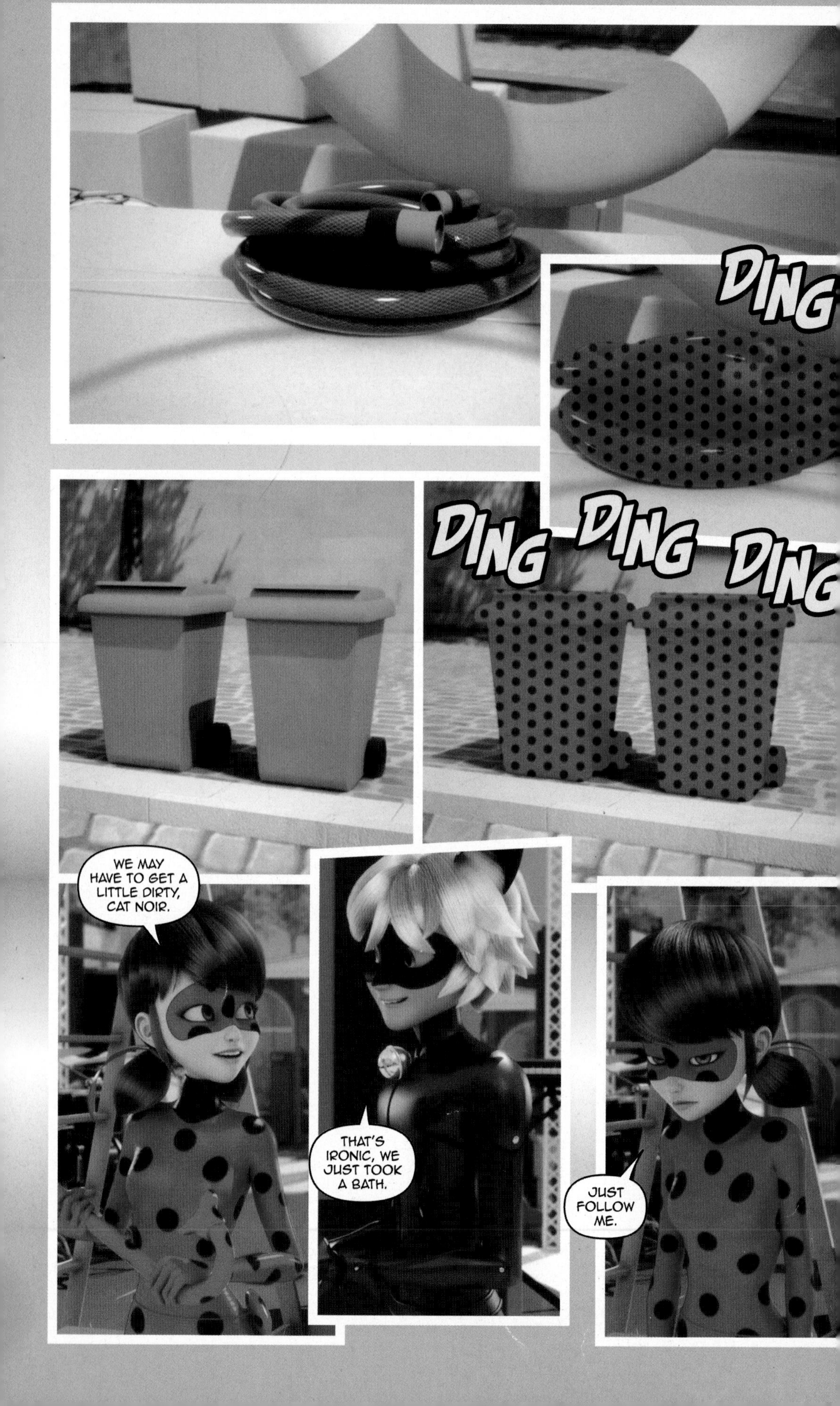
DING
DING DING DING
WE MAY HAVE TO GET A LITTLE DIRTY, CAT NOIR.
THAT'S IRONIC, WE JUST TOOK A BATH.
JUST FOLLOW ME.

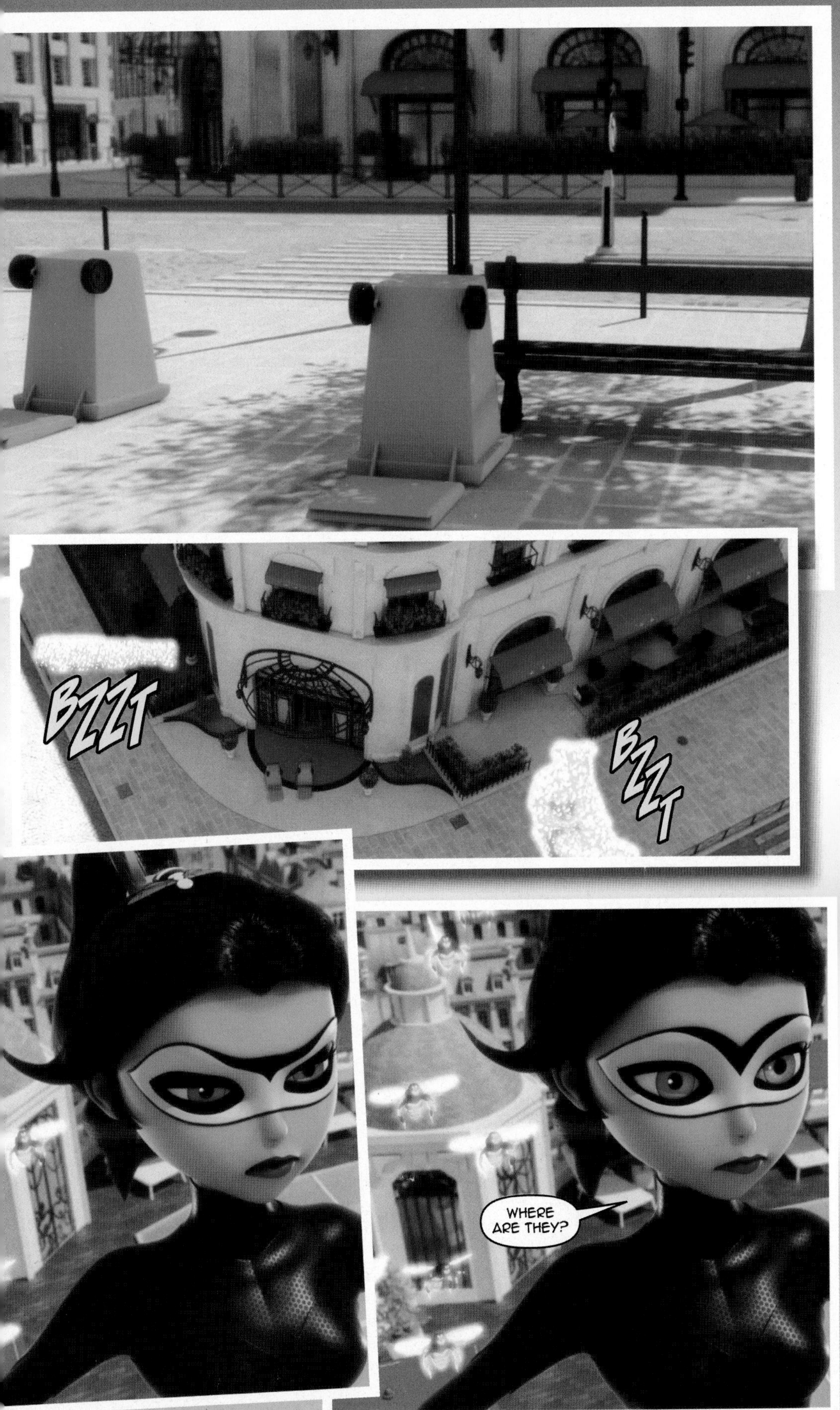
BZZT
BZZT
WHERE ARE THEY?

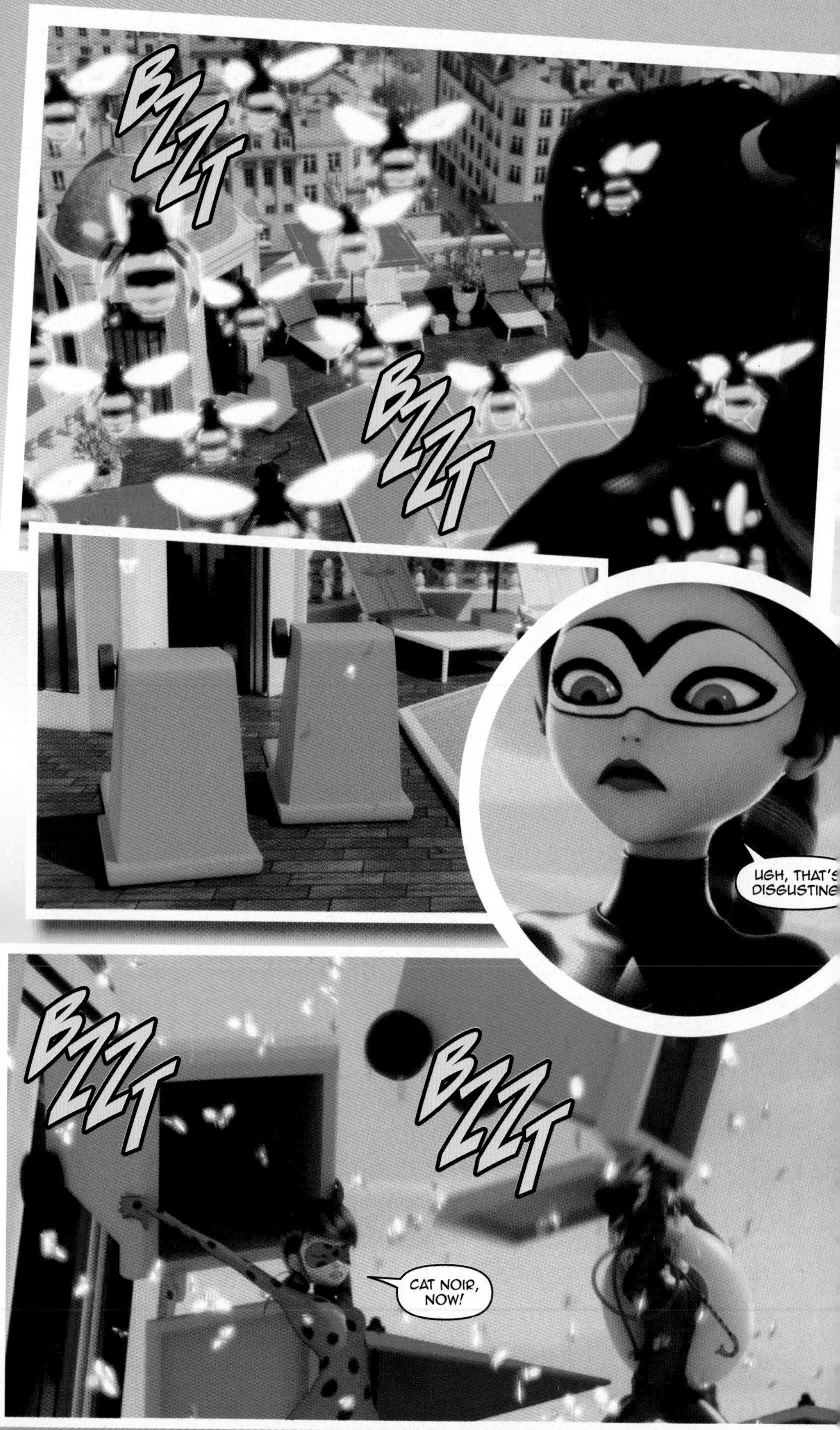
BZZZT
BZZZT
UGH, THAT'S DISGUSTING
BZZZT
BZZZT
CAT NOIR, NOW!

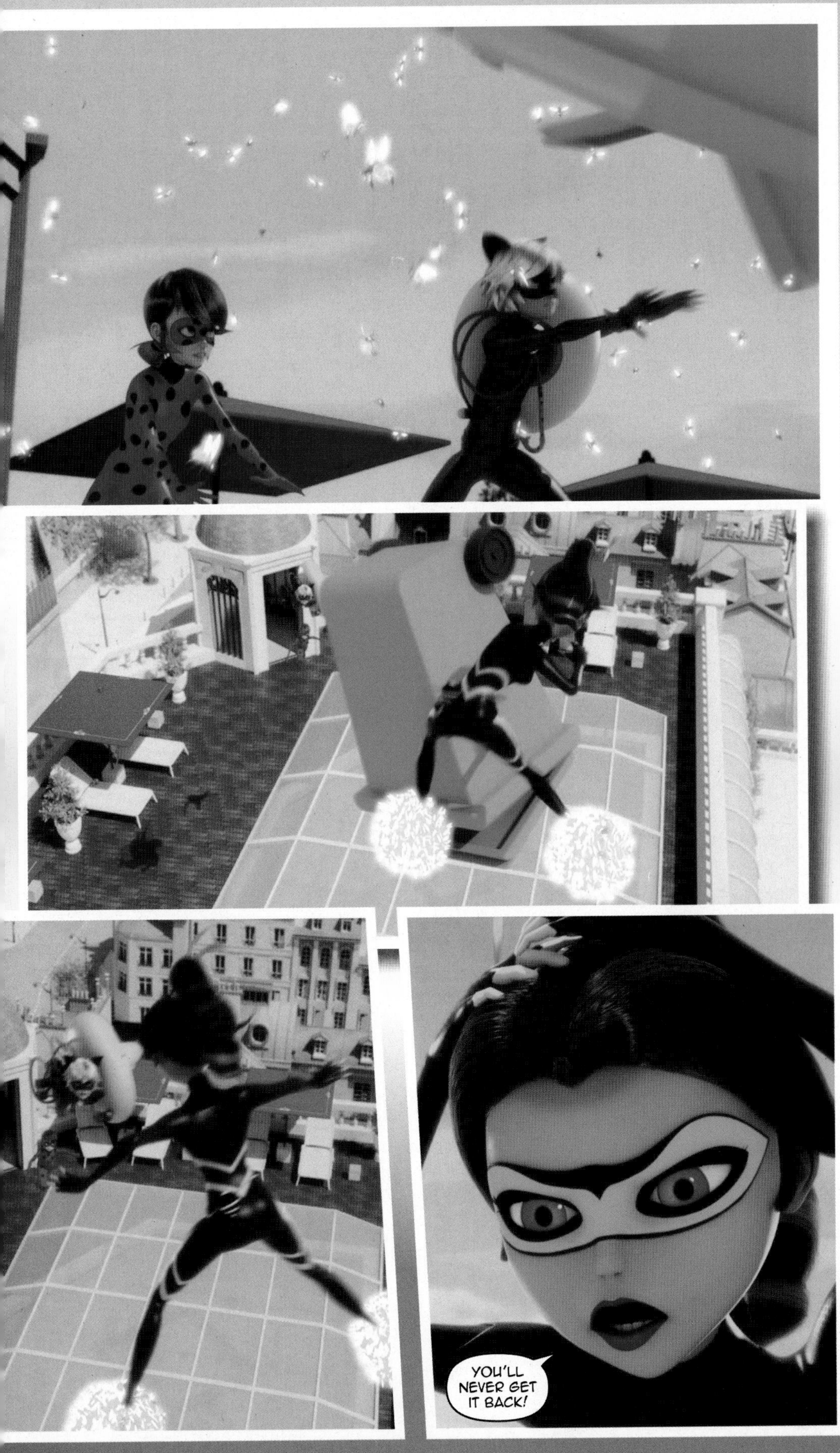
YOU'LL NEVER GET IT BACK!

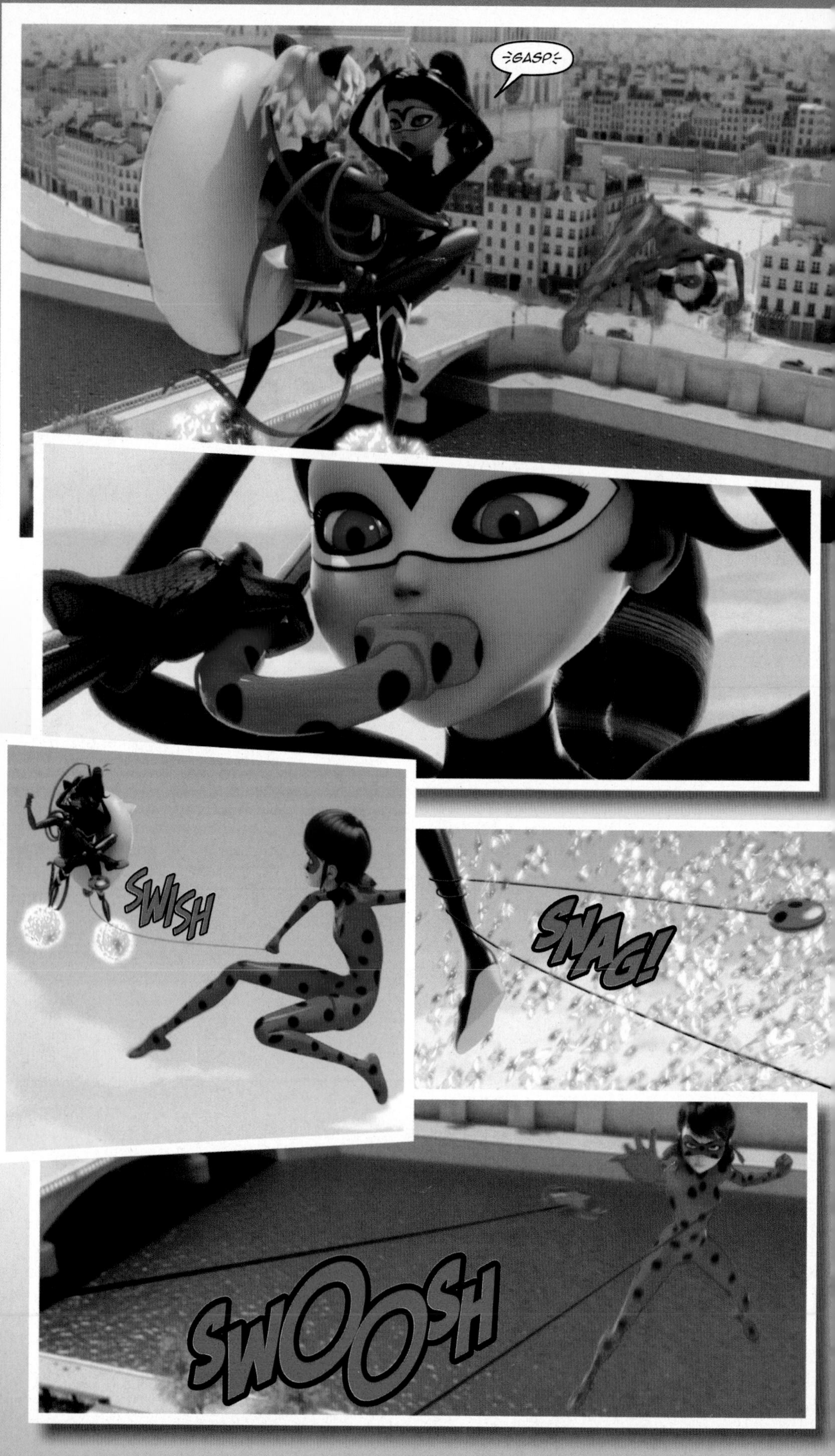
GASP
SWISH
SNAG!
SWOOSH

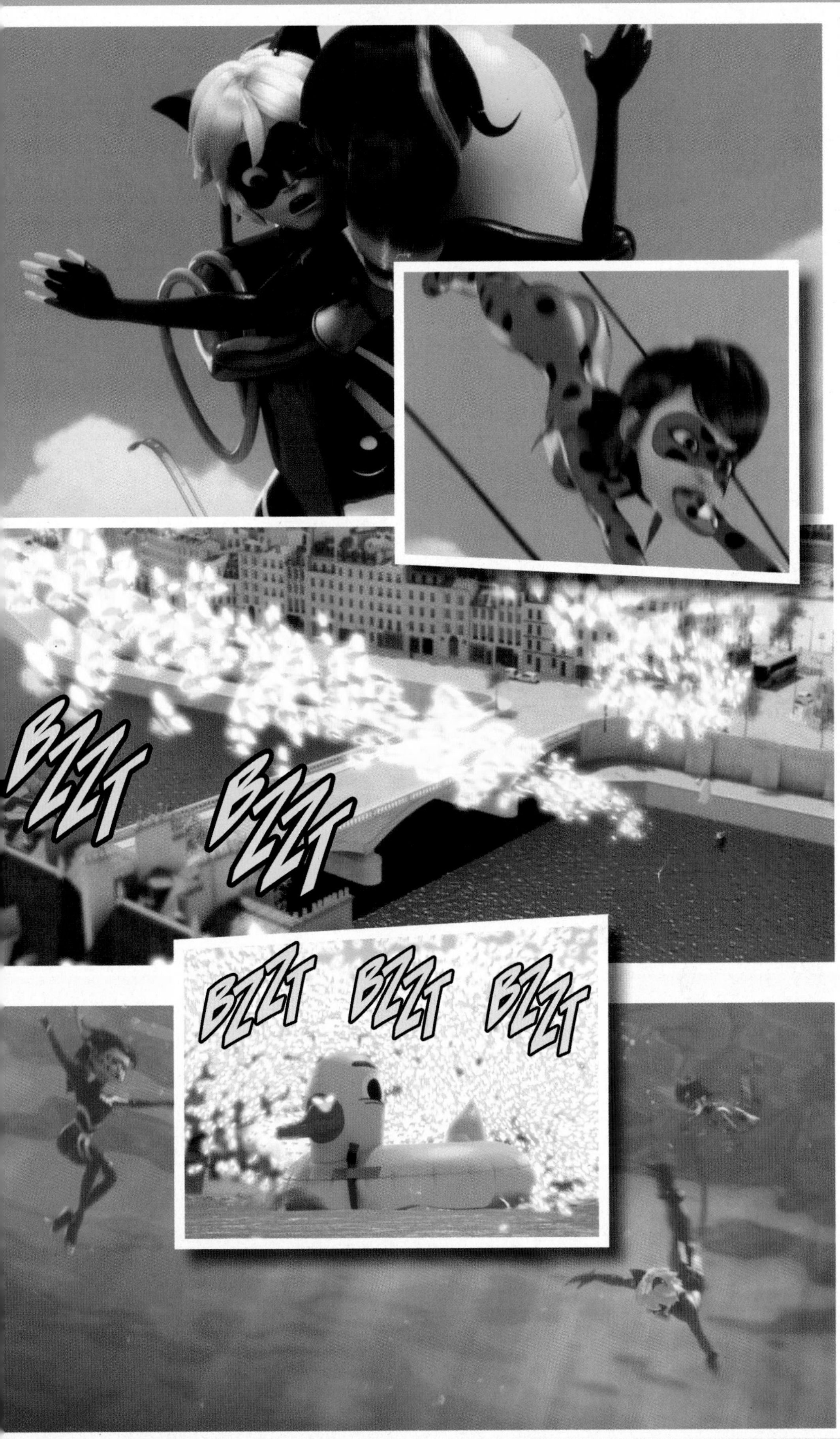
BZZT
BZZT
BZZT
BZZT
BZZT

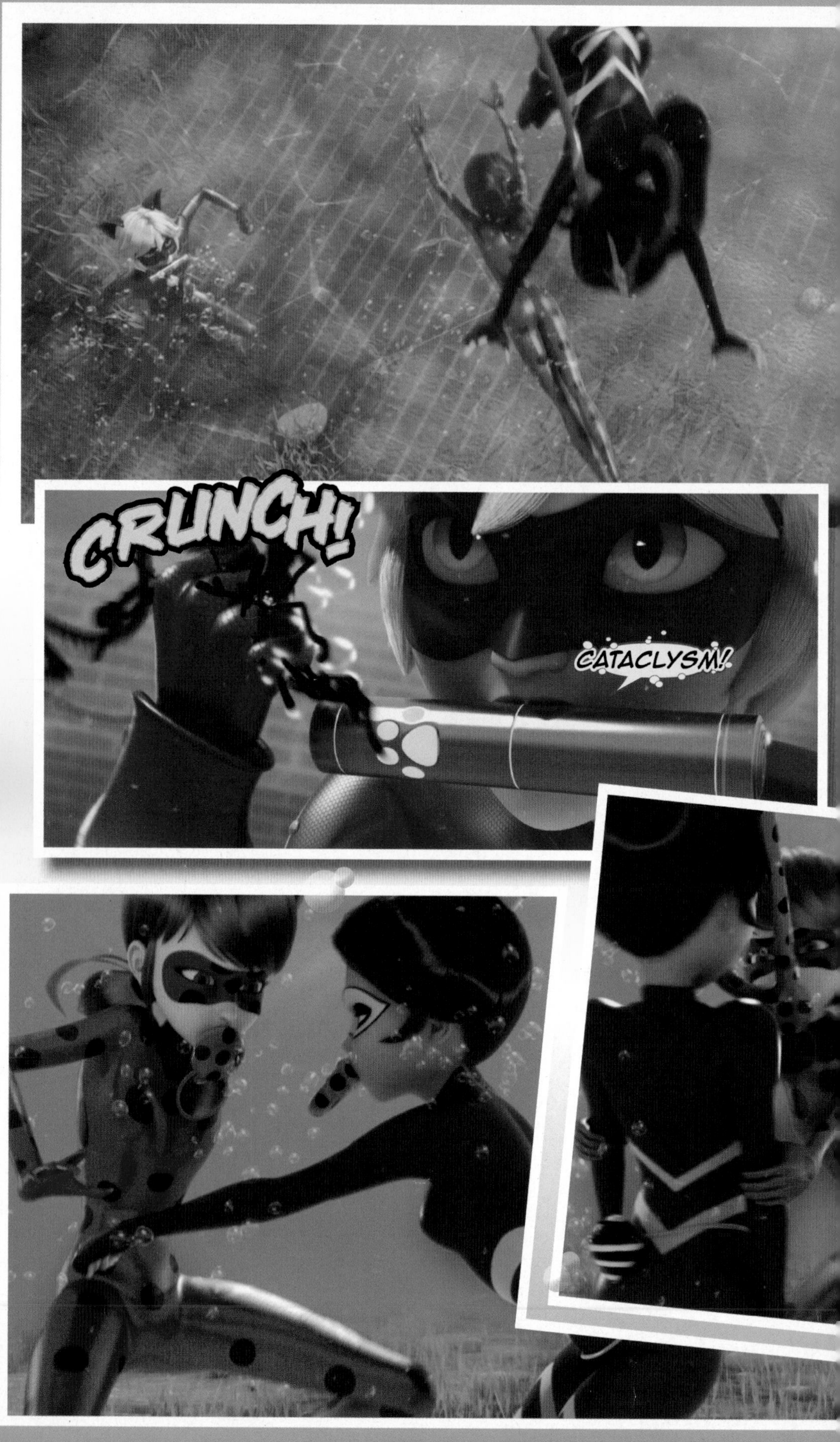
CRUNCH!
CATACLYSM!

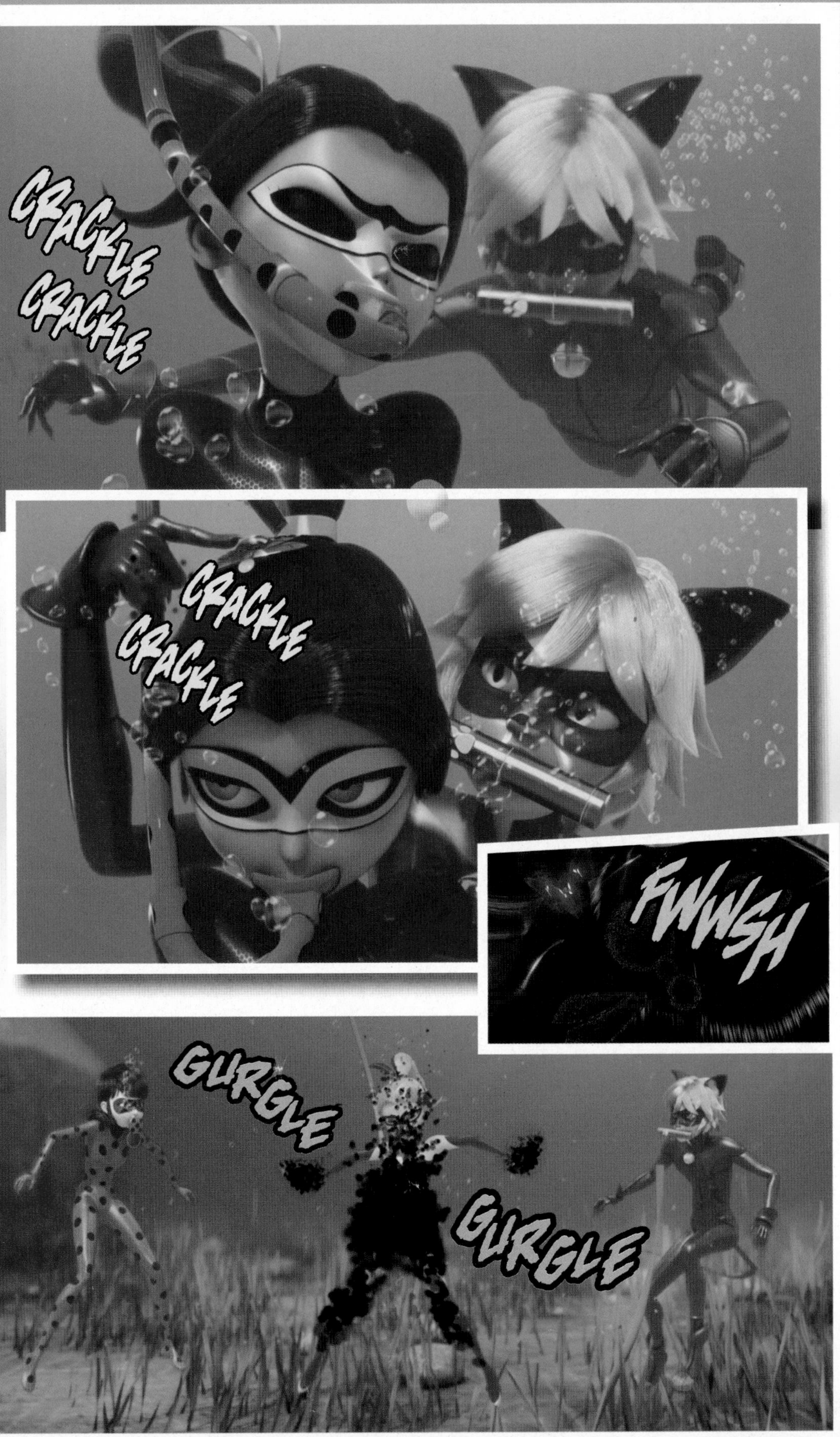
CRACKLE
CRACKLE
CRACKLE
CRACKLE
FWWSH
GURGLE
GURGLE

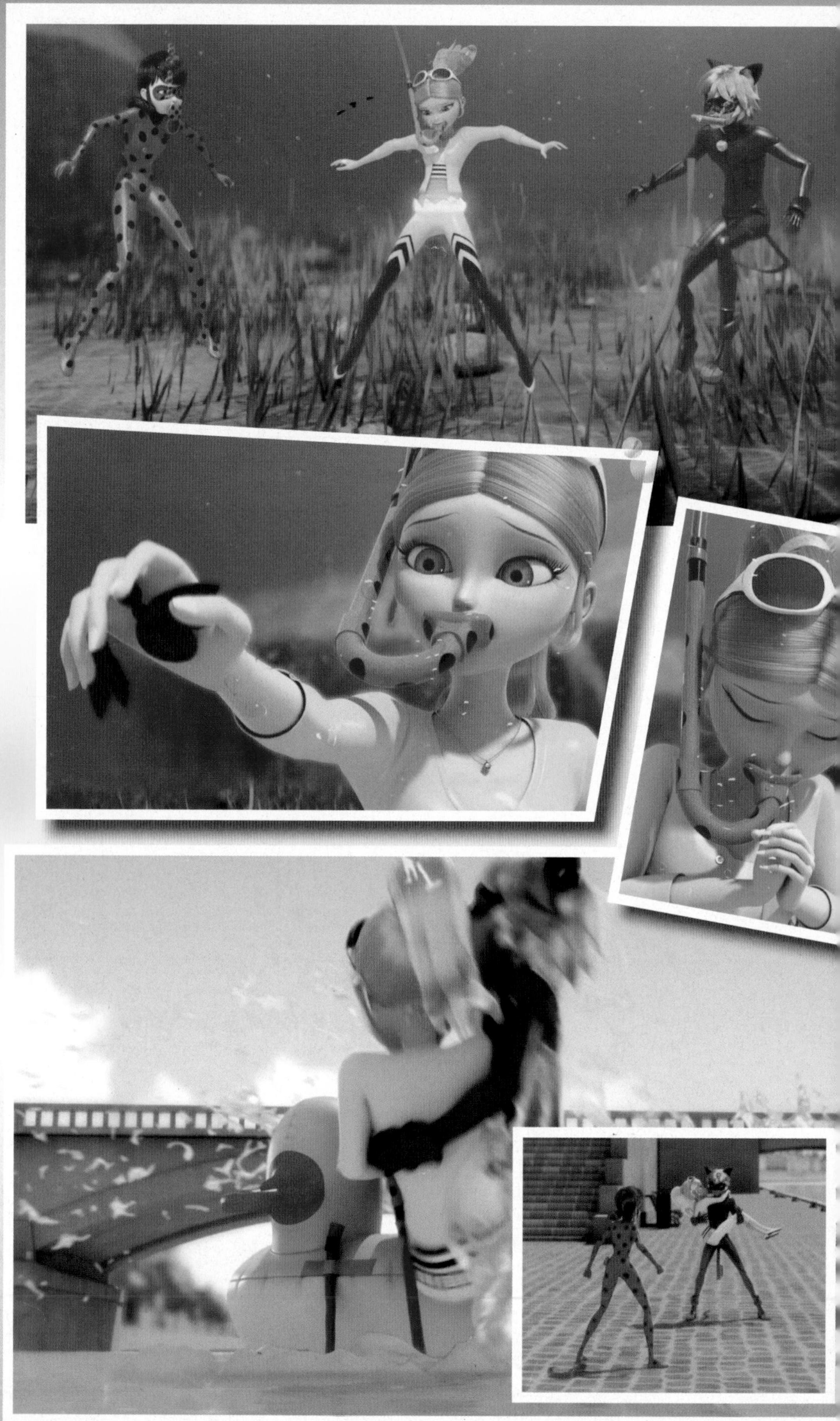

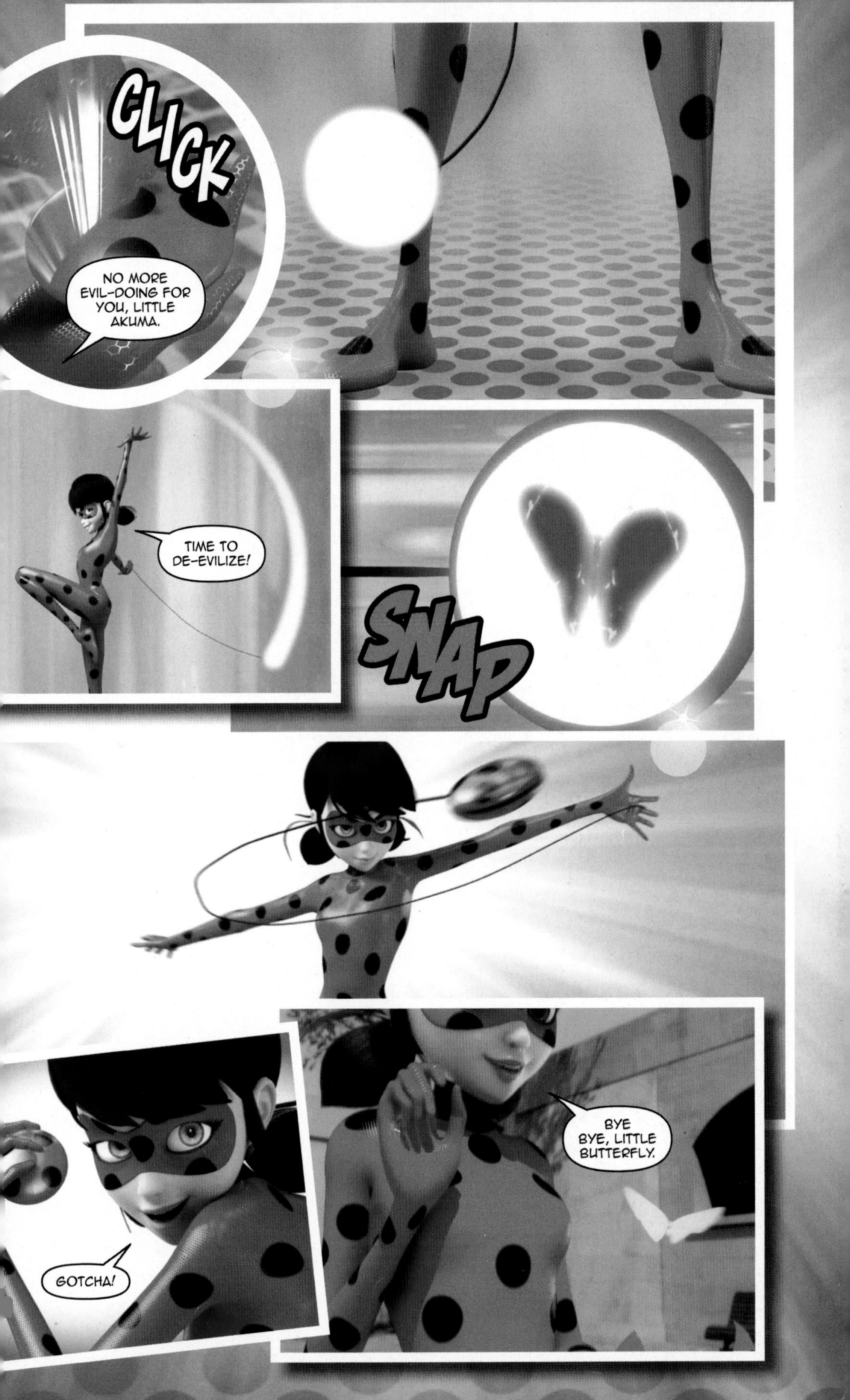
CLICK
NO MORE EVIL-DOING FOR YOU, LITTLE AKUMA.
TIME TO DE-EVILIZE!
SNAP
BYE BYE, LITTLE BUTTERFLY.
GOTCHA!

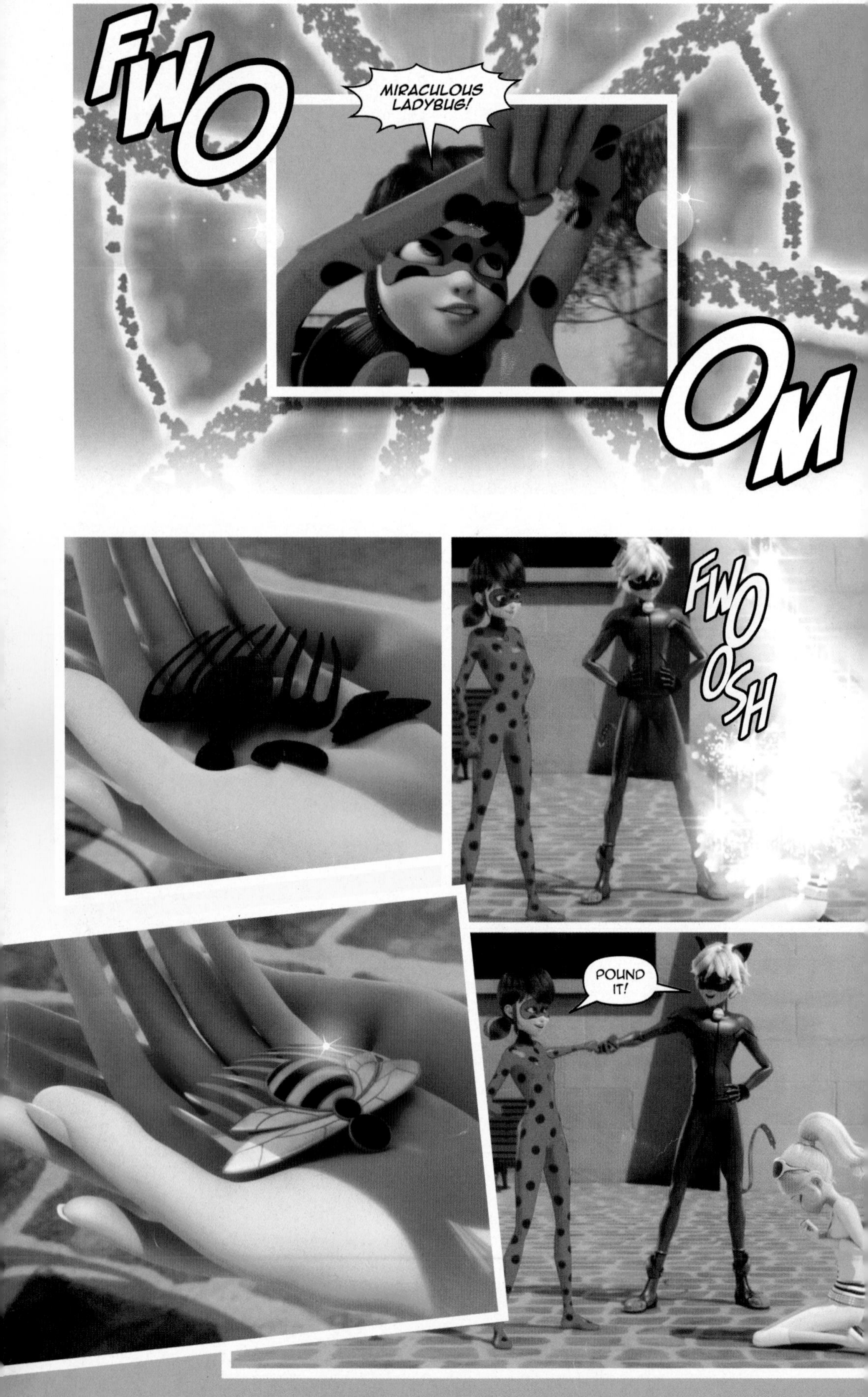
FWOOM
MIRACULOUS LADYBUG!
FWOOSH
POUND IT!

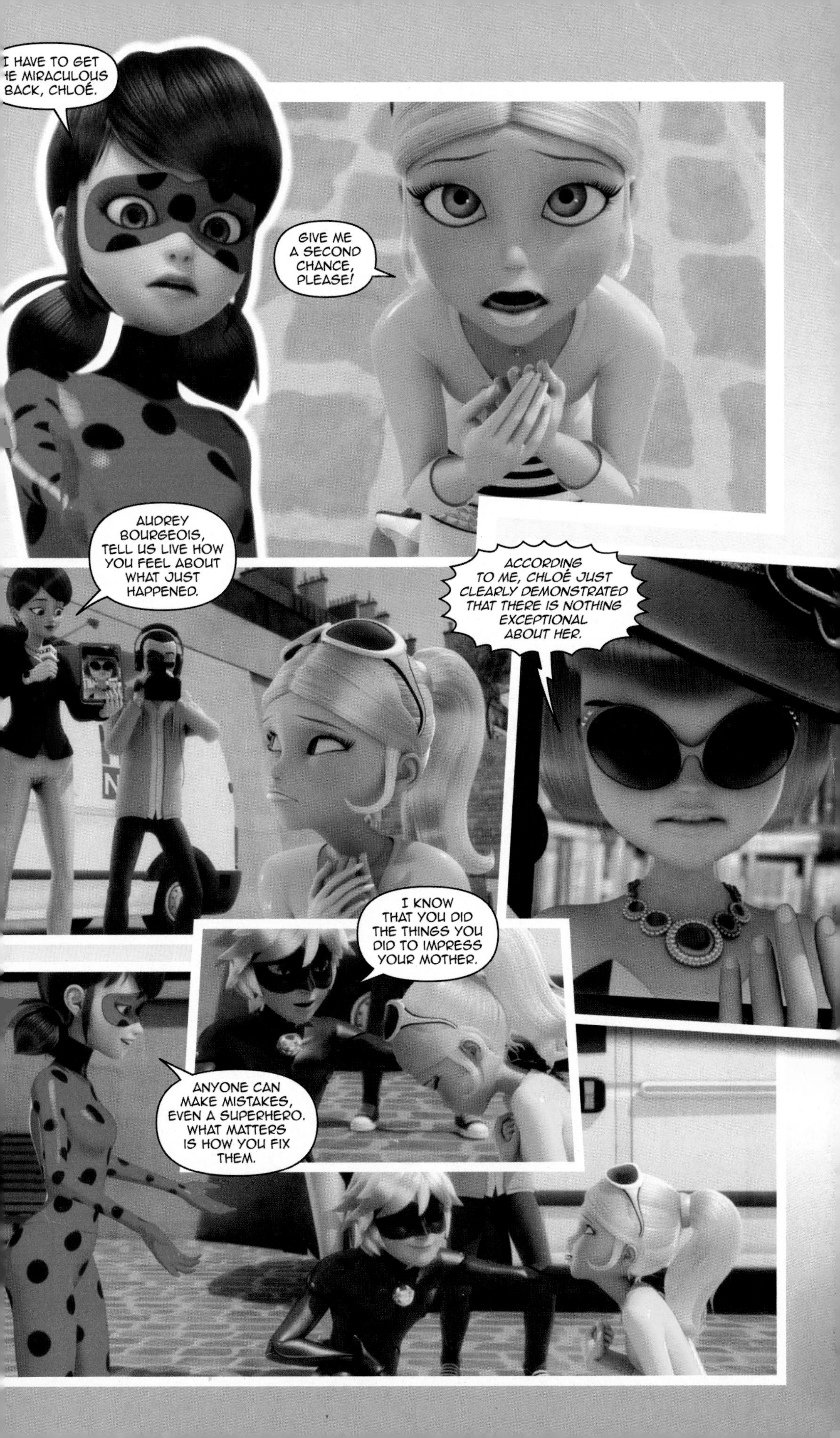
I HAVE TO GET
HE MIRACULOUS
BACK, CHLOÉ.
GIVE ME A SECOND CHANCE, PLEASE!
AUDREY BOURGEOIS, TELL US LIVE HOW YOU FEEL ABOUT WHAT JUST HAPPENED.
ACCORDING TO ME, CHLOÉ JUST CLEARLY DEMONSTRATED THAT THERE IS NOTHING EXCEPTIONAL ABOUT HER.
I KNOW THAT YOU DID THE THINGS YOU DID TO IMPRESS YOUR MOTHER.
ANYONE CAN MAKE MISTAKES, EVEN A SUPERHERO. WHAT MATTERS IS HOW YOU FIX THEM.

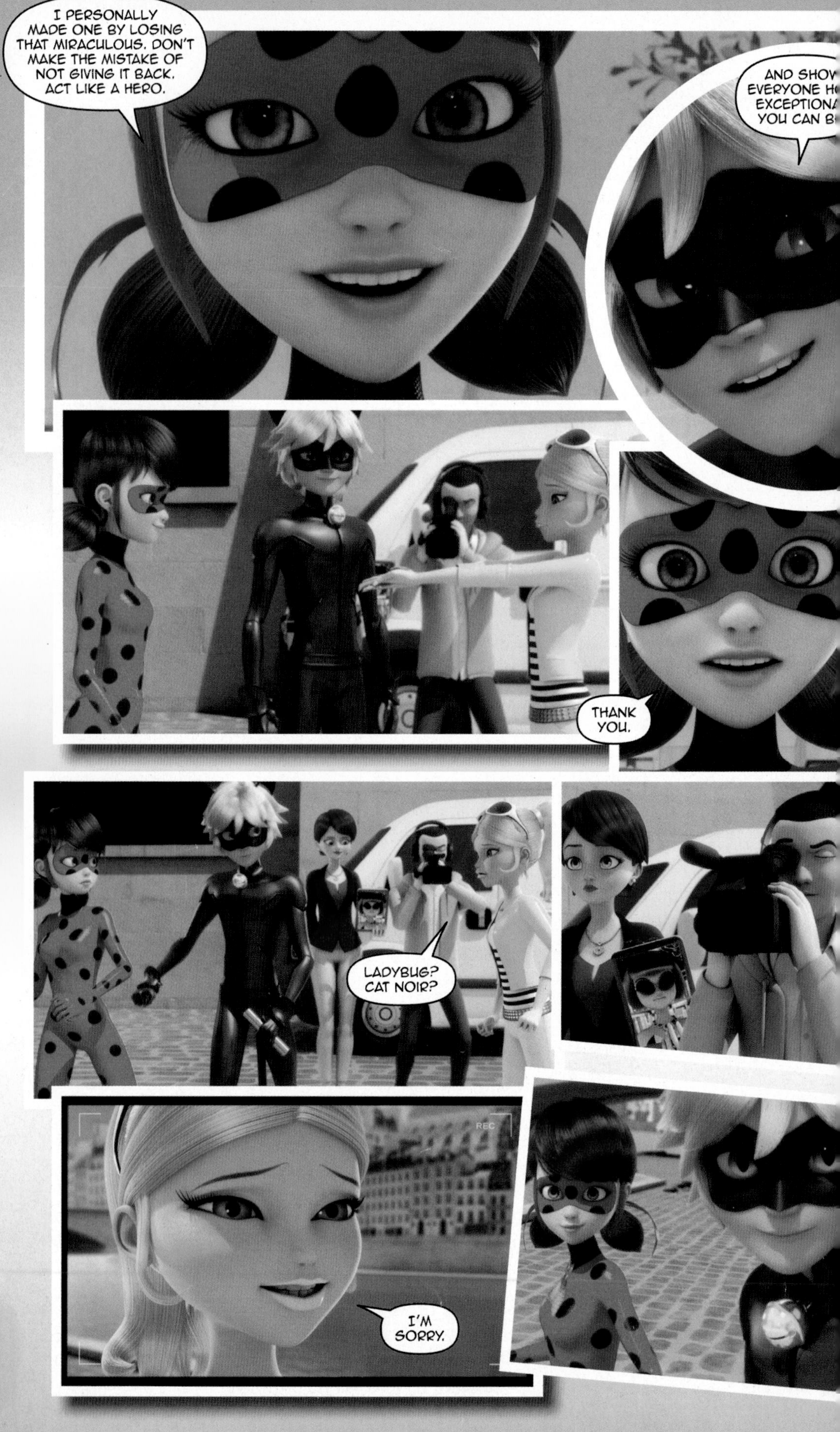
I PERSONALLY MADE ONE BY LOSING THAT MIRACULOUS. DON'T MAKE THE MISTAKE OF NOT GIVING IT BACK. ACT LIKE A HERO.
AND SHOW EVERYONE H EXCEPTIONA YOU CAN B
THANK YOU.
LADYBUG? CAT NOIR?
I'M SORRY.

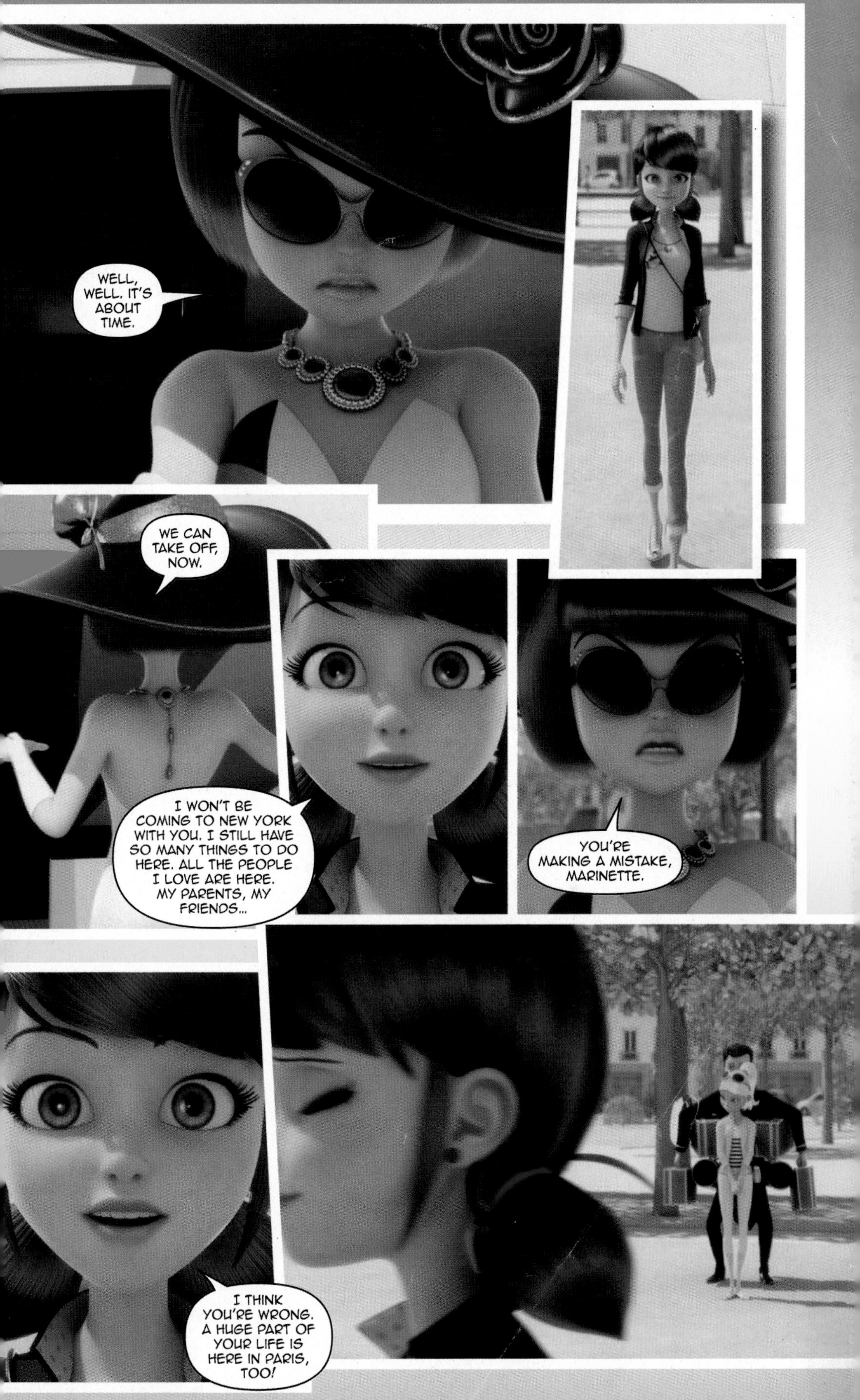
WELL, WELL. IT'S ABOUT TIME.
WE CAN TAKE OFF, NOW.
I WON'T BE COMING TO NEW YORK WITH YOU. I STILL HAVE SO MANY THINGS TO DO HERE. ALL THE PEOPLE I LOVE ARE HERE. MY PARENTS, MY FRIENDS...
YOU'RE MAKING A MISTAKE, MARINETTE.
I THINK YOU'RE WRONG. A HUGE PART OF YOUR LIFE IS HERE IN PARIS, TOO!

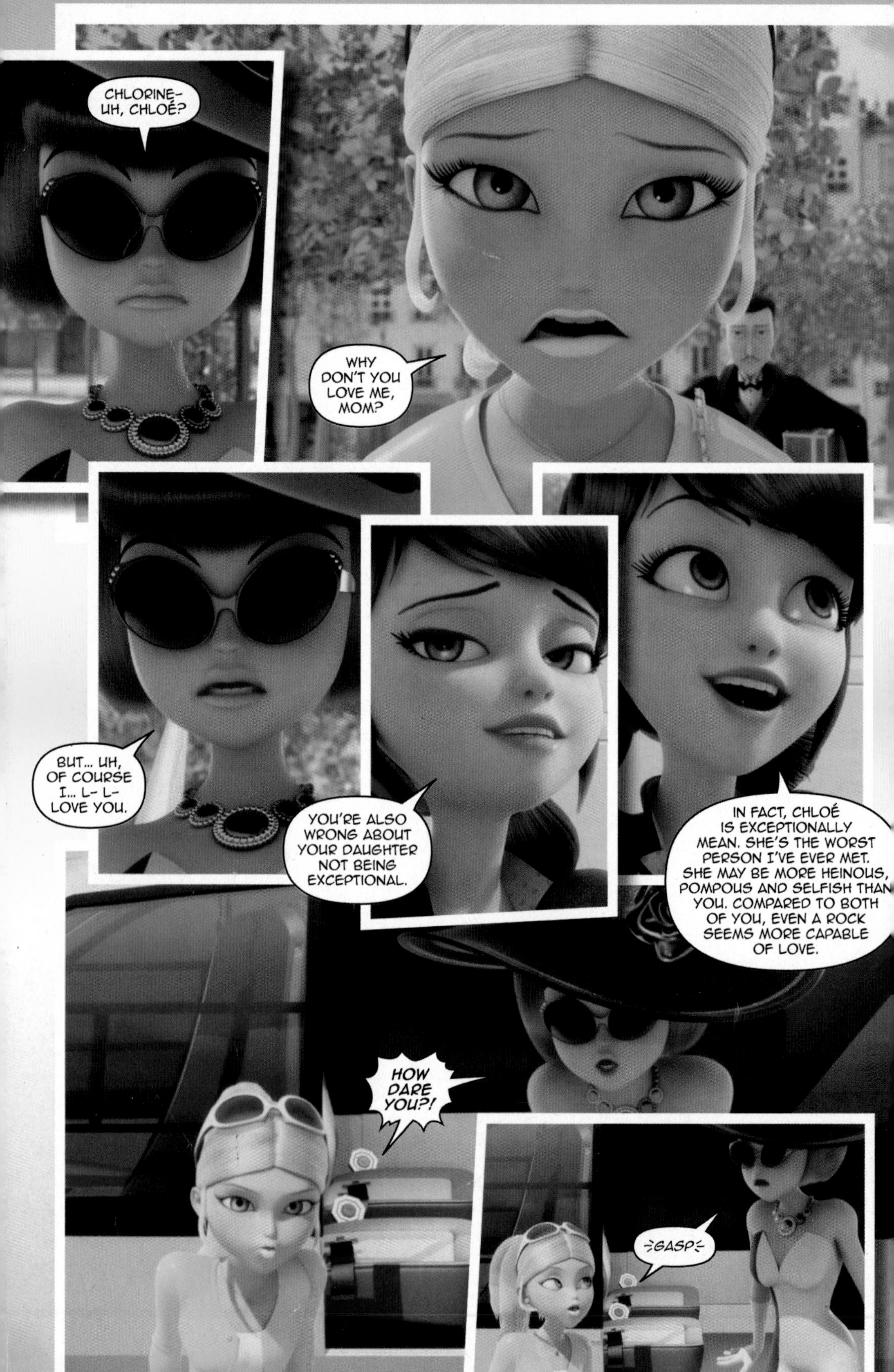
CHLORINE- UH, CHLOÉ?
WHY DON'T YOU LOVE ME, MOM?
BUT... UH, OF COURSE I... L- L- LOVE YOU.
YOU'RE ALSO WRONG ABOUT YOUR DAUGHTER NOT BEING EXCEPTIONAL.
IN FACT, CHLOÉ IS EXCEPTIONALLY MEAN. SHE'S THE WORST PERSON I'VE EVER MET. SHE MAY BE MORE HEINOUS, POMPOUS AND SELFISH THAN YOU. COMPARED TO BOTH OF YOU, EVEN A ROCK SEEMS MORE CAPABLE OF LOVE.
HOW DARE YOU?!
GASP

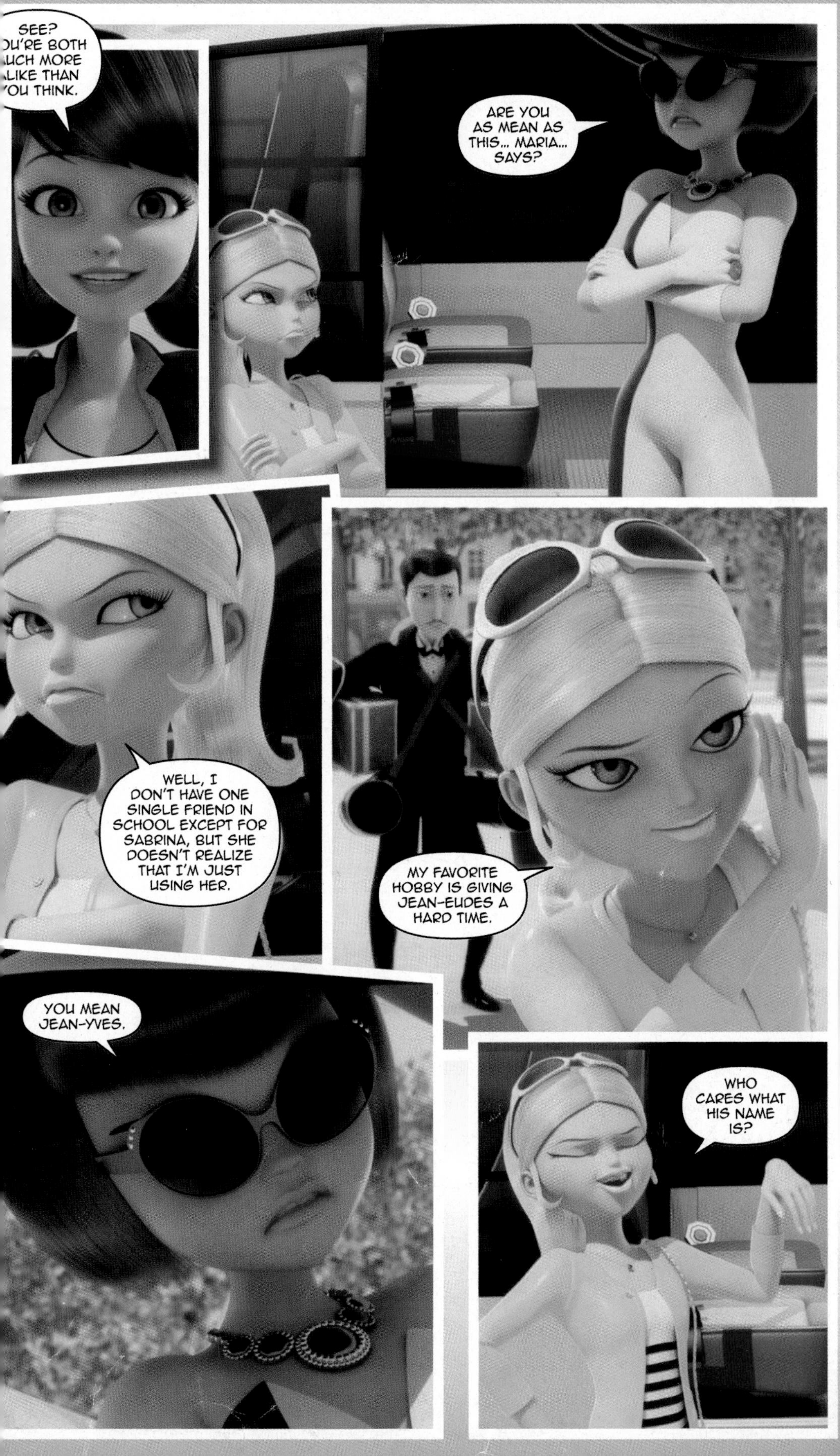
SEE? YOU'RE BOTH MUCH MORE ALIKE THAN YOU THINK.
ARE YOU AS MEAN AS THIS... MARIA... SAYS?
WELL, I DON'T HAVE ONE SINGLE FRIEND IN SCHOOL EXCEPT FOR SABRINA, BUT SHE DOESN'T REALIZE THAT I'M JUST USING HER.
MY FAVORITE HOBBY IS GIVING JEAN-EUDES A HARD TIME.
YOU MEAN JEAN-YVES.
WHO CARES WHAT HIS NAME IS?

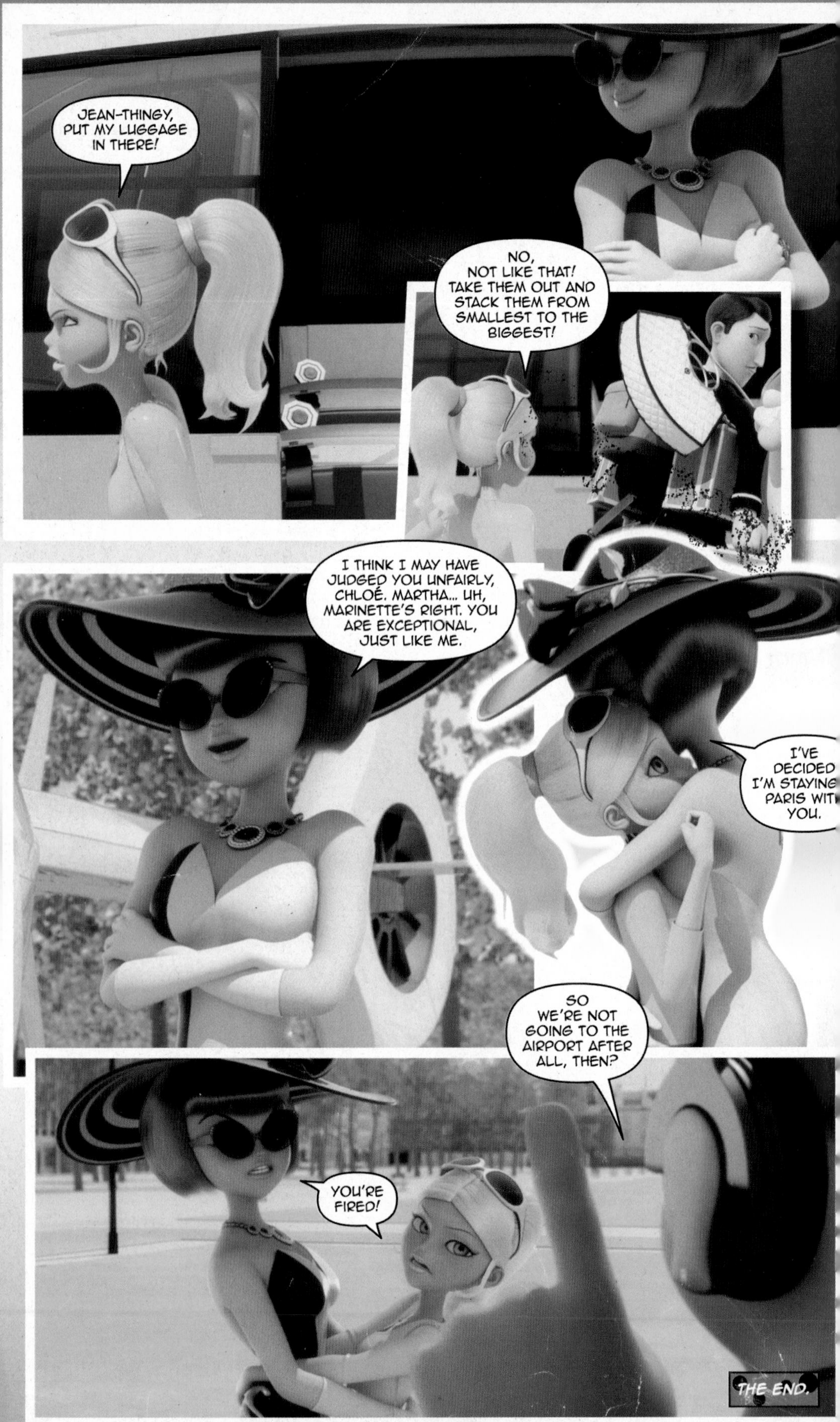

JEAN-THINGY, PUT MY LUGGAGE IN THERE!
NO, NOT LIKE THAT! TAKE THEM OUT AND STACK THEM FROM SMALLEST TO THE BIGGEST!
I THINK I MAY HAVE JUDGED YOU UNFAIRLY, CHLOÉ. MARTHA... UH, MARINETTE'S RIGHT. YOU ARE EXCEPTIONAL, JUST LIKE ME.
I'VE DECIDED I'M STAYING PARIS WIT YOU.
SO WE'RE NOT GOING TO THE AIRPORT AFTER ALL, THEN?
YOU'RE FIRED!
THE END.